Collision

A novel

By John Donoghue

About the author

John Donoghue worked in mental health for nearly twenty years and was the author of numerous articles concerning the treatment of mental conditions before writing *Collision*, his first novel. He lives in Liverpool with his wife, four children and one dog.

For my wife and children, without whom none of this would have been possible.

Acknowledgements

Thanks and love to Alison, Lynn and Marion for their assistance with proof-reading and helpful suggestions. Also to the 'regulars' at Lark Lane Writers in Liverpool go my thanks for their patience, wine, and unfailingly constructive comments.

Author's note

Collision is a work of fiction. The characters and settings are the fictitious products of an overactive imagination. No similarities with real people and places were intended. If any similarities exist, they are entirely coincidental.

Is Demonic Possession Real?

In March 2008, Dr. Richard Gallagher, Associate Professor of Clinical Psychiatry at New York Medical College wrote an article in the New Oxford Review (*Volume LXXV, Number 2*), documenting what he regarded to be 'a contemporary and clear-cut case of demonic possession.'

Although, on closer examination, many cases of purported possession have been found to be psychiatric conditions with understandable origins and predictable outcomes, this does not prove or even suggest that possession is a but a figment of an obsolete imagination. Dr. Gallagher tells us that Demonic possession is rare, but is more common than might be imagined. Even the strongest sceptics might be convinced were they to witness the 'massive and unequivocal' onslaught of a genuine demonic assault.

Though convinced that demonic possession is a real phenomenon, Dr. Gallagher cautions those involved in spiritual or mental health care to beware of falsely or mistakenly attributing counterfeit signs as true possession, particularly in circumstances where the vulnerable or the gullible may fall prey to the unscrupulous. Disentangling the widely variable manifestations of mental illness from possible possession requires the close co-operation of psychiatrists, psychologists and ministers of religion if real cases of demonic possession are to be recognised for what they are and handled appropriately.

Prologue: two fragments

"I know how it ends now," she said, her eyes shining. "He showed me. Isn't it glorious?"

*

I was falling in the blackest, darkest pit you can conceive. There's no light, but you're aware that you're falling just the same; you can feel it in the pit of your stomach. You have no control, your arms and legs are flailing, trying to latch on to something, anything, but you know there's no hope really. To make matters worse it's raining, and the deluge is falling faster than you, hitting you again and again with fat drops that are bitter and sullen so that in moments you are soaked to the skin and freezing, yet they care nothing for what they add to your mounting sense of fear. You're wondering what's waiting for you at the bottom, if there is a bottom.

Then you sense it: a brooding malice that surrounds you, that penetrates to the depths of your awareness, to the most sacred gates of your being. The voices, with their incessant gnawing at your consciousness, their remorseless assault on your soul, are constant. You try to convince yourself that they will never breach those sacred gates, that you have some inner strength, some fire in your spirit that will stop them; but in your heart of hearts you know it's not true. That's when you start to pray. To pray with all your heart and all your soul and all your mind. To pray as though not just your life depended on it, but your very soul. Then you remember the words of the Saviour. 'My God, my God. Why have you forsaken me?'

Interview with Joan Archer, 4th September 2007

1
His and Hers

God, he was beautiful. This thought so took her by surprise that it pushed her rising orgasm out of reach so that she had to reconnect with it, pull it back to the front of her mind. She was astride the most beautiful man she had ever seen, pumping up and down on him, all self-awareness long since discarded. However, now it had penetrated into her consciousness, the thought was not so easily dismissed, no matter how she tried to push it aside, to surrender to the moment. She knew that *beautiful* was not the normal way to think of a man, but he was, even with his face screwed up as he summoned his own supreme moment. In the dim light cast by the bedside lamp she could not see the colour of his eyes, but remembered their perfect piercing blue. His lips were full and luscious, with a smile so sensual it hinted at much even before a word was spoken.

Not that her own looks could be thought of as modest. She was eye candy, but not in his league. He belonged in a painting by an old master, the light of his features made sublime by a dark background. She had been aware of him almost as soon as he walked into the bar, alone, but so completely self-possessed, brushing his dark curls out of his eyes as he ordered a drink. When she caught him looking at her in the mirror behind the bar her heart leapt. She felt the adrenaline surge and when he smiled she knew she had to have him. In a moment of madness she left her friends and joined him.

They left the bar laughing, almost dancing down the street in search of a cab. Later, in the club, she danced herself almost to a frenzy, not from alcohol, but from sheer desire, caressing him in the most lascivious of ways, not caring that they were in full view of any who cared to watch. By the time they got back to his flat she was desperate for him. They had tumbled giggling up the stairs, with him telling her to shush before collapsing in a fit of laughter himself He fumbled noisily for his keys, succeeding in getting the door open only for it to slam behind them. Their clothes were thrown to the floor and she gave no thought to the condoms she had in her handbag.

Her breath was now coming in little gasps, the cadence and the pitch both rising. She was aware that he was now thrusting with her, letting her ride up off him then pushing into her as deeply as he could, faster and faster. Her orgasm was starting its gushing rush, a thrill of such joy she could not prevent herself from crying out, and then his shouts joined hers as for brief moments they were locked together in rapture.

Afterwards, he slept. A bungee-like fall into a deep carefree oblivion. Idly her fingers traced the contours of his face and down his chest until she too succumbed to the same blessed darkness.

*

God is Beauty. That thought would not let Joan alone as she knelt in the front pew of the church in silent contemplation before the alabaster statue of Christ. She wondered where the thought had come from. She had heard stories of 'Jesus spinsters' who entertained erotic fantasies of their saviour while pretending piety. She had sometimes (perish the thought!) wondered whether nuns might have sexual desires involving the Lord: what else did they have? She knew there was an unspoken gay undercurrent in the clergy, suppressed though it was by the Church. But that was nothing to her. What consenting adults got up to in private was their own business.

But how could God be Beauty? Was this even a fruitful meditation? She asked herself. His creation was certainly beautiful – parts of it, at least – but if God was the creator of everything, how could Beauty be responsible for the creation of so much that was cruel and hideous? She shook her head, trying to dismiss these distractions. She did not want to permit the slightest doubt about her beloved Lord to enter her head. Better to meditate on something more positive. God is *Truth*. There. That at least was incontrovertible.

A sudden draught blew through the church. The candles set in the wrought iron grille in front of the statue flickered, throwing points of light and shadow across its surface. For a split second, the statue looked like it had shivered, startling Joan, and making her look closely at it. But there was nothing unusual about it. Carved in white stone, it showed a benevolent Jesus, his bearded face smiling at his people, one hand raised in blessing, the other pulling his robe aside to reveal his sacred heart – one of the holy mysteries of the faith. A figure of devotion for the Catholic faithful for centuries, similar statues could be found in churches throughout the world.

Quiet footsteps sounded close by, and a man sat himself heavily in the pew beside her.

"Hello, Joan," he said.

"Hello Father."

"A penny for your thoughts?"

She smiled self-consciously. She had known Father O'Hanlon all her life. He had guided her through all the important landmarks of her faith, from her baptism to her first communion and confirmation. If ever she were to marry, she would want him to conduct the wedding.

"My thoughts?" she said in a hushed voice, "I don't think they're worth a penny, Father, not tonight."

"Would you care to share them with me anyway?" He smiled. A gentle smile born of long years of service to his parish, to the people he genuinely thought of as his flock.

She didn't answer immediately. Then she plunged straight in. "If God is Beauty, how come there's so much ugliness and pain in the world, Father?"

"Dear Lord, Joan," the priest chuckled. "You don't muck about, do you? No easy questions like 'Why is the Pope infallible?' for you, eh?" He peered at her, trying to gauge how serious she was. "It wasn't a theology degree you did, by any chance, was it?"

"No. History and politics."

"Do you mind if I ask – why did you not finish it, Joan?"

She sighed. "It's a long story Father."

He understood. He placed a hand lightly on hers, squeezing it gently. "It's okay Joan. You don't have to tell me. Not if you don't want to."

She pulled her hand away, rubbing it self-consciously. "No Father, it's not that. I don't think I've fully worked it out for myself why I dropped out." She paused. "I don't think I was prepared for all the ideology, the cant, the idea of 'realpolitik' and expediency. It just struck me that there is precious little altruism around; it was just all about power. Sometimes it was a naked overwhelming obtain-at-all-costs pursuit of power for its own sake; sometimes it was disguised by a veneer of civilisation and respectability – even democracy – but, at bottom, power was what mattered. That was quite a revelation for me, an epiphany of sorts, I suppose. I just realised that none of it mattered to me."

The priest raised his eyes to the statue before them. "And what does matter to you, Joan?"

"Faith."

2
Saturday morning

Edward had never needed an alarm clock to awaken him. He had the uncanny knack of always waking up on time, no matter what he had been up to the night before. It was a talent that had gotten him out of a number of scrapes through the years, and it served him well again today. With no insistent ringing or chiming to wake her, the girl remained comatose as Edward stumbled out of bed. Rubbing his eyes he pulled on a dressing gown before shuffling down a poorly-lit passage to the bathroom for a pee before slouching his way to the kitchen to find his flat-mate Peter sitting at the table, a mug of coffee placed before him, reading the morning's sport pages. He glanced up when Ed walked in. "Out late again were we?"

Edward responded by shaking his head before yawning and dragging the back of his hand across his gaping mouth. "What time is it?"

Peter glanced over his shoulder at the kitchen clock. "Twenty past eight."

"Shit. Later than I thought."

"Calm down, it's Saturday. I thought you didn't actually have to go in today, you were only on call?" Crisis over, Peter returned to his paper.

"Yeah, but I have to go in and write up the changes to the meds. I should have done them last night, but I wanted to get off early. Got to go, mate." Edward dragged himself back to his room.

In his bedroom Edward took a long appreciative look at the naked girl curled up on the bed. She did not stir as he pulled clothes out of drawers and dressed hastily. Peter pushed the door open and deposited a mug of coffee on the dresser. Edward wondered whether he should leave a note. *Great time last night. Afraid something came up at work. Leave me your number and I'll call you.* He decided it wasn't worth the bother, plenty more where she came from. He hurried back to the bathroom where he brushed his teeth not noticing in his rush the splodge of toothpaste that stuck to his chin.

He was standing at the front door checking his pockets for cash, keys, mobile phone when Peter called out.

"What about her?" He jerked his thumb in the direction of the bedroom.

"She's still out for the count. Could you . . . ?" Ed gave him his *if-you-were-a-mate-you-would-help-me-out-here* look.

"Again? You training for the Olympics or something?" Peter sipped his coffee as if contemplating what price he would exact. He sighed, shaking his head. Ed knew he had won. "Fine, fine!" Peter held up a hand in mock defeat. "You go. I'll take her some tea and toast and tell her there was somebody's life that needed to be saved and there was nobody but you could do it."

Ed grinned. "Cheers, mate. I owe you one."

"One? And the rest!" He heaped marmalade onto his toast. "And which list does this one go on? Wannabe or Call-back? Only I like to know whether I should be brutal or offer a few crumbs of hope."

Ed was a veteran of such decisions. It took only a moment to weigh up the events of the previous night. "She was as fit as a butcher's dog and a damn fine shag, but . . ."

"But?" Peter knew that Ed habitually employed the *'everything before the but is bullshit'* principle.

"Nothing upstairs. Definitely Wannabe."

Peter laughed. "You are all fucking heart mate. Now fuck off and save some lives, and try not to breath on them while you're doing it – you've got dog's breath!"

*

Mornings sat heavily on Sean Archer. This was the time when the trembling in his hands was at its worse. It had started a few years ago. At first it hadn't been all that noticeable; he had started to drop things, something he had never done before. He had never been clumsy, but now he was cursed with it, affecting his ability to work. He had always liked the most intricate jobs, and had developed a real skill for working with small, inaccessible circuits, but he could no longer rely on the steadiness of his touch, and his hands, which had always been so sure, were no longer fully his to command. A diagnosis of Parkinson's disease forced him into early retirement. Bernadette, as he had known she would be, was wonderfully supportive, but to Sean, whose deftness of touch had been such a source of pride, it might as well have been a death sentence. His confidence went, and with it any sense of optimism for the future. Their GP diagnosed depression – a completely understandable response to what had happened, she tried to reassure him – but Sean felt diminished. From now on he knew that what remained of his life would be an ever increasing burden on his wife and daughters. Even the smallest decision was now a major obstacle standing in his way. Despite all the medication he was now obliged to take he felt hopeless and helpless.

Most of this had happened while Joan had been away at university, but her unexpected early return caught him unprepared. He simply didn't know how to cope with a young woman who had problems of her own. Her sister Caroline thought that Joan should have found somewhere else to live rather than foisting herself back on her parents, but this had cut no ice with Bernadette who said she and Sean were delighted to have Joan back. It would have been fine if he hadn't felt so damned useless.

Although his illness had rocked Sean's faith, the Archers had always been devout, if conventional, Catholics. To their sorrow, since getting married, Caroline hadn't set foot in a church, and, despite the urging of their grandparents, the twins hadn't been baptised. In her turn Joan had shocked her parents by announcing that religion was a sham, a counterfeit comfort for people who couldn't face the realities of life. But something had happened to her during her time in Sheffield, and in the year since she had returned, Joan had shown a renewed interest and commitment to religion, and attended church regularly, almost every day, in fact. Despite their own devotion, her parents were uneasy about this, and Joan's new-found *über* piety was rarely far from their thoughts.

Now Sean spent most mornings wondering what to do with himself. He had worked all his life; he was skilled at his job and enjoyed the esteem of his workmates and having an involvement with the wider world. Despite his wife's urging to get involved with a charity, or get a part-time job, he found it difficult to get motivated these days, and usually confined himself to ruminating on the world's problems, including Joan and her obsession with religion.

"Would you like another cup of tea?" His wife called from the kitchen.

"Have you seen this?" He replied, folding his newspaper to make it more manageable. "That bloody woman's joining the Catholic Church because she doesn't want women priests, and we're stupid enough to let her in!"

"What bloody woman?" Bernadette took his empty cup into the kitchen.

"That flamin' Baroness somebody-or-other. The one with the whining voice. You know the one."

A fresh cup was placed before him. "Does it really matter Sean? It's not something to get worked up about, is it? Haven't we got problems enough without taking on other peoples' as well?"

"I suppose so," he agreed. He took a sip of the hot tea before returning to the worry that gnawed at him constantly. "It wouldn't be so bad if Joan would get herself sorted out."

Bernadette sighed. Sean seemed unable to talk about much else these days. Now she regretted distracting him from his news story. "There's no need to keep going on about it so much, she's not hurting anyone."

Sean put down his paper. "So what? It's not right at her age. She should be going out with her mates, clubbing, having a good time, meeting boys – worrying us sick by staying out till all hours. Not spending every minute of the day in that bloody church."

"Please don't go on about her and the church again, Sean. It's like you're *looking* for something to worry about. She doesn't cause us any problems, she doesn't drink or do drugs; she hasn't got any friends that we don't approve of . . ."

Sean did not allow his wife to finish. "But that's just it! She hasn't got *any* friends," he said excitedly. "She won't let anyone get close to her any more. And over the past few months it's got worse. She practically lives in that feckin' church."

Bernadette shook her head. "She's always been a bit of a loner. Always kept herself to herself. She's just a very private person and we ought to respect that."

"I know that. But how many girls her age lock their bedroom doors in their own home? When was the last time you went in her bedroom? Last month? Last year, more like! She doesn't even have her tea with us any more."

Sean's hands had started to shake. Usually the medication kept them under some control, but when he got agitated, it seemed to lose its effectiveness. Bernadette reached across to take them in hers. "You'd be worried sick no matter what she did. I know she's been a bit off recently, but what if she's got a boyfriend and is too embarrassed to tell us about him? Have you thought of that?"

"As long as she's not pregnant."

Upstairs, Joan could hear her parents' voices. It was nearly nine, and there was a mass at nine-thirty, so she started down the stairs. As she stepped down from the landing she could hear her mother quite clearly.

"Oh for God's sake, Sean. Now you're just being ridiculous!"

"Am I? It was you who said she might have a boyfriend."

Joan had noticed that her father seemed to raise his voice far more frequently of late than he had used to. She hated confrontation, and tried not to get involved, but they were obviously talking about her. She walked into the parlour.

"Who's got a boyfriend?" Her voice was harsh, accusing.

Her mum tried to make light of it. "Nobody love." She stood, picking up the empty mugs. "Want some breakfast?"

Joan was suddenly angry. She was sick of her parents interfering in her life. "You were talking about me again, weren't you?" Her anger continued to rise. "Well you've no right. You're always poking your nose into my business. It's not fair!" She glared at them, fearful of saying more. "I'm going out!"

Joan was not the only one with a quick temper. Sean no longer had the insight to reflect on whether it stemmed from feelings of inadequacy, resentment or just sheer fear, or it may just have been guilt that Joan had been right in what she said. Whatever the reason, he spoke without thinking.

"Going out are you? Again? You come in, you barely say a word about where you've been, spend all night locked in your room, won't have any breakfast, and then you're off out again? You want to talk about what's not fair? Well it's not fair having you treat this house like some sort of private hotel and me and your mum as your servants!"

Joan had heard enough. She turned her back on her father, and, trembling, walked quickly down the hall and out onto the street slamming the door behind her. Not to be outdone, Sean followed her into the hall, shouting after her as the door slammed in his face:

"That's what's not fair!"

He stood watching the door for a moment, as if expecting his daughter to come back with a tearful apology. It was not to be. He looked helplessly at his hands, once the source of so many skills, now useless pieces of meat; the tremor was worse than ever.

Bernadette tried to comfort him.

"You shouldn't go on at her like that. You only upset yourself. She's just not your little girl any more; you have to let her grow up. You're going to have to let go sooner or later."

Without replying, he went to their front window, pulling the curtain back to watch Joan walk down the street.

"I know," he sighed, his anger broken. "But I can't help it. She's my little girl and I can't stop myself thinking she's in trouble, and there's nothing I can do about it."

*

St. Peter's was not the most modern hospital in Britain, nonetheless, the staff on Maple ward tried to make it bright and welcoming. There were plenty of indoor plants and pictures of landscapes dotted about. The intention was to create an atmosphere of calm, of serenity – at least as calm and serene as could be managed on an acute psychiatric ward. The dress code on the unit was informal, and Edward did not look particularly out of place as he walked onto the ward looking like something that the cat had dragged in. Although the nursing station was open-plan, the staff had done their best to create an illusion of privacy by screening it with potted plants; Edward's arrival went unnoticed.

"Hi Maria," he said, his voice sounding louder than he had intended.

Maria, a nurse in her forties, jumped, then scowled self-consciously as she realised who it was. "Do you have to creep up on people like that? Look what you've gone and made me do!" She pointed to the book she was writing in, where her neat script had suddenly gone askew.

"Hi Ed." They were joined by another nurse: young, golden blond, fresh as a daisy. "Late night?"

Edward gave a brittle laugh. "Is it that obvious?"

"You've got toothpaste on your chin."

He groaned. "Oh, Christ. Thank God I haven't bumped into doctor Marwan yet."

Ignoring Maria, she fished in her pocket for a tissue, moistened it with spit, and wiped the toothpaste away, grinning with mock sympathy. "Is everything alright Edward? You can tell me you know - in complete confidence – I'm a *nurse*."

Edward was too hung-over to respond in kind. "A nurse? Then why are you acting like you were my mother?" He replied, sarcasm dripping.

Maria couldn't hold back. "Your mother? You mean you've got one?" She jibed.

Edward was used to Maria's frostiness. He was above responding to her supposed witticisms. Ignoring her he looked vaguely around the nursing station. "I don't suppose there's any aspirin around here?"

Maria, in a rather caustic tone replied "You're a doctor. Why don't you write yourself a prescription?"

"Ha bloody ha." He continued to look around the office. "Did Viv leave the medication changes out for me to write up? That's all I've come in for, really."

"I didn't think you'd come in just to get some aspirin," Maria said primly, turning back to her ledger.

"Do you know where she might have left them, Sue?" Edward asked, turning to the other nurse.

"I'm afraid not. She didn't mention anything at hand-over."

"Bloody typical." He started to rummage through the files and sheaves of paper stacked along the work top.

While he was occupied with this task another nurse popped her head over the counter.

"Oh, hi Ed. Glad I bumped into you." She winked at Susan who in return raised her eyebrows in mock disapproval. "Doctor Marwan is looking for you."

"What? Oh hell. That's all I needed. Bang goes my Saturday. I'm not actually supposed to be in, you know. I've already done over fifty hours this week."

Maria saw an opportunity to have the last word. "Welcome to my world!" She said, raising her eyes to the ceiling in a mock appeal to the Almighty.

It was lost on Edward. "Do you know what he wants, Cathy?"

"A new patient was admitted from A&E last night. He wants to talk to you about him and get his meds written up. He's on the ICU now."

"Who? Doctor Marwan or the patient?"

"Both of them, I think. You'd better get over there."

He left his half-hearted attempt to find the notes he needed and headed for the corridor that would take him to the intensive care unit. Susan walked with him.

"So did you have a very late night last night?"

"No later than usual," he replied, wondering where the conversation was leading.

"Was it anyone I know?"

"Anyone you know?"

Susan smiled conspiratorially. "Ed, if you think we don't all know about your reputation, you're deluded. We just need to fill in the details for the gossip mill."

He could not prevent a half smile, shaking his head in wry amusement. "No, it's not anyone you know. At least, I don't think it is."

They reached the swing doors that marked the ward's exit and stopped. Susan held the door open for him, smiling brightly. "Good!" She said.

Edward could not help feeling somewhat bemused. "Good? Why good?"

"Because then I won't have to feel guilty about taking her place in your affections."

She walked away before he could respond, leaving him looking after her, shaking his head before letting the door spring shut behind him as he exited onto the corridor. She was quite attractive, and had great tits, he told himself as he slouched along, but was getting involved with someone at work worth all the complications that would inevitably ensue? Probably not, he told himself. Occupied by these thoughts, he found himself at the ICU without being aware of how he had got there.

*

The house was peaceful with both of them out. Sean had gone for a walk. Bernadette didn't expect him to be very long. Perhaps they hadn't done the right thing just letting Joan move back in, but it was hard to say no to your own daughter, wasn't it? No matter how grown up they appeared to be, they were still your children. She heard the front door open and close, then footsteps going up the stairs. So Joan was back. Mass must have finished early. Bernadette followed her up the stairs and knocked softly on her bedroom door.

"Joan, would you like a cup of tea love?"

In the bedroom, Joan was in turmoil. The argument with her dad had left her feeling both hurt and confused. She knew she was being unreasonable: her parents had a right to expect some sort of relationship with her, but there was something within her that wouldn't let her, that wanted her to be by herself. It was true that she felt at peace only when she was alone and could devote her attention to the Saviour, and hadn't He said that He came to divide father from son, mother from daughter? But that didn't mean she didn't still love her mum and dad. She sensed she was at some sort of crossroads, but needed a clear sign to tell her which way she should go, but so far, it had not been forthcoming.

Her mum knocked again, more insistently this time.

"Joan. Come on love, you've had nothing this morning. You'll make yourself ill."

Joan didn't want any breakfast. Not now. She didn't even want to open the bedroom door. But she had to say something. "Mum, I'm sorry about this morning. But it just seems that everybody thinks it's okay to poke their noses into my business these days. I'm just a bit fed up with it."

"I know love. And your dad didn't mean any of those things he said either. He's just worried about you."

"If Dad is so worried, why doesn't he talk to me about it?"

Bernadette sighed. She hated having a conversation through a closed door.

"You know what he's like. He finds it hard to talk about how he feels. But you know that he does really care. He just doesn't know how to say it. And it's not easy for him these days. You know how the Parkinson's disease has affected him. No matter what I say to him, after over thirty years of doing a job he loved, now he just feels like he's a spare part.

"Won't you at least try and talk to him without losing your temper and storming off again? At least try and get him to understand that he's worrying over nothing."

In her room, Joan was almost in tears. Her mum really knew how to hit the right buttons.

"Mum, I don't know how to make him understand. If it wasn't for you I don't think he'd bother with church at all any more. If his faith isn't strong enough to make him want to go to church on his own account, how will he be able to understand my faith in God?" She paused, not sure of how to continue. "I think I might have a vocation, I'm just not sure yet."

Bernadette almost breathed a sigh of relief. If that was what God wanted for her daughter, she would not try to stand in her way

"Is that what you've decided? Are you sure?" She leant against the wall beside the door. "Joan, this is big decision, you know, love. And this isn't right, talking through the door like this. It's not normal. Can't you open the door and talk about this like a mother and daughter should?"

Now Joan did have to choke back a tear. She wasn't ready for this to be out in the open yet. In a small, almost frightened voice she replied "I can't. Not yet. Not until I'm ready."

"Ready? And when will that be?"

"I don't know."

Bernadette turned away from the door and walked slowly along the landing to the stairs. As she reached the top of the stairs she was stopped by the noise of a key turning in a lock. The bedroom door opened. Bernadette's face brightened. She stayed where she was, hoping that Joan might have changed her mind, but she was to be disappointed. Joan locked the door behind her and brushed past her mother.

"Joan . . . I . . ."

"Sorry mum, I have to go. The Prayer for Peace Group starts soon; I need to hurry."

As she pushed past, the key to her bedroom fell from her pocket. She was too preoccupied to notice and didn't see her mother stoop to pick it up.

Security at the psychiatric ICU was important: its doors were kept locked and Edward had to use his swipe card and PIN code to enter. Dr. Marwan was waiting for him.

"Oh, Edward. Glad I bumped into you. Did you get my message about our new visitor?"

Edward had to suppress a yawn. "Er . . . Yeah. Cathy told me. I came over straight away."

Marwan looked closely at his senior house officer. "You look knackered, Edward. Bloody awful, in fact. Out on the piss again last night were we?"

"Something like that."

Marwan was not impressed. "Edward, you're promising material, you know that. But you're never going to pass your College exams if you're out painting the town red every night of the week. A little bit of moderation goes a long way."

It wasn't the first time that Ed had heard this particular lecture, or a variation on it. He tried not to sound bored. "Thanks," he said. "I'll bear it in mind."

Marwan shrugged. It wasn't his job to wrap the juniors in cotton wool. "Well as soon as we've sorted this fellow out, you can go. Why don't you get yourself a coffee and I'll see you back here in ten minutes?" He opened the ICU door and walked away.

Ed was rarely impressed by the well-intentioned advice of senior staff members. "Why don't I indeed?" He muttered to himself as Marwan left.

Thirty minutes later, Edward had finished his cup of instant coffee and was kicking his heels in the ward manager's office. He was not in a good place: the pleasures of last night were all but forgotten as he looked repeatedly at his watch, not caring that Tony, the unit manager, was witness to his growing irritation.

"Ten bloody minutes he said. That was half a sodding hour ago. I'm not even supposed to be in today. Got a banging headache and I'm starving."

The unit manager was not entirely sympathetic. "No breakfast?" Ed shook his head. "Again?" He could not keep his mild amusement at Ed's predicament from showing.

"Why do they always have to do this, eh? I mean, he's not the only one with things to do today, is he?"

Tony gave Ed a half-smile. "Keep the plebs waiting? Because they can, I suppose."

Dr. Marwan arrived, a thick folder in his grasp, which he handed to Edward. He frowned at the noise coming from people chatting in the corridor. "Do you think we could have a little quiet, Tony?" He asked.

Without replying, Tony put his head out of the door and called: "We're having a meeting in here – can we not be disturbed please?"

"How has he been?" Marwan asked after he had settled himself.

"Mr. Kendrick? He was pretty restless for most of the night. Up and down like a bloody yo-yo. The night staff had to sedate him at one and again at four. He's sleeping now, but fitfully. We've got him on fifteen minute obs."

Marwan turned to Edward. "Mr. Kendrick is an old customer of ours. We do our best to patch him up and send him home, but a few months later and he'll be back," he said by way of explanation. "You can count on it." Then he asked Tony "How long is it since his last admission?"

Tony consulted a file. "Nearly five months. He's done quite well this time."

Edward was becoming mildly interested. "What's his problem? Why does he keep having to come in?"

"If you have a look in his notes you'll see Mr. Kendrick has bipolar-one disorder," Marwan explained. "He experiences predominantly manic symptoms, with occasional depression. His problem is compounded by the fact that once he's out of hospital he doesn't take his medication, and he likes a drink."

This was something Edward could relate to. "Don't we all?" He grinned.

Marwan was not particularly amused by Ed's feeble attempt at a witticism. "The occasional drink would not be a problem. Mr. Kendrick likes to down a bottle of whisky a day."

"Right."

"So what's the plan this time?" Tony asked. "Dry him out and send him home again?"

Marwan looked thoughtful. "You know, I'm not sure. I think we should see what he's like when he's not under the influence. Somewhere under all the layers that he's built up over the years is a person. A person I would like to think we can help. I think it's time we went back to basics with Mr. Kendrick. What do you think Tony?"

Tony understood Dr. Marwan's instincts were right, but as the unit manager, he had to make sure that there were always enough beds available for whatever emergencies might arise.

"That depends on what you mean by basics, Salim. The ICU isn't intended for long admissions, and generally, the pressure on beds is as high as it's ever been."

Marwan sympathised. He had complained several times that running the unit on the minimal number of beds was not serving the interests of either patients or staff. But it was about time they did something more than just another patch-up job on Mr. Kendrick.

"This time I'm thinking of a long admission to try and get him properly sorted, so that when we do send him back out he'll be able to cope better."

Edward had been skimming through the notes. "What about his key worker?" He suggested.

Tony was all too familiar with the problems Mr. Kendrick posed. "The problem with Mr. Kendrick is that he doesn't keep regular hours. It's a nightmare trying to keep up with him."

"Which is exactly why I want to spend some time getting him properly settled." Marwan concluded.

Edward tried to bring them both back to the immediate point of their discussion. "So what would you like me to do?"

"Not a lot for now," Marwan said, "but this is exactly the sort of case with multiple complex problems that will stand you in good stead when you come to do your exams."

"It's just that I'm off duty tomorrow and the day after. If there's anything that needs to be done it would be best to get it done now rather than wait."

Marwan turned back to Tony. "Did he get started on the alcohol detox regime last night?"

Tony consulted his notes. "Yes, but it was interrupted because of the mirazepam we had to give him to calm him down."

"Right. When he wakes, we had better start again from scratch." He paused. "Edward, can you please make sure that gets written up before you go off?"

Edward found the prescription sheet in the notes that Marwan had given him. "Sure. What about the bipolar disorder? Does he get a mood stabiliser or an antipsychotic, or both?"

Marwan's eyebrows rose. Was he getting Edward's attention at last? "Good question. What do you think?"

"I've read the guidelines, and if I remember rightly, they recommend a mood stabiliser, with an antipsychotic added if the mood stabiliser isn't effective by itself."

Marwan exchanged a look with Tony. "Excellent. Which mood stabiliser?"

Edward scanned the notes again, but couldn't find the information he wanted. "I'm not sure." He turned to Tony. "What's he been on before?"

"I think that the last time he was in he was discharged on valproate, but I think I saw a note from pharmacy about that."

"From pharmacy?" Edward was slightly irritated that they should be pushing their noses in. "What about?"

"They think it's probably not a good idea to restart valproate until we've got more information on his liver function, what with his drinking and everything."

Edward took this information on board. "Right."

"So which mood stabiliser do you think we should give him?" Marwan asked.

Edward shook his head.

"I haven't a clue. I thought that basically it was either lithium or valproate. If he can't have valproate, it looks like lithium doesn't it? But doesn't that take a long time before it works?"

Marwan was almost pleased with Edward's response. "Depends what you mean by a long time. Anyway, I won't start lithium until we know what his kidney function is like. I think the best thing we can do for now is to start an antipsychotic. As soon as his alcohol detox is finished, start haldene five milligrams three times a day. Write it up so that it can be given by mouth or I-M." He turned back to Tony. "He's on a section, so if he refuses oral, give it by injection." He stood to go and announced "We'll review his progress in a week. If he's not in your face too much, he can be transferred off the ICU onto Sycamore ward – if they've got a bed available."

Edward was writing furiously in the notes even before his boss had left. At the door, Marwan had an afterthought and turned back.

"Edward, seeing that you *are* in today, how about we do that tutorial on schizophrenia for the new juniors? We've been putting it off for ages – seems like too good an opportunity to miss?"

Edward did his best not to show his irritation. "Er . . . no problem, I'll round them up. What time?"

"Let's make it eleven; no, eleven-thirty. I'll arrange for coffee and biscuits. Who says consultants don't look after their juniors properly?"

*

The Prayer for Peace meeting had not been the uplifting experience that Joan had hoped for. The group was dominated by an older woman called Theresa who seemed to be *against* an awful lot of things. She was against most of the regimes in the Middle East, and Africa, and parts of Asia, especially Burma and North Korea. Wouldn't it be better, Joan had suggested tentatively, to be *for* things instead. Evil regimes could raise their heads anywhere, so shouldn't they just pray for peace and justice everywhere? This had caused a short, but heated, debate. Theresa had been rather aggressive. But did this mean, she had asked, that Joan was in favour of the happenings in places like Afghanistan or Syria? No, Joan had insisted, of course not. But what about injustices in places like Israel or even at home in England? They couldn't pick and choose what they were against, so wasn't it better, as Joan had already said, not to pray that certain regimes and their practices would come to an ignominious end, but to pray for human rights and justice to be available to all? To her disappointment, Theresa had won the day. Revelling in her victory, she told them to remember how the Church had prayed for years for the downfall of the communist regime in Russia – and how those prayers had been answered. She led them in prayers for the destruction of the communists in North Korea and China, and the collapse of regimes from Afghanistan to Zimbabwe. The prayers brought no sense of peace to Joan. They were hateful – the antithesis of what she believed Christianity should be about. What about the power of love and forgiveness? She wanted to shout at them, but she felt overwhelmed. Maybe next time. If there was a next time.

Now the church was empty, as it usually was at this time of day. By lunch-time, the cleaners had finished, and whatever groups used the church as a meeting place had left. Joan took her usual place before the statue of Jesus and prayed for the music to come again.

She had first heard the music a few months after coming back from Sheffield. Sat alone in the church, trying to sort out her thoughts, she had heard the lone voice of a man singing. His song was wonderful, at the same time both comforting and rousing. Joyous. That was how she had eventually come to think of it. She didn't recognise or understand the language he was singing but it was such a thing of beauty that she made sure she was in the church every day to hear it. It only ever came when she was alone, so she resented any intrusion.

Gradually, the music had become fuller. There was now an orchestra behind it, and a chorus. In her mind's eye she saw Jesus as the singer of this amazing song, and that he was surrounded by a choir of shining angels. Today, she was not disappointed. As she prayed for guidance about what her future should be, the lone voice entered her consciousness and she followed its melody without hesitation, waiting for the moment when the orchestra would add to its texture before the choir raised it to its beautiful climax. She didn't understand where the music came from, or why or how it came only to her, but she accepted it – as humbly as she was able - as a miracle – a gift from her Saviour. If anyone had witnessed it they would have seen her face and eyes raised to the statue of Jesus in complete rapture, but they would not have heard any music. They might also have described a sheen of light around her head that looked like a halo from some religious painting. But that would have been too much to believe, wouldn't it?

3
Faith

Dr. Marwan's office had been hurriedly rearranged to make space for the new S.H.O.s. A tray bearing paper cups of coffee and a plate of cheap biscuits had been placed on his desk and the juniors each helped themselves after bringing in a chair and finding a space to sit down. Marwan was quite pleased with himself. It was terribly difficult to find time for a tutorial during the week, what with ward rounds, clinics and the interminable meetings he had to attend, so putting it together at short notice during the one week-end in six when he was the duty consultant had been a stroke of genius.

Edward had been able to round up four of the current crop of six new starters. Marwan immediately asked him to stay and help. The best way to learn is to teach, he had told him. He was busy describing the signs and symptoms of schizophrenia, oblivious to Ed's scowl and muttered complaints at being made to stay.

"No – Moira, is it?" Marwan said, addressing one of the juniors. "It's a misconception that schizophrenia is a split personality."

Moira almost blushed. This was her first psychy job, and she felt as though she'd just made a major blunder. "So is it possible to sum schizophrenia up in a brief description?" she asked.

Marwan paused briefly to get his thoughts in order. "It's difficult to describe schizophrenia, and not entirely correct to talk about 'typical' symptoms. Schizophrenia is a syndrome. What allows you to make a diagnosis is the picture that you get both from the presence of symptoms – you see a combination of symptoms taken from a wide constellation – and the patient's behaviour, which is usually erratic and increasingly isolated in the period leading up to admission to hospital."

"If schizophrenia isn't about having a split personality, why do so many people think it is?"

The question had come from another of the junior doctors. Edward looked incredulously at him. Was he stupid or what? What difference did it make? Marwan had more patience.

"It's just a very common misconception. The term schizophrenia actually means 'split mind', and was coined to describe the inability of the sufferer to distinguish between reality and fantasy. Then, of course, the media got involved and the rest is history."

Another junior asked "Does that mean the experience of schizophrenia is like a trip induced by a drug like LSD?"

Edward could barely conceal his disdain at this question.

Marwan shook his head. "Again, that analogy is a pale imitation of what the patient is actually going through. Let me give you a real example. I had a patient, a young man of twenty years, presenting with classic symptoms. He was experiencing auditory hallucinations – he could hear voices that nobody else could. At times they just whispered in a quite sinister way, at other times he could hear multiple voices shouting at him. They stopped only when he was asleep. The voices were often disparaging and threatening. He didn't know where they were coming from, and was understandably very frightened."

"How did he respond to them?" Moira asked.

"According to his parents, at first, all he did was to isolate himself in his bedroom refusing to come out. He ate and drank very little, and stopped paying any attention to his personal hygiene. But what eventually prompted them to ask for help from the mental health service was when he started to knock holes in his bedroom wall. He had convinced himself that the voices were coming from loudspeakers that someone had inserted into the walls, and he was determined to find them."

"So the voices weren't like disembodied ghostly whispers?"

"No. Quite the reverse. He said he could hear them just as clearly as you and I can hear each other. That's one of the reasons why patients are so convinced they're real, and not a hallucination, which, of course, is what they are."

Ed felt it was time someone asked a sensible question. "Were there any other symptoms?"

Marwan gave a half smile, pleased that Ed seemed to be taking an interest.

"Yes. As is very common in schizophrenia, the voices were accompanied by delusions."

"Delusions?" Amy Pierce had not quite grasped how delusions could qualify as a symptom of a severe mental illness. "Could you explain more about them?" she asked.

"They're false beliefs that the patient insists are true despite being presented with evidence to the contrary," he replied.

"You mean like Arsenal will win the European championship?" Stephen liked to show he had a sense of humour. Marwan almost laughed, though Edward was clearly not impressed.

Smiling, Marwan shook his head. "No, that's not a delusion, merely hopeless optimism."

That brought polite laughter and a snort of derision from the fourth junior – Sanjeev knew Stephen was a Chelsea fan. They had no more chance of winning the Champions' League than Arsenal.

Edward decided it was time for another sensible question. "Do delusions follow a specific pattern?"

This got Marwan's interest. Had Edward actually been doing some serious reading? "Like what?"

"Well," he paused to think. "Like believing that God is speaking to you, or that you have some sort of special mission, or that you've been abducted by aliens?

"That's a good question, Edward," Marwan replied. He spoke to the wider group. "Delusions like the ones Edward describes are common, but are almost always shaped by pre-existing normal beliefs or experiences."

"Like what?" Moira asked.

Marwan smiled again, pleased that he had actually managed to get their attention.

"I once had a very interesting discussion with a psychologist She insisted that delusions usually had a basis in normal beliefs and experiences, while I had been trained that delusions usually had no factual basis whatever; in fact, the more bizarre and impossible they seemed to be, the more typical they were of schizophrenia. So she told me of a case she had once encountered. The patient concerned believed he had been abducted by aliens, and that alien embryos had been surgically implanted into his body so that they could be brought back to Earth undetected, where they would later form the nucleus of an invasion."

Amy, whose father was a psychologist, was puzzled. "It doesn't sound like that could have had any sort of a basis in normal beliefs or experiences."

Marwan agreed. "My thoughts exactly. However, they subsequently learned that there was a cult science-fiction movie where exactly that scenario formed the basis of the plot. The team were informed by the patient's parents that he was an avid science-fiction fan and had seen the movie in question many times."

Now all of them were puzzled. "So what should we learn from that?" Stephen asked.

"That we dismiss our patients' delusions at our – and their – peril. If we can find out the origin of their delusional beliefs, it might offer us an important insight into understanding their illness."

There was a knock on the door. Susan put her head round; her gaze lit first on Edward, who she graced with what she hoped was a winning smile, before settling on Dr. Marwan.

"Doctor Marwan? Sorry to disturb you, but Mr. Strange's GP and social worker have arrived for the case conference, and they want to get started straight away."

Marwan glanced at his watch. "I thought they weren't due until twelve-thirty?" He turned to the junior doctors. "I'm sorry about this. Did anyone have any burning questions before we end the session?"

Nobody did. With several scrapings of chairs, they deposited their used cups into the waste bin and trooped out of his office.

"Same time next week, everybody?" Marwan asked cheerily. He thought it had gone well. This morning's session might set a precedent, and a Saturday tutorial, led by the duty consultant become a regular feature of training for the juniors. He left the office, edging past Susan who was now almost blocking the doorway. Edward was the last to leave. Susan made him squeeze past, and he deliberately brushed against her breasts; she made no attempt to pull herself away. For a moment they were close enough to kiss. It was tempting, he thought to himself.

"Strange?" He said, lip curling slightly.

"What?"

"The patient's name – it really is *Strange*?

"I'm afraid so. Apt for a mental patient, don't you think?"

"I suppose it is." He laughed.

The tension broken, Susan pulled herself away from him.

"So how'd it go?" She asked him. "You know, the impromptu tutorial. Are they all as thick as they look?"

Normally Edward would have defended the junior medical staff from sarky comments from nurses, but today he was not in the mood. "Pretty much," he agreed. This time they laughed together.

*

Bernadette had been right in surmising that Sean's walk would not take him very far. Barely five minutes after Joan's departure, he returned. He found his wife seated at the dining table, holding a key in her hands, turning it over and over in her fingers.

"What's that you've got?" he asked her.

She didn't look up. "It's the key to Joan's bedroom."

Sean was surprised. "Did she give it to you?"

Bernadette shook her head. "No," she said under her breath "She dropped it and I picked it up. She doesn't know I've got it."

Sean came closer. "Have you been crying?"

She pulled a tissue from her sleeve and wiped her eyes before blowing her nose.

"I want to look in her room. But then again, I don't."

He sat down beside her. "We shouldn't you know," he ventured. "It's not right."

She turned to face him. "D'you think I don't know that? But what's happening with our Joan isn't right either, and God knows I don't want to, but I've got to see inside that room. She'll never let us, so this might be the only chance we get."

Her resolve took him a little by surprise, though he had long known she was the stronger of the two of them. He took a deep intake of breath. "Okay," he said, "let's do it then."

Bernadette's hands were shaking as she tried to push the key into the lock. "God, will you look at me," she muttered, "I'm getting as bad as you." With a snick the key turned; she pushed the door open. The curtains were drawn. Bernadette felt for the light switch. Whatever they had imagined they might find, nothing could have prepared them for the reality that was revealed when she turned on the light.

For a moment, Bernadette was stunned to silence. "Holy Mother of God!" she eventually said.

Looking over her shoulder, Sean was similarly taken aback. "Jesus!" was all he could think of to say.

"Did you have any idea?" Bernadette asked as slowly, she entered the room.

"What do you think?"

Slowly she looked round her daughter's room, trying to take it all in. Every square inch – *every* square inch of every wall and the ceiling was covered with hundreds, if not thousands of pictures of Christ. Some in black and white, some in colour; all shapes and sizes showing scenes from every aspect of his life from his birth to his crucifixion, resurrection and ascension. Dominating them all, on the wall above her bed, was a life-size picture of him revealing his sacred heart. Bernadette involuntarily crossed herself.

"This must have taken her ages" she said, awestruck.

"Months, at least." Sean agreed in hushed tones. "How many do you think there are?"

She took a step into the room. "Don't touch anything now," Sean warned her.

Bernadette just stood at the foot of the bed, scanning the pictures, identifying many of the scenes, not able to believe what they had found. "I've – we've - known for a long time that she was dedicated to her faith, but this . . . I don't know what to make of it."

Sean would not follow her into the room. It seemed unnatural to him: more clearly than his wife he could see what this portended. "This is more than dedication," he said. "This is obsession. It can't be healthy. Do you think Father James knows?"

"How could he? I'm sure that if he did he would have mentioned something. He did ask once whether I thought Joan had a vocation to the religious life, but I said I didn't know. I thought her involvement in the church was just a phase – you know – like lots of teenagers go through – some sort of idealism, like communism or helping the poor of Africa. But this . . ." she swept her hand around the room.

For a while they surveyed the room in silence. The pictures were at once familiar but unfamiliar. At another time, they might have found the images comforting, a reminder of their faith, but here, the setting and the multiplicity of them combined to make them seem utterly alien.

"Do you think we should talk to her about it?" Sean asked eventually.

This seemed to break the spell, and Bernadette backed out of the room, locking the door behind her. Now the tears came again

"How should I know?" She sobbed, leaning into his shoulder. "Oh, Sean, how on earth did it get to this? What did we do wrong?"

Sean was not very good in situations of high emotion, but this was his daughter, who, he realised, he loved dearly.

He sighed heavily. "We didn't do anything. Let's just try and think for a moment instead of letting this get the better of us. If we do confront her with it, it might just make things worse: drive her away or make her even more isolated than she already is. God, I wish I knew what to do, but where do you go for help with a thing like this? Who do you ask?"

Bernadette regained a little of her composure. "I wish I knew. Something's wrong, but I don't know what - or what we can do about it. Do you think we should ask Father James?"

"I don't see who else we could ask. You're closest to him these days — will you speak to him?"

She blew her nose. "Of course I will."

Taking her arm, he led her away from the door. "Where exactly was the key?"

She pointed to the carpet where the door jamb cast a slight shadow. He placed it to make it look as though Joan had dropped the key there and they hadn't found it. Together they walked down the stairs.

"In the meantime," he said, "I don't think we should say anything to Joan; I'm sure she needs some sort of help, but until we've got a better idea of what we should do, I think it's probably best if we just carry on as we are."

*

The canteen at St. Peter's was not known for the high quality of its cuisine. It ran to fish, chips, various pies and a few pasta dishes, with a selection of sandwiches that dwindled through the day making up the rest of the menu. Hunger had driven Edward to eat when normally he wouldn't have gone within a mile of the place. The prospect of lasagne and chips made him wince, but beggars can't be choosers, he told himself. He occupied an empty table and was finding out how poor the food actually was when several staff from the psychy unit arrived, and, to his annoyance, came across to join him. Three of the new juniors made their way to the self-serve counter (they can't have realised how crap this mush is yet, Ed thought to himself), while Cathy and Susan got coffee from the machine before sitting down and unpacking the lunches that they had brought with them.

"I'm surprised to see you in here, Ed," Cathy said, taking a bite from a terribly healthy-looking sandwich. "Didn't think you ever came in here."

"I don't if I can help it." He sounded surly, bad-tempered.

One by one, the three juniors joined them.

"Doesn't seem so bad, Marwan," Sanjeev ventured. "I heard he could be a bit of an old twerp."

"Yeah, well, he was on his best behaviour today, wasn't he?" Ed replied.

"Seems to take his training responsibilities quite seriously though" Amy added, licking gravy off her knife.

The morning's events had already worn Edward's patience thin; now this. Did he have to put up with this drivel?

"Most of the time, he's not too bad, I suppose. He's a bit of a fusspot, but his heart's usually in the right place, but today . . . he's surpassed himself." He paused. Would they even care that he should have been having a day off today, should only have been called in if there had been an emergency admission? "You know, I should have known this would happen. Marwan knows I've been on all week and just because he's the duty consultant this week-end, he wants me in to do all the fucking donkey-work for him. Then he comes up with this fucking tutorial. Can't find time for it during the week; oh no . . . that might interfere with his fucking golf. But it's the week-end, and – hey – if he has to be in he might as well make life miserable for everyone else as well."

Stephen was not entirely unsympathetic. "Tell me about it. But it *is* the same for everyone Ed. None of the consultants give a shit about how we balance our work, study and social lives."

"Or in Ed's case, his sex life!" Cathy could not resist getting that in. She laughed and exchanged a knowing glance with Susan.

Ed was not amused. "Oh! How terribly witty Cathy."

Cathy thought this might run a bit longer. She winked at Susan. "Oh, I don't know. I thought your social life and sex life were one and the same thing. Didn't you Sue?"

Susan took her cue beautifully. "So the rumours have it."

The juniors seemed to be enjoying this exchange, but they noticed that Edward did not seem to be embarrassed that his private life was the subject of lunch-time gossip, merely annoyed.

"Well the rumours aren't one hundred percent accurate, yeah?" He bit the end off a chip and threw the rest of it onto his plate in disgust. "You know, it wouldn't have been so bad if it hadn't been so bloody pointless." He waited for the SHOs to agree with him. "I mean, for Christ's sake, it wasn't fucking rocket science we were covering in there, was it? Don't you morons know anything about psychiatry? I mean, why are you bothering if you know so little about it that you have to ask such stupid questions?" He affected a whingeing sing-song voice in parody of the questions that they had asked. *"Isn't schizophrenia about having a split personality? Is schizophrenia like taking LSD?* I ask you."

Steven was not about to take the brunt of Ed's invective lying down. "Sadly Ed, not everybody is blessed with your level of genius." He responded with equal sarcasm.

Edward did not bother to conceal his temper. "What's that supposed to mean?"

Amy decided she needed to stop what had started as mild banter from getting out of hand.

"Oh come on, Ed. We all know you're pissed off at having to be in on your day off, but there's no need to be so hard on everyone else. We're only trying to get doctor Marwan to notice us, butter him up a bit, give him a chance to show his knowledge off. Not everybody can have the plum job of working for the clinical director, can they?"

If Ed was mollified by this, he did a good job of not showing it. "Plum job? Who are you trying to kid? You can have it any day."

Susan tried a different tack. "So Ed, any plans for tonight?"

He let his fork fall to his plate. "I promised I'd go for a pint with Pete this afternoon, but that's not gonna happen now, is it? And I haven't been able to call the girl I met last night, either.

Looks like I'll be having a night in with nothing on the telly but fucking *Casualty*!"

"The girl you met last night? You still haven't told me her name, you know." Susan smiled, flirting madly.

"Probably because he can't remember," Cathy added.

Amy was not impressed, no matter how good-looking he might be. "Is that right Ed?" she asked between mouthfuls. "You had a date but you can't remember her name? What kind of a way is that to start a relationship?"

Cathy had long ago decided that Ed should be brought down a peg or two. Maybe now was the time. "Oh Ed doesn't believe in relationships. As soon as any girl he's dating looks like she might be wanting anything resembling a relationship Ed drops them like a hot brick!"

"Is that true Ed?" Amy asked. "Or is it that you just haven't met the right person yet?"

Edward snarled in the most charming manner he could muster. "Both."

Stephen found the exchange quite entertaining. Ed Plant had quite a reputation, even the new starters knew about him. He wondered if he could stir this up a little more.

"You know that old chestnut that girls choose men so that they can take them and mould them into the person they would like them to be? Well I think most girls that go out with Ed start out like that, but realise they've got no chance, so that when he dumps them they're probably actually grateful for it."

If Stephen had hoped to provoke Ed, he miscalculated. Nothing could derail that ego. "Of course they're fucking grateful, you moron. Look what they're getting: I just happen to be the ultimate package. Everything a woman could wish for rolled into one. Good looking, sexy, intelligent, a good listener and I'm fucking awesome in bed."

Cathy pretended to be worried. "Ed! Keep your voice down will you! There are too many women in here for you to cope with all at once. If they knew what we know, God knows how they'd be able to resist coming over right know to have their way with you."

This brought mild laughter from all of them including Ed, dissipating the tension that had been building. Amy pushed back her chair to leave the table.

"Well, I'd love to be able to stay and listen to this fascinating conversation all day, but some of us have work to do."

"Me too," Stephen added.

Sanjeev had said nothing all through lunch. Now he decided he had a joke for them. "Did anyone hear the joke about the Irish definition of fascinate?"

It sounded like this was going to be in poor taste at best. As one, they groaned. Sanjeev was not about to let them put him off.

"It's all to do with having a coat with nine buttons but with one less hole than buttons."

He waited but got no response. "Go on then," Stephen said.

"Yeah, you see it's a coat with a superfluous button because you can only fasten eight," he continued, pronouncing 'fasten eight' as 'fascinate' in a mock Irish accent overlain with his own Midlands.

"Oh for fuck's sake!" Ed was not even mildly impressed.

His attempt at humour having failed miserably, Sanjeev scuttled away with his tray to the disposal area.

As the others left, Susan stayed with Ed, nursing the remnants of her mug of coffee.

"You know, Ed," she said, not believing that she was actually going to say this – her heart pounding but trying to sound as casual as she could. "You don't have to spend the night in watching *Casualty* if you don't want to."

Ed was a bit slow on the uptake. "Yeah, right. What else is there?"

"You could let me cook dinner for you." There. She had said it.

"What? Didn't you hear what they just said about me and my social life?" He looked closely at her. She was very pretty, for a nurse, but . . . "Anyway, I never mix pleasure and work; it just ends up being too complicated."

Susan tried to sound off-hand. "Up to you Ed, but the offer's there if you change your mind . . . only do let me know before I go off."

Well, he had tried to warn her. And it was a case of any port in a storm. He turned on the charm. It was a trick he had learned years ago; now he could do it at will. He gave her that killer smile.

"What time d'you finish?"

"Handover is at three. I should be away for about twenty past."

He couldn't appear to be too eager, that wouldn't do.

"Look, tell you what, Sue. No promises, though, okay?" She nodded, fingers crossed under the table. "I'm not terribly good at intimate dinners, but there's a nice little bistro in Lark Street – Luccini's – you know the one?" She nodded again, mute with anticipation. "How about we meet there at eight? We can go on somewhere after that if you like?"

She couldn't believe it. She was going to get what she wanted. "Ed, I do like. See you at eight." As flirtily as she could, she added "don't be late, now; I won't!"

Edward was now smiling broadly. "Can't wait!" he said, which wasn't completely true, but was close enough.

*

Despite his best efforts to get way, Edward was still in work at three. Once again he found himself in the nursing station on Maple ward, writing up some patient notes. Cathy walked in carrying a cup of steaming tea.

"God," she said. "This is the first time I've sat down since lunch. I hate doing these long days."

Ed did not respond, concentrating instead on the additions Dr. Marwan had asked him to make.

Cathy was not to be put off so easily. "So Ed, is it true you're going to go out with Sue?"

He could hear the bitchiness in her voice. He stopped writing.

"I might be. Though I don't actually see what business it is of yours, Cathy."

"Oh, it probably isn't, but Sue's a mate, and she's not as thick-skinned as she makes herself out to be."

Edward was never impressed by people who pushed their noses in where they weren't wanted, no matter how well-intentioned they might be.

"A nurse with a heart of gold, you mean? Please; that's so yesterday's stereotype."

"I'm not saying she's all sweetness and light, but she's not a hard-bitten cynic like you either, that's all; and I don't want to see her get hurt. Try and see things from her perspective Ed: the young nurse, head easily turned by the eligible young doctor. Falls in love only to have her heart broken: turns into the bitter and twisted old maid who ends up spending all of her life on the same psychiatric ward – even longer than any of the patients, in fact.

For some reason, Ed found this mildly amusing. "Like Maria, you mean?" He sniggered. "Actually, she's not so bad looking for a hard-bitten old hag. Could even go for her myself if I was desperate enough." He realised what he had just said. "No, forget I said that." He put his pen down on the desk and turned to face her. "Spare me the bleeding heart lecture will you Cath? Sue's big enough to look after herself. And if she isn't then maybe it'll do her good to learn not to get involved with a heartless bastard like me."

"Are you really so heartless Ed? Or is it all just a big act?"

Did she detect a tiny chink in that armour? For a moment, Ed seemed serious. "I wish I knew. All I know is that I'm not ready for a serious relationship, don't want a serious relationship and I make no secret of it. If Susan thinks she's the one to change me she's welcome to try, and hopefully we'll have a little fun while she learns the error of her ways. If not, well, I can't help who and what I am, and I've no intention of changing." The moment passed and he brightened, picking up his pen. "That's why I became a bloody doctor in the first place – so I could play doctors and nurses for real."

Susan popped her head around the door, coat over her arm.

"I got off a few minutes early." She smiled. "Are you ready to come now, Ed, or will we meet later?"

Edward signed the entry he had made and clicked the rings on the file closed. "No, I'm all finished here. Just give me a minute to put this away and I'll be right out. Why don't I meet you in reception?"

"Great!" She walked away with a big cheesy grin on her face

Edward placed the file onto the trolley and gave Cathy a baleful look, as if warning her to keep quiet. Cathy waited until Susan was out of earshot before she spoke.

"All right Ed! I wasn't going to say anything to Sue; she wouldn't listen to me anyway. I just thought I'd try to appeal to your better nature, that's all."

Edward grinned nonchalantly. "Nice try Cathy. Trouble is I just don't have a better nature to appeal to."

For some reason Cathy thought this sounded rather sad. "You really do have a heart of stone, don't you Ed?"

For an instant, Cathy could have sworn that Ed changed. It was as if he knew that she – probably nobody – would ever understand him. He spoke gently, surprising her so much she didn't know how to respond.

"No, not stone Cathy; sand."

*

Like many Catholic parishes, The Sacred Heart had taken to having a vigil mass on Saturday evenings to give the parishioners more options for when they might attend. Unlike Sunday mass, which tended to be a leisurely affair, Saturday evening mass was brisk, and the congregation didn't linger afterwards. This suited Joan who had taken to staying behind and taking up her station before the statue of the Sacred Heart of Jesus, praying and waiting for the music that would fill her soul with its beauty. She wondered if it could ever be too much for her, it was so sublime. She thought and hoped not, but she had never heard it to its end – there was always someone who would interrupt her reverie. She had thought of hiding in the choir loft so that she could spend a night in the church without being disturbed, but then she remembered something about a burglar alarm with movement detectors. Never mind, she told herself, if this truly was a gift from God, He would find a way to see it through to its fulfilment. As the last of the congregation departed, the lights in the church dimmed. Father O'Hanlon would be off for his tea before returning for a final look around and locking up. She thought she would have about an hour.

Tonight she wasn't sure what she should pray for or meditate on. The cross words she had exchanged with her dad that morning still rankled. She might feel better if she told him she was sorry, but the fact was she didn't feel particularly sorry for what she had said, she only felt sorry for what she knew her dad was going through. Try as she might, she just couldn't make herself think about anything that she thought was suitable. In the end she just said under her breath "Here I am. Just waiting for you, Lord." Almost instantly the music started. However, it took her by surprise. Instead of the voice singing unaccompanied, it sounded like an orchestra tuning up before reaching a harsh and brash crescendo. It did not seem to have the serene lyrical quality she had heard before, though here and there she was able to hear themes that sounded like they had some connection with the original. It was much harder to listen to this music, it was more challenging, more demanding, less forgiving of the listener. If she had thought about it, it was consistent with her confused mood, but she didn't make that connection. She didn't know how long she had been listening to it when all of a sudden it died away to reveal the sound of quiet footsteps echoing in the near-silent church.

It was Father O'Hanlon walking up the aisle towards her. He joined her in the pew, genuflecting and crossing himself as he did so.

"Hello Joan, back again?"

"Evening, Father." She replied almost under her breath.

"If anyone were to ask me how you looked just now, I would have said you looked like you were in a trance. Is everything alright?"

Joan flushed. "Yes, Father. Why wouldn't it be?"

"Are your mum and dad OK?"

"Yes Father. Well, about as well as you might expect, given the circumstances."

The priest paused. He wondered if there was anything troubling this young woman. But how to ask? "Joan," he said, "is there any particular reason why you're coming to church so often?"

"Not really, Father. I just like it here."

James O'Hanlon was perplexed. What attraction did his church hold for this young woman? "Joan, you know, I remember your mum in tears a couple of years ago after you said something about religion being a sham, a counterfeit comfort for people who couldn't face the realities of life." He waited to let his words sink in. "And now we can't get rid of you. Is there anything troubling you? Is there anything I can help you with?"

Joan's reply was an emphatic "No Father."

But the priest was not so easily put off. He knew, from long experience, that sometimes he had to coax confidences out of his parishioners. "Not that I'm sorry to see you here, of course. I wish more people would come to church, especially people your age."

"I just like it here, Father. It's just . . ." She hesitated. He looked at her quizzically, encouraging her to continue. "Well, it sounds a bit corny, that's all."

"I wouldn't worry about that, Joan. What was it you were going to say?"

She inhaled deeply, closing her eyes and taking in all the smells of the church – the polish, the burnt wax, the remains of incense. It was so familiar, so comforting. "Just that it's peaceful. I feel like I'm in the presence of God. I look at him, and he looks right back at me. And it's peaceful. Not like out there." She waved her hand at the doors at the back of the church.

He was always surprised by how deep simple sincerity could reach. "That's pretty wonderful, don't you think, Joan?" He said quietly. "The simple experience of finding peace in the presence of God. That's really quite profound when you think about it. Maybe I should talk about it one Sunday. Would you mind?"

"Mind? Mind what?"

"If I talked about finding peace in the presence of God one Sunday at mass."

Joan was surprised he had asked her such a question. "Of course I wouldn't mind, Father. Except that the way you say it makes it sound complicated. It seemed simpler before you started talking about it. Before it was just me and Him, and I thought we understood each other. Now I'm not so sure."

Now it was the priest who was not so sure. "Well, since you put it that way, Joan . . ."

"No, Father, I didn't mean that you shouldn't, really. I think it would be nice if you talked about that in mass."

Some minutes passed in companionable silence while Joan plucked up the courage to ask what was really on her mind.

"Father," she asked hesitantly, "could I ask you something?"

This was what he had been waiting for. "Of course, what is it?"

"How can you tell what God's purpose for your life is? I mean, you have a vocation to be a priest. How did you know that was what God intended for you?"

He smiled. "Back on the easy questions again, I see, Joan." He straightened up, looking at the statue as if needing guidance. "How did I know I had a vocation? It's a bit of a long story, and I suspect it's different for everyone. In my case I was convinced that, in fact, a priest was the last thing I wanted to be. I suppose you could say I was in denial."

Joan suppressed a giggle. "In denial? That seems a strange thing for a priest to say, if you don't mind my saying so, Father. How were you in denial? What happened?"

"The short version is that *He* just wouldn't let me alone." He pointed a finger at the statue. "He can be very persistent, you know, and in the end, He just wore me down. When He wants you to know what He has in store for you, you can be sure He'll find a way of letting you know. I wouldn't worry about it if I were you; just let things happen in their own time."

Joan did not seem convinced. "In their own time? But that could take a lifetime, or maybe never."

"Joan, one of the most important things I've learned as a priest is never to try and hurry God, or presume to try and understand his purpose. It doesn't matter what we think or how we feel, He'll make things happen in his own good time. I know it's a bit of a cliché, but the saying that God works in mysterious ways happens to be true. Trust me, I know."

"I thought you were going to say 'Trust me, I'm a priest.'" She sighed. "Thanks, Father."

"No worries. Don't you think you'd better be getting home? Your mum will be wondering what's happened to you."

"My mum?" She shook her head. "I don't think so. I don't think she even knows I'm there these days. I hardly seem to see her at all."

"Hardly see her? That doesn't sound like your mum to me. Maybe you should ask her about how to tell what God's purpose is for your life. She has a vocation herself, after all."

This was not what she had been expecting to hear. "My mum? A vocation? So what happened?"

"She followed her vocation, of course. She has a vocation to the married life, and to be a parent. Neither of them are easy vocations to follow in this day and age, you know."

"I never thought of it that way."

"Not many people do – especially not children about their parents – until they become parents themselves, of course, and even then it doesn't occur to most people that marriage and parenthood might be vocations in their own right. As soon as the word vocation is mentioned, we just seem to think about the clergy and forget all about everyone else."

Joan gathered her few belongings together and edged her way out of the pew. Half way down the aisle she turned. "Thanks for the advice Father," she said. "You're a great help."

He shrugged and started to blow out the candles. "Can you let the snip down on the lock as you go out?"

4
Works and Days

On locking the church doors from the inside, James O'Hanlon made his way through the sacristy and along the connecting corridor to the presbytery. As he went, he could hear the phone ringing. Funny, he thought to himself, how we still think of a phone as ringing even though they now made only electronic chirping sounds. The insistence of the ringing seemed to make his progress all the slower, as if he had kept the caller waiting for ages.

Slightly out of breath, he picked up the phone. "Good evening, Sacred Heart of Jesus presbytery, James O'Hanlon speaking."

At the other end, a respectful voice asked "Hello, is that you Father?"

"This is Father James O'Hanlon speaking; who is this please?"

"It's Bernadette Archer, Father."

He could barely hear for the crackles on the line. "I'm sorry, who? Could you speak up - the line's a bit crackly."

"I'm sorry Father. Can you hear me now?"

"Yes, that's fine."

"It's Bernadette Archer, Father."

"Hello Bernadette. How are you?"

"I know you must be very busy Father, and I hate to disturb you, but I was wondering, could you spare me a few minutes of your time?"

He could sense the stress in her voice. "Of course I can," he replied softly. "What can I do for you?"

Bernadette's fears came pouring out. "It's Joan, Father. We're getting awfully worried about her, me and Sean, that is, and we don't know who to turn to for help."

James was astonished. "Joan, Bernadette? Why would you be needing help with Joan? She's a wonderful daughter, and a credit to you. She's not in any trouble is she?"

"Thank you for those kind words, Father, and no, she's not in any trouble, not that I know of, but I do think that there is something going on that's very worrying." She paused, not entirely sure how to continue. "I don't know how to tell you this Father, but we think she might have something wrong with her mentally."

Now he was shocked. Hadn't he spoken to her not five minutes ago? "Joan? No. I'm sure that can't be right. What makes you think that?"

For Bernadette, calling Father James was a two-edged sword Her relief at having someone to confide in was palpable, but telling him about their fears was not easy. "Well, Father, as you know, she's never away from the church these days, but we can't get out of her what the sudden attraction is. She won't talk about it. Just flies off the handle every time we mention it."

"I hardly think that counts as a sign of mental illness now, Bernadette. Quite a few people in the parish come to church every day, for many different reasons." He tried to relieve the stress by injecting a little light humour. "I'm quite sure that they're not all mentally ill, though now I think about it, perhaps one or two . . ."

Bernadette was oblivious to the humour. "It's not just that Father. We hardly see her now from one day to the next. She's taken to staying in her room, she hardly eats a thing, and she's put a lock on her door so we can't get in. She won't even let me in to clean."

Still, he was not convinced. "Well Bernadette, I'm no expert, but that sounds like fairly normal behaviour for a young person these days. Half the mothers in the parish complain that as their children get older, they treat their parents' house like it was a hotel."

"I thought you would probably say that, Father, but I'm afraid there's more to it than that. Joan was never the secretive sort, you know, she was always ready to talk about anything. But since she dropped out of her university course, she's been the complete opposite. She hardly talks to us and when she does it's usually to accuse us of prying into her business." She paused. The guilt at what she was about to tell him was awful. "This morning she dropped the key to her bedroom without realising it."

James sensed that here was the source of Bernadette's concern.

"And you and Sean used it to go in and found something you wish you hadn't?"

At the other end of the line, Bernadette was shedding silent tears. "Please Father, don't make it sound like we did something wrong. I feel bad enough already. I know we invaded her privacy, but we were so worried we just had to do something."

"Bernadette; what on earth could be so awful that it's got you this upset? What did you find? Drugs? A pregnancy test?"

He could hear her sobs clearly now. She took a breath. "Oh Father, it was awful. When we got in every inch of her bedroom was covered in pictures of Jesus!"

Whatever he might have been expecting, this was not it.

"Bernadette, please try and calm yourself. Pictures of Jesus? Try and listen to yourself and what you're saying. It's as if you'd just told me she was involved in devil-worship or something."

"Oh, Father. I knew you'd find it hard to understand. But she hasn't got just one or two pictures of Jesus. It's every square inch of every wall, and the ceiling. All covered, and I do mean all: there's not a square inch of the wall can be seen. There's hundreds, maybe thousands of pictures. It's not something she could have done overnight, it must have taken her weeks, maybe even months. It's just not normal. She's obsessed, and I've heard that's a form of mental illness that can lead you to do some awful things."

Whatever Bernadette and Sean had found, James O'Hanlon could not square it with the conversation he'd had with Joan that very evening.

"Bernadette," he said, trying to calm her, "believe me, I do understand, perhaps more than you know. What you've just told me explains a lot." He paused. "I had a conversation with Joan just today in church. I think she may have a vocation to the religious life but I don't think she's reached that understanding herself yet. She feels torn between the life she thinks she should have – like her parents, meeting a young man, marrying and having children – and what she thinks God might want for her. She actually asked me how you could tell whether you had a vocation." He waited for his words to sink in before continuing. "You know, if she does have a vocation, it's something we should thank God for."

Bernadette sensed a life-line and reached for it. "I know that Father, but are you sure? Did she really ask you that?"

"She really did. I'll tell you what . . . next time I see her I'll talk to her about it again. I'll tell her how worried you are about her and ask her to talk to you about it. I really don't think there's anything to get yourself into such a state about. Things will unfold as they should in God's own time. The best thing you can do is to pray – for Joan and for yourself. Ask God to make his purpose known sooner rather than later."

Bernadette felt such a surge of relief she felt almost elated by it. "If you're sure that's what's really going on, Father . . ."

"Bernadette, I'm sure. Now I suggest you go and make yourself a cup of tea, and stop worrying. Next time Joan comes into church, I'll phone you so you can come over and we can discuss everything – and pray - together."

*

On Maple ward, it was time for the evening medicines round. Maria had the prescription sheets in front of her, and was pushing the medicines trolley along the corridors looking for the patients who had their medicines due.

She popped her head into the day room, raising her voice so that it could be heard over the television.

"Has anybody seen Bob Traynor?" she asked.

"I think he was sat in the quiet corner," a voice replied.

She found him occupying an armchair that had seen better days, in a space at the back of the ward that had been given the name the 'quiet' corner. It was quiet only in the sense that it was away from the day room. There was little privacy, and no guarantee of quiet. Mr. Traynor was by himself, rocking silently backwards and forwards, his movement serving no purpose that Maria could see, though, over the years, she had seen this kind of behaviour in many patients.

"Mr. Traynor," she called. "Time for your medication."

His reply was slow and deliberate, as if speaking every word required a conscious effort. "I don't want it. It makes me feel terrible."

Maria ignored this, and decanted a pill from a brown glass bottle into a small plastic cup, holding it out for the patient to take.

"You have to take it Mr. Traynor," she said in what she thought of as her 'sympathetic but firm' voice. "It'll make you feel better."

The patient did not reach for the proffered cup. "I said I don't want it. It makes me feel worse, not better."

Maria knew from experience that it didn't do to allow patients to challenge her authority. "How does it make you feel worse, Mr. Traynor?"

"It makes me feel sleepy all the time, and I can't think straight."

Sometimes patients could be persuaded to take the medication if you were honest about the side effects. It was worth a try, she thought. "The sleepiness is a side effect of the medication. I'm afraid you have to put up with some side effects if you want to feel better."

"But it doesn't make me feel better. I told you, it makes me feel worse."

During this exchange, Cathy had walked down the corridor. She thought Maria could show a bit more sympathy than she generally did. Now was a case in point. "Is something the matter?" She asked.

Maria did not feel the need to explain herself to Cathy, even if she was the senior member of staff. "Mr. Traynor doesn't want to take his medication."

Cathy sat herself down beside the patient, and took his hand "Come on, Bob, you know you have to take it. It *will* make you feel better."

"But it doesn't make me feel better." He shrugged Cathy off "I just told her that." He said crossly.

"I just explained all that to him." Maria droned unsympathetically.

Cathy was not put off – by either of them. "Bob, do you want the voices to go away?" She asked him.

"Yeah. But how can a pill make the voices go away?"

"It's a bit difficult to explain. But just trust me – the pills do work, they just take a little time. But they won't work if you don't take them." She took the plastic cup from Maria and held it out to him. "Please?"

Reluctantly he took it, and handed the cup back.

"Thanks, Bob," she said. "Taking your medication is the right thing to do; you know that really, don't you?"

Without replying, he shuffled away. The two nurses walked the trolley back to the nursing station together.

"I won't be in again until Tuesday night," Cathy said, "so could you suggest to Ed when he's back in that it might be worth writing up Mr. Traynor's meds so they can be given by mouth or by injection. That way if he refuses to take it, we can make sure he still gets his medication."

5
The sin of pride

Ed liked having Mondays off; it helped him to recover from the exertions of the week-end. He did very little apart from spending some time shopping, without the annoyance of loads of people crowding him. A light lunch and a cappuccino later, he spent the rest of the afternoon in his flat doing some desperately-needed catching up with the Oxford textbook of psychiatry. Deep joy.

To Joan, one day was much like any other. She was back in the church for morning mass, but didn't stay. James O'Hanlon looked for her after he had taken off his vestments, but to no avail. Not to worry, he told himself. There was a novena that evening, and he was sure she would be there for that. He would catch her afterwards.

Sure enough, when the congregation had sidled out of the church after the novena, Joan had lit a candle before the statue of the Sacred Heart of Jesus, and, head bowed, was lost in prayer. The church lights were low, and, watching from the back of the church, James could have sworn that she seemed bathed in a light that had no source. He shook his head and started to walk slowly up the aisle towards the altar. Joan had no idea that she was not alone. She was listening with utter joy to the sound of her saviour singing to her. The language was unknown to her, but she had heard of people blessed by being able to sing in 'tongues' – a language that was intelligible only to them – and assumed that this was what she was hearing now. Whatever it was, it was miraculous. Suddenly the music stopped, and Joan became aware of slow steps approaching her. Once again she found her parish priest next to her in the pew.

"Hello Joan," he said, quietly.

"Hello Father."

"Joan, would you pray with me for a minute?"

He crossed himself and bowed his head. "Heavenly Father, we ask you to guide our thoughts, our hearts and our actions. Help us to understand what it is you want from us so that we may serve you as we should. We pray especially for Joan. I sense her heart is troubled: she wants to do your will but doesn't know what it is. Please send your spirit of grace and mercy to help her to understand what it is she should do with her life. Through Christ our Lord."

"Amen."

For a short while they knelt together in silence. It was the priest who broke it. "Joan, I've been thinking about the conversation we had the other day."

"Yes, Father." Joan waited for him to continue.

"The more I think about it, the more I feel that you may have a vocation to the religious life."

Joan agreed. "I think I might have too, Father." Then she hesitated. "But I'm not sure. How can I be sure?"

The priest sighed heavily. "Sometimes you can't be sure. Sometimes you just have to take a leap of faith and trust that you're doing what God wants of you."

"That's what I've been worried about."

He lifted himself up off his knees and sat on the bench. "I sensed that something was troubling you. I have a suggestion."

"What's that Father?"

"The sisters of St. Mary Magdalene are a working order. They run health and education projects both in the UK and in the third world. They concentrate on the needs of poor women. The ones we euphemistically used to call 'fallen' women."

Joan was doubtful. "I'm not sure that's what I'd want to do, Father."

But she had misunderstood. "No, Joan, that's not what I'm suggesting. They run retreats for anything up to three months that help people to explore whether or not they do have a vocation. No strings. If at any time you decide you haven't a vocation, you just leave. If, on the other hand, you do have a vocation, they can help you to find an order that best fits with what you feel you're called to do." He paused, letting the silence of the church do its work before asking: "What d'you think?"

Joan did not answer. He knew that responding to a vocation was never easy. No matter how many times he had told people how light the burden of vocation could be once you had taken that leap of faith, actually taking that first leap was almost always a decision of enormous difficulty.

"That's okay Joan," he said lightly, "I understand. It took me a long time to decide myself. There's no pressure on you Joan, it was just an idea to think about."

He started to get up, but Joan put her hand on his forearm to stop him. "It's not that Father, I'd be happy to go and stay with the sisters for a while. There's something I think I ought to tell you, that's all."

"Oh? What's that Joan?"

She didn't know how to say what she knew she had to tell him. "I really don't know how to tell you this Father, all I can do is to ask that you believe that I'm telling the truth."

"The truth Joan? You make it sound very ominous."

"I can't help it Father, I can scarcely believe it myself."

"Believe what Joan?"

It was obvious from the look on her face that she was finding it extraordinarily difficult to tell him. "Father, it's not the vocation I'm worried about." She paused before getting to the crux of the matter. Taking a deep breath she blurted "I've had visitations. That's why I keep coming back to church."

He could not prevent the consternation from showing on his face. "Visitations? From who?"

Joan bowed her head before answering in a near whisper "From Him, Father. From Jesus."

He could scarcely believe what he was hearing. "What sort of visitations?" He asked, his voice suddenly hoarse. "When?"

"It first happened not long after I came home from uni. I was on my own in the church, praying in front of his statue, and I heard somebody singing."

"Singing? What sort of singing?"

The memory of it was enough to overcome Joan's initial reluctance. "It was just one voice. But it was so wonderful. It was amazing. It was so beautiful, so calm, so perfect. I can still hardly believe it. I looked around, but there was nobody there. Then the singing stopped. I still couldn't see anyone. Then I heard a voice. It said 'Joan, you need to learn to trust.' I could hear it as if the person who said it was standing right next to me. This time I looked all round the church, but still there was no-one there. When I looked at the statue, I could have sworn He was smiling at me."

All of a sudden, the church seemed to take on a claustrophobic air. The priest took a handkerchief out of his pocket and dabbed his brow. "But weren't you scared Joan?" He asked.

"Scared?" Joan seemed surprised he should ask such a question. "No. I wasn't scared. It was strange, but I don't think I've never felt so safe and secure. It was like knowing I was in God's hands and nothing could hurt me."

"And since then?"

"A week or so later it happened again. This time I could hear music with the singing."

It was as though the conversation he had had with her mother had taken on a new and sinister garb. "Was it the same music?" It was all he could think of to say.

Now that she had started, Joan seemed eager to tell all. "Yes Every time I hear it a little more gets added. Now whole choirs of angels join in. It's just the most incredible amazing experience I've ever known."

"And this happens every time you come to church?" To his surprise, his voice sounded angry.

Joan shook her head. "No Father, only when I'm alone."

He didn't know how – or even if he should – let this conversation continue, but it seemed to have taken on a life of its own. "Do you know what the music is Joan?" He found himself saying.

"No Father. I've never heard it anywhere else, and the words are in a language I don't understand."

That gave him the opening he needed to try and bring her back to earth. "So, Joan, how do you know this is a visitation from Jesus? How do you know you're not just imagining all of this?" His words sounded harsh, almost brutal, but they did not have the effect he imagined they would.

"Because now I can see Him." She answered, full of self-assurance.

Years of dealing with the tragic and the unsavoury meant that he was a man who was not easily shocked. But he was now. Was he in the presence of sainthood, or insanity? "You see Him?" He asked, not daring to believe it might be true.

Joan was calm. "Yes. He stands right in front of me. He sings and I know that I am bathed in the light of his love and power I know that I have been granted a miracle. Why, I don't know, but I can't think of any other explanation for it."

Her naïve acceptance that it must be a miracle convinced him of her sincerity. But what Bernadette had told him hinted at mental instability. Or was it that – in his heart of hearts – his own faith was lacking? He paused, setting himself the conflicting tasks of accepting in faith while at the same time trying to think rationally.

Eventually he asked "Joan, have you told anyone else about this?"

She looked at him out of the corner of her eye as if trying to see through the motives behind his question. "No Father."

He breathed a sigh of relief. Faith would have to wait; rationality had to come first. "Good," he said, clearing his throat, anxious about how she would take what he had to say next. "I'm sorry to have to tell you Joan, that if you persist with this story you'll find that life will become very difficult for you. The Church is on her guard for false testimony, and you'll have all sorts of unpleasant accusations flung at you."

Joan could hardly believe what she had heard. "But that's wicked. Why would anyone do that?"

James O'Hanlon hated having to defend the less charitable actions of the Church, but it was a sad fact of life that there were many self-deluded believers too ready to shout 'Miracle!' on the flimsiest pretext, or charlatans all too keen to take advantage of the vulnerable and the gullible. He took one of Joan's hands in his, hoping that she would find it reassuring, understand that he was on her side in whatever might come to pass.

"Partly because the Church has been taken in so many times by the naïve and the unscrupulous," he said, his heart heavy. "Partly because of the sin of pride."

Joan was confused. "The sin of pride? I don't understand."

The priest sighed. "Not many people do. The sin of pride is a terrible sin because it cuts both ways. There is the sin of pride on the part of the Church refusing to believe the testimony of someone like you. It goes something like this: if the Lord is minded to grant visitations, why doesn't he grant them to the holy men and women living pious religious lives? Then there is the sin of pride of a young woman who believes she has been granted her own private miracle. What is there about her that makes her believe she is so special that the Lord would choose her above all others?"

The sin of pride cut Joan to the quick. "I don't know," she said, so quietly he could barely hear her. She seemed completely deflated. But then: "But what about St. Bernadette?" she asked, her confidence returning. "She wasn't anyone special. What about the children at Fatima. They were just ordinary people, like me, weren't they?"

He sensed it was time to bring their conversation to an end, at least for now; he needed time to think. He stood up, absently brushing his hands down the front of his trousers as he did so.

"Joan," he said, "all of this has become doubly worrying in the light of a conversation I had the other day with your mother. Your mum and dad are very worried about you, you know. I think we had better get her over here to think about what we need to do next."

6
A trinity of errors

It was with a sense of great foreboding that James O'Hanlon made his way back to the presbytery, leaving Joan at the foot of the statue. A brief phone call was all it took to bring Bernadette to the church. He had the odd sensation that although he knew she would be hurrying, it seemed that he waited an age before she arrived at the presbytery. Normally a patient man; now, even this short delay tried his patience. Hurriedly he told her of his conversation with Joan. With no further explanation other than Joan was waiting for them, he led her through the sacristy into the church. Bernadette was in turmoil, fearful of what might be revealed She hoped it would be confirmation of her daughter's vocation. She feared she would find more evidence of mental illness.

Priest and mother walked together from the sacristy door, passing the sanctuary rails to where Joan was seated before the statue of the Sacred Heart.

Bernadette hesitated. "Joan, is everything alright love?" She asked.

As Joan turned towards her, Bernadette could see the tears in her eyes. "Mum, I'm fine." She said. "Honestly. I'm perfectly okay. I'm just a bit confused, that's all."

Bernadette's voice was brittle. "Father James has told me everything." She paused. "I think I understand what's been going on now, and I want you to know that me and your dad love you and want to help you."

Joan's reaction surprised them all. Without any warning, she fell into a rage. She turned on the priest, shouting "What did you tell her?"

He tried to calm her, responding to her anger with a quiet voice. "I told her everything Joan. Everything we talked about. About the possibility that you may have a vocation; about the music."

If he hoped that this would placate her, he was wrong. Her fury was beyond reason.

"You had no right!" She yelled. "What I said to you was in confidence. How can I trust you if you're going to blab it all to the first person you meet?"

It was a case of hope winning out over experience. Rarely did rationality win out against strong emotions, but it was all he had.

"Joan, your mum's not just the first person I met. She's a very important person in your life. She's someone who cares deeply about you."

Bernadette was both frightened and distressed by what she was witness to. "Joan, please don't blame Father James. He's just as worried about you as I am, as your dad is. Won't you tell me about the music? Please?"

Now it was her mother who became the target of her ire. "Music?" The derision in Joan's voice was palpable. "What music? Who said anything about music?" The words echoed around the church for a moment before giving way to the stillness of silence. There was a deathly hush for several seconds until it was broken by the sound of someone rattling the church door. They all turned towards it but it stopped as abruptly as it began.

The tension snapped. It might have been the calm at the eye of a storm. Whatever it was, Father O'Hanlon took the opportunity to try and reason with Joan once more.

"I told your mum what you told me about Jesus coming to you in church and singing to you, and that you believed it was a miracle."

This time, Joan did not resort to shouting, but her resentment at the broken confidence could still be felt.

"Father, I don't know how you could do that," she said, almost spitting her words out, "'specially not after you practically accused me of having an overactive imagination."

High emotion was something Bernadette had become used to. She had seen enough of it as Sean had been forced to face up to his impending disability. But her daughter? What would fill a young woman like Joan with such rage, such scorn? She had not thought her daughter capable of it.

"Joan, what are you talking about, love?"

Once again, Bernadette found herself full square in the face of her daughter's wrath. "Isn't it obvious?" She snarled. "You tell him that you're worried about me, that you think I'm going round the bend, and he decides to put his oar in by making up this cock-and-bull story about me saying I can hear Jesus singing to me in church. It all fits doesn't it? You get rid of me nice and quietly, and

I get dismissed as someone who's coming unscrewed. Well, it's not going to work."

Tears formed at the corners of Bernadette's eyes. She tried to blink them away. "So you don't hear the voice of Jesus singing to you?" She asked, fearful of this creature that her daughter had become.

Joan's reply was almost hysterical. "No! Of course I fucking don't!" She screamed.

Father James and Bernadette might have been shocked to silence by this outburst, but that wasn't what stilled their response. It was Joan. Within seconds, she doubled over, hands over her ears as though trying to block out something she did not want to hear. She gasped, shaking her head in vehement denial. Then she screamed.

"No! It's not like that! I didn't mean it like that!" She started to cry inconsolably.

Without a glance at her mother or the priest, she picked herself up and ran for the church door. The key was still in the lock. Joan fumbled with it, struggling to get it open. Finally the key turned, and she wrenched the door wide, letting it slam against the wall. The street outside was empty and she launched herself into it.

7
Possession

Joan ran from the church reeling. She didn't know or care where she might be going. It had started to rain but she was oblivious to it. She had heard something in the church. Something that she knew was meant only for her. Something that had shocked her to her very core. It was a passage from the New Testament. The passage where Saint Peter was insisting that he would stick with his master through thick and thin, no matter what trials he might have to face. And Jesus had replied:

"I tell you solemnly, that before this night is over, you will have denied me three times."

Now those words were reverberating through her mind, echoing, tormenting, mocking her. She could not get rid of them. No matter what she tried, denial, prayer, screaming, there they were, repeating over and over, and there was no escaping them.

In the church Father O'Hanlon was the first to regain his composure. "Bernadette," he said, his words given urgency by Joan's flight, "yesterday I said I thought there was nothing wrong with Joan apart from her being a little confused about where her future lay. Now I'm not so sure. I think you may be right – she may indeed be mentally ill. She certainly needs help. Professional help. Certainly more than we can give her."

"So what should we do Father?"

The priest was no stranger to mental illness, though he had never witnessed its effects in such a personal way before. "What anybody in these circumstances would do. I think you should call the doctor and ask him to come and see Joan."

*

Towards noon on Tuesday, Bernadette and Sean were waiting for the arrival of their family doctor. Joan had eventually come home in the early hours, but they had not seen her. For the first time in months she had not made the effort to get up for morning mass. Tacitly they seemed to have agreed that it was best to leave her where she was. The doorbell rang. Sean shuffled down the hall to answer it. A woman in her late thirties was standing there carrying what he would have described as a 'doctor's bag'. Since the onset of his illness, he had been something of a 'regular' at the doctor's, so she knew him well. She gave her best professionally reassuring smile.

Sean did not return the smile, but did not forget his manners. "Oh, doctor Stanton. Thanks for coming over. Please come in."

"I came as soon as I could." She replied, following him down the hall to the parlour. "I'm afraid we had a rather busy surgery this morning: it only finished about ten minutes ago."

Bernadette was sat at the table, playing nervously with an empty tea mug. "Good morning, doctor," she said. "Would you like a cup of tea?"

"No thanks." She waited to be told why they had asked her to visit, but sensed their reluctance to begin. "What seems to be the problem?"

Bernadette was doing her best not to cry. "It's Joan, doctor."

"Your daughter?"

Bernadette nodded. "Yes doctor. I think she's having a nervous breakdown."

"Oh. Do you mind if I sit down?" She put her bag on the floor and took a chair. "A nervous breakdown? What makes you think that?"

Bernadette exchanged a glance with Sean. "She's been behaving very oddly lately, doctor. She's taken to her room, and hardly comes out. She won't let me in, not even to clean."

"And she's become completely obsessed with going to church, doctor. Hardly seems to be away from the place these days." Sean added.

The doctor nodded, but said "I don't think that really qualifies as a nervous breakdown."

Bernadette bowed her head as if in contrition. "No doctor." She didn't know how to explain. Didn't know where to start, what was important, what wasn't. She feared she might be letting Joan down but really had very little idea of what a nervous breakdown actually was.

"I assume there's more to it than this, or you wouldn't have called me out?"

"Yes doctor. She told Father James . . ."

"Father James?"

Sean felt he had to explain. "Our parish priest."

"Oh. You're Catholics then?"

"Yes."

"Practising Catholics?"

Bernadette thought they were getting away from the point. "Is that important?" She asked.

Doctor Stanton paused to consider. "I'm not sure. It might be. Are You? Practising Catholics, I mean."

"Yes."

"Anyway," the doctor continued, "you say she told your parish priest something. I assume it must have been important? Important enough for you to think something was seriously wrong?"

"You could say that." Sean said.

"What exactly did she tell him?"

Bernadette took a deep breath before replying. She had seen the effect that telling another person about her 'miracle' could have on Joan.

"She told him that when she went to church she could hear the voice of Jesus singing to her. And that's not all. She said that the angels joined in the chorus."

"I see. And did she say what song they were singing?"

"No. She said it was one she had never heard before, and that she couldn't understand the language they were singing in."

Sean interrupted. "Tell the doctor about what happened last night."

The doctor turned to him. "Last night? Something important happened?"

But it was Bernadette who replied. "I don't know whether it was important or not. Joan was in church, and Father James called to say I ought to go over, and we could try and talk to Joan about these visions she said she was having."

"And what happened?"

"Joan got all upset. No, upset isn't the right word to use. She was enraged. In a fury. Like she was possessed. I've never seen her like that before. Never. Although she told Father James that she had heard Jesus singing to her, when I asked her about it she denied everything, and ran way screaming. That's when Father James said he thought we should call you."

Doctor Stanton stood up. "He was quite right. Okay. I think I had better go and talk to Joan now."

"I don't think that will do much good doctor." Sean told her "She locked herself in her bedroom last night and she's refused to talk to us ever since. We can't get a word out of her."

"I have to at least try. Can you show me the way?"

Bernadette bustled round the doctor to lead her up the stairs "Of course, doctor. This way."

Leaving Sean in the parlour, Bernadette led the way up the stairs and onto the landing outside Joan's bedroom. She knocked on Joan's door and tried the handle, but, as usual, it was locked.

She knocked again, and called softly. "Joan? Joan! The doctor's here. She wants to talk to you."

Gently but firmly the doctor pushed past her, and called in a no-nonsense voice. "Joan? It's doctor Stanton. Can I talk to you please?"

There was no reply. Dr. Stanton tried again. "Joan, please? I have to know whether you're okay or not. If you won't answer me we'll have to call the police and get them to break into your room just to make sure that you're safe. You don't want that to happen, do you?"

Still there was no reply. Bernadette was beside herself. "Joan . . . please?"

Still they waited. Then they heard a muffled voice that sounded as if someone was talking from under the bedclothes. "Go away. I'm all right. I just want to be left alone."

Relieved to discover she hadn't been called out to a suicide, the doctor decided it was time to take control of the situation.

"I understand that Joan," she said firmly, "but you have to understand that your mum and dad are very worried about you. You have to admit that your recent behaviour has been a little unusual, to say the least." She paused to see if there would be any reply. There wasn't. "Won't you at least open your door and let me in so I can see for myself that you're okay?"

There was a long pause before the muffled voice came again "No. I know what you want. The lot of you just want to get rid of me. Well I'm not having it. All I want is to be left alone."

"I'm afraid I can't do that Joan. For all I know you might have cut your wrists in there and be slowly bleeding to death. I have to see for myself that you're all right."

That seemed to rouse Joan from her torpor. The rage of the previous evening erupted. "For fuck's sake!" Joan shouted. "Are you fucking deaf or just stupid? I don't want to talk to you and I'm not letting you in! Now will you just fuck off and leave me alone?"

Now Bernadette's patience broke. She could not allow this outburst to pass. Joan might be having a nervous breakdown - whatever that was - but there was no need for this. "Joan! There's no need to be like that! The doctor's just doing her job. She wants to help you. Why won't you let her in?" But all she had done was to stoke the flames of Joan's anger.

"Oh, you'd like that, wouldn't you?" She yelled back. "Let the doctor in so she can say I'm round the twist and have me carted off to the fucking loony bin!"

Bernadette shook her head. "Perhaps you can see what I mean now, doctor," she said. "It doesn't seem to come from anywhere. One moment she's quiet, the next moment it's like someone's lit the blue touch paper and she's exploded."

The doctor did not reply. Instead she called to Joan. "Joan, it's really not like that. If you *are* having a nervous breakdown there are things we can do to help. If you're not, then as soon as I've seen that you are okay, I really will go away and leave you alone. How about it? Are you going to let me in?"

Her efforts were rewarded by silence. They waited for what seemed an age. Just as they were about to walk away from the door they could hear a voice from inside the bedroom. Though the words were disjointed, it was clearly Joan, and it sounded like she was talking to someone in her room.

"No. No, that isn't what I did. No, Jesus does love me. If I can only just go back to the church and explain I know he'll understand. Jesus can forgive anything. Anything at all."

Bernadette stood close to the door, straining to hear whether there was another person in the room with Joan. "Joan? Joan?" She shouted. "Is there someone in there with you?"

But now there was only silence. Dr. Stanton gestured to Bernadette not to speak. "Joan? Who are you talking to?" She asked

For the first time in her life, the cosy familiar walls of her bedroom felt like those of a prison. The hundreds of pictures of Jesus with which she had covered them seemed to have withdrawn their promises of redemption. From her perspective, her bedroom door was preventing her from escaping to the everyday ordinariness of the outside world rather than keeping others out. Who in their right minds would want to enter this hell?

Joan was sat in her bed with the covers pulled up to her neck. She was still dressed in the clothes she had worn yesterday. She hadn't slept all night. At some point – she couldn't remember when - the words that had been pounding at her mind like a hammer on an anvil had abated. Then the voices had crept up on her, slowly, insidiously, so that she had hardly noticed them at first, but now they were an unrelenting clamour reverberating to the furthest recesses of her consciousness.

There was one now, nagging insistently at her. It never seemed to get tired of telling her what it thought of her over and over again.

Joan, Joan. Why won't you face up to what you've done? You know that you've denied Jesus. You know that you've turned your back on his perfect love. What do you think happens now? Everything we do has consequences, Joan. Judas denied Jesus. He betrayed his Lord with a kiss. Look what happened to him. Don't fool yourself that you can be forgiven. Some things can never be forgiven. Jesus sent you a test, and you failed.'

She could take it no longer. She screamed. "No! No! Leave me alone! It's not true. He wouldn't do that to me. I never turned my back on him, I never denied his love. I didn't! It's all a lie; a lie . . ." She started to sob uncontrollably. Self pity or remorse, she didn't know which.

On the landing outside Joan's bedroom Dr. Stanton turned to Bernadette. The alarm she was feeling was obvious from her features.

"Mrs. Archer," she said. "It's not possible at this stage to say what is wrong, but *something* certainly is. I don't think this is something I can handle by myself, we need to call in some expert help."

Bernadette was not sure who she meant. "Do you mean the police?"

"No. I just said that to try and persuade her to open the door. I think we need some advice from the mental health services. I need to make a call."

"Of course, doctor."

*

On the psychiatric unit, it was just another day. Crisis was their stock in trade, as it were. The phone rang at a nursing station and was picked up by a nurse. "Hello. Maple ward. Maria Sondha speaking."

At the other end of the line Dr. Stanton started to explain her problem. Maria could sense the worry in her voice, and interrupted. "Okay. I think you would be better to speak to one of the doctors. If you can hold on a minute, I'll go and find one for you."

She put the receiver down on the desk and walked out into the corridor and onto the ward proper. Edward Plant was walking along apparently lost in thought.

"Edward, are you busy right now?"

He looked puzzled. Wasn't it obvious he wasn't busy? "Er, no, not really. Why?"

"There's a GP on the phone. She says she needs some advice about one of her patients who's acting a bit strange. Could you have word with her?"

"Is it one of our GPs?"

"I don't know. Stanton she said her name was, I think."

"Okay, I'll speak to her. In the office?"

He walked into the nursing station and picked up the receiver lying on the desk.

"Hello," he said. "Doctor Plant speaking. Who is this please?"

"Oh, hello, it's Melanie Stanton. I'm a partner at the Elms practice in Wetherington. Am I speaking to one of the psychiatrists?"

"I'm doctor Marwan's SHO."

He could sense the caller's relief as she spoke. "Great. I know doctor Marwan - we're in your catchment area. I've got a problem with one of my patients and I need some advice."

Edward was grateful for anything to relieve the tedium. "I'll do my best. What's the problem?"

"The patient is a woman in her early twenties. No previous psychiatric history. Her parents tell me she's been acting oddly recently, and claiming to hear the voice of Jesus. She's now locked herself in her bedroom and is refusing to come out."

This didn't seem like anything too unusual to Edward, but he tried not to sound uninterested. "Doesn't sound too promising does it? How can we help?"

"I think what I would really like is a home visit from the psychiatric team. Could you possibly arrange that?"

Usually that wouldn't have been a problem, but the summer was usually the quiet time on the unit. The hospital took advantage of this to send people on training courses and, of course, people took their holidays.

"Oh. Hell. Em, sorry. Normally I wouldn't hesitate to say yes," he explained, "but half the crisis intervention team are away on a course this week, and I haven't seen doctor Marwan yet today. Can I call you back?"

In the Archer house, Joan emerged from her bedroom. Dr. Stanton and Joan's parents heard her run down the stairs making a break for the front door. Sean could not move himself quickly enough, but Bernadette managed to grasp Joan's arm just as she was opening the door. Taking her mobile phone away from her ear, the doctor shouted after her.

"Joan! Come back! Please come back and let me have a good look at you!"

At the same time, Sean and Bernadette were shouting too, pleading with her not to go out, to come back to them. Joan said nothing. She pulled herself out of her mother's grip and ran down the street, sobbing as she went, slamming the door hard behind her.

On the other end of the phone it sounded like pandemonium to Edward. "What's happening?" He asked, but got no answer. He decided he had better wait.

After a short wait Dr. Stanton came back on. "I'm afraid that was our patient. She's just made a break for it. She's managed to get out of the house and run out into the street. I really do think we need that visit as soon as possible."

Edward asked the obvious question. "Do you think she's in any danger?"

"It's impossible to say. I don't like to think so, but who knows? If nothing else, she's sure to be very vulnerable just now. Can you call me back and let me know when you can arrange a home visit?"

"Okay. What's your number?"

"07781 3962684"

"Okay. Got that. I'll call you as soon as I've been able to talk to doctor Marwan."

"Thanks. Please just let me emphasise that I think it's extremely urgent."

Edward went in search of Dr. Marwan. He found him in the reception area.

"Doctor Marwan?"

The consultant turned at the sound of his name. "Oh! Hello Edward. Everything okay?"

Edward was non-committal. "I'm not sure."

Dr. Marwan smiled knowingly. "Not sure? Anything to do with your date with Susan?"

Edward was surprised that his boss knew about that – almost. "How did you know about that?" He asked with a wry grin.

Marwan returned the smile. "Oh, I think everyone knows about it. We're all on tenterhooks to know how it went. You know what sad lives we all lead here, how important gossip is to us."

Edward knew exactly how sad their lives were. He was not about to make things more interesting for them at his expense. "Well, you know what they say . . ."

"About what?"

Edward shook his head. "A gentleman never tells."

Marwan sensed there was little point in pushing his luck. "Pity. Did you want something?"

"I did actually. Just had a call from a GP, Melanie Stanton. Do you know her?"

Marwan frowned, trying to bring her to mind. "Only in passing. She's one of our sector GPs. Our paths cross occasionally, but I wouldn't say I knew her well. What did she want?"

Edward explained. "A spot of bother with a patient of hers. Woman in her 20s, no previous psychiatric history. She appears to be having auditory hallucinations and has locked herself in her room and won't let anybody in. While I was on the phone she made a dash for it and ran out of the house."

"Well, we can't make a diagnosis on the basis of such limited information, can we," Marwan replied, "but it sounds like it might be something we should be interested in, don't you think? Have you called the crisis intervention team?"

"Not yet. When I spoke to Tony earlier he told me that half of them were away on a course for most of the week, so only limited cover would be available. The GP is asking for a domiciliary visit. I said I would speak to you and get back to her."

Marwan looked at his wristwatch. "Hell. I've got a hospital board meeting I have to attend in about half an hour. I can't get out of it: the budget for the admissions ward is up for review. Tell you what, why don't you go? It'll be good experience for you."

Edward was a little taken aback at his mentor's response. Marwan usually kept him on a tight rein. "Me? Are you sure?"

Marwan nodded. "Sure I'm sure. You won't be able to do much harm. If you think she needs admitting then you have my authority to bring her straight in. If nothing else we can get her under observation and make sure she doesn't come to any harm."

Later that afternoon, Bernadette answered the door to a very presentable young man. She couldn't keep the surprise on her face showing.

"Mrs. Archer?" He asked politely. "I'm doctor Plant. I'm from the hospital - St. Peter's? I spoke to doctor Stanton earlier today? She asked me to call and see Joan?"

He was a doctor? He looked more like a film star. Who was that one Caroline said she liked? Brad Pitt? Yes, that was him. This one could have been his double. Maybe. Fortunately, she had been brought up to treat doctors with the respect that was their due.

"Oh, hello doctor," she said. "Won't you come in?"

Edward followed her through the hall and into the parlour. "I understand that Joan ran away earlier," he said. "Has she come back?"

Sean answered him. "Yes, she's back in her bedroom. Still won't speak to anybody though."

"Is she any calmer?"

Sean looked to Bernadette to continue. "I think so," she said. She's stopped crying, and she took the cup of tea I left on the landing."

Edward nodded to himself, trying to look like a doctor should in these circumstances, however that was; he had not been oblivious to the impression he had made on Bernadette as she let him in.

"Can you tell me what happened?"

Bernadette started to explain. "Well, like I said to doctor Stanton, she's been acting rather oddly recently. She keeps herself locked in her bedroom, and only comes out to go to church. She told Father James . . ."

Sean interrupted "He's our parish priest."

Bernadette gave him an irritated look. "She told Father James that she could hear the voice of Jesus in church," she continued, "but when I asked her about it she said it was a ridiculous idea, and went all hysterical."

"Was that the first time she became very upset?" Edward asked.

"Yes."

"And when exactly was that?"

"Only last night."

Edward tried to sound like he knew what he was talking about. "Good. Could I talk to her now?"

Sean shifted in his chair, his hands lifted in a gesture that suggested trying to talk to Joan would be futile. "You can try doctor but I wouldn't be too hopeful." He said.

Bernadette led Edward up the stairs to Joan's bedroom door They could hear Joan talking.

"No. You lied to me before. I went back. I confessed. I begged for forgiveness, and he forgave me. He'll always forgive me, no matter what I do, because he loves me so much he gave his life for me. Nothing you can say to me can ever change that."

Edward exchanged a look with Bernadette before knocking on the door. For a moment, the voice inside went silent, then Joan called "What?" Her irritation at being interrupted was obvious.

Edward spoke to her through the door. "Joan? You don't know me. My name is doctor Plant. I'm a doctor. From the hospital

Doctor Stanton phoned me. She asked me to come over and have a talk with you, to see if you needed any help."

Joan seemed mildly intrigued. That was good, at least she was talking. "The hospital? Which one?"

"St. Peter's."

"Isn't that where the loony bin is?" Joan sounded dubious.

"We don't call it that any more," Edward replied. "It's the mental health unit."

"You've come to have me put away, haven't you?" Joan's voice was starting to sound hostile.

Edward tried to calm her fears. "No Joan. It doesn't work like that any more. The hospital is a place of calm and quiet where we can assess people's needs and give them the time and space they need to get better. We don't admit them unless they need to come in for their own safety."

Joan was still suspicious. "Do you think I need to be admitted?"

"I don't know. That's what I've come to find out. But even if you do come in, you'll be free to leave at any time."

"But my parents want me to be admitted, don't they?"

In his mind, Edward was adding paranoia to the list of symptoms that Joan appeared to have, but he replied "Joan, I don't think your parents know what they want. They're at their wits' end. All they want is to help you."

This brought no response from Joan. Edward tried again. "Joan? Joan, will you let me in? I promise if you ask me to leave I will."

The suspicion was still evident. "How do I know I can trust you?"

Edward tried the old cliché. "I'm a doctor, Joan. If you can't trust me, who can you trust?"

It worked. There was the sound of a key turning in the lock. A moment later Joan said "Okay. You can come in."

Edward entered the room and shut the door behind him. He was struck by the pictures on all the walls. "What a lot of pictures," he said, sitting himself on the end of the bed. "You must have a very strong belief."

Joan was not falling for his bedside manner. "You said you wanted to help me. How can you do that?"

Edward turned on his winning smile. "Well, first of all by making sure that you're physically well."

"Physically?"

"You know, that you haven't harmed yourself in any way."

Joan was not impressed. "Harmed myself? Why would I do that?"

Trying to be rational with someone who is probably not in a rational state of mind is not easy, but Edward tried anyway.

"Your GP, doctor Stanton, and your mum and dad told me you've been very upset, and acting rather oddly. People can do all sorts of things when they're upset, often without meaning to."

Joan was beginning to wish she hadn't let him in. "Well, as you can see, I'm fine. I'm perfectly alright and I don't need any help." Suddenly she winced, as if something had struck her. Unbidden, someone spoke inside her head. A voice that to her, seemed full of menace.

'Certainly not the kind of help he has to offer.'

"What?" She said, not sure of what she had heard.

"I didn't say anything," Edward said, senses alert. "Did you hear something?"

Joan looked to her left, as if that was where the sound had come from. "I thought I . . ."

"Did you hear somebody else speaking to you?" Edward asked, more insistently.

Joan seemed confused. "I'm not sure. I thought I heard something, but . . ."

Another voice spoke. Cruel, heartless. *'I wouldn't tell him anything. He can't help you anyway. The best thing he could do would be to go away.'*

Suddenly, Joan felt compelled to agree with the voice. "Yes. Why don't you go away now and leave me to get on with it?" She said to Edward.

Edward sensed that something was deeply wrong. "Get on with what, Joan?" He said gently.

The voice spoke again. *'You can't trust him. He says he wants to help, but he can't. The best thing you could do would be to ignore him.'*

Joan responded. "Yes, you're right."

Edward tried to distract her. "Joan, who are you speaking to? Can you hear someone apart from me talking to you?"

Joan did not answer.

"Your mum told me that Father James said that you could hear the voice of Jesus in church. Is that true?"

Now the second voice was back, loud, and more menacing than ever. *'Don't answer him!'*

Joan was finding it difficult to separate what Edward was saying from the voices in her head. "What? Hear what?" She asked.

Edward tried to get her to focus on his presence. He sat next to her and looked into her face. "Joan! Can you hear another voice – or voices talking to you other than mine?"

Joan shook her head. "Why don't you just leave me alone?" Her voice was starting to quiver.

But Edward was insistent. "I'm afraid I can't do that Joan, not until I'm sure you're okay, as I said earlier. Is what Father James said to your mum true?"

But Joan was distracted again. "Is what true?"

Edward took her hands. "That you told him you can hear the voice of Jesus when you go to church?"

Now Joan was angry. "No, of course it's not fucking true."

Joan could not understand what was happening to her. The voices were so frightening and intrusive that she hadn't had time to think about them calmly. No sooner had the words left her lips than she heard the sound of demonic laughter and a voice shrieking *'That's twice the bitch has done it!'*

Then the second voice was there again, cold and sinister. *'You had better get rid of him. If you don't get rid of him, something bad will happen.'*

Now Joan was frightened. She tried to talk to it. "Something bad? What? What will happen?"

It was the first voice that answered her. *'You know exactly what will happen. He will not be pleased with you. He might have forgiven you for now, but if you don't obey Him, He will get very angry. Get rid of him. Get rid of him. Get rid of him. Get rid . . .* '

Joan pulled her hands from Edward's grasp and put them over her ears screaming "Shut up! Shut up! Stop it! Stop it!"

Oblivious to Edward's presence, she started to throw things around her room, looking under her bedclothes, then the bed itself, up-turning her chair, pulling out drawers, looking in the wardrobe, as if searching for where the voice might be coming from, all the time shrieking "Where are you? Where are you, you bastard? I know you're there somewhere. Come out! Come out!"

Edward grabbed her arms and pulled her round to face him.

"Joan!" He yelled. "Look at me! You can hear other voices, can't you? What are they saying to you?"

She collapsed into his arms, sobbing. "I can't tell you. If I do He'll be angry. Please just go away and leave me alone. Please!!!"

But Edward wasn't going anywhere. "Joan, I need you to think for a moment. When do you hear the voices? In here . . . in church . . . anywhere else?"

By now, Joan was crying. "Only in here," she managed to say. "I've only heard them when I'm in my room."

She put her hands over her ears again as the second voice redoubled its assault on her bruised consciousness.

'You were told to tell him nothing! Can't you do anything right you stupid bitch? You are an utter failure, and you'll be a failure on the day you die. Nothing you do will ever matter. Failure! Failure! Failure! . . .'

With a supreme effort, Joan focused her attention on Edward, eyes wide with fear. "*Can* you make the voices go away?"

"Yes," he assured her, "but I need you to help me. The first thing we have to do is to get you to hospital. You'll be safe there. It might be that you only hear the voices when you're in your bedroom, in which case, getting you to hospital will make it stop until we work out what to do for the best. Will you agree to come into hospital?"

She hoped she might drown them out if she shouted. "Yes! Anything! Anything as long as you make the voices stop."

Now a third voice made its presence felt. Unlike the other two it spoke so quietly it was almost a whisper. For some reason this made it even more sinister.

'You're going to regret this, you bitch. You won't be safe in hospital. You won't be safe anywhere. The eye in the sky will see to that.'

Unaware of what she was doing, Joan pleaded with it. "Please. No." Then, as if coming back to reality, said to Edward "Make it go away!"

You didn't have to be a consultant psychiatrist to see how distraught and exhausted she was, Edward thought to himself. She was at her wits' end. He opened the bag he had brought and put on a pair of plastic gloves. Then he took out a syringe and extracted the contents of a small vial.

While he was doing this he said "What I can do to help you right now Joan, is to give you something to help you sleep. You don't look like you've slept all night. I can give you a small injection into your arm and it will send you off to sleep until the ambulance arrives. Would you like me to do that?"

Joan was not able to respond. She could barely hear what Edward had said. Her head was filled with one voice shouting *The bitch thinks an injection will help her!* The others were just laughing.

Finally, she willed herself to respond. "Yes, please anything. Anything to make them go away."

She held out her forearm and let Edward give her an injection into a vein. Within seconds she started to get sleepy. She could almost feel it rising up her arm, through her shoulder and up her neck. Then she was asleep. Edward lowered her gently onto the bed. Closing the medical kit he went downstairs to her parents.

They were waiting in the parlour, their anxiety obvious. "Is she alright doctor?" Bernadette asked.

Edward gave a reassuring smile. "She's going to be. She's asleep now; I've given her a sedative. You were right to be concerned, I think she's very stressed and overwrought. I want to bring her into hospital for a few days to keep her under observation."

Bernadette had to ask. "Is she having a nervous breakdown, doctor?"

Given his own experience of having to wait months to be told what was wrong with him, Sean thought it was better to get straight to the point. "Why don't you just come out and say it, Bernadette?" He said bitterly. "She's gone mental, hasn't she, doctor?"

Edward gave a slight shake of his head. "It's too early to say just yet. That's one of the reasons I want her to come into hospital. So we can have the time to make a careful assessment of her condition." He hoped that being non-committal would provoke less anxiety on their part. He pulled his mobile from his pocket. "Do you mind if I make a call?" He said.

Edward dialled the number for the ward. Bernadette stayed close by, listening to what he was saying, hoping to glean more about what was the matter with Joan.

"Hi, Maria, it's me Edward." He said. Bernadette wondered who 'Maria' might be. Edward explained what he was doing. "Doctor Marwan asked me to do a domiciliary assessment, and he said that if I thought the patient needed to be admitted, that would be okay." On the other end of the line, 'Maria' was obviously taking notes. "Yes," he continued. "The patient's name is Joan Archer and she's in her twenties." He paused to let Maria keep up with him. "The address is 27 Bramley Terrace." He paused again. Maria must have asked him a question, because he replied "Yes, that's right, just by the swimming baths." He paused again. "Can you please tell doctor Marwan that I think she needs to be admitted, and arrange for an ambulance to pick her up?" Another pause, then: "Thanks. Bye." 'Maria' must have asked him something else because he didn't hang up, but said "No, I'm finished now. I'm on-call tonight, and then back in again tomorrow afternoon." Bernadette couldn't hear what was being said to Edward, just a tinny voice, but whatever was said, it made him laugh briefly. Then he replied: "You'll have to ask *her* about that. Bye!" Then he hung up.

He turned to Bernadette to tell her what he had arranged. As he did so, the doorbell rang. Automatically Bernadette turned to open it. It was Father James. Bernadette ushered him into the hall and introduced him to Edward. They shook hands.

"How is she now?" He asked.

"She's sleeping for the moment," Edward explained. "I've given her a sedative and arranged for her to be admitted."

The priest nodded. But he knew that admission to a mental unit was no small matter. He had heard it was something that could follow Joan for the rest of her life.

"Is that absolutely necessary?"

Edward didn't reply directly. "I'm sure it will be only a temporary measure," he said quickly. "I just think she needs to be in a safe place with the right people looking after her."

"Well, if you think that's best doctor . . ."

Bernadette filled the vacuum left by his unfinished words. "The doctor's arranged for an ambulance to pick her up."

James didn't see the need for that. "Wouldn't it be easier to take her there in my car? It wouldn't be any trouble."

That was the last thing Edward wanted. It could have been some sort of emotional conflict between Joan, her mother and this priest that had been the spark that had led to Joan's current state of mind. A repeat of that had to be prevented at all costs, no matter how well-intentioned the priest might be.

"No." He said. He felt James' unspoken challenge and explained "As I said it's about having the people with the right experience to look after her. What would happen if Joan became hysterical again while she was in your car on the way to the hospital? No, it really is better this way."

*

It took Edward a while to get home. His flat was on the other side of town, and, though the hospital would have paid for a taxi, he preferred to walk. For almost the first time he felt excited by a case. First episodes of psychosis were relatively infrequent, and this case seemed fascinating, right from the beginning. The patient was clearly hearing voices and had religious delusions. He had been taught it didn't do to make a snap diagnosis of a mental condition, but it seemed pretty obvious that this was either drug-induced (which didn't seem very likely given the circumstances) or it was schizophrenia. A new case of schizophrenia, and it was his! He felt quite proprietorial about it. *His* case. The first case that he could say really was his. It was as if he had discovered the cure to some exotic disease. The sheer unexpected pleasure he felt was so foreign to him that it seemed to take no time at all to get home.

By the time Peter got home, Ed had settled himself in front of the television. "Hi Ed," Peter said in greeting. "Good day?"

"Not bad," Edward replied absently. "The usual." He paused. No it wasn't. "No, actually, not the usual." He continued. "Marwan let me do an unsupervised DV today. It was really interesting. For the first time I felt like it was really my case and I was actually in control."

Peter had never managed to come to grips with medical jargon. "DV? What's one of them when it's at home?"

"A domiciliary visit, you berk." Edward got up and took his empty cup into the kitchenette, talking as he went. "Young girl in her twenties; really quite attractive in a funny sort of way. Tragic case. Classic signs of schizophrenia." He came back into the lounge. "Want a coffee?" Peter shook his head. "Not much hope for her I wouldn't have thought." He made it sound like a death sentence.

"Not much hope?" Peter asked. "I thought medical science could work wonders these days."

Edward flopped back onto the settee, spilling coffee as he did so. He leant forward, trying ineffectually to brush the drops from his clothes. "Yeah, well, that's just the story that's put out for the media and the gullible public. The truth is there's lots of illnesses we haven't got a clue about, and schizophrenia is one of them."

"Schizophrenia? Isn't that a split personality?"

Edward shook his head. "Common misconception, mate. The truth is far more complicated. People with schizophrenia hear voices that aren't there and believe things that aren't real."

"And there aren't any treatments?"

"Oh yeah, there are plenty of treatments. They just don't work terribly well, so most people with the disease spend their lives haunted by voices that only they can hear. Frightening when you think about it really." He took a sip of his coffee. "That's why they need genius doctors like me to tell them what they need to do to get better."

Peter could sense Edward's conceit looming. "I thought you just said you didn't have a clue about it."

Edward put his cup onto a table. "I meant relatively speaking. We actually know quite a lot about the illness, we just haven't figured out how it all fits together."

"So what will happen to her?"

Edward steepled his fingers and pressed them into his chin, a habit he had when he was trying to concentrate. "It depends. I've arranged for her to be admitted, and we'll keep her under observation for a few days before deciding on the best course of treatment."

Peter often found that Edward's attitude didn't quite fit with his supposedly caring vocation. He felt it again now.

"Well, for such a tragic case you sound pretty pleased with yourself. What was it like, this domiciliary visit?"

"The main impression I have is of her shouting." Edward said without thinking.

"Shouting?"

"She could hear voices that I couldn't. I can only guess that they must have been threatening her: she kept shouting at them to leave her alone."

"Not like the girl on Saturday night then?"

Edward smiled at the memory. "No. Yeah. She was a bit loud wasn't she?"

"I couldn't catch quite everything she said, but let's just say I didn't get the impression she wanted you to leave her alone."

Edward grinned. "Quite the reverse."

"So are you planning to see her again, or is this just another of Ed Plant's "wham-bam" harem?

Edward had to think about that one.

"I don't know. I liked her . . . she was fun, and she was . . . great in bed. Yeah, I might see her again. I'll see her one way or another anyway – she's a nurse at the hospital."

That was news. Ed hadn't told him that. Up to now he had always said that sleeping with work colleagues was a bad idea – it always got messy.

"A nurse at the hospital?" Peter pretended to be shocked. "Doesn't that break one of your six golden rules?"

But Edward had an answer ready. "You've forgotten rule number seven, mate."

"Rule number seven? I thought there were only six."

Edward ignored Peter's objection. "Yeah. Rule number seven: rules one to six were made to be broken!"

"I give up!" As Edward left the room, Peter threw the remains of the morning paper at him.

Laughing, Edward dodged it. "You might as well. Just acknowledge who's the master!"

8
Nothing is real

Waking from a drug-induced sleep can be disorientating – especially if you're not used to it. Joan gradually became aware that she was lying in a darkened room. She didn't recognise it as her own She felt hot and sticky, but when she tried to throw the covers off she found she had become tangled in them, and had to twist herself and pull the covers from underneath to get out. As she sat up, she felt dizzy, and had to support herself with her arm until it passed. Only then was she able to get from under the covers and sit on the edge of the bed. She held her head in her hands. She wasn't quite sure if she had a headache, but she definitely felt groggy, and found it difficult to concentrate. She wondered how long she had slept for. She couldn't say she felt refreshed by her sleep; on the contrary, she was drained, physically and mentally. She turned to look at her clock but couldn't focus on it. *Why am I bothering?* She asked herself, before giving in to the exhaustion and going back to sleep.

When she woke again it was completely dark. This time she felt alert. Something must have woken her – a noise, or maybe she had been dreaming. She sat up and put her feet on the floor. Unconsciously she rubbed her eyes, becoming increasingly aware of the urgency in her bladder. When it came, the voice she heard shocked her.

'You thought you'd get away with it, didn't you, you little bitch!' Cold and menacing, she heard it as though there was a person standing next to her.

She looked around her, searching frantically for them. "What?"

A second voice joined the first. *'Don't try to deny it. You fancied that young doctor, didn't you, wanted to get your hands into his trousers, didn't you?'*

Joan was bewildered. All at once she realised what a blessed release sleep had been, for a while at least. "Who? No!" Was all she could say.

Now the first voice returned. *'You really are a piece of work, aren't you? You say you really love Him, but so far you've denied Him twice. Then you start making eyes at the first man to come your way. You're nothing but a filthy little piece of trash. That's all you are and that's all you've ever been!'*

All she could think of to do was to shout. "Go away! Go away! Go away!"

Then the worst voice came - so sinister and evil that the others were gentle in comparison. *'You'd like that wouldn't you? But I'll never go away. I'll never leave you alone because you're nothing but a stupid ugly little cow who'll never be able to get a man to fuck her and whose only interest in the god she says she loves is that she hopes he'll take pity on her so she'll get a fuck off him instead!'*

Downstairs, Bernadette and Sean were still waiting for the promised ambulance. They were concerned that it hadn't arrived, but rationalised that there must have been some sort of problem and that it would get here in due course. Now they could hear Joan shouting again.

"No! No! It's not true! Leave me alone!" She yelled. There was a pause, then a scream, then the sound of inconsolable wailing.

Bernadette leapt from her chair and walked rapidly to the bottom of the stairs, holding the banister, looking up, wondering what she should do.

"Something's not right Sean," she said, worry etched on her face. "I thought that doctor said he'd given her a sedative!"

"He must have." Sean replied. He glanced at the clock on the mantelpiece. "She's slept for nearly six hours. It must have worn off. When's that ambulance going to come? It should have been here by now."

Joan walked along the landing to the toilet. As she returned to her bedroom she could be heard very clearly, shouting at someone. "No, I won't! No, you can't make me, I won't let you! Leave me alone you evil bastard!"

Bernadette started up the stairs but hesitated. She turned to her husband saying "Sean, what are we going to do?"

The look on his face told her how helpless he felt. "You go upstairs to Joan," he said. "I'll phone Father James. He'll know what to do."

Edward had left a card with the hospital details on. Father James decided the best thing to do was to call them and ask what had happened to the ambulance. His voice was brusque. "Hello, this is Father James O'Hanlon from the Sacred Heart of Jesus parish in

Wetherington. I'm calling on behalf of one of my parishioners, a Miss Joan Archer."

It was Susan who answered the phone. Strictly speaking, her shift wasn't due to start for another half an hour, but everybody else was busy. "Good evening, Father. How can I help you?"

"As I said," he explained, "I'm calling about one of my parishioners. One of your doctors called out to see her today." He put his hand over the mouthpiece and asked Sean "What was his name?"

"Doctor Plant."

The priest continued "Doctor Plant he said his name was. Only a young chap."

"Just a minute, Father, let me check in the book." She put down the receiver and opened the day book that lay on the desk. She found the note that had been made earlier when Ed had called. "Yes," she confirmed, "it says here that Ed asked for her to be admitted. Her bed should be ready; we've been expecting her all afternoon apparently."

James was a little confused. "Ed?"

Susan smiled to herself. "Sorry Father. Doctor Plant. It's very informal round here, I'm afraid."

"Well doctor Plant said he would get an ambulance organised to bring her to the hospital."

Susan checked the day book again. "I'm afraid that's not what's written in the book, Father . . ."

James tutted with annoyance. "Well I know he did it," he insisted, "I was standing right next to him when he phoned."

Susan sighed. "Just a minute, Father, let me check." She put the receiver down again and shouted down the corridor. "Maria? Did you take the call from Ed before about the admission from the DV?"

Maria came from a side room into the corridor, wearing a plastic apron and her hands encased in thick rubber gloves. "Admission? Oh yes, the girl from Bramley Terrace. I took the call. I knew where it was right away; I only live round the corner myself."

"It's just that I've got the parish priest on the phone now asking where the ambulance is."

Realisation dawned on Marias' face. "The ambulance? Shit. I forgot to organise the ambulance, didn't I? I remember now, just as I put the phone down Jacky Downham insisted her watch had been stolen. I had to go off to help her find it. I completely forgot. You'll have to call one now."

Susan was not impressed. "*I'll* have to call one?" She said archly.

"Unless you want to clean up the mess in there." Maria gestured to the room she had just come out of. "Not a pretty sight, I promise you."

Everybody knew that whenever she could, Maria would avoid doing the unpleasant jobs. Susan was not about to let her off the hook over this. "Okay." She turned back into the office and picked up the phone again. "Hello, Father O'Hanlon, are you still there?"

In the bedroom, Bernadette was sitting with her arms around Joan's shoulders, trying to comfort her. Joan was sniffling quietly, seemingly oblivious to her mother's presence. Bernadette could clearly hear Father James' every word. Thank the Lord they had a priest like him.

"Yes, I'm still here," he said. "Now, what about this ambulance?"

"Yes, I'm terribly sorry about that, Father," Susan apologised. "I'm afraid it wasn't me who took the call, and the person who did had to go off on another job and forgot about it. You know how it is, we're always busy here."

James brushed his annoyance aside. "It's alright. I understand perfectly." He put one hand over the phone and said to Sean "They forgot to order the ambulance." He turned his attention back to Susan. "So what do we do now?"

"I'll arrange for the ambulance right now, Father, as soon as I get off the phone with you." She replied.

The priest thought it wouldn't hurt to confirm what would happen as a way of emphasising that the hospital had already made one glaring error. "Just let me get that straight, nurse. You'll organise an ambulance for Joan as soon as I put the phone down?"

"That's right."

"And how long will it take to get here?"

"About twenty minutes, thirty at the outside."

"So the ambulance will be here in half an hour at the latest?"

"Yes, Father. I'll do it straight away, I promise."

"Thank you." He put the phone down. He felt dreadful, but he had done everything he could. Now it would be up to the doctors.

In her bedroom Joan had slowly become aware of Father James' conversation about the ambulance. Before, it had seemed a good idea to go to the hospital. Now she was not so sure. She was frightened, and there was only one place where she felt safe – in church. She pushed herself away from her mum and pulled a pair of training shoes onto her feet, not bothering to tie the laces, and struggled into a baggy jumper. Bernadette was alarmed. "What do you think you're doing Joan?" Joan could not reply, but gave her mother an imploring look that she hoped she would understand.

Coming out of her bedroom she lurched down the stairs and straight into the arms of her parish priest. "Easy now, Joan," he said gently. "Where do you think you're going?"

Joan struggled but he held her tightly. "Please don't try and stop me Father" she gasped. "There's only one place I can go. I have to go and beg for His forgiveness, it's the only way."

Father James was not for letting go. "Beg for whose forgiveness, Joan? You have no need to beg for forgiveness. If you want absolution I can give it to you right now. Please don't try to leave the house. Your mum and dad are already worried sick about you as it is."

She kept trying to push him away. "You don't understand Father, I have to do this. Please let me go! Please!"

By now Sean had shuffled into the hall. He put himself in front of the door barring her way to the street. "Joan," he said, tears in his eyes, "you're not going anywhere lass, not until that ambulance comes."

Joan was becoming frantic. "Dad, please! Please don't try to stop me. I know there's nothing the doctors can do. Only God can help me now, and I need to go to Him, to pray. Can you understand that?"

"I can, lass, but the doctor . . ."

"I know what he said. He said it to me as well, remember! Please just let me go. Please . . . I'm begging you!"

Now Bernadette joined them. She put a hand on Father James' arm, indicating that he should let go of her daughter. "I think she should go" she said, her voice calm. "Get out of her way Sean, you too, Father." She turned to her daughter. "Joan, my love, just remember that I'll be praying for you the moment you step outside that door."

Joan wiped the tears from her mother's eyes. "I will mum, thanks."

The door opened and Joan was through it and running down the street before anyone could change their mind.

When she got to the church door she prayed it would be open. It was. She pushed against the door and it swung easily with her weight. Inside it was dimly lit, and she prayed again that there would be nobody else there. There was, but it was only Richard the organist, tidying up after the choir practice.

"The church will be closing soon," he told her.

She nodded. "I'll only be a few minutes" she said. She went to the front and knelt before the statue. All was silent. She heard the hasp on the door fall as Richard left. Then she started to pray, pleading with her god, almost babbling she was so distraught.

"Please, Lord, please Lord. If you love me, listen to my prayer, I beg you, I beg you on my knees. Please tell me it isn't true what the voices have been saying. Please find a way to let me know that you forgive me. Please."

She paused for breath, waiting, hoping for some response, but the church remained cocooned in silence.

Her desperation was growing, her voice became increasingly strident. "Oh, God. All the years I've prayed to you and you finally answered my prayer. All I wanted to do was to love you and serve you, but all I have now is this . . . torment. Please Lord, please, I beg you, make the voices go away, or at least find a way to let me know that what they're saying isn't true?"

Still there was no answer.

Now she was shouting, her shouts interspersed with tears. "You promised that if only we had faith we could move mountains. Well I do believe, I do. I believe in all the promises you made. That you would be with us until the end of time . . . only . . . where are you now? Where are you? Where are you?"

Her head fell forward to rest on her arms. She felt utterly alone. What was happening to her?

Suddenly the music started. She could hear the angels in all their glory. The music was so majestic, so full of power and beauty and sheer joy. She collapsed to the floor amid the sound.

Now she was crying with relief. "Thanks be to God. O blessed God." Then came the voice of her saviour, and she knew that she was forgiven.

*

The blue flashing light of the ambulance outside Joan's house reflected luridly on the houses in the street. The neighbours stood in their doorways, watching. Then a police car arrived.

Father O'Hanlon spoke to one of the paramedics. "Do the police have to be here as well?"

The paramedic scratched his head. It was going to be a long night. "I'm sorry Father, really I am," he said sympathetically, "but if a patient won't come of their own volition, we have to make a judgement whether they're likely to harm themselves, and from what you've told me she's been acting very erratically, hasn't she?"

"But why the police? Hasn't there been enough upset already without getting them involved? She's just a young girl, after all."

The paramedic tried to explain. "I understand how you feel, Father, really I do. But I'm only here to try and get her to the hospital safely. If she won't come quietly, the police will restrain her We're not allowed to do that."

Father O'Hanlon was not convinced. "Wouldn't it be easier just to give her another sedative?"

The paramedic agreed. "It might be, Father, but I'm not allowed to do that either. Only a doctor can do that."

"Well I'm coming with you then."

"Be my guest, Father."

They climbed into the ambulance and set off for the church followed by the police car.

In the church Joan was lying on the stone floor at the base of the statue. All she was aware of was the bliss of the music and love that enfolded her. The door at the back of the church opened.

Abruptly, the music stopped. Joan pushed herself up onto her hands to see Father O'Hanlon enter, followed by a man in a green overall. As they walked towards her, two policemen also came into the church.

The priest peered into the gloom, calling her name. She pushed herself up on her knees, and waited. Father James helped her to her feet. She was a little unsteady, and grabbed his arm to stop herself from falling. "Come on Joan, let's get you out of here," he said.

Joan could see the paramedic and the policemen. Where moments ago she had felt calm and serene, now suspicion flooded into her mind. "Who are these people?" She demanded.

Father James pointed to the paramedic. "This is the ambulance driver Joan; he's just here to take you to the hospital. Don't you remember you agreed with doctor Plant that the best place for you was in hospital for a few days?"

Joan pointed at the police. "What about them?"

The paramedic tried to explain. "I'm afraid miss, that . . ."

Father James interrupted. "They're here because you ran away, Joan, and we were all worried about you. We've been looking for you, Joan, and the police are here in case when we got here, you weren't."

He tried to coax her away from the statue and out to the ambulance. Joan was having none of it and shrugged him off. In the dark silence of the church her voice sounded harsh. "No!" She yelled.

Father James was more gentle. "No?"

Joan shook her head emphatically. "I'm not going to hospital. They won't be able to help me. I'm alright here. I'm safe here. Can't I stay here, until I've figured out what's happening to me? At least for tonight?"

The priest gave a half smile. "I'm afraid that's not possible Joan. The doctor thinks you're ill; I think you might be too. We have to respect his judgement. He thinks the best place for you right now is the hospital, and so do I. Let's go, shall we? Please?"

She looked about wildly, as if looking for a means of escape. "What about sanctuary?" She asked.

"Sanctuary?"

"Can't I claim sanctuary?"

Father James shook his head. "I'm afraid not Joan. That went out hundreds of years ago."

"Oh."

She looked defeated. Something in her seemed to give, and she slumped slightly. The paramedic stepped forward and took her arm.

As if electrified, Joan pulled away violently and shouted at him "Take your fucking hands off me!"

Father James couldn't help himself. "Joan! Please! Think of where you are!"

Joan laughed bitterly. "I thought He knew my every thought and word no matter where I was!" She gestured towards the police. "I know why you got these bastards to come. They're here to put me away, aren't they? Well it's not going to work!"

Joan launched herself down the aisle, trying to get past the police. One of them made a half-hearted attempt to rugby-tackle her, and she pushed at his face fending him off. The second officer managed to lock his arms round both of hers, pulling her backwards down the aisle while she continued to kick at the first officer as he picked himself up off the floor. He held his hands in front of his face trying to protect himself while his cap went spinning between the pews. Joan struggled furiously, trying to free herself from the encircling arms screaming "Get off me! Get off! Let me go, you bastards! Fuck off! Get your fucking hands off me you bastards!" The second officer managed to pull her away from his colleague who pulled a can of mace from a pocket in his body protector, and held it to Joan's face, indicating what would happen if she didn't calm herself. She slumped then, letting herself go limp. Putting her hands behind her back, the police handcuffed her and took her out to their car.

Joan sat quietly in back of the car all the way to the hospital. She had no memory of the passage of time since the morning, but knew it was late. The world outside passed in a blur. Her consciousness was bombarded by a hideous cacophony of hate.

*

Though there was a light on at the entrance to the psychiatric unit, the doors were locked. A card in the glass panel next to the door gave instructions that admissions after 10pm were to be taken to the side entrance, approximately 50 metres to the left of the main doors.

One officer clamped firmly on each arm, Joan half stumbled half shambled to the side entrance. She had stopped struggling and was all but oblivious to what was happening. The side entrance was an unprepossessing single glass-panelled door with a dim light above it. There was no sign to indicate that this was the way they should go.

"I think it's through here," the first officer said.

"Done this before, have you?" His partner asked.

"Once or twice. There's usually a doctor or nurse around, though." He pushed the door open against a firm spring, and they negotiated their way through, still firmly attached to Joan. It was awkward trying to shuffle three of them through together: he lost his grip on the door and, pulled by its spring, it closed on Joan's arm, its edge striking her painfully just above the elbow. This brought her out of her torpor.

"Ow! Fuck!" She yelled, shocked by the sudden unexpected pain. "Jesus Christ!" His way now blocked by the door, the officer behind let go his grip and Joan fell to one side where her arm had been hit by the door.

The officer leading the way turned back to stop her falling to the floor. "Sorry Miss," he said, not unsympathetically. "Are you alright?"

Joan was leaning against the wall. Her arm hurt like Hell, but she couldn't rub it because of the cuffs. "A lot you care, you bastards." She said, her anger rising to the surface again.

"No need to be like that, Miss," he replied. "I said I was sorry. We're only doing our job. We don't like having to do this any more than you do."

The other policeman had come through the door and, pushing past Joan and his partner, was wandering up the corridor. He turned back. "Where is everybody?" He asked of no-one in particular. Then he shouted. "Hello! Hello!"

The first one was not impressed. "Oh for God's sake! Why don't you shout it *three* times and then say 'Let's be 'avin' you' as well?"

"What?" His colleague clearly had no idea what he had done

The first officer sighed heavily. "Never mind."

The shouting was heard in the nursing station on Maple ward. Most of the patients were in bed, and Susan and Cathy were having a cup of tea. Echoing through the empty corridors, they could hear the hellos quite clearly.

Cathy put her cup down. "What's that?"

"Sounds like someone's managed to get themselves lost."

"In this place?"

Susan finished her drink. "I'll go and look." She said.

She went through the double doors at the end of the corridor, and there, to her left, in the muted nightlights she saw a young woman, hands behind her back, being hustled along by two policemen. It was obvious from her posture that the woman was in some distress, and she immediately went to her side, ignoring the two men. When she saw how Joan had been restrained her lips tightened in anger.

"I'll take over from here, thank you. Can we have the cuffs off now, please?" She said, emphasising the 'now'.

While the first officer rooted around for the key, his companion said "Thank Christ for that. I was beginning to think we'd brought her to the morgue, not the hospital."

Susan gave him a withering look and said to Joan "I'm Susan Jones. I'm one of the nurses here. Are you okay? You look like you've hurt yourself."

Joan shook her head and looked at Susan as though through a haze. "What's . . . what's okay? I'm not okay, no. Where am I?"

"You're in St. Peter's hospital." Susan told her. "You're Joan, aren't you? Joan Archer?"

Joan was perplexed. She didn't seem to understand where she was or why she was there. "How do you know who I am?"

Susan smiled reassuringly. "We've been expecting you. Why don't you come through here and we'll get you settled and you can have a nice cup of tea?"

This seemed to make some sense to Joan. But she replied "Settled? I'm not stopping. I wouldn't have come at all if these bastards hadn't dragged me here. As soon as they've gone I'm going myself."

Susan had dealt with unwilling patients many times before. The trick was to take control and lead them through their doubts.

"Why don't you come through and at least have that cup of tea, then we can talk about it. These gentlemen have some forms to sign anyway, so they won't be off just yet a while."

Grudgingly, Joan agreed. "Okay. But I'm not stopping, got that?"

"Let's wait until the doctor's seen you, shall we?"

She led all four of them through the double doors onto the ward, Joan rubbing her hands where the cuffs had chafed. This time the first policeman held the door open for her until she was through Susan pointed to the nursing station. "You two go in there and ask for the transfer forms. The nurse there will sort you out."

This brought a knowing snigger from the second officer. "Sort us out? Just what we needed!"

Susan took Joan further down the corridor into the ward and sat her in an easy chair typical of the National Health Service: open sided with plastic upholstery and hard wooden arms. Easy to clean, but they stick to you when you've been sat on them for any length of time. "You just wait here until you feel a bit calmer," she said. "I'll get you some tea. Do you take milk and sugar?"

Exhausted, Joan sank into the chair. "Just milk, thanks."

"You'll feel a lot better once they've gone, people always do."

"They?"

Susan looked back towards the nursing station. "The police," she said tartly. "I'm afraid it happens quite a lot, the police bringing people in. They have to, you see. If they suspect that someone might harm themselves, they have to take them to a place of safety. Usually that means they bring them here, though sometimes they put them in a cell for the night. You've got the better option, if you think about it."

Joan was not convinced. "If you say so." She rubbed again at her wrists as if to emphasise what she had just been through.

Susan left her and went to the kitchen area, and put the kettle on to boil. Joan curled up into a ball on the chair looking very vulnerable. It wasn't long before she had her cup of tea.

"Here we are," Susan said. "Drink it while it's hot. I'll be back in a mo'." She walked back to the nursing station to find out why it was taking Cathy so long to get rid of the policemen.

One of them was seated at the desk, filling in a form. The other was trying to look down the front of Cathy's blouse. In what he obviously thought was an ever so suave and sophisticated manner he said to her "Haven't I seen you somewhere before?"

Cathy did not look at him. "Oh God," she moaned. "Not another original one."

The one filling in the form stopped what he was doing. "What's that love?" He said.

Cathy could not keep the scorn from her voice. "How much longer are you going to be? Or did you get the job because you're the only one with a GCSE in English?"

He shook his head as if disappointed by what she had said. "I'm sorry. Did I say something?"

"Not really," Cathy acknowledged, "but your mate did."

The second officer was instantly on the defensive. "Me? What did *I* say?"

Cathy let him know what she thought of him. "Oh for God's sake," she ranted. "What is it with you lot? Does being a nurse automatically mean we're gagging for a shag with the first copper that we meet?"

She almost succeeded in embarrassing him. "Not exactly," he conceded. "I mean, of course not. No need to be so touchy. I was only trying to be friendly."

Cathy was not to be easily mollified. "Well try being 'friendly' somewhere else."

Defeated, he spoke to his colleague. "You nearly finished there, Tim?"

For some reason, Cathy found this intensely amusing. "A copper called Tim?" She laughed.

Now it was Tim's turn to show his irritation. "What's wrong with that?" He asked.

Cathy stopped laughing. "Nothing," she admitted. "You just didn't strike me as a 'Tim' that's all."

"There's nothing wrong with a copper being called Tim," he insisted.

Cathy looked him in the face. "You're right," she said. "I'm sorry. Forget about it. I just didn't like your mate eying me up like I was on display in a shop window, that's all."

"Yeah," Tim admitted. "He's always getting me into trouble doing that."

"So why do you put up with it?" She asked.

Tim gave her a wry grin. "It's not me he eyes up, is it? Anyway, I don't get any choice who I get sent out with, do I?"

Then Susan walked in. Her eyes took in the two policemen. "You two still here? You only have to tick a couple of boxes and sign the form, you know, we don't expect a PhD thesis."

The slimy one now fixed his attention on Susan. "'S alright love. We're just goin'." He picked up his cap and walked slowly out of the nursing station. As he stepped into the darkened corridor he turned back and said with some exaggeration "Evenin' all."

Tim cringed. As he followed him out, Cathy called after him "Tim . . . I'm off duty at half-seven. If you fancy breakfast, we could discuss GCSEs if you like . . ."

Tim smiled broadly. "Really? I mean yeah. Great. Brilliant. I could pick you up at about eight. Where d'you fancy going for breakfast?"

Cathy smiled back. "I'll leave that to you. You must know where all the best caffs are."

The two men were silent until they were back in the car park As he activated the remote to open the car doors, one of them spoke. "You jammy bastard! I do all the legwork, and you get the jackpot."

Tim was having none of it. "You call lookin' at her tits legwork? She couldn't stand the sight of you. She liked me because I'm the caring and sensitive one."

His colleague carried on, true to type. "In your dreams. She likes you 'cause she thinks you're gay."

Tim opened the passenger door and got in. "We'll see, won't we?"

Back in the nursing station Susan was in fits of laughter trying to keep herself from waking the patients up. "*Tim*?" She hooted. "God, you're quick. I only left you alone with them while I made a cup of tea."

Cathy could see the funny side of it too. "I only wanted to get at his mate. The bastard had his eyes all over me. Slimy get. Anyway I think he's cute. He could turn out to be that one in a million. You never know; nothing ventured, nothing gained."

"One in a million? You mean finally there's a bloke good enough for Cathy Temple?"

Cathy sobered. "No. A copper who's also a decent human being."

They paused for breath. Then Susan asked "Cath, who's on-call tonight?"

Cathy gave her a 'told-you-so' look. "You know very well it's Ed. Why?"

"It's Joan. The girl who just came in. She needs to be properly admitted. She says she doesn't want to stay and I think I succeeded in persuading her to stay until she sees a doctor. If Ed sees her, at least he can give her a sedative and she can be assessed properly in the morning."

Cathy understood. "You sure you want to call him?" She said quietly. "I thought you'd been avoiding him since the night you went out with him." She paused. "Well, have you? Been avoiding him?"

Susan shook her head. It wasn't her who had been avoiding Ed. "I'm not sure. I thought it was more like he was avoiding me. You know what it's like, I'm probably being over-sensitive. The fact that we haven't bumped into each other could be a coincidence or it could be deliberate."

"Do you want to see him again?"

Susan gave a mirthless smile. "I can hardly avoid it, really can I? Sooner or later it's bound to happen."

Cathy put her hand on her friend's arm. "I meant go out with him again."

Susan took a tissue from her pocket and blew her nose. "Yeah, I know what you meant. I don't know. I had a great time, I thought he did too. But you know what he's like. We all know what he's like. You can't say I didn't know what to expect."

"Did you sleep with him?"

Now Susan smiled like she meant it. "What do you think?"

Cathy caught her mood and laughed. "You did, didn't you, you randy cow. Was it worth it?"

Susan pretended to be coy. "What do you mean, 'was it worth it?'"

"Was he as good in bed as he thinks he is?"

"Yeah. I'm afraid he was."

"Bastard!" Once again they had a fit of the giggles, trying desperately to keep the noise down. When they had calmed down, Cathy said "Anyway, you want me to call him?"

Susan nodded. "Would you mind?"

"'Course not." She reached for the phone. "Switchboard?" She said into the receiver. "Hi-i. Could you bleep doctor Edward Plant for me? Ask him to come over to Maple ward A-S-A-P? Thanks. You too. 'bye."

9
Harsh reality

Mornings are busy times in hospitals, perhaps for no other reason than that is the way it has always been. The early shift comes in at seven, and the night staff hand over to them, reporting anything of note that has happened during the night. Nurses seem to have a constitutional dislike of lay-a-beds, even though hospitals are not the easiest of places to get to sleep. Even if a patient has spent most of the night struggling with their personal demons, the night staff will start to wake them at about six, so that by the time the day shift begins, all are awake. This makes for very long days.

On this morning, there was one lay-a-bed on the ward – for good reason: she had been heavily sedated on admission. But there were no concessions to her continuing slumber; nobody walked quietly when going past or spoke in whispers. To all intents and purposes, she was ignored, waiting for the time when the sedative, having fulfilled its narcotic purpose, simply wore off.

Two people stood at the foot of Joan's bed: Amy Pierce, one of the new SHOs, and Maria Sondha, a nurse in middle age who had never advanced past her basic qualification. She liked to say she had twenty-five years experience. Occasionally (and maliciously) it was said (behind her back) that she really had only one year of experience, but had repeated it without learning from it twenty five times. Whatever the case, she and Amy were walking from bed to bed making sure each patient's notes were up to date.

Amy was struggling to make sense of Joan's notes. "Christ," she said, exasperated. "Who wrote these notes? I can't read a bloody word! Did they have a degree in dyslexia or something?"

Maria suppressed the urge to giggle. She knew very well who had written the notes. A degree in dyslexia? Just wait until she told him that. "Her name's Joan Archer, age 24. Ed clerked her in last night after she was brought in by the police. Cathy said he wasn't keen to stay for long, that's probably why the notes look so scrappy." She took the notes from Amy to see if she could decipher them. "Suspected psychosis, cause unknown. Ed gave her two milligrams of IM mirazepam. Should sleep for a couple of hours yet

Her mum called this morning to see how she was and was told she'd had a quiet night and was sleeping peacefully."

Now it was Amy's turn to grin. "Ed? That explains everything." She took the notes back to see if she could make any more sense of them. "They must be very worried about her."

"Worried about her? Who?"

"Her parents."

"They always are," Maria agreed as she turned away from the bed.

"What time's Ed due in today?" Amy asked, for no other reason than to keep the conversation going.

Maria looked at her watch. "Should be here by lunchtime I would have thought. Apparently doctor Marwan's arranged another tutorial."

"Shit, I nearly forgot. Thanks for reminding me." Amy felt almost grateful to the nurse for telling her. It was difficult to like Maria, she was such a misery guts. Hurriedly, she signed the entry she had just made.

"I wouldn't worry about her," Maria said, indicating Joan's slumbering form. "She's actually Ed's patient anyway. I'm sure she'll keep until he gets in."

Joan's were the last notes that needed to be checked. Amy made to go off the ward. "Yeah. Well, if she wakes earlier and you think she needs to be seen, bleep me. I'll be in the library. I need to prepare for this sodding tutorial."

Maria decided to give Amy the benefit of her twenty five years' experience. "I don't know why you bother. Nobody else does. It's psychiatry, you know, not brain surgery."

This woman was unbelievable, Amy thought. How could anyone with any experience in psychiatry come up with something like that? "Someone has to take it seriously." She replied.

Maria shrugged. What did she care? "I suppose so."

Two hours or so later, Joan was starting to come to. She couldn't work out where she was. It was all she could do to push herself up from the bed, excruciatingly slowly, her limbs like lead. And her brain felt no better, it was as if it were full of porridge. She rubbed her eyes trying to get them into some sort of focus. She wasn't in her own bedroom, but in some sort of large cubicle with three other beds, all neatly made. The beds had thick metal frames –

like hospital beds, she thought groggily, though she didn't make the connection. There were various metal plates around the walls, whose function she could not even begin to guess, and frames round the beds on which were hung curtains which could be drawn around for privacy. She was the only one there. To her left was a large window, letting in bright sunlight; to her right was a print in a crooked frame that looked like some famous impressionist painting, though she couldn't remember which one: it had obviously see better days and had faded to pastel shades.

Joan pushed her legs over the side of the bed and tried to stand. A wave of dizziness swept over her and she fell back heavily. She tried again, and this time succeeded in standing, though the dizziness was still there, now accompanied by intense feelings of nausea. She looked for any sign of a bathroom, but there was none. Then the nausea passed, only now she became aware of the blood pounding in her temples. She felt like shit. Holding on to its frame, she shuffled to the end of the bed. The bay had an open entrance into a wide corridor, and she could hear sounds of activity coming from somewhere. Leaning heavily on the wall, she followed it to her left and step by step made it to the nursing station. Maria looked up from her writing.

Joan found it hard to get the words out. "Hi. Er, excuse me. Can you tell me what's going on?" She looked around for some point of reference she could recognise. "Where exactly am I?"

Maria clicked her pen and put it down before replying. She was always being interrupted. "Good morning, Joan," she said, unconcerned by the patronising tone in her voice. "You're on Maple ward, St. Peter's Hospital; I'm Maria Sondha, I'm the senior nurse on duty today. You were brought in last night. One of the doctor's gave you a sedative and you've had quite a sleep. I'm afraid one of the side effects of the sedative is that when you wake up you feel like you've got a whopping hang-over. From the look of you that's how it's affected you."

Joan yawned. "Yeah. That's exactly how I feel. Awful."

Maria nodded sagely. "I'm afraid it'll probably take a few hours for it to wear off. Why don't you have a shower and go and sit in the day room? There's a kettle in there and you can make yourself a cup of tea or coffee. The doctor will be round to see you later."

It hit Joan then exactly where she was. It might have been the matter-of-fact way that the nurse spoke to her, that someone turning up in a threadbare nightgown with a splitting head was nothing at all out of the ordinary, or it might have been that her senses had begun to work in some sort of harmony. Whatever it was she knew she didn't want to be in the hospital. "A shower? Why can't I just go home?"

The nurse tutted and stood up. "I'm afraid that won't be possible until after you've been seen by your doctor."

Joan could feel her hackles starting to rise. Had she been right to suspect that this was all part of a plan to put her away somewhere? "Won't be possible? Why not?"

Maria walked out of the nursing station and, trying to look casual, positioned herself between Joan and the doors that led from the ward to the external corridor. "I know that you won't have been told yet, but fairly soon someone will be along to explain what's happened and what your rights are." She smiled – the type of insincere smile that tells you the conversation is at an end.

"Explain what my rights are?" Joan could feel her anger building. "What the hell is going on?"

Maria sighed. In what she thought of as her kind-but-firm voice she said "Joan, I'm afraid you've been detained under one of the sections of the Mental Health Act. You can't leave the hospital unless the doctor says it's okay for you to leave. If you do try to leave you'll be restrained, and if you sneak out, we'll send the police to look for you."

Joan was visibly shocked. "You mean I've been committed? Is that what you're trying to tell me?" Her breathing had become shallow and rapid. *Don't lose it now* she told herself.

Maria was starting to become impatient. Why didn't patients listen to what they were told? "No, Joan, that's not what I'm trying to tell you. People don't get 'committed' any more, not unless they're mentally ill and guilty of some serious crime."

"Mentally ill?" Joan almost shouted the words. "Are you trying to tell me I'm mentally ill?" Then something happened because she sagged and tears welled in her eyes.

The change in Joan took Maria by surprise. She had half been expecting her to fly into a rage. Instead, she had turned in on herself, becoming transformed into a pitiful shambles of a person.

"No, Joan," Maria explained, doing her best not to lose her patience "That's not what I'm trying to tell you. You were brought in because you've been acting oddly and getting very upset. Your parents and your GP were worried you might harm yourself. To be honest I've no idea whether you're mentally ill or not, and anyway, it's not my job to decide. You're here so we can assess you in a safe environment. Believe me; we won't keep you here a moment longer than is absolutely necessary." She took Joan by the arm and steered her back into the main area of the ward. "Now why don't you try to relax and do as I suggested. The ladies bathroom is at the back of the ward, and the shower has a soap & shampoo dispenser in it. If you go and get it started, I'll bring you a towel. Okay? Like I said, after you've had a shower, you can sit in the day room and watch the telly or read, or do whatever you like. How about it?"

Joan had lost the strength to resist. "When did you say the doctor would be coming?"

"He was called out last night – to admit you actually, so he won't be in for a few hours yet, and I know they've got a tutorial they're supposed to attend with one of the consultants this afternoon, so I doubt you'll be seen until about two o'clock."

"Two o'clock?" In Joan's beleaguered state of mind Maria might as well have said 'until next month'. "As long as that?"

Maria tried her 'this conversation is at an end' smile again. "Joan, don't worry about the time. People will understand if you're not able to stick to any arrangements that you might have made before coming in here. They always do." She gestured pointedly to the bathroom.

"I suppose so" Joan said as she walked slowly away.

*

The shower helped. The hot spray and the sheer vigour of rubbing herself dry made her feel at least a little refreshed. She found the kettle and made herself a cup of tea and settled herself into an armchair. She wasn't keen on going into the day room; other patients were watching some daytime TV show: people who didn't know any better baring their souls to the world. The last thing Joan felt like doing was making polite conversation with people she didn't know or want to know. Some of them looked decidedly rough, she thought. She found a quiet corner and tried to think about something comforting. She crossed her self and tried to pray. Almost immediately she heard the voice. It sounded so close and intimate that it startled her.

'Joan, Joan. You silly bitch. You let them bring you to this place. Did you really think they could help you?'

Almost panic-stricken, Joan looked around for the source of the voice. "Who is this?" She called. "Where are you?"

A second voice joined in, sneering. *Just look at her. She's looking for us. She won't find us. What a state she's in. She's finally ended up where everybody knew she would. She's going nowhere.'*

"Please," Joan pleaded. "Please just go away and leave me alone."

The first voice returned. *'Alone? You'll never be alone again, Joan. Never. Never in your entire life. You'll never get rid of us. Never.'*

The second voice was not to be outdone. *'Pathetic! She's a pathetic little cow with ideas above her station. She wants to be left alone does she? Who does she think she is?'*

Joan could not prevent herself from shouting. "For God's sake! Shut up and leave me alone!" Head in hands, she wept.

Then the third voice entered. Its whispered quiet only made it sound all the more menacing. *'She thinks she's someone special. She thinks she's been chosen by God. But she only has these pathetic ideas because she can't get a man for herself. She's managed to convince herself that Jesus loves her.'*

'Stupid bitch!' The first voice agreed.

Joan was now crying uncontrollably.

'All she can do is sit there.' The second voice added. *'Little miss pathetic and helpless. Diddums. Look, she's crying. As if that is going to help.'*

Then the whispered *'She thinks Jesus loves her. She wants Him. Wants to fuck Him. That's what she really wants, isn't it?'*

'Dirty little bitch.' The first voice said, followed immediately by the second.

'Oh, look. She's going to deny it. But we know it's true, don't we?'

Through her tears Joan tried to answer her accusers. "No, no. It's not true, it's not true. Jesus loves me and I love Him. Our love is pure, untainted, true."

This resulted in a chorus of raucous laughter. All Joan could think of to do was to shriek "Stop it! Please, please, just stop it!"

When Edward eventually arrived it was closer to three o'clock. He found an empty interview room on the ward and Joan was brought in. She accepted a paper cup of water but didn't drink any. For a minute or so Edward occupied himself writing in a blue-covered file. Resting his pen on the open page he said "Joan, do you remember yesterday, when I came to see you at home, I asked if you could hear a voice or voices that only you could hear?

The voice spoke to her clearly and sharply. *'Don't talk to him!'*

Joan struggled to ignore it. "I remember. I remember you said you could help me. If this is what your help is like, I don't think much of it."

'I said don't talk to him, bitch!'

Edward tried another tack. "Joan, we can't do much to help you until we know what's wrong. If you won't tell us what's wrong, it's going to be very difficult for all of us, isn't it?"

"I'm not to talk to you." She told him.

This got his attention. "Not to talk to me? Why not?"

Joan could not bring herself to reply.

The second voice was almost nice to her. *'Good. At last the stupid cow is doing what she's told.'*

Edward sensed he had to push this. "Joan? Why aren't you to talk to me? Is someone telling you not to?"

Still she couldn't answer. She felt she was under the compulsion of the voices, but she did manage a slight nod, before looking intently at the paper cup in her hands.

"So is there a voice that only you can hear?" Edward asked.

Again the slight nod.

Edward's voice was surprisingly gentle. "Joan, I know that hearing a voice that nobody else can hear can be very frightening, especially if the voice is threatening you, but you're not alone, Joan, There are lots of people here, people who want to help you. People like me, and the nurses. But you have to learn to trust us, even if the voice tells you not to."

Now the first voice was angry. *'Don't listen to him!'*

The second voice also made its presence felt. *'If she knows what's good for her, she won't listen to him.'*

Edward, unaware of what the voices were saying to Joan, could see that something was going on. "So, Joan, can you tell me about the voice?"

"I'll try." She whimpered.

Edward squeezed her hand. "Good, Joan. God loves a trier." He smiled reassuringly. "Is the voice a man or a woman?"

"Which one?"

"You mean there's more than one?"

She nodded again into her cup.

"Joan, this is important," he said. "Please try to concentrate. How many voices can you hear?"

"Three, I think."

He made a quick note in the folder. "Three? And will you try to tell me about them?"

All she could manage was a muted whisper. "Yes."

"Tell me about the one you heard first. When did you first start to hear it?"

"Only yesterday."

Another quick note. "Only yesterday? Never before then?"

"No."

"And what kind of things does it say to you?"

Joan didn't know how to respond. How could she tell a complete stranger about the voices? Would they inflict some terrible punishment on her if she did? "It says horrible things," she said. "Things your worst enemy would never dream of saying to you. It tells me to do things."

"What does it tell you to do?"

"It told me not to let you bring me into hospital, and it told me not to talk to you."

There was a brief pause while Edward made more notes, then: "And if you did let us bring you into hospital, or if you did talk to me, what would happen to you?"

She could not suppress a shudder. "Something terrible."

Intuitively Edward realised he now had to probe gently. "Joan, can you tell me what, exactly?"

Now, almost defiantly, Joan looked him in the eye. "It told me that I was denying Jesus, and that Jesus would never forgive me, and would stop loving me."

Edward was relieved. He didn't believe in God, and had been much more worried that the voice might have been commanding her to harm herself or somebody else. He moved on. "What about the second voice you heard, Joan, what does that say?"

Again, she found the strength to take his question full on. "That's not very nice either. It doesn't tell me to do anything, but it says awful things about me. It calls me names, and keeps saying I'm no good."

"No good? No good at what?"

"Everything. It just keeps on and on telling me I'm nothing but a failure."

Writing furiously, he continued "I see. And is that all of the voices, or are there more?"

Joan's defiance dried up. The first two voices were bad enough, but having to think about the third one just made her feel like a lost and frightened little girl. "There's one more," she murmured. "It's the worst of the lot. It really frightens me. It's not like the other two - it comes and goes. But the things it says are just dreadful. Awful."

"What does it say? Does it threaten you?"

She shook her head, spilling a little of the water from the cup. "No. It just says the most awful things about me. Things that aren't true. Hideous things, a complete denial of everything I hold dear."

This, Edward thought to himself, would probably be the key to understanding what was happening to her. Very gently, he said "Joan, can you tell me what it says?"

Joan was very reluctant to say. "I don't think I should. What it says, is unrepeatable. It's sacrilege, an affront to God's very existence."

"Please, Joan," he insisted, "it could be important."

Finally she took a sip of the water. "Okay." She paused, seeming to lose her resolve before managing to continue. "It says that the only reason I love Jesus is because I can't get a real man for myself, and I want to have sex with Jesus instead." Now the tears came, tears of sorrow, tears of humiliation, tears of remorse for imagined transgressions.

Edward stopped writing to hand Joan a box of tissues. "Oh. I see. I'm sorry I had to ask you about that, Joan. I didn't mean to pry, but what the voices are saying to you is possibly quite important."

Joan took a tissue and blew her nose. "Why?"

Edward now found himself wishing he hadn't told her that. "I'm not entirely sure," he was forced to admit. "I need to ask my consultant, doctor Marwan. You'll meet him before long. If you have any questions, you're best asking him, he's very experienced."

For a minute or so they sat in silence while Edward continued to write in the folder. Finally he closed it on his lap, clipping the pen into his shirt pocket. "Joan, I can't be completely sure at this stage," he said, "but I do think you're probably suffering from some sort of mental illness."

Joan did not want to believe him. "Mental illness? How?"

He thought it should have been easy to explain, but it wasn't "I can't say how, exactly, probably nobody can say for sure, but the experiences you're having are consistent with a condition called psychosis."

Joan's heart went cold with fear. "Psychosis? I've seen that in the papers. Isn't that where people go mad and attack other people, or kill themselves?"

For some reason this made Edward angry. Why did so many people think that? Was it all because of sensationalist media stories about mental illness or was there more to it? "Joan, you shouldn't believe everything you read in the papers. What psychosis means is that you're having experiences that happen only to you, and that you can't explain. One of the most common of these experiences is to hear voices that nobody else can hear, and you don't know where they've come from, and can't explain why you can hear them."

Joan found it hard to take in. "So it isn't about going mad and attacking people?"

Edward wanted to be reassuring, but did not make a very good job of it. "No Joan. Only a very small number of people with psychosis ever attack other people, they're more likely to harm themselves than other people. In your case, you can hear voices, which, by your own description are threatening, unpleasant and extremely distressing. But the good news is we *can* help."

Help? The word was like a touchstone to Joan and set her thoughts racing. In her mind she was shouting 'Help! Help me!' At the same time she was praying 'Dear Jesus, please help me.' From nowhere, she heard the Beatles song. "Help?" She said. "How?"

Now Edward was on firmer ground. "There are medicines we can give you that are quite effective at getting rid of the voices. They take a little while to work, but if you persevere, most people find that the voices go away or become less intrusive, enough to let you get on with your life."

Joan tried to understand what she was being told. "You mean the voices could still be there, but I would be able to not listen to them."

"Pretty much, yes." He sounded confident. Too confident?

But she wasn't convinced. "I don't see how medication could help. I know I'm not mentally ill."

Inwardly Edward groaned. He thought he had been making progress. "Look Joan, I know you'll find this hard to believe, but most people who are mentally ill deny that they've got a mental illness, just like you just did. The important thing right now is to get you started on medication. The one doctor Marwan usually likes to prescribe is called phenylatrazine. You need to take it twice a day, and we should get you started on it as soon as possible."

Joan went off at a seeming tangent. "What about being able to go to church?" She asked.

Her question was unexpected, and he answered without thinking. "I'm afraid that won't be possible, not until you've been seen by doctor Marwan, and he's had a chance to review your case. If he thinks you're showing some improvement you might be allowed to go home at the week-end for a few hours."

Joan snorted. "Home at the week-end? For a few hours? Is that it, then? Is this all you can say, that I'm mentally ill and need medication?"

Edward realised he had not handled that very well. Her scorn was almost tangible. He rose, indicating that their interview was at an end. "For now, Joan, that's what we have to do." Automatically, she stood up and walked to the door. As she reached it he added "All I can do right now is to ask you to trust me and to take the medication. It really will help; you just need to give it a little time."

10
Cornflakes and taxis

Hospital days are long and time is difficult to fill. Wednesday passed with stultifying slowness. Joan spoke to her mother on the phone, but said she did not want visitors, not yet. That night she was given clean but worn pyjamas and a sleeping pill and managed a fitful sleep, with half-remembered dreams filled with devils pitching the unfortunate souls of condemned sinners down into hell.

Breakfast was a quiet affair: milky tea and a bowl of cornflakes sitting on her bed, not talking to anyone. Joan left the dishes on her bedside cabinet and went for a shower. So far the voices had left her alone today. She prayed they had gone. She spent a long time in the shower, letting the hot water stream over her wishing her cares washed away, her life moved back to where it had been only two days ago. Showered and dressed and it was still only eight o'clock. The other patients were scattered around the ward, some engaging in desultory conversations, though most, like Joan, were introspective, uninterested in their surroundings and what was going on around them.

Joan still had not ventured into the day room; nor did she now. She wandered around the ward, picking up various objects that were lying around, but not really taking any interest in them. At the rear of the ward, furthest from the nursing station was a small quiet area with a couple of chairs and a small table with some magazines and a couple of newspapers scattered on it. She sat down and tried to read the paper, but nothing would register. She read several paragraphs but couldn't remember any of what she had read. She found this rather disturbing and quickly put it down. What time was it now? She wandered back along the corridor. Ten past eight. Was it possible for time to pass more slowly? Perhaps the patients who were in the day room had got it right. Watching drivel on the telly while drinking endless cups of tea was the best way to pass the time here.

She wondered whether the hospital had a chapel. Most did, didn't they? The staff she had seen around hadn't said a word to her Surely they wouldn't notice if she went to look for it? She sidled up to the doors at the ward entrance and opened one of them looking out into the corridor.

This brought an immediate response from the nursing station. "Joan?" She did not respond. "Joan!" This time it was louder, more insistent. She turned to see one of the nurses walking towards her. Her badge said she was 'Maureen Kerwan, Nursing Assistant'. She loomed over Joan, looking large and formidable. "Joan, where do you think you're going?" She asked, her voice having the authoritative tone of a teacher feared by her pupils for her strictness.

"I want to go to the chapel." Joan mumbled.

Speaking loudly and slowly, enunciating every word clearly as if Joan were hard of hearing, Maureen said "Joan, you know that you're not allowed to leave the ward. Not until you're more settled. You know that, don't you?"

Joan felt like a child caught doing something she shouldn't. But she had a streak of stubbornness in her and she wanted to go to the chapel. "Doctor Plant said I would be able to go to the chapel." She said.

Maureen Kirwan gave her a *don't-think-you're-going-to-put-one-over-on-me* look. "No Joan," she said, still using her 'does she take sugar?' voice. "He didn't say anything about that to me. Not today, at any rate. Perhaps tomorrow, Joan, after you've seen doctor Marwan. Definitely *not* before tomorrow. Until then you have to stay on the ward. It's for your own safety Joan – just until you're settled – okay?" She took Joan's hand. Her grip was surprisingly firm. Joan would have had to struggle to free herself from it. "Why don't you go and sit in the day room for a bit?" Maureen continued. "Maybe you can have a chat with one of the other patients?"

Before Joan could resist, she led her in the direction of the day room – slowly, like she was helping an invalid. The day room was already occupied by several other patients, all glued to the TV. The room was supposed to offer a calm relaxing environment to the patients, with pastel shades and pictures of various country scenes hung on the walls. To Joan it was drab; there was nothing in it she found remotely attractive.

Maureen led her to an empty chair. "The best thing for you to do now Joan is to try and relax. Take your mind off things. You deserve some time to yourself, you can put your feet up for a bit, watch some telly. There's magazines if you want something to read. In a couple of days one of the occupational therapists will organise a programme of activities for you and you'll be kept busy then I can tell you. You just take it easy while you can." Without another word, she turned her back on Joan.

"How can I take it easy when they won't give me a minute's peace?" Joan called after her, but was ignored.

"Wha's that love? Won't give you a minute's peace? I'd complain if I was you." One of the other patients was talking to her, leaning across from her chair, jabbing the air with her forefinger to make her point. The woman looked about fifty, and was dressed in oddly-matched clothes that looked like they had come from a charity shop. Her hair looked like it hadn't been brushed in years. Joan didn't want to talk to anyone, and ignored her, but this didn't put her off. "What you in for love?" She made it sound like they were in a prison. Her voice was rough and cracked. "They told you yet? They won't tell me why I'm in here." She looked round furtively, as if to make sure what she was saying would not be overheard. She pulled her chair closer to Joan's. "I've been in for weeks. They say I'm ill and they keep givin' me this injection. Doesn't seem to make much difference 's far 's I can tell." She looked around again, scanning the room for eavesdroppers. "Don't know what all the fuss is about. I was doin' okay until I told me nurse 'bout the fuckin' taxi drivers."

Joan wanted to be left alone, but what the woman was saying was so unbelievable she felt compelled to respond. "Taxi drivers?"

The woman seemed delighted to have found someone who would listen. "Tha's right love. They bin followin' me - everywhere." She passed her hand slowly through the air in a gesture to show she literally did mean *everywhere*. "Plottin' to do me in they are. Just waitin' for the right moment, then – they'll 'ave me." She paused as if to make sure Joan had got every word. Then she relaxed. "I'm safe in 'ere though," she continued. "Tha's why I'm 'appy to stay put. The food's alright an' all."

Despite herself, Joan wanted to know more of this woman's bizarre tale. "How did you work all that out?"

To some, the tone of Joan's voice might have conveyed that she found what the woman had to say was hard to believe. The woman herself was oblivious to it. "Stands to reason, love. Everywhere I went, there they was, followin' me. I couldn't nip out to the shops without seein' at least a couple of the bastards keepin' tabs on me, just waitin' for the right moment to pounce. Y'know wha' I mean?"

Joan decided she had heard enough. "Not really, no." However, when she stood up, the woman reached across and tugged her sleeve.

"Wha's yer name then, love?" She asked.

"Joan."

"Not a name you 'ear a lo' of these days, is it?" The woman smacked her lips and seemed to be sucking something. "Pleased to mee' cha." She said. "I'm Carrie, Carrie Locklin." She paused as if considering something then asked "What you in for then?"

In the nursing station, Maria tapped Maureen on the shoulder and gestured towards the day room. "Looks like our Carrie's found a new friend," she observed drily. Maureen suppressed a laugh as Joan left the day room and walked back to the bay where her bed was. She glanced at the clock. It was just gone half past eight.

*

Dr. Marwan's afternoon ward rounds were marathon affairs. He insisted that all the patients had a right to a full review of their cases and progress, no matter how long it took, so it was the one day of the week that Ed made sure he had a good lunch. 'Good', of course being relative – the food was generally lousy, but he needed something filling to get him through the tedious afternoon ahead. Ed had come in late yesterday, the usual day for the ward round, so Dr. Marwan had put if off until today. Just because he's too sodding lazy to write up the case notes himself, Ed told himself.

He edged his tray along the shelf that ran the length of the canteen's self-selection area, helping himself to a 'Salad Provencale' and a yogurt before getting a coffee. Once he had paid for it he looked for somewhere to eat his lunch. He could see Maria at a table with a couple of the other psychy SHOs and decided that was the last place he wanted to sit. Looking over to the other side he saw a female in a white coat sitting by herself. He didn't know her, but that didn't matter to Ed: he soon would. As he got closer he saw the tell-tale stethoscope that proclaimed her status. She had a book on the table that she was holding flat with one hand while she spooned food into her mouth with the other. She didn't hear him approach.

Ed pulled a chair back from the table, scraping its feet on the floor as he did so, which made her look up. He smiled. He knew how good he looked when he smiled and he gave her the full treatment. "Hi. Mind if I join you?"

The effect was striking. As she glanced up at him her jaw dropped open. All of a sudden she was inexplicably tongue-tied. "Er no; er, not at all." She almost stammered. "Feel free." God, he was gorgeous! Was he real?

Putting his tray down on the table, Ed leant across holding out his hand. "I don't think we've met," he said. "I'm Ed. Ed Plant."

Again, the effect was startling. She ignored his outstretched hand as she gagged and almost choked on her food. Quickly Ed picked up the plastic water jug on the table and poured her a drink. "Are you okay?" He sounded concerned.

She took the paper cup off him, and sipped at it between coughs, waiting for them to subside. She blushed, sheepish. "Thanks. I'm fine; really." She started to laugh, then saw the look on his face. She tried to explain. "I just read your name badge." She laughed again, rather loudly this time. "Edward Plant." She took another sip. "I thought you said 'Eggplant'." She laughed again and took another drink of water. "I'm sorry," she coughed again, but waved her hand at him to indicate she was really alright before adding "God, what must you think of me?" Only then did she hold out her own hand, still continuing to chuckle between words. "Joan, Joan Arkwright. SHO in orthopaedics." Her voice had a northern twang – Yorkshire? Geordie?

They shook hands. Both were grinning broadly. She was not the sort that Ed would normally have gone for, not blonde for a start, and that accent was, well . . . but she was kind of attractive in a quirky sort of way. Snub nose, freckles, eyes that laughed, and a smile that was just full of life.

Ed sat down. "Hi, Joan. Actually, I think you must have read the name on my badge wrong. I really am Egg, as in Egg Plant, my close friends call me 'Gene'."

Her eyes crinkled in amusement. "Gene?"

He kept his face completely deadpan. "Short for aubergine."

She laughed again. Edward forked a potato into his mouth. "You did say Arkwright – as in 'Open All Hours' Arkwright?" He asked, still trying to be his witty amusing self.

Her reply surprised him. "'Fraid so." She sighed. "The old fart was my uncle – once removed."

"The old fart?"

She ate a piece of cold ravioli and made a face. "You know – Ronnie Barker? Well, he wasn't really my uncle – but apparently my dad knew him from years ago. The story goes that he chose the name Arkwright because he knew it would piss my dad off no end – at least that's what me dad says. Anyway, as soon as you mention that your name's Arkwright these days, some clever clogs starts stammering 'Ger – Ger – Granville, stop mer-messing about and help this ler-lady with her der-drawers'." She did a very poor imitation of Ronnie Barker. "Very droll - until you've heard it for the seven hundred and twelfth time."

Edward was grinning broadly. It was fairly obvious he found it very funny. "I can imagine. Obviously I wouldn't do anything so crass."

There was a hint of irony in Joan's reply as she said "Obviously."

Ed took another mouthful of food. She threw her fork down on her plate and sipped at her coffee.

"Well, Gene," she asked, "what do you do in this God-forsaken place?"

"I'm like you – an SHO – but in psychiatry. I work for doctor Marwan." He continued to champ away at his lettuce.

Her eyes widened playfully. "A trick-cyclist? How interesting. Never really appealed to me, though." She paused as if considering something. "Is it true you spend all of your time analysing people?" She pretended to look shocked and looked around furtively. "God, I hope no-one sees me with you. They might think I'm seeking your professional advice about something."

"I wouldn't worry about that," Edward said, shaking his head. "Actually it's a ker-common mer-misconception that psychiatrists try to analyse per-people." He could imitate Ronnie Barker very well. He paused to gauge her response. She smiled in a disapproving sort of way as if she did find it funny, but couldn't quite bring herself to show it. "I spend most of my time trying to get laid," he added.

Joan laughed abruptly and rather loudly. "If that's meant to be a chat-up line, Gene, I have to tell you it's not the best, or the most original one I've ever heard."

Edward seemed surprised. "Really?" He feigned annoyance. "Blimey! That must be where I must have been going wrong. I read this book, you see, by some terribly eminent psychologist, who said that if you wanted your relationships to last, you had to start by being honest."

"And you decided to take his advice to heart? How very enterprising of you."

Ed pulled the top off his yogurt. "Well," he said, licking the lid, "not all of it exactly."

"So which bits *did* you take to heart?"

He had to think fast. He sensed she would give as good as she would get. "Erm . . . mostly the bits that said if you wanted to be a successful psychiatrist, sucking up to your consultant was a good place to start."

She nodded sagely in mock agreement. "Mmmm. Actually, that sounds like terribly good advice to me. Has he written anything on the subject of becoming a successful orthopaedic surgeon?"

Now it was Ed's turn to nod. "I believe he has, but I'm pretty sure you couldn't have read it."

Joan pretended to look aggrieved. "Oh? What makes you say that?"

"'Cause he said that the key to success as an orthopod was to develop muscles like Arnold Schwarzenegger!"

Now they both laughed. Ed tried to scoop another spoonful of yogurt but only succeeded in spilling it down his tie. Joan wiped it off with a tissue dipped in water and left a big wet stain. By now they were both almost helpless with laughter. Then Joan looked at her watch. The spell was broken.

"Oh shit. I've got to go. Ward round at two. Mr. Weston is a stickler for starting on time." She pushed her chair back and stood up, gathering the debris of her meal back onto her tray.

Edward also stood. "Well, doctor Arkwright," he said with mock formality, "it was very nice meeting you. We really mer-must do it again ser-sometime."

She looked at him. He was very attractive – and funny. "Yes I think we mer-must." She smiled. "Tell you what: I have an early outpatients tomorrow morning, then an afternoon list starting at one. I'll be in here for lunch at 11.45 prompt." She started to walk away carrying her tray to the trolley standing by the exit. She called back over her shoulder "Don't be late!"

Something of the sunshine in her smile seemed to reach out and touch him. He didn't know why, but he knew he had to see her again. "Der-don't worry, I won't be!" He called after her.

11
Two evenings

No afternoon had ever passed so slowly. Making a break with habit, Ed went to the canteen for an early lunch. And now, since meeting Joan for the second time, he was on tenterhooks, wanting time to pass quickly, wishing his life away so that his date with her would come all the sooner. He couldn't remember the last time – if ever - he had felt so excited about a date. After work he had shaved and showered, and was now trying to decide what to wear. He had taken the extraordinary step of asking Peter for his opinion. Peter didn't know whether he should be amused or bemused as he stood in the bedroom doorway, beer in hand, watching Ed picking out clothes and trying various combinations in the mirror. He had never seen him like this before.

"She must be some girl, to have this effect on you, Ed. So tell me again: how and when did you meet this one?"

Ed pulled off a t-shirt and put it back in the draw. "She's not 'this one' you peasant." He replied, pushing his arm into a shirt sleeve. "Her name is Joan. And I met her in the hospital canteen."

Peter shook his head in mock amazement. "See what I mean? Usually you can't remember their name after you've spent an entire night with them. You haven't even been out with this one yet."

Ed stopped what he was doing. "Stop calling her 'this one' will you? Her name is Joan!"

Peter held his hands up as if to defend himself. "Okay! Joan! So when did you meet her?"

"Yesterday."

"Only yesterday?" Peter pretended to be horrified. "My God! Does this mean the world is about to end?"

Edward threw a towel at Peter, nearly knocking the can out of his hand. "Maybe. Who knows? But there *is* something about this one. I don't know what . . ."

Now it was Peter's turn. "This one?"

Ed grinned. "Alright, you win. But there *is* something extraordinary about her. I was only with her for about fifteen seconds when I knew I was going to enjoy our conversation."

"Fifteen seconds? Isn't that about how long your conversations with women usually last?"

Edward was used to Peter's pseudo-ironic observations. "Ha, ha. No. I mean . . ." For some reason he found he didn't know what he wanted to say.

Peter sensed his friend's difficulty. "Come on man, spit it out," he said, sounding like some military type.

Unusually, Edward found himself on the defensive. "It's alright for you, you're already deep under the thumb." Immediately he knew that wasn't what he had intended to say. It just came out.

As usual, Peter didn't take offence, but responded seriously. "Is that what you think is happening? You only met her yesterday and already you're under the thumb?"

Edward sat on the bed. "No. That's not what I think at all. I just found myself instantly enjoying her company. You know, just being with her. I suddenly felt . . . I don't know . . . *real.* Yeah, that's how I felt; I felt real. Authentic. For once I wasn't just acting out the stereotype that is Ed Plant. Suddenly it was the real me on show like I had been wanting to get out of this shell for years but had never been able to do it before, but now I could. And it happened because she made it happen."

Peter was awestruck. He had never seen Ed like this before. Ed Plant and his six golden rules for the conquest of women had turned into Edward Plant the philosopher. "Fuckin' hell, mate," he said. "That's incredible."

Ed took this entirely the wrong way. "Pete, you're my best mate. I'm never bothered by anything you say, but please don't patronise me, not over this, okay?"

"No, Ed, I really mean it. She really must be something else to have that effect on you."

Ed smiled, more to himself than at his friend. "Just wait till you meet her."

"When were you planning for that to happen?"

"Well, if the old charm's still working, should be at about half ten tonight."

Peter was reassured. "Thank God for that."

This remark puzzled Ed. "Thank God? For what?"

"I was beginning to think you were doomed, but maybe there is a ray of hope in there somewhere."

This attempt at an explanation was lost on Ed. "Ray of hope? Pete, what are you talking about?"

"This one – sorry, Joan – might have brought out the authentic you, but underneath, the old you is still very much alive and kicking."

The old easy-going camaraderie was restored. Ed laughed and threw a shoe at Peter. "Why don't you just piss off and let me get ready?"

*

It was visiting time on Maple ward. Joan had finally relented and agreed that she would have visitors. Shortly before seven, her parents and her sister Caroline had arrived, but after greeting Joan with forced cheerfulness, the conversation had quickly hit a lull. Joan was lying on her bed. She felt exhausted. It was a real battle to keep her eyes open, a battle she thought she would lose. She was finding it extremely difficult to concentrate, and her replies to her visitors' questions were monosyllabic. To her visitors Joan appeared uninterested. It seemed such an effort for her to concentrate and find the words she wanted, and her eyes kept dropping shut.

As ever, Bernadette tried to put a brave face on things. "Well it's nice to see you settled in so quickly love, we were really worried about you, weren't we Sean?" She looked pointedly at her husband.

"That's right love," he said. "We just didn't know what to do until that young doctor chap came – what was his name?"

Bernadette took the baton up again. "Doctor Plant. That's right, isn't it Joan? Is he your doctor in here too?"

Joan could barely think. "Yeah . . . think so," she mumbled.

Sean hadn't been able to hear what his daughter had said. "What did you say, love?"

Bernadette answered for her. "She said she thinks he's her doctor, didn't you love?"

Joan did not reply. The conversation stalled again. Then Caroline had an inspiration. "Hospital food's supposed to be really crap, isn't it?" She tried. "What's it like in here?"

It was all Joan could do to say "Dono."

Caroline tried to cajole her sister into livening up a little. "Oh come on Joan, try to make an effort."

"Can't."

Bernadette glared at Caroline before asking "So how are you feeling now Joan, are you feeling any better?"

Joan shook her head slowly. "Dono. Not really."

Bernadette tried a different tack. "Have you seen the doctor since you came in, love?"

"Yeah. Saw him 'safternoon."

"Did he tell you what he thought was the matter with you?"

"Oh Mum!" Caroline interjected. "They're hardly going to know yet, are they? I bet they've got all sorts of tests to do, haven't they Joan?"

Joan seemed to take a moment to think about her reply. "Dono. He said I might be mentally ill."

Bernadette was quite shocked. "No, Joan. I'm sure they wouldn't say that so soon." She looked for affirmation from Sean and Caroline before adding "Would they?"

Sean thought Joan had definitely gone mental, but he had kept his thoughts to himself. Now he found himself agreeing with his daughter. "If that's what Joan says was said . . ."

Caroline was not sure that what Joan said could be relied on. "Maybe we should ask one of the nurses."

Quietly, Joan started to sob. Bernadette reached for her hand. "Joan love . . . what's the matter. Please tell me. I only want to help."

Joan shook her head, wiping the tears away on her sleeve. "Can't help. No-one can. I'm just so tired. I want to sleep, but I'm afraid."

Fear was something that Sean could understand. Fear of facing an uncertain future, fear of being thought useless. "Afraid of what, love?" He asked.

Her answer surprised them all. "Them." She looked frightened.

"Them? Who?" Bernadette asked the question for all of them.

Joan spoke in a small, tremulous voice. "The voices in my head. Only I can hear them. They're horrible. Just . . . awful. Oh

Mum, I'm so frightened." She pulled herself into her mother's arms and sobbed quietly. Bernadette found herself crying with her.

Caroline had had enough. "This isn't right, mum. I'm going to ask one of the nurses what's going on."

*

To Peter's relief, Ed was almost ready. "So just how did you manage to persuade Joan to go out with you?" He asked.

Ed looked up from fastening his shoes. "D'you know, I'm not sure I did. The more I think about it, the more I'm convinced it was her who stage managed the whole thing."

"But I thought you said you only saw her for the first time yesterday. How *could* she have set it up? Unless she's been stalking you." Ed threw him a withering look. "Bloody hell," he continued, "that's impressive. Not exactly the normal state of affairs, is it?"

Ed stood up and took a last look in the mirror. "Normal? What d'you mean, normal?"

Peter stood away from the door to let Ed out of the bedroom. "Well I know women are usually falling over themselves to go out with you, but I thought you usually had to ask them, rather than the other way around."

Edward smiled at that. "Yeah, see what you mean. No, this was really quite different. We spoke in the canteen for all of ten minutes, then she had to dash off for a ward round. Apparently her consultant is a real pain about starting on time. She said she'd be in the canteen again today, at quarter to twelve, and I just knew I had to be there as well."

"So how did tonight come about?"

"Strange as it may sound, I couldn't wait until tomorrow to see her again. So I had her bleeped."

"Bleeped?"

"Yeah, called her personal bleep: you get the switchboard to do it – the extension number they have to call appears on the bleep. All the juniors have them; the hospital would stop working if we didn't."

"What then?"

"I asked her out."

"And she said yes?"

"Not exactly. She said she'd only go out with me if she could pick where we went."

Ed moved into the narrow hallway, looking for his keys. Peter followed him. "So where are you going?"

Ed shrugged. "I've no idea. I'm meeting her at the corner of Cross Street and Furnace Road at seven."

Peter found Ed's keys and handed them to him. "Didn't know there was anywhere decent to eat 'round that part of town."

"Me either, but you live and learn, don't you?"

*

Her steps firm and purposeful, Caroline walked from Joan's bed to the nursing station. She put her head round the entrance. There were two nurses inside, drinking tea. "Hi. I'm Caroline Roberts – Joan Archer's sister?" She announced.

One of the nurses put down her tea. "Hello Mrs. Roberts." She said politely. "I'm Susan Jones. I'm the acting ward manager tonight. How can I help you?"

"I'm here visiting Joan with my Mum and Dad," Caroline explained. "We're all desperately worried about her. Is there anything you can tell me?"

Susan stood and walked to where Caroline was standing. "Was there anything in particular you wanted to know? I'm afraid I'm not allowed to discuss any patient's confidential details unless they give their consent. The hospital is very hot on that, I'm afraid."

"But she's my sister!" Caroline was quite appalled.

Susan gave a sort of half smile. Relatives often found it difficult to come to terms with the rules of confidentiality. "I'm afraid it doesn't make any difference. We're not allowed to give out any information unless the patient says we can."

"Well, can you at least tell me whether she's seen a doctor yet?"

Susan gave a brief nod. "Yes, she saw doctor Marwan in the ward round yesterday afternoon."

The only doctor Caroline had heard tell of up to now was Dr. Plant. "Doctor Marwan? Who's he?"

"He's the consultant psychiatrist in charge of Joan's care."

Being told that Joan had been seen by a consultant psychiatrist seemed to mollify Caroline a little. "Okay. What does Joan have to do to give her permission for you to talk to me and my parents about her case?"

Susan brightened. She didn't want to appear uncooperative, but she had to follow procedure. "We have a standard form she has to sign."

"Could I have one?" Caroline asked. "I'll get her to sign it now."

Susan frowned. "I'm afraid it's not that simple. I have to be there when you ask her to sign it, just to make sure she's not put under any pressure to agree to something she doesn't want to."

Caroline was quite upset by this. "But . . . that's terrible! We wouldn't try to make Joan do something she didn't want to do! We're her family, for pity's sake!"

Susan stood firm. "I'm afraid it's hospital policy. And as acting ward manager, it's more than my job's worth not to do it."

"Job's worth?" Caroline's voice rang with scorn. "Oh don't tell me we have to go through that rigmarole here as well?"

Susan felt she didn't have to answer. She merely shrugged and went to the filing cabinet from which she extracted a pink form. Wordlessly she accompanied Caroline to Joan's bed. When they arrived, it was Caroline who spoke.

"Mum . . . This is the acting ward manager – Nurse Jones? She says she isn't allowed to tell us anything about Joan unless Joan gives her permission."

Bernadette reacted in the same way as Caroline. "But we're her family! Don't we have a right to know what's going on?"

Susan knew this wasn't going to be easy. "I know how you must feel," she said, "but it's hospital policy. One of the most important things we have to do is to respect all of our patients' right to confidentiality. Mostly it's just a formality, but one we have to observe."

Caroline spoke to Joan. "Joan – you have to sign this form to say you give your permission for the doctors and nurses to tell us what's going on." She turned to Susan. "Where exactly does she have to sign it?"

"Just here at the bottom." Susan held the form out to Joan. "But before she signs it I have to explain it to her." She spoke quietly to Joan. "Joan – this form is a release form. If you sign it, it means we have your permission to discuss your case with the people that you specify. In this case it would be your mum and dad and your sister."

Joan roused herself, wanting to understand. "What exactly would you tell them?" She asked, her words coming slowly.

"We would answer any questions they might ask, and keep them fully informed about your treatment and anything that occurred during your stay with us." Susan told her.

"But what if I don't want you to tell them?"

"Then you don't have to sign the form. If you don't sign it, we won't give out any confidential information – to anyone."

"I don't want to sign it."

Bernadette was aghast. "Joan! It's not just anyone we're talking about here – it's me, and your dad, and Caroline. We're just very anxious about you, love. We just want to know what's happening. Have you any idea how worrying it is, not knowing what's going on?"

Susan felt she had to intervene. She couldn't permit Joan to be put under any pressure, not when she was so vulnerable. "I'm sorry Mrs. Archer, I really am. But Joan's made her wishes known very clearly. I have to respect them. Don't feel too bad about it – it often happens that patients don't want even their loved ones to know what they're going through. They think it's too painful for them. Sometimes, it's part of their illness to want to keep everything to themselves."

Caroline was outraged. "Is that what's happening here? It's part of Joan's illness? 'Cause if it is, shouldn't you take that into account when deciding whether or not you can talk to us about it?"

Caroline might have thought she had a point, but Susan could not rise to it. "I'm really sorry, but I can't discuss it with you. Not now. I could make an appointment for you to see doctor Marwan if you like. He's probably the best person for you to ask."

"And how soon would that be?" Sean demanded, his ire also rising.

Susan remained calm. "I don't know. I would have to ask his secretary, and she's finished work for today. If you leave me a number I can reach you on, I can ask her to contact you tomorrow to arrange it. Would you like me to do that?"

Sean thought they were being given the run-around. He had experienced it before, with his Parkinson's disease. He scowled. "Feckin' right I would!"

"Sean! Language!" Bernadette chided. She turned to face Susan. "I'm sorry. But you can understand how worried we all are, can't you?"

"I can," Susan said sympathetically, "and I do feel for you, but you have to try and understand my position too. My first responsibility is to Joan. It's her wishes I have to respect in this."

Something occurred to Caroline. "Nurse – before you go, can you answer one question for me? Joan said she was taking medication – so that's not a secret is it?"

"No, not if she's already told you that herself," Susan agreed

"This sleepiness – is that because of the medication she's taking?"

Caroline watched Susan closely, looking for signs of her being evasive. She saw none. "Yes, it is. I'm afraid that sedation is a common side effect with the medication she's taking."

Caroline wanted to know more. "And how long will the sedation last? Is it something that will wear off, or is it something she's going to have to learn to live with?"

Susan shook her head. "That's impossible to say at this stage For some people, the sedation wears off in a few weeks, for some people it doesn't. We just have to wait and see."

Caroline smiled grudgingly. "Thank you."

"If you want more information about the medication, I can arrange for a pharmacist to see you, if you like."

"Could you?"

Susan relaxed. "I'll put a note in the day book for them to contact you."

"Thanks nurse. I'm sure you're doing everything you can. We're really very grateful." Bernadette said, trying to hide the worry she was feeling.

"That's okay. I ought to get back to the ward office. I'll be there all evening if you want to see me again before you leave."

*

The junction of Cross Street and Furnace Road was not in the most up-market part of town; in fact, it was old and dilapidated, with a palpable air of decay, but Joan Arkwright loved it. She thought the area had character, with its venerable tall buildings, with glazed brickwork in different colours, wide streets, many still with cobbled surfaces, and old mansions stepped well back from the road, now mostly converted into flats and bedsits. The streets were not terribly well lit, and she was standing in the yellow halo of a street lamp about ten yards from a corner shop called 'Khan's L8 Stores'. She glanced at her watch. He was late. She had been so sure he would come. She would give him fifteen minutes longer, but no more. A mini-cab approached from the direction of Furnace Road and stopped outside the shop. Edward stepped out. He looked up and down the street as if to get his bearings, and when his eyes lit on Joan they beamed with delight.

He half ran to her, smiling broadly and gave her a hesitant peck on the cheek. "Joan, Hello. I'm sorry I'm a bit late, couldn't get a cab." He looked around. "I didn't know this part of town even existed."

Joan looked him coolly up and down, appraising him, then smiled in her turn as if she liked what she saw. "Hello yourself, Gene," she said. "Not many people know this part of town, not many doctors anyway." She looked wistful. "It's like they've forgotten it ever existed, but it used to be a vibrant part of town a hundred years or so ago. You can guess the local industry from the street names: Furnace Road, Cutler Street, Smith Lane – metal working mainly. It's a shame that it's down on its luck now, some of the local buildings are quite spectacular – if you're prepared to look beneath the surface."

Ed was impressed, or at least gave the impression of it. "You seem to know a lot about it. Do you live round here, or do you have an interest in local history?"

"Both, actually."

He turned on the boyish charm. "Wow, cosmic. So where are you taking me? I didn't think there'd be any place round here to eat."

"There isn't really. I thought we could go back to my place – unless you'd rather go somewhere else?" She walked past him heading towards the corner shop.

"No, that would be great." He enthused, catching up with her. "So where do you live?"

Joan stopped dead. "Not so fast, Gene. I haven't exactly had weeks to prepare for this, have I? We've got to get the stuff before I can cook it, okay?" She took his hand and led him into the shop.

A bell rang as they pushed the door open. An Asian man was standing behind the counter reading the local free paper. He looked bored and gave them only a cursory glance as they passed. The shop was fairly typical in its layout, with racks of magazines and cigarettes behind the counter, shelves along the walls with a motley display of groceries and household goods, and, at the back, a dairy cabinet, a meat counter and a freezer.

Joan stopped before the vegetable rack. "What would you like to eat? The choice isn't too bad as long as you don't want anything too exotic."

Edward was a little taken aback. Whatever it was he had been expecting it wasn't this. "Exotic? Er, no. Actually I'm fairly catholic in my tastes; I'm up for pretty much anything."

"Catholic?" Joan looked at him quizzically. "That's an unusual choice of adjective. Nothing Freudian behind it, I hope?"

"Freudian? I don't think so. Funnily enough I had a patient admitted the other night who's a Catholic, but I don't think I'd read anything into that. Why?"

"'Cause I'm a Catholic myself."

This was definitely not what he had been expecting. He wasn't sure how he should respond. Religion had never been a topic of discussion with any of his previous conquests. "Oh. That's very, er, devout. Practising?"

Joan's reply was instant – like she had been working at it. "Constantly – only the Pope ever gets it perfect."

They both laughed.

Joan brought them back to the task at hand. "So come on Gene, what do you fancy?" He smiled. "I meant to eat!" She gave him a playful look that at the same time told him to behave.

What did he fancy? Hadn't he just said he was up for anything? He thought quickly. They were in front of the fruit and vegetable section. "Okay. Er, how about something vegetarian – with rice, or maybe pasta?"

Joan raised her eyebrows. "Don't tell me – *brown* rice?"

Ed pretended to be surprised. "How did you know?"

She gave him an 'I'm not stupid' look. "Funny, I didn't take you for a veggie," she said.

"Actually, I'm not," he admitted, "but I didn't want anything too heavy, not when I've got to be in early tomorrow."

Joan was not buying his explanation. Not yet. "And, of course, some women find that sort of thing terribly attractive."

"What sort of thing?"

"Men who appear sensitive and caring."

He stepped back. "Joan Arkwright, you're not a cynic, are you?"

"Me? No, not a practising one, anyway."

He shook his head, smiling to himself. "Tell you what, why don't you buy something terribly macrobiotic and wholesome, with lashings of natural yoghurt, and I'll sort out some wine."

The awkward moment passed. "Cool!"

"Red or white?" He asked.

"Oh, I think I'll let you decide – you look like a sophisticated man of the world!"

From the meat counter Joan selected two packs before picking out some frozen vegetables, a tub of yogurt and some herbs and spices. She had them paid for and packed into a carrier bag while Edward was still in the limited wine section trying to make his mind up.

She looked over his shoulder. "What's the matter? Spoilt for choice?"

Edward frowned, his face a mask of indecision. "I can't quite make my mind up whether to go for the '95 or the '99."

"Would that be pence or pounds?"

He laughed and picked up a bottle of champagne.

"Don't be too extravagant now, Gene." But even if he was trying to impress her, she was glad to see he wasn't a cheapskate.

"Always start as you mean to go on, is what I say," he said, taking the bottle to the counter to pay.

On leaving the shop Edward insisted on carrying the shopping. Joan linked her arm into his as they made their way between the pools of yellow light that showed their way.

In the hospital, Bernadette reached into a carrier bag and brought out a bunch of grapes and some peaches. "I didn't know what to bring, so I brought you these. You like grapes, don't you, Joan?"

The sleepiness seemed to have abated a little. "S'pose so." She replied.

"Father James was asking after you," her dad told her. "He said to remember him to you. Said he'd be praying for you."

"Did he?"

Caroline was still seething from the way that Susan had acted over Joan's right to confidentiality. "What are the staff like? That nurse who was over here just now seems a right pain in the backside."

Joan pushed herself up on the bed to face Caroline. "No, she's nice really, Car. She was very good to me the other night when I was really frightened and confused about what was going on."

This did not satisfy Caroline. "She must have taken a narky pill or something today, then." She observed cattily.

Sean continued as if Caroline had not uttered a word. "Your uncle Joe was asking about you too." He said.

This irritated Joan. "Uncle Joe? Why did you have to tell him I was in here?"

Sean did not notice his daughter's irritation. "Not just Joe, love," he said, "everybody's worried about you."

"Everybody?" This made her cross. "Oh for God's sake, Dad. Why don't you just put an advert in the fucking paper?"

Bernadette had been delving into a bag at her feet. "Joan! Just remember who you're talking to. There's nothing wrong in having people care about you."

Once again the conversation reached a low ebb. Bernadette gestured to Sean and he lifted a small travel case onto the bed. "I knew you wouldn't have any of the stuff you need, love," she said chattily as if nothing untoward had been said, "so I've brought your toilet bag, and some clean clothes, and a couple of nighties and your dressing gown and slippers."

If she thought that Joan would be pleased by this, she was way off the mark. "You went into my room?" She could feel her anger rising. First, they had blabbed about her to anyone who was prepared to listen, and then they had invaded her precious sacred space.

Her dad came to the rescue. "We had to, love. What else were we supposed to do?"

The moment passed. Her mum carried on in the same chatty tone. "Is there anything else you need love? Have you got no idea how long you're going to be in for?"

The moments of anger seemed to have revitalised Joan. "They said I can't leave the ward until after I've seen by the consultant again. But I'm not staying after that."

Sean could not keep the worry out of his voice. "Don't you think you ought to let the doctor be the judge of that, love?"

Joan almost laughed. "The doctor?" She barked contemptuously. "And what is he going to be able to do?"

Her mother could not bear to hear Joan talk this way. "That young doctor who came to the house said they would be able to help you, but that you had to let them help you; they couldn't help if you wouldn't cooperate."

The conversation stalled again. Caroline pulled some magazines out of a carrier bag. "I brought you some magazines Joan I wasn't sure which ones you liked to read so I bought a few."

Joan had not the slightest interest in any magazines. "Thanks. Just put them on my locker."

Caroline could see her sister wasn't really interested, but she persevered, asking "D'you like those crossword and puzzle magazines? They've got loads of them in the shop in the hospital foyer. I could get you some of those if you like?"

Joan almost smiled. A 'thanks, but no thanks' sort of smile. "Not really."

"Is there anything else you'd like us to bring in for you, love?" Bernadette asked.

"My rosary. Can you bring me my rosary?"

"No problem, love. Where did you put it?"

Joan ignored her. "And some mineral water. The tea and coffee they have here is disgusting."

"What about the food? Is that okay? Would you like us to bring you something to eat?" Her mum continued.

Joan shook her head slowly. "Not really bothered about having anything to eat."

"You've got to eat love, keep your strength up, or you'll never get better." Her dad's worry was still obvious.

"When little Sean was in hospital last year, we weren't allowed to take food in. Before we bring anything, maybe we ought to ask the nurses if it's okay," Caroline said, "that's assuming they'll tell us," she added.

A bell sounded. "Is that the end of visiting already?" Bernadette asked.

One of the staff walked along the corridor not quite shouting "Visiting time is over now please, can you please leave and make sure you take everything with you, thank you. Visiting is at the same time tomorrow, and from two to four pm and six to nine pm at the week-end. Visiting time is now over, please leave quietly and take all personal items with you, thank you."

As her visitors made to leave Joan blurted out "Can you ask them if I can go to the chapel?"

Bernadette was surprised by her daughter's request. "The chapel? Why wouldn't they let you go to the chapel?"

"They wouldn't let me go when I asked before." Joan explained. "They said I couldn't leave the ward until after I had seen the consultant again. Said it was for my own safety, but I only want to go to the chapel." Her eyes filled with tears.

Bernadette turned to Sean. "Not allowed to visit the chapel? That's terrible! You go and talk to them about it, Sean!"

Caroline was having difficulty getting out of her chair; her bottom had stuck to the plastic seat. "We can go and ask," she said, "but what's the betting that they tell us it's just another one of their procedures they have to follow?"

"Please, will you just ask them?" Joan pleaded. She got off her bed, and together they walked slowly along the corridor towards the nursing station.

*

For Ed, Joan's flat was something of a nightmare. Although his was better situated for the centre of town and all that went with it, hers was bigger and more comfortable, and the walls were adorned with all sorts of prints, mostly modern art. But her untidiness made him cringe. The place was a mess. Articles about various aspects of surgery were strewn on every available surface, and there were items of clothing lying all over the place. And it was filled with books, hundreds of them: paperbacks, hardbacks, new, second-hand, on every subject under the sun. On this, he realised, they would never see eye-to-eye. He was tidiness personified, but Joan seemed to have no regard for it whatsoever. It was as if her living space was a shrine dedicated to chaos and she was determined not to permit any vestige of order to intrude. It struck him as strange that it was so unexpected: why had he been so ready to assume that she would be tidy? Unconsciously, he had already started to think about how their worlds might fit together, but he wondered whether he would ever be able to cope with such unbridled disregard for orderliness.

While she was preparing their meal, he learned that her favourite artist was Miro, and that she had no favourite author, but was willing to give anyone the chance to be read. She generally had three or four books on the go at any one time, she admitted, with at least one history book, and usually one fiction. That was why there were books all over the place, including the toilet. She thought of modern art as a sort of visual poetry, she told him, and liked to contemplate pictures for hours at a time, often combining the experience with music. He was awestruck. He knew little about art: his appreciation of it more or less stopped with the old masters. He thought of it as mere adornment, slightly above wallpaper, but not by much: he had never even heard of Miro. She told him to put some music on. He investigated her CD collection. The breadth of her musical taste was as wide as her taste in literature. Her collection ranged from renaissance madrigals to punk and from jazz and swing to pop and avant-garde. He began to feel that his own interest in late sixties pop was parochial in comparison. He chose an artist he had never heard of, supposing, correctly, that their music would be obscure. It was. A haunting female voice filled the room, sometimes with orchestral accompaniment, sometimes rhythmic, with lyrics he would never be able to decipher. The experience was strangely sensual, with the vocal rising and falling sometimes with a sense of urgency, but mostly with a feeling of extraordinary fulfilment. He had never heard anything like it. Joan walked into the room. "I see you found Lisa Gerrard," she said dreamily. "Isn't she fantastic? She's one of my all-time favourites."

Ed searched for something to say. If modern art was visual poetry, could this be musical poetry? That was a nice way to think of it, Joan agreed, but she had a more personal take on it. To her, this was what she called 'flying carpet' music. It helped her to soar above the humdrum cares of the world and find her inner self. She laughed self-consciously as if she had given too much of herself away too soon, and then went back to her cooking.

She made room for them on her small sofa by the simple expedient of sweeping everything that was on it onto the floor. Now they were side by side. The music was less exotic - Van the Man - and the debris of their meal lay scattered on a low table in front of them. Edward went to the fridge and returned with what was left of the champagne and emptied it into their glasses. He took a sip before putting his glass on the table.

He clasped his hands behind his head and looked at the ceiling. "You have to hand it to them, don't you? They can do marvels with that textured soya protein stuff these days. I couldn't tell that it wasn't meat, and it tasted really quite like chicken." He looked at Joan. "What d'you call that stuff we just ate, anyway?"

Joan lifted her glass to her lips. "I call it chicken curry and chips – what do you call it?"

As casually as he could, Ed put his arm around her shoulder "I call it absolutely amazing that you have the energy to whip up something like that after a putting in a full day at the hospital. I never do. I usually just have something out of a packet or a tin or have a take-away."

She took another sip of her drink. "I bet you do. Do you live alone?"

Ed shook his head. "Not exactly. I live with my mate Peter. We were at Oxford together."

"Oxford?" She nodded to herself as though this were a key piece of a puzzle she was struggling to complete. "You did medicine at Oxford?" Edward nodded. "And where were you before that?"

Now it was Ed's turn to feel self-conscious. "I'm not sure I want to tell you."

"Why not? Come on, Gene, no need to be shy." She edged closer to him.

"I was at Winchester school."

"Is that posh?"

Never before in his life had he felt sheepish about telling someone where he had gone to school. "Very." He waited to see if there would be any reaction. There wasn't. "Where did you go to school and Uni?"

Joan slouched down into the couch. "School – St. Hilda's RC High School for girls in Sunderland. It wasn't a high school really, but they couldn't call it a comp because it was girls only. Then I did medicine at Leeds. Fab place, Leeds, so much going on."

"So why did you come all the way down here?" Ed wanted to know.

This was a question she had never been able to answer. A year or so ago she had felt unaccountably restless. Something within her had prompted her to make the move, and she had simply gone with it. "I don't know really, I think I wanted a change, explore my options, see a few new horizons. What about you?"

Edward frowned. "Not exactly miles away from my roots here, am I? Actually, I'm thinking of going into forensic psychiatry, and the regional secure unit is part of the SHO and registrar rotation – great experience if that's what you want to do."

Joan moved closer. "What about your mate – the one you share your flat with?"

"Peter? He was coming here anyway. He wanted a job in marketing and got offered a fantastic package straight from Uni, so he was all set to come here."

"What did he do?"

"At Uni? Psychology. Perfect start for a career in marketing, and he got a first, so he had plenty of options when it came to prospective employers."

She moved closer still to Edward, their mouths only inches apart. "I got a first too." She murmured. "Double first actually, MB *and* ChB."

"Blimey." It was all he could think of to say.

"Oh, do shut up." She kissed him. It was wonderful. His heart was pounding fit to burst out of his chest, like it was his first kiss ever and he had no idea what it was going to be like. She didn't keep it going for long before she pulled away. He tried to prolong it, but she turned her face away so that his lips landed on her cheek.

He felt a little foolish, but she just whispered "Not so fast, Gene. There's plenty of time."

"Sorry."

She put her fingers to his lips. "No need to apologise, I just like things to move a little more slowly than perhaps you do." She reached for her glass and emptied it. "I'm fascinated by psychiatry really," she continued, "it's so different from setting broken bones and doing hip replacements. What made you want to do it?"

Ed tried to make it sound interesting. "When I first went into it I thought it was completely absorbing, and the more you get into it, the more you realise how much we really don't know about the mind and how it works. I don't think I could work in any other branch of medicine now."

She snuggled herself down to make herself more comfortable in his arms, her head resting on his chest. "Tell me about the patient you admitted the other day – the Catholic one."

Edward pursed his lips. "I'm not really supposed to discuss cases."

She twisted her head so she could see his face. "I don't want to know who they are or anything, I just want to know a bit more – doctor to doctor; just between us. If I understand how you see your patients, it helps me to get to know you better."

He shrugged. "OK. Well, the patient is a young female, early twenties. No previous psychiatric history that we know of, and recently she started to act rather oddly. She dropped out of uni, came back to live with her parents and started spending a great deal of time in her local church."

"That doesn't sound too odd. Lots of people drop out of uni, and plenty of students get religion."

Edward felt the need to explain. "Absolutely. But where odd behaviour crosses the line into mental illness is when it becomes distressing to the individual and prevents them from living a normal productive life."

Joan grimaced like she'd just bitten into something sour. "That sounds like you've eaten a textbook of psychiatry."

"I suppose it does a bit" he admitted sheepishly. "Sorry."

But she wanted to hear more. "So presumably there's more to this than just dropping out of uni and going to church?"

He nodded. "Yeah. She also hears some pretty distressing voices that tell her to do things and constantly criticise her in the strongest possible terms."

"You mean auditory hallucinations, just like the text books?"

"Absolutely classic symptoms of schizophrenia."

Joan had a flash of intuition. "But there's something special about this case, isn't there?" She asked.

Edward hadn't really thought about it since he had felt so elated after doing the domiciliary visit. He tried to put his thoughts into some semblance of order. "Well, it's tragic that she's so young. People rarely make a complete recovery from an episode of schizophrenia, so she's likely to have the illness for the rest of her life."

"Is that it?"

"Yes," he admitted. "It was the first time I had seen a first episode of schizophrenia. They're quite rare, and I felt like I had done something monumental, and felt like I owned it in some way."

Still her intuition told her there was more than he was telling her. "But there's something else, there's got to be," she insisted.

He hesitated. "I'm not sure yet. The voices have a religious dimension to them. They're obscene in the way they refer to her Catholic faith, and I've never heard of that before. But there is something I can't quite put my finger on about the way I feel about Joan . . ."

She sat bolt upright. "Joan? The same as me?"

Edward was a little surprised by her reaction. It was a common enough name, wasn't it? "Yes." Was all he said.

But she said "That's quite a coincidence, don't you think? Not such a common name these days, and she's Catholic too. If I didn't know better I'd say it was almost creepy."

Ed didn't know what to make of it. "You think so? I never gave it any thought, really. Anyway, what makes her different is that she seems to have some kind of inner resource, a belief in something greater than she is that gives her strength when other people might just give up the ghost. I couldn't recognise it before, but it suddenly became clear to me . . . like she has some kind of aura, a presence . . ." He stopped, embarrassed. "Listen to me, talking nonsense. I'm not very good at talking about feelings and stuff."

"A psychiatrist no good at talking about feelings and stuff? I predict you'll go far, young man." She kissed him again, this time not pulling away.

*

On Maple ward Joan and her relatives reached the nursing station. Caroline looked to see if anyone was inside. Susan was writing something in a folder, but looked up immediately.

"I'm sorry to disturb you again," Caroline started to say.

"Not at all," Susan replied.

"It's just that Joan asked me to ask if it was alright for her to go to the chapel for a while."

"Yes, she asked to go earlier," Susan told her, "but I'm afraid our instructions are that she should stay on the ward until she's been seen by doctor Plant tomorrow."

"And then?"

"Doctor Plant will decide whether it's appropriate for her to go." Susan could see the concern etched on Caroline's face. "Don't worry, we'll make sure that he's reminded that Joan wants to go to the chapel, even if Joan herself forgets to ask."

Joan had come up behind Caroline. "Is that okay?" Caroline asked her.

"I suppose it'll have to be, won't it?" She replied, shuffling away.

At the ward entrance, Joan hugged each of her visitors in turn.

"'Bye, love." Her mother said, trying to hold back her tears. "See you tomorrow."

Her dad was surprisingly gruff, but then he was trying to keep his own tears in check. "See you, pet. You take care of yourself now, hear?"

"I will, dad." She said.

"Promise?"

"I promise."

Caroline, ever practical said "See you, Joan. I probably won't be able to get in tomorrow, Martin's got to work late, and I can't exactly ask mum to mind the kids, can I?"

"Don't worry about me Caroline; I'll be fine, you'll see."

As soon as the swing doors had closed behind them, Joan walked back to the nursing station. "Nurse . . . Please nurse, please . . ." She pleaded. "Let me go to the chapel. Just for a few minutes. I promise I'll be back as soon as I've said some prayers."

Susan had to be firm. "I'm sorry Joan, I really am, but you already know I'm not allowed to let you go. Why don't you have a cup of tea and watch telly for a bit, eh? Then have an early night. I'm sure you'll have no trouble sleeping tonight, and you'll feel all the better for your case review tomorrow."

*

For once Ed did not mind doing the washing up. Joan was drying. It was more practical that way, she had said, since he did not know where the dishes lived. Joan was still curious about her mentally ill counterpart. "You said that at first you couldn't work out what was different about your new patient, but that it came to you all of a sudden what it was. When was that?"

Edward answered without thinking. "You're not going to believe this, but it was just after I met you in the canteen. I couldn't begin to put it into words, but all of a sudden I had a flash of intuition."

"A man with intuition? Scary!" She put the plate she was drying into the cupboard. "So what brought on this flash of intuition?"

"I didn't know it at the time, but I see exactly the same thing in you."

This did not seem much of a compliment to Joan. "What? Madness? Insanity? Thanks a bunch!"

"No, not that, you doofus!" He turned away from the sink and pulled her into an embrace, wet hands and all. "It was this aura, this sense of purpose, serenity, even. Somehow I sense exactly the same things in you." He brushed his lips on hers. "Maybe that's why I'm so attracted to you." He kissed her again, a deep, long kiss.

She pulled away and resumed drying the dishes. "As long as you're not attracted to her as well."

"Of course not." He put the last dish on the drainer.

She left it where it was and put her arms around his waist, pulling herself close. "Would you like a coffee before you go?" She asked.

"Do I have to go?" He sounded so plaintive she almost took pity on him.

"I'm afraid you do."

He sighed. "In that case, I won't have a coffee, if you don't mind. If I do, I'll just be awake all night."

She wrapped her arms tightly around him, her head snuggling into his chin. "I think I'll be awake all night anyway." They kissed again. A clock chimed midnight. Reluctantly she pushed him away. "Gene – it's midnight. I hate to be a killjoy but I do have a busy day tomorrow."

This was unprecedented, but strangely, he was glad of it. He felt serene, even happy as he opened the door to leave. "It's okay. I understand, really I do." Holding the door open he turned back. "Joan – I had a brilliant time tonight. In fact, I can't remember when I've ever had such a good time just being with somebody." He recalled a line in one of the songs they had listened to earlier. "Wouldn't it be great if it was like this all the time?"

"Careful what you wish for, Gene," she replied. His saying that seemed to have made her a little wistful.

"Can I see you again?" He said.

She was right behind him. She took his hand in hers as if she might be persuaded to relent. "What an idiot you are." She said. "How on earth did you manage to get into to Oxford?"

He grinned. "I cheated, naturally."

"Naturally!" She gave him a last kiss and pushed him out.

12
The power of love

Ed slept fitfully. When he woke he remembered having dreams, but couldn't remember what they were. Unperturbed he went through his morning routine knowing that by the time he was dressed Peter would have the coffee on. As usual, Peter was reading the paper and barely glanced in Ed's direction when he made his appearance. Ed poured himself a coffee and refilled Peter's cup.

"So, how did it go last night? Anything favourable to report?" Peter asked, flicking a page over, affecting little more than a passing interest.

Edward cut two slices from a loaf and put them into the toaster. "Not a lot really," he said. Then he stopped himself. "God, listen to me. No, as a matter of fact I had an absolutely fantastic time. We met outside a Pakky shop; that's where she does her shopping: she chose the food, I chose the wine. We went back to her place, and she cooked for me. It was just brilliant. Really."

Peter folded his paper closed. "Does she live in that part of town? I thought the only people who lived there were smack-heads and immigrants."

"You'd be surprised," Ed replied, hunting in the fridge for the marmalade. "Once you look around there's quite a lot going on in the area. It's interesting both historically and architecturally, and there's quite a bohemian feel to it. Her place was . . ." He wondered whether he should tell Peter the whole truth about Joan's flat. He decided against it. ". . . quite remarkable."

He turned round to find Peter looking at him askance. "Since when have you been interested in history and architecture? And you're about as bohemian as the Beckhams!"

Edward grinned. He knew this was completely out of character for him, but strangely, he found himself enjoying it. "It's Joan. She's quite passionate about it. It's obviously important to her, and she doesn't care who knows."

Peter put his psychology hat on. "Maybe it's a test or something."

Ed was dubious. "A test? Why would she do that? Anyway, what kind of test?"

"It could be she's looking to see how malleable you are, how far she can push you. There isn't a woman alive who doesn't believe she can't change her man for the better."

Playfully, Ed adopted his Jedi persona. "Ah, my young apprentice. You still have much to learn." The toast popped up, and putting it on a plate, he brought it to the table and sat down. While he buttered it he said "Have you forgotten the six rules of conquest? I draw your attention in particular to rule number three: *Always show an interest in the person you're pursuing, and be sensitive to the things they claim to find interesting. That is the path to true enlightenment.*"

Now it was Peter's turn to mock. "Enlightenment? I thought it was all about sex?"

"It's always about sex." Ed took a bite of toast, marmalade running down his chin.

"So . . ." Peter asked slyly, "did you?"

Edward was walking back from the kitchenette, mopping at his chin with kitchen roll. "God, you can be an insensitive sod at times you know." He said.

"Insensitive?" Peter replied, incredulous. "Pots and kettles going on here I think, mate. Blimey, usually you can't wait to give me a blow-by-blow account of your conquests. I always thought it was your sadistic streak coming out."

"Sadistic? Me?"

Peter was happy to explain. "You know, dangling the temptations of the flesh before me, making me envious of what I was missing, trying to tempt me from the straight and narrow."

Ed shook his head, picked up his second piece of toast and grinned. "You've got it wrong mate. I wouldn't try that on you, I know you're beyond temptation."

"So, I take it you didn't, then?"

Ed laughed at his friend's persistence, crumbs exploding over the table. The toast was put down as he brushed the crumbs into his cupped hand. "Okay," he said eventually. "For your information, no, I didn't."

Peter was awestruck. "I knew it!" He said. "That's got to be a first?"

"Not quite," Ed conceded, "but not far off."

"And presumably you want to see her again?"

The banter was over. "What do you think?"

Peter could sense a change in his friend. "I think it's finally hit you." He said, equally serious.

"Hit me? What?"

"You know, Cupid's arrow, the love-bug, call it what you want. I think a member of the opposite sex has finally succeeded in getting through that armour-plate that masquerades as your personality."

Ed paused to ponder what Peter had said. "I never thought of it that way before, but when you put it like that, you could be right, I guess."

The moment passed. Peter grinned. "I doubt it. I'm sure it's just a phase that will pass soon enough. Once you've got her into bed you'll lose interest like you always do."

But Ed was still in a thoughtful mood. "Do you think so? I'm not so sure. In fact, I don't think I'll get anywhere near her bed until she's sure about me and about herself. She seems to have an uncanny intuition, like she knew the way everything would happen, long beforehand."

Peter had never seen this side of Ed before. "So are you going to see her again?" He asked, all jocularity abandoned.

Ed thought the answer was obvious. "Are you kidding?"

"But this time it's your turn to take her somewhere."

Edward popped the last morsel into his mouth. "Yep. That's the plan."

"So where will you take her?" Peter suggested a couple of places Ed favoured when he wanted to impress the ladies. "La Maison d'Or? Marelli's?"

Ed shook his head. "No. I don't think so. I want it to be somewhere really special."

Peter was somewhat taken aback by his reply. "It doesn't get much more special than La Maison d'Or, I wouldn't have thought."

Ed was looking thoughtful again. "I know, but I've got to find somewhere."

*

Although the Friday review, as Dr. Marwan liked to call it, was less formal than the ward round, still he liked to see all his patients and consider whether they might benefit from being allowed to go home for the week-end. Yesterday he had been accompanied by Ed and Cathy as together they saw each patient in turn. They had occupied one of the small interview rooms, a pile of patients' files at Ed's feet. As each case was discussed, Ed wrote in the notes, and on a separate pad, kept a list of everything that he would have to do afterwards. Cathy had brought Joan in, and Dr. Marwan had questioned her at length. Joan had obviously found it difficult to respond. On top of being sedated she appeared distracted, and occasionally cocked her head as if listening to something, though she didn't respond to it, at least not while she was in with them.

Dr. Marwan had tried to explain to Joan why he had gone on at such length. "Thank you for trying to answer all my questions, Joan," he had said. "I do know how difficult it can be, especially when I'm sure you must have had similar discussions several times already with other people, but it's important for me to come to my own conclusions: I hope you understand."

Joan had been preoccupied with the paper cup in her hands. It had become her constant companion; her mouth was dry all the time, and she sipped at it repeatedly. "Yes, I think so," she said.

Marwan sat back in his chair. "Now Joan, are there any questions you would like to ask me?"

She looked up. "Yes. When can I go home?"

Marwan had been anticipating this question. In theory this was the whole point of the review, but it was far too early to contemplate her being discharged or even going home on weekend leave: she was clearly disturbed and therefore unpredictable. "I think it's too early to say just yet, Joan. You were brought into hospital for three reasons, Joan, and all of them still pertain."

Joan seemed mystified. "Three reasons? What were they?"

Marwan was happy to explain. "The first was because we had reason to fear for your safety. The second was to monitor you to try and ascertain exactly what problems you were facing. And the third was so we could offer you treatment should you need it."

Joan either hadn't understood or thought his explanation irrelevant. "So why can't I go home?" She persisted.

Marwan shifted slightly in his chair, moving forward. "Doctor Plant and the nursing staff are still concerned that it might not be safe for you to be allowed home so early. And as far as assessing you and starting treatment, it's still very early days. I'd like you to stay with us for at least another week, and we can re-assess the situation then. Is that acceptable to you?"

Joan's suspicions about why she had been brought in had not abated. "What if it's not?" Her question sounded surly.

Marwan sighed. "Then I'm afraid we would have to use the provisions of the Mental Health Act to insist that you stay with us. And believe me when I say I really would rather not have to resort to that."

Joan had strength for only a token resistance. But if she couldn't go home, there was something else she wanted. "Okay. Well, can I go to the chapel then?"

Marwan glanced at Ed and Cathy to see if they might voice any objections. Neither of them said anything. "I don't see why not," he said. "Do you have any special reason for wanting to go there?"

Now Cathy spoke up. "She's been asking to go to the chapel since she was admitted. Last night she got quite upset when we told her she had to stay on the ward."

Marwan nodded as though this information was significant. "I see. Joan – is there a special reason why you want to go to the chapel?" He asked again.

"Yes. When I pray, and can focus my thoughts on Jesus, the voices are less troublesome." She avoided looking him in the face when she said this.

Marwan seemed satisfied by her explanation. "In that case I think it's an excellent idea for you to go to the chapel." He spoke to Cathy: "She can go for half an hour at a time, but not unaccompanied." He turned back to Joan. "Is that acceptable?" When she nodded he added "Thank you Joan, you can go now."

She felt like she had been dismissed. Slowly, she had come to her feet, waited a moment to be sure of her balance, then left the room. Once she had gone, Marwan had turned to Ed. "So, Ed. What do you think?"

Edward was fairly sure of himself. "I know we shouldn't make assumptions, but it seems to be a fairly classic case of psychosis – probably schizophrenia?"

"What leads you to that conclusion?"

Edward paused briefly to gather his thoughts. "It's mainly the voices. She's hearing multiple voices in a triad of command, comment and argument. Her blood tests have all come back negative for illicit substances, so I think we can rule out drug-induced psychosis, and there are no signs to suggest any metabolic or organic involvement."

Marwan beamed like a teacher with his star pupil. "Excellent We'll make a psychiatrist of you yet, Edward. As a provisional diagnosis, schizophrenia seems reasonable, but there's one major problem with it. Any idea what it may be?"

Ed was taking a particular interest in Joan's case – his case, as he saw it. He had done his homework. "Yes. It's the time factor. If we were using American diagnostic guidelines, the voices would have to have been present for at least two weeks, but in her case they've been apparent for less than a week."

"Good. Go on."

"On the other hand, according to ICD-10*, the time factor isn't considered to be so important to the diagnosis. And the voices are very intrusive and distressing."

"Have you written a diagnosis of schizophrenia in her notes?"

Ed shook his head. "No, not yet. I was waiting until I had spoken to you about it."

Marwan was pleased that Ed seemed to be developing a sense of professional discretion at last. He had spoken to him several times about his impulsivity: he was sometimes too sure of himself, too ready to assign a diagnostic label prematurely. "Thank you, Edward. Though I find nothing to disagree with in your assessment, I still think it's early days for this patient. I would prefer to make a provisional diagnosis of psychosis, cause unknown. Should that influence our decision about treatment?"

"I wouldn't have thought so. An antipsychotic medicine should still be given."

"Right." Marwan asked Cathy "What medication is she on right now?"

---

* Note for reader – International Classification of Diseases, 10th Edition: a standard diagnostic manual for mental disorders used by psychiatrists in the UK.

Cathy checked the medication sheet. "She's on phenylatrazine, twenty milligrams at bedtime."

"You prescribed that?" Marwan asked Edward.

Ed took the medication sheet from Cathy. "Yes."

"And how long has she been taking it?"

Cathy knew the answer without consulting the sheet again. "She's only had a couple of doses – started Wednesday night."

Marwan leaned back in his chair, looking at the ceiling while he considered this information. "Okay. Obviously we need to give her some time to respond, but Edward is quite right about the severity of the voices she's hearing. I think we should increase the dose. What do you think?"

Cathy wasn't sure. "Well, she was very sedated last night, and you could see how drowsy she still is just now."

But Edward agreed with his boss. "I think at least part of that is due to her lack of sleep over the past few days. She's been frightened to shut her eyes because of the voices. I agree with doctor Marwan, I think we should increase the dose."

Marwan was pleased to have his junior's support. "Thank you Ed. Would you increase the dose to twenty milligrams twice a day starting tonight?"

Ed wrote quickly in the notes. "And review in one week?"

"That sounds reasonable." As an afterthought he added "And as for her going to the chapel, can you take a quick look at her in the morning, and make a decision then about whether she's fit to go?" He turned in his chair to pick up the coffee he had suddenly remembered. He grimaced; it was cold: he was always doing this. It was poor form to ask for another. "Now, who have we got next?" He asked.

"It's Carrie Locklin." Cathy told him.

Carrie was an old customer. He smiled to himself. "Oh yes. And has she seen any taxis while she's been on the ward?"

Now it was Cathy's turn to smile. "Not this time."

"Do you think she's ready to be allowed home for a short time, perhaps over the week-end?" He asked her.

"I wouldn't have any problem with that," she replied, "but her CPN's waiting outside, perhaps we'd better ask him what the home situation's like first?"

Marwan shifted his weight to make himself more comfortable. "Fine. Shall we have them in?"

Cathy had left the room to return a minute later with Carrie and her community psychiatric nurse.

Carrie had been all smiles. "'allo, doctor Marwan," she said affably. She glared at the community nurse. "Yer not makin' me go 'ome awready are yeh?"

*

It wasn't far from the ward to the chapel – seven or eight minutes taken at invalid pace. On Saturday afternoon Joan was taken there by Maureen, who was glad of an opportunity to sit and do nothing for half an hour or so. Wordlessly she opened the chapel door and indicated to Joan that she should enter. It was non-denominational and was sparsely furnished so that its only ornament was a plain crucifix on the far wall. There were four narrow pews on either side and a wooden lectern at the front. But it felt tranquil, and that was all that mattered to Joan.

"Here we are, Joan," Maureen said without much interest. "It's not much, but it's the hospital chapel. It's nice to come here occasionally just for a bit of peace and quiet. Remember, doctor Marwan said you could stay for half an hour."

The chapel was dimly lit with cheap stained glass in two windows. There were no candles, and no statues. Hesitantly, Joan walked down the aisle, saying nothing. Above the door behind her was a white clock, the same as could be found on all the wards: the time was just past three o'clock. Maureen settled herself in a pew at the back. Joan went to the front pew, knelt, and crossed herself. Silently she started to pray. Suddenly she looked up and around as if searching for something. Her movements were quite exaggerated.

"Are you alright Joan?" Maureen called.

Joan's voice was hushed, but full of surprise. "It's the voices," was all she said.

"What about them?"

"They've gone."

Maureen was sceptical. Voices didn't just go like that. "Gone? You mean gone completely?"

"Yes." The relief in her voice was obvious.

Joan knelt in the first pew, holding her head in her hands. It was a paradox, but the silence in the spaces in her mind was now so loud it was as if she could hear it, like the passage of an echo. No vestige of the voices remained. She could not even remember what they sounded like. It was miraculous. For the first time in days she could gather her thoughts enough to pray. Whenever she had tried before, the voices had assaulted her, preventing her from finding that place where prayer could exert its healing grace. Then, so quietly she wasn't sure she had heard it, she could hear singing. One moment it seemed too far away to hear clearly; then it was upon her The rush of it almost overwhelmed her. She felt transfigured by it, basking in the glorious music of Heaven. Slowly she raised her head. The physical appearance of the chapel was unchanged, but she could swear that where a short while ago the chapel had been in semi-darkness, it was now bathed in a light that seemed suffused with a divine presence radiating the power of love and joy. As she listened, the song flowed into her and through her. She was in a state of rapture that she had never before experienced. Was this what it was like to be in the true presence of God? She wondered. Tears of joy ran down her cheeks. She had not been abandoned. She could not even begin to fathom God's purpose for her in the dark places where she had been cast away, but she was not alone. He was with her, as He had promised.

As the power of the divine Word coursed through her and welled up in her, now she felt she could pray. "Blessed Jesus, blessed Jesus." She whispered, not wanting Maureen to hear. "Thank you Lord, thank you. Please, I beg you, help me now. I am surrounded by evil and don't know what to do. Please send your Holy Spirit to bless and guide me, send your blessed angels to watch over me and protect me. Please God, please, just help me . . . please . . . ."

As abruptly as it had come, the music ceased. Two people had entered the chapel, a male patient wearing pyjamas and a dressing gown, accompanied by a woman, presumably his wife. They sat together on the side away from Joan. Grateful and strengthened by her glimpse of God's presence, Joan continued to pray silently. The couple left, but the music did not return. Joan did not resent this. Its presence had been the most intense and personal she had ever felt. It had comforted her very soul, and she knew she would never be afraid of anything again. The fact that the voices had departed was consolation enough. She glanced round at the clock. She had five minutes left. A feeling of panic took her by surprise. What if the voices came back when she left the chapel? Doubts began to assail her. She knew that without help she would never be able to resist them. The moment of her epiphany had passed. She was alone again.

At three-thirty, Maureen came out of her pew and walked slowly to where Joan was kneeling. She grasped her shoulder gently. In a quiet, reverent voice she said "Come on Joan, time to go. We can come back at the same time tomorrow."

Joan pulled away. "Not yet, please." She pleaded. "It's . . . I'm at peace here. The voices have gone. Can't I have just a little more time? Please?"

Maureen was not completely without sympathy, but she had her instructions. "Joan, I'm sorry, I really am, but doctor Marwan was quite clear – half an hour, no more. I have to do what he said." Still Joan stayed put. Tears were running freely down her cheeks. More firmly, Maureen said "Come on Joan, please. If you won't co-operate, they'll just make you. It'll be worse for you in the end. They might even stop you from coming to the chapel again. Please?"

Joan was helpless. She knew she couldn't leave the chapel. To do so would be to invite the unspeakable horror to return. "I can't." She sobbed. "I'm scared. I know what will happen as soon as I set foot outside that door."

Maureen was losing patience. "What's that Joan?"

"The voices will come back. Only they'll be worse than ever. They'll give me hell because I went to the chapel. I can't do it, I just can't. Please let me stay here just a little longer."

Maureen sighed. She hadn't had much to do with Joan on the ward, but she could see how distraught the poor girl was now. Terrified, more like. "I'm sorry Joan, you know I can't."

She took a firm grip on Joan's upper arm and tried to pull her to her feet. Maureen was a big woman and Joan only slightly built, but her fear gave her a strength she did not know she had. "Get off me!" She screamed. She threw the older woman off easily.

Maureen knew she could not force Joan to leave the chapel, not by herself. "Joan. You've got to come. If you make a fuss, believe me, they'll just come along, give you an injection to tranquillise you and haul you back to the ward. If that's what you want to happen, just carry on behaving like this. Now for the last time, are you going to come back to the ward with me or do I have to get them to drag you back?"

Joan was almost beside herself. "Don't you understand you stupid cow?" She yelled. "I don't have any choice in the matter. Spending a few more minutes in here is infinitely preferable to hearing those voices again, even if I delay them for only a few more minutes. If you knew what it was like you wouldn't ask me to leave. Nobody would."

She collapsed into the pew, crying into her hands. Maureen decided she had better go for help. At the door she turned back for one last attempt at reasoning with Joan. "I'm sorry Joan, I really am, but this is your last chance. Are you going to come with me or not?" She didn't know whether Joan had heard her or not, but enough was enough.

It took about fifteen minutes for Maureen to get back to the ward, enlist some help and then return to the chapel. At her side, Tony, grim-faced, walked as fast as decorum would permit through the warren of corridors that led to the chapel followed closely by Maria and Viv. Ed had been bleeped in case they needed to use tranquillisation. From what Maureen had told him, Tony's main fear was that Joan might have absconded and be at risk of harming herself. The chapel doors were pushed aside unceremoniously. To their relief, Joan was still kneeling in the front pew.

Tony sat down beside her. "Joan," he said calmly, trying to get her attention. "Please! This sort of behaviour isn't going to help you. We know you're not well, but you have to trust that we do know what's best for your welfare. You have to come back to the ward with us now. If you won't, we'll take you forcibly, and you won't be allowed back. Do you understand?"

She turned to face him. She looked awful; her eyes red with crying. Her face crumpled. "It's you who doesn't understand. None of you do. How could you possibly understand what I'm going through?"

There was no point in trying to reason with her, he decided. He turned to the other nurses who had come with him. "I don't think she's going to co-operate." He said. "Do we all agree?"

They did. He turned back to Joan speaking slowly and clearly. "Joan, because you're refusing to co-operate with us, we're going to escort you back to the ward whether you like it or not. Please do not resist us." To the others he said "Maria, Viv, you take her arms and make her stand up. Me and Maureen will open the doors as we go. Okay?"

At first Joan did not resist, and allowed herself to be guided along the short aisle. But as she approached the doors she stiffened and started pushing back, determined not to go through. Desperation gave her strength as she struggled to break free of their grip, but the nurses were experienced at restraining disturbed patients and their combined efforts were too strong for her. As they came level with the door frame Joan's eyes widened in terror and she screamed "No! Get your fucking hands off me! You fucking bastards! No . . ." But, ignoring her protests, they pulled her through. As they left the chapel something extraordinary happened. As if controlled by a switch Joan fell abruptly silent. A look of abject horror passed across her face and she fell limp in their arms. As they half walked, half carried her along she roused herself for an instant to mumble "No, please. No more, no more. Please God, please . . ."

His bleep had brought Edward to the ward just in time to see Joan being guided past the nursing station. Tony seemed quite relieved to see him. "Ed, have you got a moment?" He asked.

Edward glanced at his watch. "Yeah, 's long as it doesn't take too long. "I was just about to go down to A&E to assess an N-A-I*."

Tony pointed to one of the interview rooms. "It won't take a moment, but it is important."

Edward followed Tony in. "What's the problem?"

Tony looked grim. "You saw Joan just now?" Edward nodded. Tony continued. "That was her coming back from her visit to the chapel. We had to remove her and bring her back forcibly."

Edward's reply was a little flippant. "Didn't look like she was resisting very much to me," he said. As soon as the words had left his mouth he regretted them.

---

* Non-accidental injury

Tony's tone was almost angry. Didn't this pompous arse know what risk was? "She doesn't seem to be responding to the treatment she's been given. I think she needs something stronger."

Edward realised he had undervalued Tony's concerns; he had his staff to think about as well as the patients, but Ed had jumped to the conclusion he was over-reacting. "Be fair Tony, she's only been on the medication for a few days . . . it takes a bit longer than that to work, you know."

Tony stood his ground. "I know that, but she's shown no sign whatever of any response. Nothing. Can't you give something to keep her calm in the meantime?"

Edward considered. Tony had a point, and a lot of experience. "Like some p-r-n* benzos?" He asked.

But Tony wanted something a bit more emphatic than the occasional minor tranquilliser. "If you think it would help, yes. I was thinking more about upping the dose of her antipsychotic."

Edward wasn't happy about that. "I don't think Marwan would go for that. She's already on 40 milligrams of phenylatrazine a day, and she's treatment naïve – we really ought to be going easy rather than diving in with the heavy stuff, you know?"

Still Tony was not satisfied. "That's all very well for you to say, Ed. You and Marwan aren't the ones who have to pick up the pieces when a patient goes AWOL."

Edward tried to be diplomatic. "Okay. Look, I'll speak to Marwan, alright? I can't really do much more than that. Now I really do have to get going."

Tony knew when to stop pushing, but he had one last point to make. "Fair enough. But one last thing. No more visits to the chapel – okay? At least not until she shows some sign of responding to the treatment."

This was something Edward felt he could safely agree to. "Yes. That sounds reasonable. I'll write it up in the notes as soon as I get back from A&E."

As he made to leave, Tony added "Ed - don't forget it's me and my staff in the firing line, and I just have a feeling about this one."

That sounded ominous. "A feeling? What sort of feeling?"

---

* prn = medical jargon for "when needed"

"That it's going to get very messy before the end, and I don't want any of my staff hurt in the process."

13
Not your normal Saturday night

Never in his entire life had Ed been to a place like this. The building was like a long shed, low-roofed, shedding light into the surrounding darkness through cheap-looking windows, paint peeling from the frames. Though it was set back from the road, the lack of any curtains or blinds meant the interior could be seen by any passer-by. It was fronted by a large parking area in which stood two articulated lorries, lights out. Standing like a commissionaire at the entrance to the car park was a large brash neon sign which told anyone who cared to read it that this establishment was none other than '*Vinny's No-Nonsense Diner*'.

Looking in from the outside, Ed wondered whether he was doing the right thing coming here, but, he told himself, only time would tell. The entrance was brightly lit so as to be clearly visible from the darkened parking lot. Inside there was a long counter with a cash register at one end, a blackboard bearing the day's 'menu' and various diners eating fried food and drinking enormous mugs of tea. Nearly all of them were men. There were a couple of bikers and their girlfriends in one corner, noticeable for the noise they were making. As Ed pushed against the spring on the door a bell announced his arrival, though nobody looked up. Walking to the counter he rested a large carrier bag on its surface. As he allowed it to settle, the clinking of an indeterminate number of bottles could clearly be heard.

A plump middle-aged woman with dyed platinum blond hair and wearing an old and faded pink overall was putting away cups and plates from a dishwasher. Although Edward was sure she had seen him, she ignored him.

He coughed to get her attention. "Excuse me?"

She did not seem pleased to be interrupted. "Oh, 'allo." She looked him up and down without showing the vaguest interest in him, which was not the response his film-star looks usually elicited. "C'n I get yer somethin' dear?"

Edward was not sure of the etiquette in such establishments "Er, not exactly," he said.

She shrugged and went back to her task. "Fair enough, dear. When you've decided what you want, just let me know, okay?"

They seemed to have reached an impasse. There was an awkward silence that both seemed reluctant to break. Eventually Edward spoke again. "Is the owner in?"

She did not answer him, but instead yelled at the top of her voice "Vinny!"

A reply came from behind a hatch in the wall. "What now?" It sounded mildly annoyed.

"Somebody askin' for yer!" She shouted back.

A man walked out of the kitchen wiping his hands on a greasy cloth. He was wearing a chef's outfit but without the hat, and an apron so festooned with stains it was as if they were badges of achievement. "Who wants me then?" He asked.

Edward was suddenly a little nervous. "Actually it's me. Are you the owner?"

The man immediately looked suspicious. "Who wants to know?"

"My name is Edward Plant." Ed didn't know why he had said that. It didn't seem to get them anywhere.

The man looked at him from the corner of his eye. "Plant?" He said, as though it were a name he should have found familiar. "Where you from?"

Ed was starting to catch on. "I'm not from anywhere really, not anywhere official, if that's what you mean." The man continued to eye him with evident suspicion. "I just wanted to ask you something," Ed continued, warming to his task, "and perhaps put a little business your way."

"Ask me somethin'? Like what?"

Edward put on his charming smile. "Vinny – do you mind if I call you Vinny?" When the man did not answer he continued "Do you like a drink?"

This seemed to make Vinny relax a little. "A drink? Yeah, I s'pose so. 'bout as much as the next man, anyway." He winked at the waitress who was no longer even pretending to be busy so intent was she on listening to their conversation.

Edward beamed. "Oh, good. Do you mind me asking what's your favourite tipple? Whisky? Vodka? Gin?"

Vinny took a moment to consider. "Rum. Bacardi."

Edward delved into his carrier bag. It contained several bottles of spirits – whisky, brandy, gin, - and a bottle of Bacardi.

With a flourish he took it out and placed it on the counter. Vinny looked at it covetously, but made no move to take it. "Please take it," Edward said. "It's yours. Call it a token of my appreciation."

"A token of your appreciation?" Vinny's suspicion deepened. "What are you after?"

Edward had to talk fast. "Not a lot, really. I want to ask you a small favour, and like I said, put a little business your way, that's all. And I'm prepared to pay – handsomely."

The waitress laughed or it might have been more of a shriek. "'kin 'ell Vinny." She rasped. "Pick up the bottle before 'e disappears in a puff o' smoke!"

A customer walked to the counter. He did not seem amused "'s my dinner gonna be much longer?" He grumbled. "I've gotta be in Sarfhamp'on before ten."

Vinny sized the situation up instantly. "Sorry mate," he said to the trucker, "it'll just be two minutes." He turned quickly to Ed. "You mind waitin' for two minutes?" Edward shook his head. "Good." Pointing at Edward, he turned his attention to the waitress "Tess, give 'im a cup o' tea." He turned back to Ed saying "You 'ave a cup o' tea, mate. On the 'ouse, like, okay?" He finished with the trucker: "You too, mate, for bein' so patient. 'ow's that?"

While he returned to the kitchen Tess poured two cups of milky tea and gave one each to the trucker and Edward before going back to putting the dishes away. Edward sat at a table near the counter and sipped his tea gingerly. Had they really added the milk in the teapot? Yuch. Soon a plate of mixed grill and chips appeared on the serving hatch, which the waitress picked up and took to the customer.

Vinny emerged and sat with Edward. He lifted the Bacardi and rolled it over in his hands as though it were an objet d'art. "So, Edward, or would you prefer to be called Mr. Plant? What's this favour you want me to do for you that's worth a bottle of Bacardi?"

Ed grinned. "Two bottles, actually. There'll be another bottle if you agree to go through with it."

Vinny thrust out his bottom lip – a habit he had developed over the years. He thought it made him appear reasonable without being a pushover. "Fair enough. Now what is *it*?"

"I want some help to set up a bit of a practical joke." Ed explained.

Vinny seemed dubious. "A practical joke? Don't see too many of them around here. Nobody will get hurt will they?"

Edward hadn't been sure how to explain what he really wanted. It all sounded a bit pathetic, and describing it as a 'bit of a practical joke' had seemed a good idea at the time, but now he realised it had been a mistake. "Absolutely not! No, that's not the intention at all." He wasn't very good at this. "No, the thing is, I'm going out with this girl, and I wanted to take her out for a really special meal."

For some reason, Vinny found the whole idea very amusing. "An' you wanted to bring her here? 'ckin 'ell, mate, you got a funny idea of what special means, that's all I can say."

Edward was anxious to explain. "No, you don't understand. She'll expect me to take her somewhere expensive or exotic, somewhere that I'll think will really impress her. It's too obvious. So I asked myself, where's the place she'd least expect me to take her? And here I am."

This seemed to impress Vinny. "So you want to bring this girl here for a meal? What do you want me to do? I can't do no special menu or nothin'. I'm not a bad cook, but I know me limitations. I'm a dab hand at mixed grill, a bit o' gammon, steak and chips, a good fry up ..."

Edward started to relax. "No." He said. "That's the whole point. She wouldn't expect anything special. It's coming here that would make it special. We'll just pick something off the menu same as everybody else. What I want from you is something different."

Vinny's eyebrows rose. "Like what?"

"All I want is for you and your staff to treat me as though I were a regular customer, that's all."

Vinny shook his head. This was never going to work. "A regular customer? She'll never fall for that – unless she's blind. Is she blind?"

Nervously Edward took another sip of the tea, then wished he hadn't. "No, she's not blind, but that's not the point. She'll work out that it's all an act, but she'll appreciate the effort and thought I've put into it and that'll impress her far more than taking her to any posh restaurant would."

Vinny seemed convinced. "Okay. Let's suppose I do decide to help you out. What exactly would you want me to do?"

"All you have to do is to welcome me by name, ask me how work's going, what do I think of the latest political scandal, nice weather for the time of year, that sort of thing."

"And I suppose you'd want a nice bottle of wine thrown in?"

This was more like it. "That would be great – if you could."

With great exaggeration Vinny shook his head. "'fraid not. Don't 'ave a licence for drink. Wouldn't be appropriate in a transport caff would it?"

Ed hadn't thought of that. "I s'pose not, no."

But Vinny had other ideas. "That doesn't mean you couldn't bring your own though – we could charge you corkage for openin' it for you."

"Yeah. That's a great idea." Ed enthused.

"Better make it a screw-top though, don't think we've got a corkscrew."

Vinny held the Bacardi up to the light as if worried it might not be real. "So let's get this right," he said slowly. "You're gonna bring this girl here, and we act like you're one of our regulars. You 'ave a meal like everybody else, and pay in the normal way."

Ed shook his head. "Not exactly. I want to be able to say to you that I want you to put it on my tab."

"Sorry mate," Vinny replied, "can't do that. 'ouse rule. No credit." In a sing-song voice as though he was quoting from something he announced "Please do not ask for credit as a smack in the mouth often offends."

And it had all been going so well. Then Ed had a brainwave. "Don't worry. I'll pay in advance."

Vinny brightened. "Now you're talking. 'ow much?"

"Would fifty pounds cover it?" He pulled out his wallet and put five ten-pound notes on the table. Vinny pocketed them immediately.

"Fifty squid? For that kind o' money I'll get ol' Tess there dressed up all nice in a proper waitress outfit."

Now it was Edward's turn to smile. "That really won't be necessary."

Vinny's manner became brisk and business-like. "Okay matey, you got yourself a deal. When was you plannin' on bringin' this young lady to my 'igh class establishment, then?"

"How about Monday? Around seven-thirty?"

Vinny proffered his hand. "Look forward to seein' ya, Mr. Plant."

Edward couldn't resist saying "It's doctor Plant, actually."

Vinny was impressed. "Doctor? Jeez!"

Edward retrieved his hand from Vinny's iron grip. "Yeah, but don't stand on ceremony, please just call me Ed, okay?"

Vinny grinned hugely. "No worries, mate - Ed. You just turn up on Monday – we'll see ya right, never fear."

Ed stood to go, leaving the rest of his tea untouched. Chuckling quietly to himself, Vinny picked up the cup and returned to the kitchen with it. Without thinking he took a drink from it and gagged, almost spitting it out. Tess looked at him with alarm. "Yuch!" He grimaced. "I shoulda known - no bleedin' sugar!"

14
Fair of face

Edward didn't see Joan over the weekend. She had been on call and had called him briefly to let him know that the orthopaedic department had been unseasonably busy. Unknown to him she had worked late on Sunday, and was not due in until Monday lunchtime. He had bleeped her, but had received no response. Wondering why she had not responded kept intruding into his mind all morning. He had talked to Dr. Marwan about his conversation with Tony about Joan Archer's refusal to come back from the chapel voluntarily. As he expected, Marwan was reluctant for the dose of her medication to be increased so soon, and had suggested to Edward that he might spend some time with Joan trying to find out the reasons for her behaviour.

They were seated together in the quiet corner. He had her notes on his knee and she was holding the paper cup of water that had become her constant companion. Although she kept putting it to her lips, its contents did not seem to diminish. They spoke in undertones, pausing self-consciously whenever a patient or member of staff walked past. It was obvious to Ed that Joan was having difficulty in concentrating.

"Do you want to tell me about what happened on Friday?" He probed gently.

"Friday? What about Friday?" She yawned, absently passing her hand across her mouth. "Don't really remember much about it."

"The chapel?" Ed prompted. "What really happened? Why wouldn't you just come back after half an hour - like you agreed with doctor Marwan?"

Joan looked at him through red-rimmed eyes. "I told you that if I was allowed to go to the chapel that it would make the voices go away." Her voice was angry, as if she felt she had been let down.

Ed shook his head. "No, Joan, I'm sure that's not you said." He went back a few pages in the notes and read from them. "What you actually said was . . . if you were allowed to go to the chapel to pray, it would help you to ignore the voices. So did going to the chapel actually make them go away?"

She took another sip of water. "Yes." Now her voice was that of a frightened child.

Edward wanted to be sure. "Completely?"

"Yes."

"I'm afraid I find that a little hard to believe."

Joan shot him the 'let down' look again. "Why? Why would I lie about something like that?"

There was no reason that Edward could think of, but still . . "I've never heard of anything like this before. I think it's something I should tell doctor Marwan about."

"If you like." Now she sounded like it was a matter of complete indifference to her. What was going on in that head of hers?

"So if the voices had gone away, does that mean you were back to your old self?"

Joan wasn't sure how to answer that. "Yes. No. Not completely. I was very confused and I found it really hard to think. I couldn't work out why this was happening to me."

Edward made a note that she still would not accept that she was mentally ill. "Joan - I don't think there's anything *to* work out." He explained patiently. "You're suffering from a mental illness. You just have to learn to accept it. Only then will you be able to deal with it. Until then we have to persist with the medication."

This provoked a bitter response. "We?" Her anger was close beneath the surface now, ready to emerge at the slightest cause. "Who's this we? I don't see *you* taking any medication. Don't you get it? It just makes me feel worse. Look at me, for God's sake. I can't think straight, I'm so tired I could fall asleep at any moment, and I can hardly hold this cup for my hands shaking." Briefly she put down her water and held out her hands; he could see a marked tremor.

Edward made another note in her file. "You just have to trust us Joan. I know it's hard, but it takes a while for the medication to start to work. We have to give it time to get into your system."

This did nothing to calm her. "And until then?"

"Until then I'm afraid you just have to put up with it. I'm sorry. It's the best I can do for now." He didn't have anything else to offer.

Now her bitterness and frustration poured out. "You're sorry? Is that all you've got to say? You're fucking sorry? Jesus!"

She burst into tears. Ed pulled a tissue from a box on a low table and passed it to her. "Tell me more about the voices, Joan. The more you tell me, the more I'll be able to understand."

At least being angry made it easier to talk about them. "They're just totally evil. That's the only way I can describe them. Pure, undiluted, cruel, relentless, evil." Now she had started, the words just poured out. "They torture me. Sometimes they take me by surprise, catch me off guard. That really amuses them, when they're able to do that. Other times, they just take it in turns to torment me. I've worked out why they've come, but not where they've come from."

This was what he wanted her to tell him. "Why do you think they've come, Joan?"

She looked at him incredulously. "Isn't it obvious? To make me lose my faith. To make me abandon my trust in God. To get me to burn my bridges with Jesus so that I'll be totally, completely alone. Only then will they be able to consume me. That's what they've come for, so that I can be made so vulnerable that I'll have no defences against being eaten up by this vile, hideous force of evil that's somehow taken up residence inside of me. But I won't let that happen. My strength comes from Jesus, who promises that we're never truly alone. If my strength fails, He'll send his angels to guard me."

Edward tried again to get her to understand what was happening to her. "I know it's hard to accept right now Joan," he said quietly, hoping that his calmness would give his words authority, "but that belief you've just described is what we call a delusion – a belief that has no basis in fact. It's part of the pattern of your illness, and as the medication starts to work, that too will fade, and you'll wonder why you ever believed it."

He was rewarded with a baleful glare. "Oh for God's sake. Can you not just listen for a moment instead of being so fucking pompous? I'm not mentally ill. If I was, I wouldn't be able to get rid of these voices by going to the chapel, would I? Don't you see? I *can* control them. I just have to learn how to control them when I'm not in a church or a chapel, then I'll have them beaten. Somehow, for some reason, my mind has become a battleground between the forces of good and evil. Somewhere there'll be an answer to it, but I'm never going to find the answer stuck in this hole taking your phony medication."

Edward shook his head as she displayed this further evidence of her psychotic thinking. "I'm afraid that what you've just said is also very common in people with a mental illness," he insisted. "They nearly always deny that they're mentally ill, but try to find some other reason for what's happening to them. Please Joan, just trust us for a few days longer. Then you'll see a difference, I promise you. Just give the medication time to work, that's all I ask."

As quickly as it had arisen, her rage evaporated. Once again she was a frightened young girl. "When will I be allowed to go back to the chapel?"

Another question Ed for which had no proper answer. Instead he prevaricated. "When we can be sure that you're ready to co-operate. It *is* for your safety you know. While you're in here we're responsible. We have a responsibility to make sure that anything that might lead to your being harmed is avoided. When we can be sure it's safe for you to go to the chapel, then you can be allowed to go back."

But Joan was not put off so easily. "And when will that be?"

Now it was Ed's turn to show his exasperation. She didn't seem to realise that she was his special case, and he wanted everything to go perfectly. "Joan, why did you have to refuse to leave the chapel in the first place? Why did you make them bring you back forcibly? It's not very clever you know, making four members of staff go off the ward because of the concerns that you caused. It might leave other patients on the ward at risk because there aren't enough staff around. It's quite serious."

Joan was looking at him as if she couldn't believe he was saying what he was saying. "If you knew what it was really like . . ."

Ed was so involved he forgot about the importance of keeping his professional distance. He reached out and took one of her hands, squeezing it gently. "So tell me."

For a second, Joan looked up and to the left, before focusing her eyes firmly on Edward's. "The voices are so bad, that if you can get them to go away you just want to prolong that moment at all costs. I didn't care about the consequences; I just wanted a few more precious moments when the voices were being held at bay by the power of that place."

Edward sat closer, returning her gaze. "But now you've lost the privilege of being able to go back every day. Isn't that worse?"

She pulled away. "Until you've been through it yourself, you'll never be able to understand."

*

Ed was on his way back to the nursing station when his bleep went. It had to be Joan - his other Joan. There was no-one on the nursing station to eavesdrop his conversation. Smiling with anticipation he dumped the file he was carrying on the trolley and dialled the extension number his bleep was showing.

It was answered almost immediately. "Joan? Hi. It's Ed."

He could picture the smile on her face. "Hi Gene. How are you? Good day?"

"So-so. Could be better. Had an interesting chat with a patient."

"Would that be your Catholic patient?" She asked.

"Might be," he admitted. "Anyway, how's your day?"

"Nothing special. Fractured tib & fib came in from A & E last night. Nothing out of the ordinary really."

He wasn't really listening, so eager was he to see her. "Joan, are you free tonight?"

"Yeah, I've got an outpatient clinic this afternoon, so should be able to get away for half five, maybe earlier."

"Would you like to go out to dinner? I know this really interesting place. The choice of food is a bit limited, but it really is a bit out of the ordinary."

He sounded so keen she felt she could almost reach out and touch it. "Sounds great. I'd love to. What should I wear?"

What a question. How should he know what she should wear? "What should you wear? Wear whatever you like."

"No, Ed. What I mean is should I dress up or down? Posh or casual? Town or country? A girl needs to know these things."

Why did women always make things so complicated? "Right Er . . Casual I think. Yeah, I think that would be best. Definitely casual."

"Casual it is then. Where are you taking me?"

Now it was his turn to be mysterious. "That's my surprise. I'll pick you up, about seven-thirty, okay?"

"How did you know I liked surprises? Seven-thirty sounds great." It sounded almost as if she was singing.

Ed laughed. "Brilliant! See you later."

She laughed too. "Can't wait!"

*

That afternoon Edward managed to corner Marwan and discuss Joan's case with him. Marwan appeared to be a little preoccupied. Ed put it down to his managerial responsibilities, which seemed to be eating up more and more of his time.

"I had a long chat with Joan earlier," Ed told him. "I asked why she refused to leave the chapel of her own volition."

Marwan pricked up his ears. "What did she say?"

Edward tried not to sound smug, but he did feel that what he had learned this morning confirmed the provisional diagnosis he had suggested to Marwan last week. "Quite a lot actually, most of which strengthens the case for a diagnosis of schizophrenia, but there is one aspect that I found puzzling. I had a look in the text-books but couldn't find any mention of it."

Marwan put his pen down and sat back, giving Edward his full attention. "Okay. First tell me about those aspects which strengthen the case for schizophrenia, then tell about what's puzzling you."

"Well first, she volunteered to having quite an elaborate delusional belief system that her mind had become a battleground between good and evil, and that the voices had a specific purpose – to make her lose her faith in God. Once that was accomplished, she would be truly alone and the voices – which are nothing less than the personification of evil – would be able to consume her."

Marwan considered this for a moment. "You're right – very elaborate, and clearly delusional in nature. What else was there?"

Ed warmed to his task. "Her complete lack of insight and her total denial of being mentally ill."

The older man agreed with his junior's reasoning. "That's good. I think you're right. The clinical picture is becoming better defined. I still want to be a little cautious about our diagnosis, however. We'll wait a little longer before we settle on schizophrenia I think."

Edward did not allow his disappointment to show. "Okay. No problem."

Marwan had not forgotten that Edward had mentioned something that he had found puzzling. "What's this other thing you mentioned? This thing that's perplexing you?"

He could see from his junior's body language that Ed had developed a particular interest in this case; Ed leaned forward, making vivid hand movements. "It's this business of her being in control of the voices. She says she can get rid of them at will providing we allow her to go to the chapel."

This was fascinating. Something he had not encountered in over twenty years as a consultant psychiatrist. "Completely, you mean?"

"So she says."

"That's *very* interesting." Marwan pondered what Ed had just told him. He rose to take a book from a one of the cases lining his office walls. He consulted the text before passing it to Ed. "You might find this useful," he said, indicating a particular passage. "According to Keane, what we need to think about here is the broader picture of the clinical phenomenology, rather than the specific issue of her having control of the voices."

Ed was trying to scan the passage, but he couldn't read it and take in what his boss was saying at the same time. "In what way?"

Marwan leaned forward. "It seems to me that it would be extremely unlikely that she would actually have real control over the voices. It's more likely that the voices, although usually a distinct and independent part of the syndrome, are in this case subordinate to her delusional system. Part of her delusion is that in this struggle between good and evil, the voices represent evil. Therefore, when she finds herself in a place that she perceives as 'good', the voices are repelled. It is not she who has control of the voices; it is the voices behaving in a manner that is consistent with her delusional beliefs about her situation. It is very interesting – and rare – but completely explainable. I think you should write it up, it would make a very useful case study for the juniors – and consultants - to discuss. Good work Ed. Anything else?"

Ed made a quick note of the title and author of the book. He would get it from the library later and read it when he had some spare time. "She's persistently asking to be allowed to go back to the chapel. If we don't relent, I think she'll try to sneak out and go by herself."

Marwan sat back, trying to weigh up the pros and cons of this decision. It did seem somewhat draconian to deny access to a place of worship to someone with such a strong faith. "Very well." He said. "Let her stew for the rest of today – just so that the message gets home that she can't just expect to have everything her own way. She can go back again tomorrow."

Ed agreed with his mentor. "Yes. I have explained to her that it's a matter of her own – and other patients' safety. I think she understood."

He stood to leave. Then Marwan had an afterthought. "Oh, Edward, I think you should go with her – to observe this interesting phenomenon of the voices being dismissed as she enters the chapel."

Ed rested his hand on the doorknob. Marwan was presenting him with a superb opportunity. Writing this case up and getting it published could be a defining moment in his career. "Of course. I'll make sure I find time to go with her."

15
And then I go and spoil it all

Joan couldn't remember the last time she'd had gammon and chips, but, she had to admit, it tasted as good as she remembered, even if the pineapple ring was obviously out of a tin. She also couldn't remember the last time she had been in a transport cafe, but she was delighted at the thought that Ed had so obviously put into bringing her here. They had been seated in a dimly lit alcove, at a small table covered in a red cloth with a candle and a small vase with a single rose at its centre. Not your usual transport caff. She chuckled again at the wonderful incongruousness of it all. Ed gave her a quizzical look.

"You don't really bring dates here as a rule, Gene, do you?" She asked, smiling.

Ed looked hurt. "What makes you say that? Don't you like the place?"

She turned in her seat to look around and take it all in. In other circumstances it would have seemed functional, basic, perhaps even grim, but tonight it had an allure that would have been unrecognizable to anyone else. But was it romance, or a calculated gambit? "I love it" she said, turning back to him. "It just seems a bit out of character, that's all."

"Out of character?"

"You know. Not exactly what you'd expect from the boy who went to public school and then Oxford, is it? I'd have thought The Savoy was more your cup of tea."

Ed unscrewed the cap from their wine and refilled her glass. "Claridge's, actually." He said without thinking.

Joan was a little incredulous at his obtuseness. "Claridge's?"

"Yeah," he said, amused that it had been so easy to wind her up. "Tea at Claridge's, *dinner* at The Savoy."

She got the joke, but persisted with the point she was trying to make. "So you do agree – a little out of character?"

For the first time in his life, Edward was starting to feel that his privileged background might be more of a hindrance than a help "What exactly are you getting at?"

Joan put her cutlery on her empty plate. "I'm not sure. I just have an uneasy feeling at the back of my mind that won't leave me alone. It keeps telling me you're trying to work a number on me or something."

Edward decided that pretending to be dense was probably the best thing to do. "Work a number on you?"

Although she was enjoying herself, Joan couldn't help herself: she had to make her point. "You know, get me off balance, let my guard down so that you can get in and get what you want."

This seemed to amuse him still further. "Oh. So you know what I want, then, do you?" He chuckled.

"Well, I know what most men want," she insisted.

Suddenly Ed became serious. "What if I'm not most men?"

It threw her. "You know, I so hope that you aren't."

"Aren't what?" He was no longer pretending to be dense.

"Aren't most men." She explained.

Now he smiled. "Me too."

She was smiling too, but there was hesitation behind her smile. "There you go again, Gene, turning on the charm, giving me that winning smile. It's – it's like it's instinctive – you know it's a killer combination, guaranteed to get you to exactly where you want to go."

He reached across the table to take her hand. "Sounds like we're back where we were a minute ago, doesn't it? Let's try something different. What about you, what do you want?"

She looked into his crystal-blue eyes and almost groaned. "I want you not to be most men."

There was that connection again. Ed sensed it, but it was new to him, and he didn't recognise it for what it was. But though it was elusive, it had the result of making him say the right thing. "You know, I'm trying so hard not to be, but it's not easy."

It made him sound almost vulnerable; a quality that most people who knew him would have said was new – or even foreign - to him. But Joan had only her intuition to rely on. "Not easy? Why not? You don't have to do anything to impress me, I'm not impressed by the usual sort of things that a man might do."

The connection was there again, but still as ethereal as a will o' the wisp. Instinctively Ed followed it. "I know . . . at least I sensed you wouldn't be. That's why I brought you here. I knew you wouldn't be impressed by going somewhere posh or trendy or just plain expensive, so I had to think of something that was out of the ordinary, and this is where I ended up. Don't be too hard on me; it was the best I could come up with."

She reached across and caressed his face with the back of her fingers. "It's perfect."

"Perfect?"

She took a sip of her wine. "It's the most thoughtful thing I think anyone's ever done for me. Just look at the place. I love it!" She laughed aloud.

This brought Vinny to their table. "Is evryfin' awright doctor Plant?" He asked, eager to please. "C'n I get you any'fin' else?"

Ed exchanged an amused glance with Joan before replying "We're fine, thanks, Vinny. Fine. Really, great, in fact, thank you."

Vinny was delighted. "You're welcome, mate, I mean, doctor. Would you like to see the sweet menu?"

Edward turned back to Joan. "Would you like a sweet?" He asked.

Joan gave Vinny her best smile. "I'd love one."

Now it was Vinny's turn to smile. "I'll bring it over then."

Almost immediately he returned with a scrap of paper on which was typed:

Heinz jam sponge pudding and custard
Treacle tart and custard
Apple pie and custard
Jam roly-poly and custard
All £3.25

They looked it over with as much consideration as if they were in a Michelin-starred establishment. "See anything you like?"

Now she had an audience, Joan was taken by a flirty mood. She looked directly at Ed. "Oh yes." Her eyebrows flicked upward. Then she turned to Vinny. "I'd like the jam roly-poly please, with lashings of custard."

Ed laughed. "And I'll have the apple pie please Vinny – but go easy on the custard for me, won't you?"

Vinny caught their mood perfectly. "I'd 'ave fought the treacle tart would 'a bin more up your street tonight, doc!" He winked at Ed before shouting "One roly-poly special and one apple pie wiv' on'y a bit o' custard." Then he spoke to Joan: "It'll be over in 'arf a mo, miss." His voice had taken on a respectful tone that was usually absent when he addressed his other customers. He picked up the scrap of paper and had started to walk away when something else occurred to him. He turned on his heel. "C'n I get yer anyfin' else?" He asked. "Tea? Coffee?"

In the orthopaedics department, Joan had become known – affectionately - as the tea monster. She had never been known to refuse a cup of tea. Nor did she now. "Mmm." She murmured appreciatively. "Yes; tea. Black, please, not very strong. No sugar."

"Can you do that?" Ed asked Vinny.

Vinny's face was a picture of remorse. "Sorry, doc." Mournfully he shook his head. "The tea comes 'ow it comes. The milk gets added in the pot. It's 'ow ve uvver punters like it. Can't change a winnin' formula just to suit one customer who's a bit partic'lar. Know what I mean? Could be the start o' somefin'. 'oo knows where we might end up?"

It was all Ed and Joan could do to conceal their amusement.

"How about it?" Ed asked Joan. "Are you willing to give it a try?"

She pretended to think long and hard about such a momentous decision. "Okay. As long as I can have it without sugar?" She looked at Vinny expectantly.

Vinny was almost indignant. "What do you take me for darlin'? Course you can 'ave it wivout sugar, we're not totally unsophisticated you know." He went back to his kitchen.

"So where were we?" Ed asked.

Joan shut her eyes. "I can't remember. Erm, I think we were hoping that you weren't most men."

"Yeah. I don't know what to say, really."

Joan pretended to be shocked by what he had just said. "What? The great doctor Edward Plant, tongue-tied by a mere slip of a girl?"

By unspoken consent they said nothing while the waitress brought their sweets and two mugs of milky tea.

It was Ed who broke the silence. "You know Joan, you're going to find this hard to believe, but I'm not usually tongue-tied. Usually I can think of plenty of witty, amusing things to say right up to . . ."

"When you get them to your bedroom and conversation becomes a bit redundant, is that it?" Joan interrupted.

"More or less, yes."

Joan pushed her spoon into her sweet, playing with it. "But now?"

Talking about how he felt did not come easily to Ed. "Will it sound horribly cheesy if I say I'm not sure, I'm confused, my feelings are in a whirl?"

"God, yes."

Edward suddenly realized the time for kidding around was over. "I thought so. Joan, I want to be honest with you, I want to take the risk that you might find the real me so repulsive that you'll have nothing further to do with me, but on the other hand, there's the chance that you might find something in me worth saving, something that's worth redeeming."

Joan's eyes opened wide. She had sensed from their first meeting that there were depths to this man that were hidden even from him, but she had not expected to see anything other than glimpses, at least not for a long time, and she had half expected that she wouldn't be part of his plans for that long. Now she wasn't so sure. Neither was she sure she was ready to get in so deep so quickly.

"There you go with those big words again, Gene" she said. "That's some risk you're taking there. How do you know I don't just want to shag your brains out, same as any other girl?"

But Ed ignored her attempt to make light of it. "Trust me, I just know. Look, I've been with loads of girls. It's fun. I love having sex. But I've never in my life made a connection with a girl. It's always been about partying, sex, until I get bored and meet the next one. But with you . . ."

His sudden intensity was amazing. It was as if he was on fire "What?" She whispered, praying silently that the spell would not be broken by some intrusion.

It wasn't. "You're different," Ed continued. "For the first time in my life I know there's a connection. Don't ask me how I know, I just do. It's not about sex any more, it's not about having a good time, it's just about being. Being with you. Really. Just being with you is amazing, wonderful, incredible. I don't know why, or how, I can't even describe it . . . . It just is."

His words were sheer joy. Pure adrenaline. She almost had to pause for breath before replying. "God, Gene," she said, smiling broadly. "You know how I said I didn't think much of your chat-up line?"

"Yeah?"

"I take it all back. Your chat-up line is fantastic."

*

On Maple ward, Susan and Cathy were on the late shift again. Cathy quite liked working lates; two hours of the shift were taken up with visiting. There wasn't much to be done then, apart from just being around, and it gave the opportunity for a nice sit-down, a cup of tea, and a good long chin-wag, as long as you were on with a mate.

"So how did your date with Tim go?" Susan asked.

"I see you remembered his name then."

"Of course." But Susan wasn't letting her friend off the hook. "So how was it?"

Cathy tried to play it down. "Well it wasn't a date exactly – we only had breakfast. Actually he took me to the Marlborough hotel."

Susan was impressed. "The Marlborough? That's posh. I didn't know they served breakfast to non-residents."

"Neither did I, but they didn't bat an eyelid. They seemed to know Tim, though, and the service was great - and the food."

"I suppose hotels like to keep on the good side of the police," Susan observed.

"Yeah," Cathy agreed. "Anyway, it was quite nice really. He seems quite a decent sort. Being in the police is all he's ever wanted to do, a real career for him. He hates the bloke he was on with the other night, but says he doesn't have any say in the duty roster and gets lumbered with him as a partner more than he really likes. He says that although there are still quite a few arseholes like him about the police are slowly changing for the better.

Susan took a sip of her tea. "Sounds like he made quite an impression on you."

Cathy thought for a moment. "Yeah. I quite liked him really. Nice that for once doing something on a whim seems to have worked out alright."

Susan was pleased for her friend. "When are you seeing him again?"

"Who says I'm seeing him again?" Cathy pretended to be non-committal, but Susan saw right through it.

"You are though, aren't you?"

"I'm not sure. He promised to call me, but he said it's impossible to know what any shift will throw up, so he couldn't say when. Anyway, since he's been on nights all week . . ."

Susan leaned in conspiratorially. "You know, Cath, if you really do like him, if he doesn't call you . . . you know what men are like, so make sure you call him."

They were interrupted by the sound of someone coughing. Whoever it was, they were standing just outside the nursing station, hidden from their view by the potted plants. Cathy stepped out. It was Joan Archer. She hadn't been well all afternoon, and her mum and dad had left early, obviously upset at Joan's condition. Now Joan had got into her pyjamas and dressing gown and was just standing there, she wasn't weeping, tears were merely flowing in rivulets down her cheeks. She looked dreadful.

"Hello Joan," Cathy said. "Is something the matter?" Her voice was full of concern.

"They won't leave me alone," Joan sobbed. "It's horrible. I don't think I can stand them any more."

"You mean the voices?"

"They're not just voices. They're evil. It's the Devil himself. And I'm not strong enough. They're just pitiless. Soon I won't have the strength to resist any more, and then I'll be lost."

Joan's voice was rising, getting loud enough to be heard by other patients and visitors. Best try and stop Joan from upsetting them as well, Susan thought as she came out into the corridor. "Joan, would you like something to help you to sleep?"

Joan's gratitude was pitiful. "Yes, please. Anything that will give me some relief from this torture."

*

Somehow Ed and Joan managed to get from Vinny's to her flat without incident, and were now snuggled together on the couch, nursing mugs of tea.

"Did I tell you," Ed asked, "about how I used to feel about women and how they fitted into my life – my other life - before I met you?"

The floodgates seemed to have opened. She sensed this was an important moment that would have its own momentum, but that she was the catalyst that would set it free. "I don't think you did," she said. "Tell me."

Ed dived in. "I thought life was like a journey across a desert. A journey with no end because you could never get to the other side. All you could do was stumble through the relentless wasteland and hope to come across the occasional oasis. That's all there was."

She squirmed round to look at him. "God, Gene, that's a terribly bleak view of life, isn't it?" She waited, but he didn't answer. "But now something's changed, has it?"

He smiled. Not a smile of mirth or joy, but of discovery. "God knows how, but I've reached the other side; and it's wonderful."

Joan put her cup on the floor then lay back across his lap so she could look up at him without having to strain. "My God, you have so much to learn, don't you? Don't you understand that it's the journey that's important, not the arrival? Life changes all the time, so every time you think you've arrived at your destination, the destination just up and changes. I can't remember who said it, but I do remember reading once that you should embark on the journey like a madman, without any regard for whether you might eventually reach your destination."

This was such a revelation to Edward. How had he missed it before? It was so obvious, now. "That's entirely the story of my life. I've been so intent on not thinking about the destination that I've missed the whole point of the journey. But you . . . how come you know so much about it? How is it that when I'm with you I can feel so complete and so inadequate all at the same time?"

She could see tears breaking into the corners of his eyes. He tried manfully to blink them back, but they were too much. As if from nowhere she conjured a tissue and reached up to wipe his eyes "God, look at me" he sniffed. "I'm sorry."

She pulled herself up and kissed him, feather-light, on his lips. "Now Gene, don't go getting all mushy on me. I don't think I could stand that. Maybe we need to inject a little female cynicism into this conversation before it gets too dewy-eyed."

This brought him back from the brink. "Female cynicism? Like what? I thought women liked all that dewy-eyed stuff."

"We do," she acknowledged, "but only up to a point. Let's see, what can I dredge up from the depths? Oh I know. I can't remember where I saw this, probably in some girly magazine or somewhere. Something some female pop-star or other is supposed to have said about what men want from women."

"That's probably more straightforward than what women want from men," he said, recovering his smile. He noticed she was looking at him intently. "So . . . what exactly do men want from women?" He asked.

Joan had a triumphant look on her face. "They want women to be great cooks, wonderful mothers for their children, but most of all, in the bedroom, they want their women to be outrageous whores."

"Really?" Ed said, grinning. "And is that what you think too?"

"It might be." She said it as if she wanted to be convinced of it, but wouldn't take too much convincing.

Ed decided she didn't need any convincing at all, she was just playing coy. "And is that what I can expect from you?"

Now she went past coy at speed and straight to coquettish. "It might be."

Edward thought he understood the rules of this particular game. "Well . . . I've sampled the cooking, and it was pretty damned good. It's a bit premature to be thinking about children. Are you an outrageous whore in the bedroom?"

Coquettish was discarded as old hat. Now she was a seductress. "I might be."

"When do I get to find out?" How long could he wait?

All of a sudden she was Marlene Dietrich and Greta Garbo and Sophia Loren and Audrey Hepburn and every Hollywood temptress rolled into one. She shot straight from the hip. "Well Gene, that depends on what you're offering yourself."

"What I'm offering?" A moment ago it was he who had been in control – or so he had thought. Now he was floundering.

"Yeah. I don't let just anyone into my bedroom to see what an outrageous whore I am. You've got to convince me that it would be worth my while."

Now he got it. "Oh it would, I promise you."

But she was having none of it. "Yeah, Gene. That's what they all say." That took the wind out of his sails. She kissed him. "So, Gene . . . convince me."

That brought him back to familiar territory. "Okay. Well, where should we start?" He took a moment to think. "Yes. We start with the lighting. No lights at all to start with, until I light the candles."

"Then what?"

"Then we kiss." He kissed her, gently letting his tongue trace the contours of her lips, no more. He pulled away. "Slowly," he said, "not furiously, not in a frenzy. Slow, like a long slow dance."

She brushed her lips across his cheek to nibble his earlobe. "Gene, this is good," she whispered. "Keep going. What next?"

"Then we open the champagne – we've got to have champagne – before I start to undress you. Again, very slowly. None of this can't-wait-to-rip-your-clothes-off nonsense, though that is nice sometimes." He paused to kiss her; again, just very lightly, almost teasing. "And every time I take off an item of clothing, I kiss your body underneath as I peel it away."

Joan didn't think this was entirely fair. "You undress me? Don't I get to undress you as well?"

He smiled, confident in this at least. "Not yet. First I want you to be naked in my arms, I want to feel the touch of your skin, the curve of your back, your belly, your breasts, everything, all just for me, just to indulge myself for a moment or two of selfishness."

"That kind of selfishness I can live with. Where do we go from there?"

He thought for a moment before answering. "The bathroom. There's something just so amazingly sensuous about washing another person, and being washed by another person. A nice rich bath oil – and a natural sponge."

She pushed herself up until her face was level with his, and, taking his face in her hands she kissed him; slowly, deeply, sensuously. "And then?" She asked when she surfaced.

"Back to the bedroom. Still only lit by candles. Everything has to be perfect; I want to make love to you, but not yet. A massage. A long, slow, head-to-toe massage with some aromatic oil."

She had pushed her hand inside his shirt and was stroking his chest, playing with his nipples. "Aromatic oil? Which one?"

"Patchouli."

This surprised her. She stopped what she was doing. "Patchouli? Why patchouli?"

He grinned. "I don't know. I just said the first thing that came into my head."

She pulled out a cushion and hit him with it. "Never mind. So far, so good. What next?"

"Then I give you the most sensual massage you can imagine. I start with your feet, move up your legs, then up your back, then turn you over and start at your feet again. Then I kiss every bit of your body, inch by perfect inch."

"And then?" She purred.

Now he laughed. "And then? Then I give you the best oral sex you ever had in your life and I keep on giving it to you until you beg me to stop."

Now she sat up so she could look him in the eye. She looked stern like she was going to tell him off or warn him about something. "Gene. Are you sure you know what you're committing yourself to here? It might be quite some time before I beg you to stop. Have you got what it takes?"

But he had the smile of one who knows what they're doing. "The longer the better. Trust me; I love to give oral sex."

She shook her head. "I bet it's not as much as I like to get it."

"It's a good job I'm not a betting man then, isn't it?"

Again, they kissed. It seemed natural that for the moment there was a line they would not cross. "There's just something about oral sex," she mused, her chin nuzzled into his shoulder. "It makes me feel like my body is no longer my own. It's as if I'm a stranger who's been borrowing it, and now the real owner wants it back. Any shame I might once have harboured is abandoned because my whole being is changing – it's as if I'm metamorphosing into a new creature. Sometimes it's like ice melting; sometimes it's hot like molten metal. Either way, I'm lost in a rapture of desire. I become more than I was before. I flow around my lover, and we dissolve into each other, becoming one, complete." She shivered at the thought of it before adding "the new me that I have become is nothing less than desire itself."

Ed was quite taken aback. "You are just . . . incredible. I've never heard anybody talk about love-making like that before. I never stopped even to think about it like that myself."

She smiled to herself. "You've just never made love to the right person before," she murmured. "Do I shock you?"

He shook his head. "No. You amaze me."

But she was straight back to business. "So - then we make love?"

"Oh no, not yet. First we cuddle for a while until you've had time to get over your first orgasm. Then we make love."

"Sounds perfect," she whispered. "Got any candles?"

This provoked a quiet laugh. "No. Not right now."

Abruptly, she sat up. "What?" She cried, disappointment written all over her face. "God, Gene. What were you thinking of, leading me on like that when you knew all along you didn't have any bloody candles?"

He looked crestfallen. "I'm sorry. I didn't know I'd need them tonight." He rearranged his rumpled shirt. "I didn't want to . . you know, presume."

Smiling, she pulled him back into their embrace "God, you're such an idiot" she said. "But I can't be doing with anything less than what you've promised now, can I? You've got a hell of a lot to live up to there."

They kissed again. "So when should I get the candles?"

For a second time she pushed him away. "Hang on a minute Gene. Don't think you're getting away with just candles. I seem to remember mention of champagne, bath oil, a natural sponge, and sensual massage oil."

This time it was Ed who pulled her into his arms. "Don't worry. I'll make sure I don't forget a thing. When?"

She had a surprise for him. "I know a place that would be perfect for lighting candles, and I've got this week-end off. How about you?"

This was all happening so fast. As soon as the thought entered his brain, Ed recognised it for the cliché it was; images of Dustin Hoffman and Mrs. Robinson came into his mind. He shook his head to clear it. "Shit. I don't know . . . I'll have to ask . . . Oh fuck it. Yes. Definitely, yes. I'll move hell and high water, and Marwan owes me a few favours - all I've done for him covering his on-call and everything. If the worst comes to the worst I'll call in sick. When are you actually off?"

"I'll be finished at one on Friday. How about you?"

"It'll depend on whether we get any admissions, but definitely no later than three. Where's this place that's perfect for lighting candles?"

She smiled. The knowing smile of a conspirator whose plans have just come to fruition without incurring even the merest hint of suspicion. "Why don't we keep that a surprise?"

Ed was not usually one for surprises, but now he found the sense of anticipation was intensely pleasurable. What was it that made Joan so different from all the other women he had known? Whatever it was she intended to surprise him with, he instinctively knew he would enjoy it. "That's . . . brilliant." He couldn't think of what else to say. "Where and when shall we meet?"

"Can you pick me up in a taxi?" She asked. "But no later than four. There's a train we have to be on at twenty-five past."

He could feel goose-pimples rising in the back of his neck. "You've had this planned all along!" He pretended to be shocked.

She grinned. "I might have," she admitted.

"Shit. I can't believe this is happening." He said.

She pulled herself tightly into his arms. "Neither can I, but maybe now is our time for believing."

16
Confessional

Tuesday morning began normally for Edward. He entered the kitchen in his apartment just as Peter was pouring boiling water into a cafetière. As usual, Edward was in a hurry.

"Hi Ed," Peter said without looking up. "Coffee?"

"Yes please, mate. Any toast?"

Peter pointed with the kettle. "In the toaster."

The toaster popped almost immediately. Ed dropped two more slices of bread in and put the toast on a plate to bring to the table. They each took a slice. Peter spooned a generous helping of marmalade onto his, but Ed ate his with only butter for a topping.

"So . . . how was last night?" Peter asked between chews.

He had to wait while Ed swallowed his toast. "Oh mate . . . it was just fantastic. Joan is just the most amazing . . ."

Peter stopped pouring coffee into his cup to interrupt Ed. "The most amazing . . . but you still haven't let me meet her? I wonder why?"

Ed reached across to steal Peter's cup. "Don't read anything into it mate. I just think she doesn't want to feel pressured into anything she isn't sure of, so she prefers to go back to her place: home ground and all that."

Peter didn't care. This aspect of Ed was new and fascinating He was consumed with curiosity. "So tell me about it. Did you . . . ?"

Ed laughed, nearly choking on the toast at the back of his mouth. "Did I? God, when did you get so bloody interested in my sex life? You'll be telling me you've started reading 'Hello' next."

"Actually, it's not your sex life I'm interested in. It's just that I've never seen you in so deep before. I keep asking myself - can it really be happening? Is he going to snap out of it? Has this just become a challenge, or is Edward finally showing signs of growing up?"

Ed went to the fridge to get the milk. "You tell me – you're the psychologist, remember?" He said over his shoulder.

Peter frowned. "Sad to say, I think I detect signs of growing up."

Ed put the milk on the table. He was wearing his cocky look "I don't think I'd go quite that far." He sat down.

Peter's curiosity was growing. It was as if Ed were teasing him. "So how *did* it go last night? I'm beginning to think you're trying to evade the question."

"Taking her to the transport cafe was a stroke of genius – I recommend it. I have a feeling it's a place I'm going to get to know quite well. Afterwards we went back to her place; it got pretty passionate, but she asked me to leave before it went too far."

That surprised Peter – almost. "And you left – just like that?"

Ed grinned. "Not exactly."

"Not exactly?" Peter tried to keep his expression neutral.

"We're going away. A whole week-end with that incredible woman. God, I can hardly believe it's happening."

"Where to?"

The toaster popped again. Ed was so excited he almost jumped. "Dunno, mate. She said it was going to be a surprise. The only thing she would tell me was that I would need my passport." He threw the toast on the table and shrugged himself into his jacket.

Peter reached for the marmalade jar. "Fantastic! So are you serious about her, or is this just testing the water?"

Edward was about to open the front door but paused to consider. "How can I tell if it's serious? I think it is, but this is all new to me, you know."

"Yeah, I do know." Peter replied, taking a bite of toast.

Ed looked at his watch. "Sorry mate, gotta dash."

*

Edward had promised Marwan that he would accompany Joan to the chapel. After checking that there was nothing else he needed to be doing, he went and found her. She looked dreadful. The night staff had said she had slept poorly, even though she had been given a sleeping pill, but that didn't prepare him for what he found. She had a look of haggard exhaustion on her face, and her hair was matted. She looked at him with the detached hopelessness of the starving, and when he asked if she would like to go to the chapel she showed no emotion whatever. They walked along the corridors with a slowness that was almost painful, as if Joan had to struggle for every step she took. But when they entered the chapel, Edward was astonished by the change that came over her. She was transformed, as if she had been able to put down an enormous burden that had been forced on her. Although she was tired, her conversation was lucid and rational.

There was no question that the voices were gone, though according to Joan they had been tormenting her remorselessly for the past thirty six hours. Now she could not even remember what it was like for them to be there, she said, like the memory of pain: you can remember experiencing pain, but it's impossible to bring to mind exactly what it was like or recreate the agony of it.

Joan said she wanted to pray, so they sat together quietly for a few minutes. Then her voice broke the silence. "I'm ready now," she said.

"Can you describe for me exactly what it is you've been going through?" He asked.

She shuddered. "Do I have to?"

"That's why I came here with you."

She sighed then plunged in. "Imagine you're falling in the blackest, darkest pit you can conceive. There's no light, but you're aware that you're falling just the same . . ." Edward wrote at furious pace, trying to keep up. After she had finished she fell quiet. He could think of nothing to say, so deeply had her words affected him. Eventually it was she who spoke.

"Doctor Plant, d'you mind if I ask you something?" Telling him of her experience must have been cathartic, for her voice had taken on a calm, serene quality.

Edward shrugged. "Depends what it is, I suppose."

She was looking at him intently, as if by doing so she would better be able to gauge his response. "How can you tell what purpose God has for your life?"

Edward gave a sad smile. "I think you're asking the wrong person. I don't believe in God."

"You're an atheist?" She seemed surprised, shocked, almost.

Edward shook his head wryly. "I suppose so. I haven't really given it that much thought, I suppose. I guess I'm an agnostic really."

"So what do you believe in?"

Edward shook his head again, more assertively this time. "I'm not really here to discuss my own personal beliefs, you know Joan. I'm supposed to be finding out what your problems are to see how we can help you."

She would not be put off. "But this is important. If you don't believe in God, what else is there to believe in?"

Edward decided it would probably be easier to tell her what she wanted to know. "I believe in the evidence of my senses, in what I can see and hear for myself. And I believe in myself, in my abilities." Now he warmed to his subject. "More than anything I believe that I should use my own intelligence to work through any problems I might encounter rather than rely on some mystical hocus-pocus."

She was staring at him aghast. "Isn't that horribly empty? Bleak, even. I think it must be. I know that not everybody believes in God, but you have to believe in something beyond yourself. They say that no man is an island, and I think that's true."

Edward had never faced such a sincere challenge to his professed atheism. "What do you think I should believe in?" He asked, curious to know how she would answer.

She took a moment to consider his question. "I don't really know. What about the power of love in the world; the struggle between good and evil? Family? The people you love?"

He shook his head again. "Like I said: I believe in myself and the evidence of my senses. I don't think there's much else to it."

"Much else to what?"

"To life generally."

Joan turned to face the front of the chapel, letting her gaze rest on the crucifix. "That's so sad," she said. "Are you a sad person doctor Plant?"

Edward told himself that he shouldn't be letting the conversation drift in this direction, but he half-convinced himself that by doing so he would learn more about Joan. He could feel a connection. He didn't know what it was, but in some way he didn't comprehend, she was guiding him into uncharted emotional territory, and he wanted the journey to continue, sensing that for some reason it was important that it did. He wasn't sure he wanted to talk about being sad, however, and his reply was more abrupt than he intended. "I don't think so. I'm just a realist, that's all."

But Joan stuck unerringly to the path she had found. "So what's it all about then, this life of ours?"

Almost trance-like, Edward found himself replying "This is the strangest life I've ever known."

She turned back to face him. It was evident that she thought his answer shocking. Had he meant it to be? "What's that supposed to mean?"

Edward rubbed his eyes as if he were waking from a deep sleep. "What?" He seemed disorientated. "I dunno. It wasn't actually me who said it, anyway."

Joan peered at him like this was a crucial question. "Who *did* say it, then, and what did *he* mean?"

Ed found her intensity amusing. "How do you know it was a he?" He asked.

She wondered if he was trying to brush her off, but decided he wasn't. "I didn't know it was a he, but I had a guess and had a 50-50 chance of being right." She paused. "Am I right?"

He grinned self-consciously. "Yeah, you're right. It was a bloke called Jim Morrison; he was singer with a band called the Doors in the 1960s. They were quite notorious. He had a habit of getting himself arrested."

"Arrested? What for? Doing drugs and stuff? I wouldn't have thought that was the way to become notorious in the 60s."

"Not drugs, no. At least, that's not what he became notorious for."

Even though he had started to tell this particular story, he now found himself reluctant to continue, but he had aroused Joan's curiosity. "What was it then?" She asked.

Edward shrugged. In for a penny . . . "It was for indecent exposure - on stage. He was pissed, apparently, and not exactly giving the performance of his life, so the audience started heckling him. All of a sudden he shouted at them *'You wanna see my prick?'* and without waiting for an answer, he pulled it out then and there and waved it at them, until the police pulled him off stage."

A look of distaste crossed Joan's face. "That's an odd thing to tell me, isn't it?" She asked. "Why did it enter your head to talk to me about that?"

Edward shrugged again. "I don't know" he admitted. "Maybe because it's because I'm interested in the inadequacies of celebrities and how they cope with them – always being on display, never being able to relax in public for a moment." He paused, and looked down at his hands in embarrassment. "Maybe it's because you unsettled me, asking about my own inadequacies."

This admission of vulnerability took Joan by surprise. Weren't doctors supposed to have all the answers? "*Your* inadequacies? Jesus, if you start off having inadequacies, God help the rest of us."

This seemed to bring Edward back to his senses. "Lots of people put doctors on pedestals. If they only knew that most of us have feet of clay."

Joan snuggled up closely to him. She pushed her arm through his and rested her hand on his thigh. She felt safe with him now, the trauma of the past few days relegated to the back of her mind. "Don't think I'm letting you off that easily" she said lightly, almost playfully. "You were about to tell me about your philosophy on life."

The reluctance to reveal his inner self returned. "It's really not very interesting."

But she was not going to let him put her off. "I think I should be the judge of that. What makes you think that you're not interesting or that someone wouldn't be interested in you?"

How did she know how to prod his ego? Was it intuition, or merely chance? Either way, it brought the response she wanted. "I didn't say that I wasn't interesting, exactly," he said, turning to face her.

She took his hand. He didn't try to pull it away. "Please?" She said.

There was that connection again. What was happening to him? He felt caught in the coils of predestination. "Okay," he sighed. "You asked for it, but don't say I didn't warn you. For as long as I can remember I've thought that life was just a journey without any destination. We live, we die, and life is what happens in between. Personally it seems to me that our journey is like crossing a desert; we can never reach the other side. We might come across the occasional oasis, but that's about as good as it gets. My purpose has always been to find and enjoy as many oases as I can."

She wasn't convinced. "But what about your *real* purpose in life. Have you worked out what that is?"

"I don't think my life has any particular purpose. It's mainly just about survival. And having a good time along the way if you can."

Edward's response had been a little too vehement, too well-rehearsed. It was as if he were telling her about something that was in the past, not about now. She shook her head. "No, there has to be more to it than that. What about your vocation?"

"My vocation?"

"To be a doctor. Didn't you become a doctor because you wanted to help people?"

Edward gave her a wry smile. "It might have been that way once, but not any more. Medical school and life as a junior doctor knock all that idealism out of you. Now I just want to make consultant as quickly as I can."

Still she could not bring herself to believe what he was telling her. "I don't know why, but I don't think that you really believe that. Not deep down."

She was trying to delve too deep. She had led him a long way, but he could not go any further down that particular road, not yet. He reverted to his doctor role. "You can believe whatever you like Joan. But I think that's enough about me. I need to talk more about your voices, so I can understand where they're coming from and how we can help you." The change was so abrupt that it took Joan off guard.

"I don't think I want to talk about them any more just now."

"I'm sorry to insist," Edward said, "but I think it's really important that we do while you can have a conversation about inconsequential things – like normal people do." He paused, watching his words penetrate her tortured mind. "Do they ever stop completely outside of a church or a chapel?"

She shook her head. Even trying to think about the voices was excruciatingly painful, but she knew she had to. "I don't know."

"Surely you know whether they stop or not?"

"Yes, it's just that . . ." She stopped speaking.

"What?" She didn't respond, but he could see her lips moving. "Joan?"

She held up her hand. She needed a space for prayer, and she knew he would not understand. Thank God for the Lord's Prayer. It was a source of both solace and rescue. Finally she spoke. "It's not like I've had them for a long time. I only heard them for the first time just a few days ago, and they change all the time. Sometimes they pretty much go away, but mostly they just torture me."

It had dawned on Edward what she had been doing. "Are there any particular times when the voices go away?"

She looked down into her lap. "Not really. The only time I can be sure of it is when I'm in church, or here, in the chapel."

"And that's why you like to come here, that's why you had to be dragged out the other day, because you knew that as soon as you left, the voices would come back?"

Her response was to cup his face in her hands and look intently into his eyes as if searching for something. She felt safe with him here, she told herself, but how far could she really trust him, a self-confessed atheist? Could she trust him with the keeping of her very soul? She could not tell him outright, she decided, but if he was as perceptive as he thought he was, he would realise that there was more to her story. "Partly", she said. "You're right that I don't hear the voices when I'm in church, but that's not the only reason I like to go there."

Edward replied without any thought for what she had just said. He heard what he wanted to hear and what she said fitted in perfectly with the discussion he had had with Dr. Marwan yesterday "No, of course not," he agreed. "You go to pray as well." A pang of doubt flitted briefly through his brain, a feeling of absence, loss almost. Had he missed something? He dismissed it. "Joan," he continued, "what would you say if we could get rid of the voices for you for all or most of the time?"

But Joan was sceptical. "And how would you do that?"

"Modern treatments are very effective." He said it in his most reassuring voice.

She felt only patronised. He was back on the same tired hobby-horse. "Treatments? You mean drugs?"

"Not drugs, medicines. I know it's difficult to understand that they could do something like take voices away, but I can only ask you to believe me that they do."

Her mind shrieked. No, no, no, no, no! "But the voices are a visitation from the Devil. How on earth could medicines stop that?" The pitch of her voice was rising.

Edward was astonished by her reaction. For half an hour she had been lucid, rational. How could she react like this after all they had talked about? He tried to calm her. "Joan, I know that it's difficult for you to understand or accept this, but your voices are not a visitation from the Devil," he told her with a quiet authority. "They're what we call auditory hallucinations. The voices are inside your head and they happen because of an imbalance of the chemicals in your brain. The medicines correct the imbalance and the voices go away."

Joan pulled away from him, and stood in the aisle keeping a safe distance from him. Her voice was shrill. "No, doctor Plant, it's you who doesn't understand. The voices are real. I can hear them as clearly as I can hear you. I don't have a chemical imbalance; I really do have the Devil talking to me."

But he persisted in trying to convince her. "No Joan, you don't. Listen to me. You have an illness called schizophrenia. One of the signs of schizophrenia is hearing voices that aren't really there; another is having beliefs about things that aren't real. You have the classic symptoms – voices and false beliefs, and the medicines will help to take them both away."

As if she knew that she could never persuade him to believe her she sank to her knees in a gesture of defeat. "But I don't want you to take my beliefs away. They're the most important thing in my life."

To Edward it was obvious that she had misunderstood what he had been trying to tell her. "The medicines won't take away any *real* beliefs, only false ones. You'll continue to believe in God, they won't affect that, but they will help you to understand that the voices you hear are the product of your own mind, and not the voice of the Devil." She didn't respond. Was she thinking seriously about what he had said, or was she being passive-aggressive? That other possibilities might exist did not occur to him, so fixated was he now on convincing her that he was right. "Will you agree to continue with the medication?"

Tears were flowing down Joan's cheeks again. She felt that her tears were old, having been shed so many times over the same thing. She could no longer distinguish self-pity from real pain. Did he have no pity? She asked herself. They had been so close only a few short minutes ago. Now she wondered whether she would ever be able to convince him of the truth or was he utterly impregnable behind his self-important beliefs about mental illness? It was a while before she could bring herself to speak. "I'm not sure," she said, the words forming with painful slowness in her mind. "I don't really think I want to take medication. I have been taking it because people told me I had to, but I don't think it's doing me any good and it makes me feel awful."

Edward sensed a small victory. "I know," he said, oozing sympathy. "I really do, but will you please just keep taking it at least until doctor Marwan sees you again?"

She swallowed. "Okay," she said, in a small frightened voice.

Edward stood. "It's time to go now. Will you come quietly this time? If you do, you'll be allowed to come back again tomorrow."

She looked up at him. He could see the red in her eyes. He found himself wishing he could do something to stop her crying. "Will you come too?" She asked.

He felt in his pocket. Why did he never carry tissues? "It depends - on how busy I am. But I can see how helpful it is to you to come here, and I will tell doctor Marwan that. I will definitely recommend that you should be allowed to come here – more frequently, and for longer periods of time if staffing allows. As you improve, you'll be allowed to come by yourself. That's something to work towards, isn't it?"

He led her to the door, holding it open for her. On the threshold she paused, looking back as if to imprint the appearance of the chapel on her memory. Then she took a purposeful step into the corridor. Almost at once she winced. Her torment was no longer a memory but an ever-present reality.

17
Schizophrenia

The ward round was its usual semi-organised affair, with the hospital staff arranged in chairs in a semi-circle around the patient. Mental illness is so complex, and the needs of the sufferer are so varied that it takes a multitude to decide what's best and to act upon it. Or it could be just that there's safety in numbers. Today was no different. Dr. Marwan's team had taken over the group therapy room for the morning, and had arranged themselves in their usual order. Flanking Marwan were Edward and the ward manager. Then came the occupational therapist and the pharmacist. As each patient was seen there was a seat for their ward primary nurse, and, if discharge was being contemplated, spaces for their community nurse and social worker.

Marwan had been droning on all morning. Edward was trying to maintain his interest, occasionally making entries in the patients' notes, but to relieve the crippling tedium he was musing now on the words of a *Doors* song.

'Five to one, baby, one in five.
No-one here gets out alive . . .'

A few minutes before, Joan had been brought in, and there they were – five of them to her one, and she looked as if she really might not get out alive.

Marwan was talking to Joan. She was seated in a low armchair facing the assembled professionals as though she were being interviewed by captains of industry for some high-flying job and they had told her to be at her ease. If only. She was slouched to one side, and looked like she was hugging one of the chair's arms, staring at the floor. Her eyes had a vacant look that suggested she was either drugged almost to the point of insensibility or that she had been transfixed by some inner eye that kept her entirely captive. Either way she took little interest in what was going on around her.

So far she had replied to Dr. Marwan's questions in monosyllables, if at all. She did not appear distracted, merely incapable of responding. Marwan tried again. "Doctor Plant tells me that he went with you to the chapel and that you were calm and lucid and able to have quite an in-depth conversation about what's been happening to you. Have I got that right, Joan?"

She raised her eyes a fraction. For an instant her eyes met his. "Yeah. S'pose," she mumbled. "Hard to remember."

"Is it hard to remember because you're hearing voices?" Marwan raised his voice as if this might help to penetrate the barriers that had been erected in her mind. Joan did not respond. "Or is it something else?"

The group could almost feel what it was costing Joan to rouse herself to reply. "Not sure. The voices are there most of the time I'm awake, but it's hard to concentrate, y'know? And I feel so sleepy most of the time."

Edward broke in. "I did explain to Joan that the sleepiness is a side effect of the medication, and that it will probably wear off eventually. In the meantime it helps her to get to sleep at night; isn't that right Joan?"

Joan's look told everyone that he had told her no such thing "'f you say so."

Marwan did not pursue it. Sleepiness was of little concern at this time. "Edward also tells me that you discussed your belief that the voices you hear come from the Devil, and that you think you might be possessed?"

This roused Joan's interest. She pushed herself up on her arms. "Yeah. I worked it all out. The voices are some sort of test. I have to be strong and resist. As long as I keep my faith in Jesus I'll eventually be alright."

Marwan spoke as if this were an entirely reasonable hypothesis. "How long do you think it's likely to last, this test?" He asked.

"How should I know?" No sooner had she said it than she lowered her head and whispered to herself, the words not quite inaudible to those gathered round her. "No, He will come, I know it; then you'll see."

Marwan waited to see if she would say more. When she didn't he said "Joan, who were you talking to just then? Was it one of the voices?"

Joan looked at him, seemingly surprised. "How did you know?"

"I heard you talking to someone. We all did." He looked round the staff members who, as one, nodded in agreement. Joan showed no reaction. "Did doctor Plant explain to you about a condition called schizophrenia?"

She frowned. This was something she did not want to talk about. "Can't remember." Her voice was sullen. "He might have done."

Edward spoke again. "Try to remember Joan. Think – we talked about the two common symptoms of schizophrenia – hearing voices that no-one else can hear, and having bizarre beliefs that don't have any basis in fact. Do you remember now?"

She closed her eyes. What struggle she was enduring could only be guessed at. With an almost explosive effort she said "I remember you saying that the medication could take the voices and beliefs away. Something about a chemical balance."

"A chemical *im*balance, Joan. In your brain. It causes the voices and delusions to happen, and is corrected by the medication. You do remember, don't you?"

But Joan seemed to have suffered a setback. She collapsed into the chair again. "'f you say so."

Marwan thought they had seen enough. "Joan, is there anything else you want to talk to us about? Anything about the conversation you had in the chapel with doctor Plant?"

She shook her head. "Don't think so." She could not look at them.

Marwan turned to his trainee. "Edward?"

Edward thought it was important for them all to know more about the visit he had made with Joan to the chapel. The nursing staff were still reluctant to support future visits despite the one with him that had gone off without incident. She was due another that afternoon. "What really struck me was how obvious it was that the voices stopped when we entered the chapel, and came back as soon as we left. Once we were inside, she was clear-headed and lucid. Her mood was low and she was apprehensive about what she believed would happen when it was time for us to leave, but for a while she was cogent and completely cognitively competent. It was then that she denied being mentally ill, and told me about her belief that the voices came from the Devil."

Marwan turned his attention back to Joan. "Joan, doctor Plant thinks you may have a condition called schizophrenia. What do you think?"

Now she roused herself to glare at Edward. "He's wrong. I just know he's wrong."

But Marwan had reached the same conclusion himself. "Did he also tell you that most people who have schizophrenia find it hard to believe it's an illness because the voices they hear are as real as my voice now, and the beliefs seem to them to be completely reasonable?"

But she was implacable. "I just know he's wrong."

Marwan gave her a dismissive smile that told her he was sympathetic, but that on this he was siding with Edward. "Are you sure you don't have any questions you would like to ask me or any of the other staff, Joan?" He asked.

"No." She seemed defeated. She understood she had no power to gainsay what might be decided about her.

"Then you are free to go back to the ward," he told her with a brief smile. "Thank you for coming in to the ward round today. If you want to see myself or doctor Plant at any time, just ask one of the nurses, and they'll make sure you are seen quickly. Is that okay?" He waited until she had left the room before asking "What medication is she on now?"

The pharmacist consulted her file. "She's now on 20 milligrams of phenylatrazine twice a day, trinazilor 10 milligrams at night if required, and cyclidil 5 milligrams twice a day for the side effects."

Briefly Marwan considered this information. "Has she been getting the trinazilor regularly?"

Susan was Joan's primary nurse on the ward. So far she had not contributed to the discussion, but she spoke now. "Yes. She's so tormented by the voices that she can't get to sleep without it, despite the drowsiness that the phenylatrazine is causing."

"So, does everyone agree with Edward's diagnosis of schizophrenia?" Marwan looked to his team for their comments, but there were no disagreements. The symptoms were indeed vivid, and all the tests for possible physical causes of her condition had come back negative. "Me too," he continued. Edward smiled to himself, pleased that Marwan had finally given in to the obvious. "I think it's become increasingly clear that schizophrenia is the only reasonable conclusion we can draw, though I must admit I find this business about her becoming symptom free when she goes to the chapel intriguing and a little disturbing. This isn't something I've ever come across before. I do think we should consider writing this one up as a case study." He lowered his glasses and looked at Edward. "She's been on treatment for a week or so now, so do we all agree that we should continue as we are and review again next week?"

Now Edward voiced a concern that had been nagging at him. "What if there's no improvement?"

His mentor's was the voice of experience. "Let's cross that bridge when – and if – we come to it, eh?"

However, something in the intensity of Joan's belief that she had become a battleground between the forces of good and evil had created a nagging doubt in Ed's mind that would not be silenced. "Shouldn't we have seen at least a little improvement in her symptoms by now?" He insisted.

"Possibly," Marwan half conceded. "But don't forget - some people just need to be given more time than others to respond." He looked from one member of the team to another. "Let's try and retain some optimism for this young lady, eh?"

The question was closed. Then Susan asked "Before we move on to the next patient, can she continue her visits to the chapel, and can she be allowed to go home on leave at the week-end?"

"What does everybody think?" Marwan asked.

Before anyone else could speak, Edward blurted "I think her visits to the chapel are definitely therapeutic, I think she should be allowed to go at least once a day, if someone can go with her."

"Given the strength of her appropriate religious beliefs, that doesn't seem unreasonable," Marwan agreed.

Now Susan echoed the concerns of the other nurses on the unit. "The problem is we're a bit short at the moment. Jan's on maternity leave, and there's a freeze on bank staff unless it's an emergency."

Marwan sighed. That the psychiatric unit was run with minimum numbers of nurses was a constant complaint of his. It clearly was not in the best interests of patients, and here was another example of it. But it wasn't Susan's fault, she didn't decide on the staffing levels. "Very well. She can go to the chapel, but only if there's someone to go with her." He made a mental note to put it on the agenda for the next management meeting – again.

Susan made a note in Joan's nursing record. "And week-end leave?"

"I think it's too soon for that," Edward said. He thought it a good idea for Joan to be allowed to go to the chapel, but home? "She's still not settled, and there's precious little sign that the medication is working yet."

Marwan agreed. "Anything else?" He asked. There was nothing. "Then who's next on the list today?"

*

It had been a busy list that day which had included a repair to a torn Achilles tendon, a hip replacement, a knee cartilage repair and several fractures. Joan was enjoying a well-earned soak in the bath, thinking about the coming week-end. 'You are one crazy woman,' she told herself. What was she thinking of, throwing herself at a man like this? It was probably because he would be the first man she had slept with since moving down here, she rationalised. But even that was out of character for her. In her life she had slept with only three men, one of whom had turned out to be an arsehole, but the other two had been long satisfying affairs, if perhaps a little too comfortable and lacking in passion. In Edward she sensed something different. She could feel a connection that she had never made with any other man. Where did it come from? She had no idea. He was totally not the kind of man she had gone for in the past. He didn't seem dependable or particularly caring or even share her interests. But she could almost touch the life that was in him, his energy, his spark, his inherent dangerousness. Although he was completely unconscious of it he carried it with him like an aura, and only she could see it. Now she understood the truth in the idea of setting off on a journey like a madman, with no concern for where it might take you. This was an adventure, and it might prove to be the adventure of her life. God, she was tingling with the anticipation of her need for him. She had almost given in to it the other night, but she was glad she hadn't.

The phone rang. She knew it would be him. She stepped out of the bath and into the hall and stood there dripping on the rug. "Hi Gene," she said brightly. Maybe too brightly.

"Hi Joan, It's me, Ed."

"Yeah, I know," she said. "What's up? Couldn't you wait until the weekend?"

"Sort of. I had to make sure that Monday night wasn't a dream and that I wasn't going to wake up and find it was just a figment of my imagination."

She could picture his face as he talked. The little creases at the corner of his mouth when he smiled that killer smile of his. "Maybe you should consider talking to a psychiatrist."

He laughed. "Touché; you got me fair and square there. I just wanted to know exactly what was going to be happening at the weekend."

"Oh no, Gene. You don't get to know until the last minute. It's a surprise, remember? Just pick me up at four, as we arranged, okay?"

Now was his opportunity to get his own back. "But what should I wear?" He asked plaintively. "A man needs to know these things. You know; town or country, posh or casual?"

He had her. "Who said you were going to need clothes?"

So it was going to be like that. "You're enjoying this, aren't you? Just tell me. Warm or cool?"

"Warm, Gene. Sizzling, in fact."

He laughed again. "You are a tease doctor Arkwright, and I predict that one day it will be your undoing."

"And what day do you think that might be exactly?"

"Friday, hopefully." They both laughed.

The water evaporating from her skin was making her cold. She shivered. "Can you just hang on a minute," she asked. "You got me out of the bath and I'm standing here naked. I just need to get my dressing gown."

"I wish you hadn't told me that," he said. "Now I won't be able to get the picture of you standing talking to me naked out of my mind all night."

She was back less than a minute later, cradling the phone under her chin as she tried to comb her hair before it started to dry. "When exactly will we be back?" Ed asked. "My mate Pete is dying to meet you. He thinks I'm being all mysterious, keeping you away from him. I reckon he thinks I'm having some sort of a crisis, making the whole thing up."

Joan tugged the comb against a knot. "Well, we can't have that: we'd better put him out of his misery soon, hadn't we?"

"I thought maybe we could have dinner with Pete and his girlfriend on Sunday if we were back early enough, if that's okay."

She dropped the phone. She hated it when that happened. She put the comb down. "Sound's great," she said when she had retrieved the receiver. "What time do you think you'll be able to get away on Friday?"

"If it all goes according to plan, two at the latest. I'm getting all my paperwork up to date, and I've arranged cover for all my patients."

She felt the tingle of anticipation again, stronger this time. "Brilliant. Outpatients on Friday finishes at one, so I'll be away handy too."

"I can't wait," Edward said, and he meant it.

"Me either." She meant it too.

"See you," he said.

"Not if I see you first Gene."

"'bye then."

"'bye Gene."

18
Lives in the balance

Friday eventually arrived. Edward packed light. 'What the hell,' he thought. 'If I need anything, I can just get it when we get there, wherever "there" is.' The morning passed in slow motion. Never had he known time to dawdle so. He wondered if Joan was experiencing this same sense of being motionless in her outpatient clinic. The Friday morning review of Marwan's patients seemed never-ending, and Marwan noticed his junior seemed unusually distracted. But minute by unhurried minute the clock wound its way round to two.

Maria was in the Maple ward nursing station. There had been a minor accident. A patient had scalded himself making a cup of tea and to Maria fell the responsibility of recording it in the accident book. It was a duty she took on willingly, too willingly, some thought. It meant she could be sitting down not having to deal with patients. Any excuse to hide in the nursing station was welcome and she was known for her lengthy entries in the notes. Some said they thought she must be writing a novel, so much of her time seemed to be taken up in this way. She was so absorbed in her task she didn't hear Joan until she was standing in front of her.

Not wanting to be interrupted, Maria did not put her pen down, but tilted her head to look at Joan. As usual, she looked drained, standing with her head down and her shoulders bowed. "Hello Joan. What do you want?" Maria asked, not bothering to keep her irritation from showing.

If Joan was aware of Maria's impatience she did not react to it. "I want to speak to doctor Plant, please."

Maria looked back to the accident book and continued writing where she had left off. She did not look up as she replied. "I know he's a bit busy today. He's got the weekend off and he's trying to get everything sorted before he leaves. Is it something I can help you with?"

Joan shook her head. "I don't think so."

With a sigh Maria put her pen down. "Could you tell me what it is?"

Joan was adamant. "No. But doctor Marwan said I could speak to him any time. Please?" The tears started.

Ed was nowhere to be seen, but his bag was where he had left it in the nursing station, he had to be around somewhere. "Okay," Maria relented. "I'll bleep him for you. I'll get him to come and find you when he gets here."

Minutes later the phone rang. Maria answered. "Hello, Maple ward. Maria Sondha speaking."

She could hear Ed's tinny voice from somewhere in the hospital. "Maria, it's Ed. You bleeped me?"

"Yes. Where are you? It's Joan Archer. She's asking to see you."

"I'm in A and E. Can't she see one of the other SHOs?"

But Joan was Ed's patient. It was like he owned her; none of the other juniors would want to step in. "It's you who's got the therapeutic relationship with her Ed; I doubt she'd want to see anyone else."

"But didn't you tell her it was my week-end off and I was trying to get away early?"

"I did," Maria replied wearily, "but she was quite insistent." She paused, waiting for Ed to capitulate. He was entitled to his time off, but Maria knew that if he didn't see Joan the rest of them would have a hard time from her all week-end. It was a long shot, she knew, Ed didn't usually go much for sympathy, but it was worth a try. "She's really having a hard time, you know. She's quite distressed and she's just moping around the ward trying not to burst into tears."

"Okay. Okay. Tell her I'll come over as soon as I've finished here. Then I'm going, so don't fall for any more sob stories on my behalf, okay?"

In the orthopaedic outpatients department the phone rang. It was picked up by one of the receptionists, her voice clipped and efficient. She peered along the corridor in each direction before replying. "Doctor Arkwright? I think she might have gone. Just bear with me and I'll see if she's still here." She put the receiver onto the desk and walked out of the reception booth. Just then Joan emerged from one of the examination rooms. "Oh! Doctor Arkwright!" The receptionist called. "Phone for you." She went back into the booth and passed the receiver over the counter top.

"Hello?"

It was Edward. "Joan? It's me, Ed. Listen, I'm really sorry, but I won't be able to get away as early as I hoped. I was trying to get everything done and dusted when one of the patients insisted on seeing me. It shouldn't take too long and I'll pick you up as soon as I can."

Joan frowned. "One of the patients? Is it who I think it is?"

"Yeah. I was in A and E when the ward called me to say she's really distressed and is being very insistent on seeing me."

"Just be careful Ed. She might really be distressed, but there's always the possibility it could be attention-seeking behaviour or it might be that she's forming an attachment to you. It does happen you know."

She sensed he wasn't really listening; he was too caught up in trying to prevent his week-end from being spoiled. "Yeah, I know. I'll be careful, and I'll get away as soon as I can, okay?"

When Edward got back to the ward, Joan was waiting for him in the quiet corner. He took the chair next to hers.

He tried not to let his irritation at being delayed show. "You wanted to see me Joan?" She nodded but said nothing. "Maria told me it was pretty important?"

Very softly she said "Yes."

Joan was still not sure what she should tell him. The day that Edward had gone to the chapel with her was the only day he had been able to go. She had an intuition that their time together had been the beginning of something, and something within her was urging her to confide in him, but still she was plagued by doubt. Could she trust him - someone who didn't believe in God? As she sat there next to him, the voices were screaming at her, commanding her not to talk to him. She was trying to build up the courage to tell him the whole story of what was happening to her but the assault on her mind was implacable and trying to find the strength to gainsay the voices was so, so exhausting. But it was this more than anything that convinced her. She reasoned that the voices would try to stop her from doing what they feared the most. If she was to defeat them, she would have to do exactly what it was they were telling her *not* to; she would tell him everything.

Edward could not know the conflict that was taking place in her mind. As calmly as he could he said "Please Joan, if there was something important you needed to ask or wanted to tell me, can we get on with it? It's supposed to be my weekend off."

"I don't want to take the medication any more." That wasn't what she had meant to say, but the words were out of her mouth before she could stop them.

Edward's response was perhaps predictable. "Is that it? You made me come all the way back just to tell me you didn't want to take the medication any more?"

Silent tears started down Joan's cheeks. She made no attempt to wipe them away. "No."

Now he felt guilty. There was a box of tissues on the table between them. He pulled one out and passed it to her. "Here. I'm sorry. What's troubling you so much you had to see me?"

"You said I was mentally ill; you said if I took the medication it would make the voices go away."

He could feel the reproof in her voice, but he couldn't accept what she was implying. "That's right Joan. I said I thought you had schizophrenia, and doctor Marwan agrees with me. The medication will help to get rid of the voices."

"Well it's not fucking working!" She was angry. Probably with him, he reasoned.

He leaned forward and took one of her hands. "Not yet, Joan. But it will. It takes time. You just need to give it a chance to work. You promised me you would."

Exasperated, she pulled her hand away. "I know. But I've been on it now for nearly two weeks and all it does is make me feel worse. And what if it takes away the music as well as the voices?"

"Music?" She had never mentioned this before. "What music?"

Her tears were not from pity, but from anger and the sheer effort of defying the voices. "God's music!"

Edward was torn between being exasperated himself and gripped by what she was telling him. He had been expecting that any real breakthrough, if there were to be one, would happen in the chapel. And now, at the worst possible moment, she seemed determined to pour her soul out. "But you didn't say anything about any music before. Can you hear music now?"

She looked at him as though he was stupid. "No. Of course not."

Edward tried another tack. "So did the medication make the music go away?"

"No!" Why was he being so dense?

But Edward persisted. "And you're sure you're not hearing music now?"

Could he not see what this was costing her? "No," she whimpered.

To Edward it looked as though she was collapsing from the inside. He sensed he had missed something, but what? "What about the voices, are they still there?"

She gave a hesitant nod.

"And are they still telling you that Jesus doesn't want you any more?"

She nodded again, unable to look at him. Telling him about the music had taken all her strength and now she had no reserves left. The voices were gleeful. She had not succeeded.

Edward dithered. She had been about to tell him something important and he had mishandled it. Now she was withdrawing back into her shell. She would not tell him now. He looked at his watch. He decided to try one last time to get her to tell him, but so distracted was he by his need to get away that he did not ask the right question. "So there's no music now?"

"Not any more." She pulled her legs up to her chest and curled into a ball, rocking slowly in the chair.

There was nothing more he could do now. She had given him a tantalising glimpse that there might be something going on inside her head beside the voices. But it would have to wait. If she was hearing music it wouldn't alter the diagnosis or the treatment. He made a final attempt to reassure her. "Joan - that's what the medication is for – to take away the voices *and* the music. Okay?"

He left her there to face her tormentors alone. But he was perplexed that the medication seemed to be having no effect whatever. Picking up his bag from the nursing station he told Maria what had happened. Not that she showed any particular interest. "I've done my best," he said, "but she's not making very much sense. I just think she needs someone to sit with her for a bit, give her some sympathy. I really do have to go, okay?"

"It's fine Ed, you just go," she replied through pursed lips before settling herself back down to make another of her interminable entries, this time in Joan's nursing notes.

19
Out on the weekend

The taxi took them from Joan's flat to the station. After a short wait the train that would take them to the airport pulled in. Only at the check-in desk did Ed finally discover where he was being taken: Barcelona. He had been there before. Once on a stag night, and another time with Peter. He hadn't really been that interested in what the city had to offer apart from its bars and night life. Naturally he had pulled both times. This time would be different, he knew. Burdened only with cabin baggage they were soon through check-in and security. He realised he was ravenous. Pity there's no Vinny's diner here, Joan had teased, but joined with him in sharing a soggy burger and fries. Their flight was slightly delayed, but such was their delight in simply being in each other's company that they made light of it, and chuckled at the impatience of the other passengers at the gate. On the flight she showed him a map of where they would be staying, in a small apartment on one of the narrow streets off the *Avenida Diagonal*. Her parents were divorced, she told him, and the apartment was her dad's. He had bought it only last year, and this would be her first time there.

In the queue for immigration and on the train into the city they acted like teenagers in the first flush of love, holding hands and kissing at the slightest provocation. They were joyous and carefree and they basked in its wonderful glow.

The apartment was not in any of the tourist areas, and was reached by climbing a steep *carrer*, walking all the way from the metro stop. Having to find their own way was part of the adventure. It was on a second floor overlooking the street below, and they tumbled up worn narrow steps with their senses so heightened with anticipation that every detail was imprinted on their memory. Although the lock was fiddly, Joan insisted that she would be the one to open it. They were drunk with joy and laughed without restraint at her clumsy efforts. At last the door swung open and they fell in.

It was Joan that instigated their love-making. No sooner were they through the door than she locked her arms round his neck and kissed him, hungry for him. Giggling they raced round the apartment until they found the bedroom. She pulled him in, unbuttoning his shirt, fingers fumbling at their task in her haste. It was Edward who suggested they take it more slowly. But her need had risen within her so acutely that to have waited any longer would surely have been a sin.

"But . . . I thought you wanted candles, and oil and . . ." he tried to say.

Her breath was already coming in gasps. "That can wait," she said. "For now, I just want to shag your brains out."

Afterwards they lay entwined on the bed, letting the evening air cool their skin, wanting to preserve every precious moment as though it were their last, not their first. They were truly one flesh now and each of them knew it, and, for the first time in their lives, understood the mystery of it. The peace and serenity of that knowledge gave them a power they had never experienced before. No matter that the rest of the world might rage at their door, they were safe within and always would be.

Ed was up early the next morning and left Joan sleeping. He couldn't explain what he was feeling. He only knew he had never felt so good. It was a feeling of completeness, of all the pieces now being in place. It was power and beauty and confidence and exhilaration and . . . He was running out of words to describe his emotions. Was this love? If it was, it was glorious.

He ran down the hill and into the square at the bottom. It was empty. The cafés lining its sides were closed. He thought he remembered seeing a small supermarket and headed off to find it. He returned loaded with orange juice, coffee and bread, marmalade, apricots and peaches, cheese and ham, and – most importantly – a bottle of champagne. Candles and oil would have to wait until later.

*

On Maple ward, the phone rang. It was the OT. Was Joan Archer there? She should have come down for her occupational therapy session. Maria put her head out of the nursing station. Viv was there talking to Amy, one of the SHOs. Maria didn't get on too well with Viv – she was one of those nurses who didn't take kindly to colleagues who didn't pull their weight, and over the years she had made a number of remarks about Maria and her 'novel writing'. Bitch. Maria was in a sour mood and not the least bit interested in having to go running after a patient. But on second thoughts she decided it would be easier to look for Joan herself rather than ask Viv to do it. She found Joan in the corridor between the ward and the occupational therapy department. She had stopped in one of the chairs that stood in pairs dotted around the unit, holding her head in her hands.

"Joan?" Maria called as soon as she saw her. When she didn't get a response, she came closer and shouted more sharply. "Joan! You're supposed to be in OT." It wasn't uncommon for Maria to raise her voice to uncooperative patients, but today she seemed more testy than usual.

"Can't," Joan protested weakly.

Maria had had enough of this nonsense. "No, Joan," she said, sounding like a school mistress talking to a pupil who was being impertinent, "what you really mean is 'won't'. Well we're not having it." She gripped Joan's upper arm so tightly that the pain of it made her wince. "You're going to OT whether you like it or not. It's for your own good, understand?"

*

She was still asleep when he got back. He put some coffee on and got back into bed with her. He woke her by repeatedly kissing the nape of her neck. She stretched languorously, like a cat, before turning to kiss him. "Hello, you," she said, smiling. "How did you know I liked that?"

"It's no big deal," he replied. "Everybody likes it."

They made love again, slowly exploring each other, delighting in their discoveries, learning about their new state of being.

They took the metro to *Catalunya*. Ed was impressed that the train was air-conditioned. They climbed the steps to the street and strolled hand in hand down *Las Ramblas* towards the sea, admiring the performance artists in their garish costumes before turning left into an ancient street that led to a grand square with colonnades on each side. For the rest of the morning they explored the old city, finding the market and the cathedral, which Joan said she thought a little disappointing, not so much a sanctuary of Christian worship, rather a setting for an *auto da fé*. It was creepy rather than comforting, and she did not want to linger there. After lunch at a street side café they took the funicular railway up the hill to the Joan Miro institute. Ed had never had much time for modern art, dismissing it as the kind of rubbish that most kids could do, but now, for the first time, he was able to experience something of the poetry and emotion in Miro's work. It might have had something to do with his heightened emotional awareness, but he sensed it helping him to become aware of the change that was taking place in him.

Later in the afternoon they imitated the citizens of Barcelona and slept, waking in the early evening as the city started to stir again after its siesta. When they awoke they lay in bed together listening to the sounds of the neighbourhood: the motorcycles roaring in the street below, children laughing, crying, their parents sometimes shouting; radios playing in nearby apartments – the sounds of salsa and samba and awful Spanish pop music, no longer awful: for them it had taken on a new significance. At the bottom of the hill was a small square – more of a triangle really, with trees around its edge, and a news stand, the young men posing, swigging bottles of San Miguel, cigarettes drooping from James Dean lips, the old men playing backgammon, and the local senoras sitting on the benches that stood round the edges swapping gossip, keeping a watchful eye on their children. It was a magical place to be. So exotic, so rare, so far removed from normal existence: so full of life. Complete; for a while at least.

*

It was nearing the end of Maria's shift. It had been a long day and her mood had not improved with its passing. It suddenly occurred to her that she hadn't seen Joan since marching her to the OT room. But that had been hours ago, where could she have got to since then?

Amy Pierce was on the other side of the nursing station, a folder open before her, reading through the hospital policy on tranquillisation for disturbed patients. She had read it before, but its complicated flow charts never seemed to penetrate.

"You haven't seen Joan Archer have you?" Maria asked.

Amy stopped to think for a moment. "That's the patient Ed asked me to keep an eye on, isn't it?"

"Yes. I haven't seen her since she went down to OT."

Amy closed the folder. "You're sure she's not on the ward?"

"Pretty sure."

"Do you think we ought to check?" Together they did the rounds of the ward. Joan was nowhere to be seen. "Could she have gone down to reception to get a paper or something?"

Maria shook her head. "I doubt it, she's never done that before, and anyway, she's not supposed to leave the ward without permission."

Amy Pierce reached for the phone. "I s'pose we ought to start phoning around to see if anyone has seen her. I'll start with reception."

It was Tony who organised the search of the hospital. Fortunately for them there were only two high dependency patients on the unit, but still he resented having to send his staff out on such a task when it could have been avoided – should have been avoided. He still thought that allowing Joan to continue going to the chapel after the way she had acted up was nothing short of indulging her. Bloody doctors. They were never the ones who had to pick up the pieces when things went wrong. Typical that Ed had gone away for the weekend. If he had been around, he would have asked him to come in, day off or no day off.

Joan was in the chapel. She was at peace, giving grateful thanks for the miracle that banished the voices while she was in here. She had suffered hell for most of the morning. Maria telling her that there were not enough staff on duty for someone to go with her to the chapel had been the signal for the voices to wreak havoc in her consciousness, leaving her almost incapable of coherent thought. Occupational therapy had been a waste of time. Art therapy, the OT had called it, giving Joan paper, an easel, a box containing water-colour paints and a brush. Joan had stood before her easel and daubed three angry brush-strokes of black paint on it. The OT had clucked her tongue and told Joan she didn't think she was trying. Joan almost despaired. She wanted to tell the stupid vacant woman that she was trying to show her what it was like to have three demons tormenting your every waking minute. Her picture represented three jagged gashes in the fabric of her existence through which every vestige of her being was leaching away. Soon there would be nothing left of her, only the devils who would claim residence of her empty shell.

The OT should have gone back to the ward with her, but Joan said she could find her own way. She had had an idea. She would stay in the chapel for only a few minutes; nobody would know she had even been in here. That had been about four hours ago, though by now she had lost track of the time. After this prolonged period of respite she felt almost normal again, and began to think about visiting that night. Caroline had said she was going out tonight, so it would just be her mum and dad. She felt so sorry for them. Dad's illness gave her mum enough to cope with without this, but there was nothing she could do about it, not while she was in here. She should never have gone back home, but her mother would never have understood if she had gone elsewhere. Dad's illness had affected him badly, leaving him almost incapable of making a decision, but her mum was strong. Joan wished she had some of her mum's inner strength herself. The more time she had to think in this sacred place, the more she became convinced that the voices really were manifestations of evil, sent by the Devil, and permitted by the Lord as a test. She knew she would come out of it stronger than when she went in, if only she could keep her resolve and hold onto her faith. She knew that if only she had the courage and the fortitude to command them to be gone, then it would be so. But that was the problem. They were so sure of themselves, so contemptuous of her puny will that she knew she was powerless, that it would take some external power to banish them.

But that was then, not now. Now she was wrapped in the perfect bliss of her Saviour, and she was safe. Over the hours she had been in the chapel, the music had come and gone several times. She wondered about that too. There was no doubt in her mind that it was a miracle, but why had it been granted to her? God's ways were mysterious, but sometimes faith was not quite enough. If only she was able to understand what it was that was happening to her, what God's purpose in it was.

On the ward it finally occurred to Tony where Joan would be. "Has anyone checked the chapel?"

Maria was the first out of the door, seething. She had been made to look a fool, and that was something that she would not tolerate.

*

That evening they retraced their steps to *Las Ramblas*, exploring more of the narrow streets on either side. They found a shop that among a cornucopia of tourist t-shirts and Gaudi figurines sold candles. Ed bought a dozen. Then into a bazaar where the shelves were filled with birth stones and quartz and other new-age paraphernalia including a whole range of aromatic oils. They even managed to find patchouli. As it grew dark, the city took on a new identity, putting on its glamour like a prima donna readying herself for a gala performance. Like flowers opening their petals the street lights on their elegant wrought-iron pedestals blossomed slowly to become brilliant oases of light which attracted people like a full moon attracts moths. Along the entire length of the *Ramblas* the multitudes were promenading, enjoying the sights, enjoying being part of this exquisite vibrant migration even if only for one night before falling back to earth and whatever travails tomorrow might bring. Never before had either Ed or Joan been aware of this organic life and its seething pulsating force pumping its vitality through their veins, but now they were so much a part of it they were reluctant to leave. In one of the restaurants pitched along the central island they shared paella and a bottle of wine simply watching the crowds surging around them, until, sated in their hunger for both food and this extraordinary existence, they took the metro back to the apartment.

*

The lack of dignity of it notwithstanding, Maria practically ran to the chapel. She was easily the first there. She wrenched open the door. "Joan!" She yelled. "What the hell do you think you're doing?" Without waiting for a reply she strode forward and yanked Joan to her feet.

Joan pulled away from her. "Don't touch me!"

"Have you got any idea of the rouble you've caused you silly girl? We've had staff looking all over the hospital for you!"

Joan rubbed her arm. It was still sore from the morning. Warily she glared at Maria. "Doctor Marwan said I could come to the chapel every day."

It did not occur to Maria that Joan was talking normally. She was so angry at being made to look stupid that she responded without noticing that Joan was able to converse without having to fight the voices. "Only if there was someone available to come with you. You knew that."

But Joan was not having this. "And today there was nobody, was there? Why should I have to miss out on coming to the chapel just because there was no-one to supervise me?"

"You know very well why. It's not because you need to be supervised, it's to make sure you don't come to any harm."

Joan screamed. A combination of frustration and rage. "For God's sake! Just listen to yourself you stupid cow! What harm could I possibly come to here? It's the one place in this dump where I feel safe and secure. It's the only place I get any peace."

Maria was not used to being confronted in this way. Disturbed patients who were incoherent in their thoughts and actions she had been trained to deal with, but how should she react to a patient who, though angry, appeared to be rational? She felt uneasy. Where were the others? Surely they should have been here by now? She tried to impose some authority on the situation. "This is not the right place for this conversation, Joan," she said.

"And I suppose the right place is on the ward, is that it?" Joan asked, her derision at Maria's denseness almost tangible. "On the ward where I'm so consumed by the voices that I can scarcely remember my own name?"

Maria licked her lips, her anxiety starting to show. It was a commonly held belief that patients who became temporarily lucid could be unpredictable, even dangerous. "You have to come back to the ward. Now."

Joan shook her head. "And if I don't want to come, you're going to make me – is that it?"

Maria thought she could hear footsteps outside. Her voice took on a hectoring tone. "I don't want to have to do that Joan, but if that's the way you want it, yes."

Joan had not wanted to become angry, but Maria had taken her by surprise. Now was her only chance to reason with the woman. With an effort she controlled herself. She held her hands out, palms upwards in a gesture of supplication. "Look Maria," she said. "You can see how it is for me down here. I'm normal again. The voices have gone. As soon as I step one foot out of that door I step back into my own private version of Hell. You saw I wasn't doing anything I shouldn't be. I was just having some quiet time to myself. Please don't force me to go back. Please."

Maria was uncertain how to respond to this sudden turn about. "I can't. I can't take that responsibility. If anything should happen . . ."

Joan lost her patience. "What could possibly happen you stupid woman?"

This outburst brought Maria back to her senses. What had she been thinking of? There was nothing to be negotiated until they were back on the ward. The arrival of Tony and two other nurses lent her voice the authority it had been lacking. "That's enough! If you won't come of your own accord we'll remove you forcibly. Now, Joan; are you going to come of your own accord?"

Joan was incredulous. She had heard stories of how patients were ill-treated in mental institutions, but she had never really believed them. Slowly she shook her head. "No."

*

Joan awoke. It was still dark. Slowly she waited for her senses to become attuned to their surroundings. She was in bed – with a man – and the air was rich with the smells of candles and aromatic oil. She could hear quiet breathing next to her, and moved her body slightly until she was cradled in his warmth. For a while she allowed herself to luxuriate in the memories of the previous evening. Feeding each other paella in the midst of a seething mass of humanity as if they were the only ones actually aware of the joy of their existence, and then racing each other up the *carrer* after getting off the metro – he with the handicap of having to try and leapfrog the garbage bins that stood like statues on the street corners. Then they had done everything – and more – that they had talked about on that night – had it really been less than a week ago?

She smiled at the memory of the disappointment on Ed's face when she had made him go home after getting him to promise so much. But it had been worth the waiting. Now she was wrapped in the bliss of love and nothing in her life had ever been so perfect.

Very lightly she ran the tips of her fingers up his arm, along his shoulder and down onto his chest. He stiffened and stretched. He turned to face her and caressed the length of her back letting his fingers rest on the cleft of her buttocks. "Hi," he said.

"Hi yourself, Gene." Her eyes were smiling. In little more than a week her life had been transformed. Something had happened. She was his, and he was hers. She was certain there would never be any going back. Why it had happened she did not know, but it had happened all the same. He pulled her to him and kissed her, revelling in the touch of her skin on his from lip to toe. She was eager for him again and her fingers pushed down to his groin until they found the expectant surge of his penis. She stroked its tip between her thumb and forefinger.

"I seem to remember," he said, "that I made good on my promise to give you oral sex until you begged me to stop."

She loved the way his lips crinkled at the corners when he smiled. God, he was so fucking good looking. "So you did, Gene," she admitted, heart thumping at the memory.

"I wondered if you might like to repay the favour."

"What's in it for me?" She asked, teasing.

He pushed her back onto the bed and took a nipple into his mouth, sucking firmly. At the same time, he pushed a hand between her legs, and brushed her clitoris feather-light with the tip of his finger. "How's that for starters?"

A shiver of expectation ran through her belly. How did he know how to do that? Ever practical, she glanced at the clock. They had plenty of time. "That'll do for now," she told him, "But there had better be more where that came from." Now it was her turn to push him back. She had never thought much about men's penises before, but his, she realised, was perfect. She pulled back his foreskin and licked the end. Slowly she ran her tongue round the ridge before taking him fully into her mouth. 'Should she?' She thought. 'Why not?' Quickly she lifted her body across his to make a sixty-nine. Then she resumed her task, confident that he would take the hint.

*

Maria was on the early shift. On a Sunday. Still, she was off tomorrow. Ed would be back. She hoped he'd had a shitty weekend off after all the trouble his patient had caused. Tony had given her a right bollocking for not noticing that Joan had been gone for so long. Okay, so she *had* been in the chapel; but what if she hadn't? She could have been anywhere, and saying you were short-staffed was little more than hiding behind an excuse. She wondered what had really happened when Ed had seen Joan on the Friday afternoon when he had been so eager to get away. It would not have surprised her if Ed had told Joan that if there was nobody available to take her to the chapel, it would be okay for her to sneak off and spend some time there anyway, as long as she came back before she was missed. He must have done, she reasoned. Joan would never have thought of it by herself, not in her state. Well, his little plan has misfired, she told herself, and now it was highly unlikely that Joan Archer would ever be allowed to go back.

On Sundays the patients were usually allowed to lie in, which meant that they would be woken at eight rather than six-thirty. Maria decided she would look in on Joan, and see if she couldn't find some reason to wake her early. She didn't need to. Although she was still lying in her bed, Joan was awake, silent tears streaming down her face. She looked like she hadn't slept for hours. Maria was a little surprised by this. They'd had to sedate Joan yesterday to bring her back from the chapel, and Maria thought this should have had an additive effect with her regular medication, and that she would have slept the night through comfortably. Her parents had been disappointed and concerned to find Joan unconscious during visiting, and had asked that they be called when she woke up. Maria wondered (not a little spitefully) whether she should call them now.

"Are you awake, Joan?" She asked.

Joan had been semi-conscious when she had been taken out of the chapel, but now she was fully awake. It felt as if she had been awake for hours, though in all probability it hadn't been very long. That she felt no vestige of the sedative effects of the drugs she had been given was due to one thing. The voices were exacting a terrible revenge for her escape into the chapel, and had seemed to insinuate themselves into the corners of her mind as she was waking so that now they were at the very forefront, shouting and shrieking at her with all the vile hateful poison they had at their command.

"Joan, are you awake?" Maria repeated crossly. She could see Joan was awake, and assumed, wrongly, that Joan was being deliberately uncooperative.

For days Joan had been finding it increasingly difficult to do anything of any purpose. Each act of defiance against the voices required a major effort of will, and each one had to be paid for. She found she could use anger to force the voices aside temporarily, but that the effort required necessarily meant that such respites were short-lived.

Maria shook her roughly. "Joan! Come on! If you're awake you should get up."

Now the anger managed to break through to the surface. "And why the fuck would I want to do that?" She shouted back. "What's the point? What's the fucking point? Why don't you just fuck off and leave me alone?"

Susan and Cathy were also on the early shift. They were having a quiet cup of tea in the lull before the day got going. They heard Joan shouting. "What's that?" Susan asked.

"I bet it's Maria with Joan Archer," Cathy said. "I heard she got a right telling off yesterday. I wouldn't put it past her to take it out on Joan."

Susan put her cup down. "Not while I'm in charge." She went in search of Maria.

Maria was nowhere to be seen when Susan reached Joan's bed. Joan looked worse than ever. Susan hadn't seen her for the past two days; when was the medication going to start working? Couldn't Marwan see that it was having no effect? Even Ed was starting to come round to that conclusion. Privately Susan thought Joan should have been given something stronger – perhaps one of the newer drugs – but phenylatrazine was Marwan's favourite, and no doubt he would have said 'no' if anything else had been suggested.

Joan was vaguely aware that Maria had gone and someone else had taken her place. The voices seemed to be able to sense the effort that it now cost Joan to respond when she was spoken to and were pleased by it. *'Very soon, now, Joan,'* said one.

'Very soon,' echoed another.

These two voices paled before the sibilant whisper of the frightening voice. *'You will be mine,'* it said. *'And they can do nothing – nothing – to help you.'*

This last statement registered with Joan. 'No,' she told herself. 'I will not give in to them. My saviour will rescue me, I know he will.' She tried to summon the will to pray. Two words were all she could manage. "Please, Lord," she said under her breath.

Susan could hear that Joan was saying something, but could not catch what it was.

"Are you alright, Joan?" She asked. "Can I get you anything?"

Joan shook her head and closed her eyes. She hoped that Susan would leave her alone. She did. But what the voice had said was still with her. *'They can do nothing to help you.'* It was right. What had they done? All they had done was give her medication. Medication and so-called art therapy. It hadn't worked. It had made her feel worse. Much worse. It made her feel tired all the time, and it was a constant struggle to think. She had told Edward she didn't want to take it any more. Well now she had made her mind up. She would take no more, and then they could see whether she got any worse. She couldn't see how she could. She was possessed. The voices she heard came from Hell. She was convinced that the evil one that spoke in a whisper was Satan himself. Drugs couldn't exorcise demonic possession. There were only two avenues open to her, she reasoned. The first was to take shelter within the protective boundaries of a sacred place. But, blessed relief though it was, that protection could only be temporary. The other was exorcism. But how could she arrange for that to happen? Nobody believed her. Everyone thought she was mad. They believed the doctors who said she had schizophrenia. But what did they know? How did they come to be the ones to dismiss the power of evil in the world and replace it with their own conceited theories? How could any puny human invention like *medication* replace the dreadful power of bell, book and candle? But, she told herself, one thing at a time. First she would stop taking the drugs. Then she would figure out how she would get an exorcism. She would find a way. Jesus would show her the way.

Though she was unable to go back to sleep, Joan kept her eyes closed and Maria did not disturb her again until eight o'clock when she came into Joan's bay with the breakfast trolley. Two of the beds were empty – their usual occupants had gone home on week-end leave. The woman in the third bed rarely ate breakfast, and today was no exception. She helped herself to a mug of tea and heaped three sugars into it.

"What would *you* like Joan? Rice crispies or cornflakes?" Maria lifted up a box of each. "It's the biggest decision you'll have to make all day," she taunted her.

*

Packing one's bags after a break is usually something of an anticlimax, but for Ed and Joan it was the opposite. They were conscious that it represented a new beginning for each of them, an adventure, a journey where their destination was as yet undiscovered. They ate a hasty breakfast and quickly cleaned the apartment, putting the bedding into the washing machine. Joan's dad said a housekeeper would take care of anything they missed. At the airport they strolled round the shops looking for something to take back to their respective departments. Both decided on chocolate, hoping that it wouldn't melt en route. Their flight was on time. They would be home late that afternoon, in time for dinner with Peter and Karen. Both were looking forward to it. Joan was eager to meet Ed's friend and Ed wanted to show her off. If Peter was the only real friend he had, she was the only woman he'd ever found love with.

*

Sundays were quiet days on the psychiatric unit. Sometimes as many as half of the patients went home on leave, there were no ward rounds, no occupational therapy, no planned admissions, and there were two sessions for visiting – three hours in the afternoon, and two in the evening. The usual routine was suspended. The idea was to make a slow day pass as agreeably as possible for both patients and staff. When Maria had finished the rounds with the breakfast trolley Susan and Cathy gave out the medicines. When they got to Joan, she put her plan into action. When she was handed the medication, with a supreme effort of concentration she managed to palm it and swallowed nothing but water. She waited until they were in the next bay then went into the bathroom and flushed the pill down the toilet. After that she went to the day room hoping to catch the Sunday service on the radio. She was disappointed. The hi-fi unit that usually lived there had developed a fault and had been taken away for maintenance. Nobody knew when it would be back. Stoically Joan stayed where she was, enduring the venom of the voices, which were now gloating at the absence of the radio.

There was another radio in the nursing station, though its presence was unofficial. Other than at week-ends and during visiting it was silent. At nine Maria announced she would be taking her break in the canteen. Cathy and Susan exchanged glances. "Bit early for a break, isn't it?" Cathy said, voice hushed.

"Oh just let her go," Susan replied. "There's nothing doing here, she might as well be miserable by herself rather than spoil our day as well."

The local station they were listening to had a Sunday morning request show called 'Endless Love'. The show was a monument to slushy sentimentality but they listened anyway – mostly out of habit – it was what they did on Sunday mornings. The show's presenter called himself DJ Mike, and, in a strangely compelling if tacky style, he broadcast the hopes and aspirations and sometimes the woes of the lovelorn to whoever cared to listen.

Susan had an idea to break the monotony. "Cath, I've just had a thought. Why don't you phone in a request?"

"Me? Who for?"

"You know, you and the old Bill."

"The old Bill?"

Susan gave her friend a playful push. "Duh . . . Tim, nice but dim?"

Cathy was appalled at the prospect. "Put in a request for a love song for Tim? Are you kidding? His mates would take the piss forever. He'd never forgive me."

Susan played all innocent. "Well if you won't, I think I will."

Cathy looked aghast at Susan. What had gotten into her? "You? Who for?"

"Ed, of course." It was what she had intended all along. The idea had germinated shortly after the show began and had been growing in her mind, convincing her that if nothing else it would be a good laugh.

But Cathy could see only the down side. Did Susan want the whole unit to know that she was throwing herself at Ed? "Sue, I think that's a very bad idea. You went out with him once, and he's never asked you out again, has he? You know what he's like – Mr. 'one night stand', Mr. 'not ready for commitment'. The best thing you can do is to forget him: he's already forgotten you. Trust me."

But Susan was not deterred. "I just want him to know that I'm still interested, that I'm not going to give up so easily."

"And what makes you think he'll even be listening to this drivel?"

"I'd be surprised if he was. What I'm banking on is that someone will tell him."

Cathy couldn't believe what she was hearing. "Why don't you just jump on him in the corridor and pull him into the linen room if you're that desperate?"

Susan smiled. She knew Cathy's advice was well-intentioned, but she wasn't listening. "I'm not desperate," she assured her, "just determined." She picked up the phone and dialled the number.

A production assistant took the call. She took a note of the track Susan wanted to request and told her she would be called back in about fifteen minutes. Cathy still could not believe that Susan could be so stupid and absented herself, deciding that the treatment room needed a good clean, something that would occupy her for at least an hour. She did not want to witness the exchange between nurse and DJ.

Susan had been told to turn the radio off to prevent feedback. Anyone in the vicinity of the nursing station would have heard a rather odd one-sided telephone conversation.

It sounded odd even to Susan, who had the distinct impression that she was being talked about rather than talked to. First the production assistant told her that DJ Mike would be the next voice she would hear, then, in an overly loud, overly familiar voice she heard "And on the line we've got Susan, who's a nurse, is that right?"

She had often wondered at people who got tongue-tied when interviewed in similar circumstances. Now she hoped it would not happen to her. "Yes Mike," she answered.

"And is it Susan or Sue?"

"It's Sue – to my friends."

Now came the inevitable "Can I be your friend Sue?"

You'll have to do better than that, she thought. "Maybe . . . If you play my request."

"That's what we're here for," he assured her. His voice was too jolly, too friendly for this time on a Sunday morning. It wasn't so bad listening to it when it was just on in the background, she realised, but actually being part of it, now she was not so sure of herself. But it was not DJ Mike's style to give his victims time to think. "Tell us a bit about yourself, Sue. What exactly do you do? Where do you work?"

"I work at St. Peter's hospital, in the psychy unit."

The DJ's voice took on a wary tone. "Psychy? Is that Psychiatry? Isn't that a bit scary? Don't you have to deal with violent crazy people?"

Susan hated it when people tried to sensationalise mental health. "No, Mike," she said, her voice firm. She hoped she wouldn't come across too much like she was preaching. "It's not at all like that these days. Most people who have a psychiatric problem are scared and lonely. They'd no more think of being violent than you or me. Violence can sometimes happen, but as a matter of fact you're more likely to be attacked by a member of your own family than by a person with a mental illness."

Still he tried to trivialise it. "You've obviously met some of my family! Scary! But seriously, that sort of puts it into some sort of perspective, doesn't it? So tell me Sue, why is it that we all associate violence with mental illness?"

Susan thought for a moment. "I think it's because whenever a tragic incident does happen, the press blow it up out of all proportion. That might sell papers, but it doesn't paint a sympathetic or even true picture of people who have a mental illness. That's why people with a mental illness are so stigmatised and why so many of them don't want to admit they're mentally ill or even talk about it."

She had evidently gone too far. DJ Mike did not want to hear any more of that. She could almost see him in the studio miming a yawn to his producer. It was too depressing. But his "Blimey! Well folks, how about that?" Showed no sign of it. "Tune into DJ Mike and get educated as well as entertained!" He continued. "Thanks for that Sue. Okay! Well, who do you want to dedicate your request to?"

She took a quick breath. "I want to dedicate a song to one of the doctors who works here."

The DJ continued in the same inane way. "Doctors and nurses eh? Always wanted to play that game, but it never quite worked for me. So what's his name, this lucky doctor?"

"Edward. Edward Plant."

"And is there anything you want to say to doctor Plant?"

Here goes, she thought, crossing her fingers as she spoke. "I just wanted to let him know that I had a great time when we went out the other day, and that I'd like to do it again some time."

"And is there any particular song you'd like?"

"When will I see you again?"

With a click the line went dead. A second later the production assistant was back on thanking her for calling in to 'Endless Love'.

Only the show's listeners heard the rest of Sue's request as the DJ's vacuous voice carried on. "Cool. And here we have it, a dedication from nurse Sue at St. Peter's hospital to doctor Edward Plant – if you're listening, doctor Plant – it's the Three Degrees with 'When will I see you again?'"

20
Trust

For the first time since being admitted, Joan was looking forward to visiting. The medication was starting to wear off and she didn't feel half so drowsy, though her increasing alertness meant she was more acutely aware of the voices. She had been careful to conceal her thoughts from them, they would have become incandescent if they'd had an inkling of what she intended. She caught herself smiling at that. Wasn't the Devil already incandescent? She would find out soon enough. At two o'clock the visitors started to arrive. Her parents were first in, anxious because of yesterday's episode. Her mum was expecting Joan to be withdrawn and vague, and was pleasantly surprised to see her looking a little better. After a brief hug Joan took them down to the quiet corner. She did not intend that their conversation would be overheard.

"Do you think Father James would visit me tonight, if you asked him?" She said. No sooner were the words spoken than the voices renewed their onslaught. With a great effort she pushed them to the back of her mind.

"I don't know love," her mother replied. "Why do you want to see him?"

Joan closed her eyes. *'Concentrate!'* she told herself. "Mum, I can't keep this up for very long, the voices are giving me hell, and soon I won't be able to concentrate. But I need to ask Father James about having an exorcism."

"Exorcism?" Sean exclaimed.

Joan took a fierce grip on his hand. "Dad! I don't want anyone to hear, alright?" She jerked her head towards the nursing station. "If they knew what I was planning they would just put a stop to it."

"But why do you want to talk to Father James about an exorcism?" He hissed.

"Isn't it obvious?" She frowned, her forehead creasing with the effort of ignoring the voices. "Listen," she continued, "I've been taking their medication for two weeks and it hasn't done a thing. They say I'm mentally ill and I have to wait for the medication to work. But I know I'm not mentally ill, I'm possessed.

If I was mentally ill, I wouldn't be able to talk to you like this, would I?"

Bernadette reached for her daughter's hand. "Joan love, it's wonderful that you're able to talk to us normally again, but you have to admit you have been very ill this past couple of weeks. Maybe the reason you're feeling better is because the medication is starting to work?"

Joan shook her head. "No mum. It was the medication that made me worse. The staff here don't know yet, but I stopped taking it, and that's when I started to feel better. The voices are there, but I've learned I can keep them penned in for short periods of time, if I'm angry or if I can concentrate hard enough. It was the medication that affected my concentration." She closed her eyes, breathing hard as if in great pain. "I can't hold them off for much longer. Just promise me you'll ask Father James, then stay with me for as long as you can. I won't be much company, but just knowing you're here is a greater comfort than you can know."

"Of course we'll ask Father James," Bernadette said. "As soon as we get home."

"Thanks be to God." She let go. It was as if someone had pulled a plug. Joan's eyes rolled up and she collapsed backwards into her chair.

For the next two and a half hours she said nothing, but occasionally squeezed her mother's hand. When visiting was over she roused herself sufficiently to accompany her parents to the exit, but could say nothing. They hugged as if she were about to embark on the most dangerous journey of her life.

By unspoken consent her parents said nothing until Bernadette had driven the car past the hospital gates.

"Shall we go home first?" She asked.

All through this ordeal Sean had felt like a helpless spectator His little girl was in trouble so deep he didn't know how he could help her. Now for the first time he could see clearly what needed to be done. "Let's not," he said. "We'll go straight to see Father James."

"Shouldn't we phone first?" Bernadette objected. "What if he's busy?"

"He'll see us," Sean insisted. "Christ, all the years we've been going to that feckin' church, it's the least he can do."

"Sean!" She scolded him, but did not disagree.

When Sean Archer had come over from Ireland all those years ago, he had been a devil-may-care harum-scarum teenager. Though he was under age he talked his way into a job in a bar in Liverpool and for two years enjoyed everything the city had to offer It was great craic, but when a pal suggested they go down to the Smoke Sean had gone with him without a second thought. If he had thought Liverpool was big compared with his home in Drogheda, it was like a peanut next to London. For teenagers on the razz, it was perfect. A foreman at one of the sites where he got work took him to the Kilburn rugby club, and he became one of its star players with a reputation for being completely fearless (or was it brainless?) in the tackle. The combination of heavy labour, the gym and the free-flowing Guinness had finally put some weight on him. He had no qualifications, but then again he had enough money and virtually no responsibilities: in London the craic was mighty.

Then he met Bernadette. He thought her the loveliest thing he had ever laid eyes on. A friend had brought her to the club after a game one Saturday and he had been smitten. Little did he know then how his pal Brendan had played Cupid to bring them together. At first, he thought Bernadette had not been convinced that he was such a catch. As he was to discover, she had a gift of being able to weigh people up in moments, and she was never wrong. She must have seen something in him, because for the next two years they went everywhere together. But that didn't mean she was sleeping with him. That wasn't going to happen until after they were married And she had no intention of marrying him until he had better prospects. That meant a qualification and a proper career.

It said much about his feelings for Bernadette that during the three years it took him to qualify as an electrician, he never tried it on with her. This gave them plenty of time to save for the wedding which happened in riotous Irish style, with his family coming over from Ireland and taking an instant liking to his new in-laws.

Shortly after a job had come up with the electricity board and they had moved out of London. They had been here ever since.

James O'Hanlon had been a curate in the parish then, had gone abroad to spend some years in the missions, but, when the incumbent fell ill unexpectedly, he had returned to the Sacred Heart and there he had stayed. He thought of Sean and Bernadette as more than just parishioners, they were almost family, and he and Sean had enjoyed many a pint at the church social club watching the rugby before going back to the meal that Bernadette had prepared for them. Even so he was surprised to find them knocking at the presbytery door that afternoon to ask if he would visit Joan. His first reaction had been to say he would be more than glad to, and that he would bring her the Sacrament, but then they told him about Joan's request, and his heart went cold.

Exorcism. The very word brought dread. For Catholics it was nothing less than an open acknowledgement of the presence and power of Satan in the world. He had once heard a bishop preaching at an ecumenical service. "The Devil's greatest achievement," he had said, "would be to convince us that he does not exist." How right he was. But that did not mean that he expected to be confronted by his evil presence so directly. He was not sure he was up to the task. Anyway, exorcisms could not be performed without the direct permission of the bishop, and he wondered how easy that would be to obtain. But he would try. He owed it to Sean and Bernadette – and to Joan - to do at least that.

He invited them to stay in the presbytery until it was time to return to the hospital. They couldn't think of anything to say to each other, so he suggested they go into the church to pray. A single candle was burning in a red glass lantern, its light flickering before the statue of the Sacred Heart. "This is the spot Joan always liked to pray," he told them. "Maybe this is where we should pray too." He led them in saying the Lord 's Prayer and a decade of the rosary, but prayer brought little comfort. He felt for them. After all that Sean had been through, now this. Was Joan really possessed or was she mentally ill? The doctors had seemed pretty convinced according to what he had heard. He would have to get some help. The bishop would be able to put him in touch with a priest trained in identifying cases of possession and in performing the rite of exorcism. In the end it was in God's hands.

Joan was pitifully happy to see Father James. Despite his entreaties being added to those of Joan and her parents she was not allowed to visit the chapel, even if they went with her, so they settled on the quiet corner again. The priest laid his hand on Joan's head saying "I absolve you of your sins, in the name of the Father and of the Son and of the Holy Spirit." Then he gave her a communion wafer. Joan was grateful to receive the Sacrament, but her hopes that it would exert a calming effect on the voices came to nothing. If anything, the voices took their assault on her will to new heights. They were determined to prevent any meaningful conversation taking place. They reviled Joan, cursed Father James and poured scorn on the worry shown by Sean and Bernadette. But despite remaining passive since her efforts earlier in the day, Joan thought that without the effects of the medication to hamper her she was better able to defy them, for a while, at least, and she was building up her resolve once more.

"About the question of exorcism, Joan," the priest began. "It's not that it can't be done, but first we have to get permission from the bishop, and then we have to find a priest who's properly qualified."

"Not you, Father?" She asked.

He shook his head. "I'm afraid not." He wondered if it would have been more honest simply to say 'I'm afraid.' "And there's also the question of the doctors. If they insist you are mentally ill, legally we have very little power to gainsay them."

"What if I discharge myself?" She countered.

"It's not that easy. If you've been detained under one of the sections of the Mental Health Act, you can't leave without their permission, and you won't get that unless they think you're getting better."

Joan gave a short bitter laugh. "How would they know? They might think they have a monopoly on mental illness, but they know nothing about possession. I'll bet they won't even acknowledge it as a possibility." She had to pause for a minute or so to concentrate on driving the voices back. Her breathing was laboured. Her mother moved forward as if to comfort her but she held up her hand to ward her off. "I'm alright," She insisted. She opened her eyes. "How soon could you get an answer from the bishop?" She asked.

"I'm sorry Joan, I just don't know. A few days I should think, even supposing the doctors give their blessing, which I doubt."

By now the onslaught of the voices was like a physical pain. She could not hold out much longer. "Promise me . . ." She started to speak but had to stop, screwing up her eyes with pain or effort, possibly both. Her knuckles were white. "Promise me you will ask," she said, forcing the words out.

"I do promise Joan. You can trust me on that."

"I do Father. Trust you, that is."

*

Edward had phoned for a taxi and now they were waiting for it to arrive. They were stood just inside the porch at the entrance to his building. It looked like rain, but they didn't care.

"You sure you can't stay?" Ed asked, stroking her hair.

She smiled. "'Fraid not. I'd love to, I really would, but we always have a big list on a Monday morning and I need to get home, changed and then in early." She paused. "Ed, I just wanted you to know I really had a fabulous time."

He glanced back towards the stairs that led up to the flat. "Yeah, I told you Pete wasn't such a bad guy, even if Karen is a bit of a control freak."

She punched him playfully on the chest. "No, you twit, not just this evening. I meant the whole week-end. It was wonderful. It was very special to me."

"Me too."

He tried to kiss her but she pulled her face back just out of his reach. "So be honest with me Ed – please. Now that you've had your wicked way with me, will I be wasting my time if I wait for you to call me?"

He was shocked that she could even ask him. "God, no. Are you kidding?"

But she was nothing if not practical. "Ed – please tell me the truth. You know your reputation precedes you."

But he had never been so sure of anything. "No. I mean it. If it had been anyone else, I would have done my usual thing and never called them again, but you're different. Being with you is perfect. I want to see you again more than anything I've wanted in my entire life."

"And I want to trust you more than anything I've ever wanted in my life." Outside a car beeped its horn. "That'll be my taxi." She said.

He picked up her bag and carried it out to the car. "I'll call you tomorrow sometime, yeah?"

She gave him a last kiss. "You won't catch me during the day, try me at home on the evening."

"It's a promise," he said. "G'night!"

21
Consequences

The Monday morning orthopaedic surgical list always started early. Mr. Weston, Joan's consultant, liked to have the first patient being wheeled in at eight. At seven-thirty, Joan was in the scrub room next to the operating theatre in her greens and clogs about to scrub her hands. She waited briefly for a theatre nurse to finish before taking her place at the sink.

"Hi Joan," the nurse said. "Good week-end?"

Joan could not help smiling. "Brilliant actually."

"Looks like it," the nurse observed. "What did you get up to?"

"Had a romantic week-end in Barcelona with my boyfriend."

"Oh yeah? Do tell."

Joan let the hot water stream over her hands and pumped the soap dispenser. "Not that much to tell; he's an SHO in psychiatry. Bit of a lad really, but somehow we seem to make a connection. I suppose you could call it chemistry. Anyway, we had a really great time."

"Psychiatry? The nurse seemed surprised that Joan would take up with a shrink. "One of the nurses from the psychy unit was on the radio on Sunday morning."

Joan wasn't paying too much attention. She was just making conversation until Mr. Weston arrived. "On the radio? Really?"

The nurse rattled on in the same vein. "Yeah. You know, the DJ Mike request show. 'Endless Love' they call it. She requested a song for one of the doctors she's got the hots for."

Joan laughed. "You're kidding me."

"No. She said that she was disappointed he hadn't called her back after their last date, but that she wanted him to know she was still interested. 'When will I see you again' is what she requested."

Joan suddenly felt sick. "Can you remember the name of the doctor she requested it for?" She didn't need to ask, she already knew what the answer would be.

"Yeah. Unusual name. Plant."

*

On Maple ward Edward was getting chapter and verse about Joan absconding to the chapel and having to be sedated before she could be brought back to the ward.

"I didn't want to sedate her," Amy Pierce told him, "but she was obviously very distressed and I didn't think there was anything else I could do."

"No, I suppose not," he agreed. It was probably the lesser of two evils. "Thanks, Amy. I owe you one. How has she been since?"

It was Cathy who brought him up to date. "Since she was brought back to the ward she's been totally withdrawn and miserable. Don't be too hard on her Ed, I think she's really going through it, you know?"

"Is she still asking to go to the chapel?"

"That's pretty much all she does. We've told her it's out of the question until doctor Marwan has gone through her case in this morning's review."

And that's it, he told himself. Although we're fully aware of how great her need to go to the chapel is, all we seem to do is to stop her from going. It's like we're punishing her. He berated himself for not having been able to spend the time she needed on Friday afternoon. Well, he would make up for it. He went in search of Joan. Cathy followed him.

"She's still in bed, I think. She hasn't moved since last night."

They found her curled up on her bed in the foetal position. She did not respond when they spoke to her. Edward's brow furrowed with concern. "You know," he said, "I think we're missing something here. I don't think we should let this drag on. I'm going to see doctor Marwan now."

Edward found Marwan in his office. As usual, he was trying to catch up on reading background notes for a management meeting later that day. He got straight to the point. "Did you hear about what happened over the weekend with Joan?"

Marwan looked up. "Joan Archer?"

"Yes." Marwan scrutinised his junior closely. Edward looked angry. "For the record I think that the actions taken by the staff were entirely appropriate."

"Yeah. I don't think there was much else they could have done in the circumstances," Edward agreed. "It's just that on Friday before I went off, I had a brief conversation with Joan. I'm sure she was trying to tell me something important, but I was in a rush and didn't have time to think about it properly. I'm convinced that there's something going on that we don't know about yet. I'd like to try and explore it with her, but the only way it's possible to have a sensible conversation with her is if we stop the sedation and let her go back to the chapel. I wanted to clear it with you before I took her back there."

Marwan didn't reply immediately. Instead, he started to polish his glasses. It was a habit he had developed when he needed time to think before he spoke. "Edward; do you perhaps think you're getting a little too involved in this? Are you being entirely objective, or are you allowing your judgement to be clouded by the fact that beneath her distress this patient is an attractive young woman? Maintaining a professional distance is essential; without it we wouldn't be able to help our patients."

Edward considered what Marwan had said. He might have a point, but this was his case. Nobody knew Joan as well as he did. "If that's what you think," he said, "you could ask someone else to take over the case."

Marwan examined his lenses closely, breathing on them and polishing them still more, making Edward wait. "Edward, that's not what I think, but you need to be aware that your reputation with respect to young women is well known among your colleagues. Tongues might wag, and I want to protect you from that."

Edward felt angry. Had someone said something? If they had, and he found out who it was . . . He did not complete the thought. "I assure you that what you are implying has never so much as crossed my mind."

Now Marwan gave Edward his full attention. "Good. In that case, you have my blessing. Stop the sedation, give her twenty four hours and then go with her to the chapel for as long as you think is appropriate."

When Bernadette and Sean arrived at Maple ward for visiting that evening, Edward was waiting for them. "Excuse me," he said, "Mr. and Mrs. Archer?" He remembered the mother from the domiciliary visit.

"Yes?" Bernadette hadn't been expecting to be met by a doctor. "Is anything wrong?"

Edward shook his head. "I don't know if you remember me? I'm doctor Plant, one of the doctors looking after Joan?"

Bernadette gave him a polite smile. "Oh yes." She stood to one side to allow her husband to join them. "You remember, Sean, this is the young doctor who came round to the house to see Joan when she first took ill."

Sean held out his hand. "Doctor," was all he said, hoping that his handshake would not betray him.

"I wondered if I could have a word?"

"About Joan?" The question seemed obvious, but Bernadette wondered whether something might have happened during the day.

"How is she, doctor?" Sean asked.

Edward frowned. "Not very well. But there's something we don't quite understand and I'm hoping you can shed a little light on it." He led them to one of the interview rooms. "Would you like a cup of tea?" He asked them.

"I wouldn't, thanks all the same," Sean replied for both of them. It would have been like accepting a gift from the enemy.

Edward pulled up a chair to sit facing them. "Do you remember when I came to your house that you told me that Joan had said she could hear some sort of music, but when you asked her about it, she denied it?"

Bernadette became quite animated. "Yes, that's right. Father James told us Joan told him that she could hear Jesus singing to her. But when I asked her about it she denied all knowledge and became hysterical."

"Was that the first time you noticed anything unusual?"

They exchanged an almost guilty look. "No, not exactly, doctor." Sean said.

Bernadette disagreed. "Yes it was Sean."

But Sean was sure of himself. "What about the time we went into her room?"

"Her room? What happened when you went into her room?" Edward wanted to know.

Sean shifted uncomfortably in his chair. "Nothing 'happened' exactly, doctor. But you must have seen it yourself when you went up there – all the pictures of Jesus?"

Now Edward remembered. "Yes, of course." He hadn't paid much attention to them at the time. "But coming back to Joan's behaviour, can we be clear on this – the first time she showed any signs of real distress was the time she denied being able to hear Jesus singing to her?"

Bernadette took over. "Yes, that's quite right. At least that's the first time we ever saw her acting like she was losing her mind."

Edward stood up. "That's been very helpful, thank you."

"Is that all you wanted to know?" Sean asked. Meeting them at the door to talk to them in private – in secret, it seemed like - was a bit melodramatic for such a small thing, he thought.

"No, really, it's been really useful," Edward assured them.

But Sean wasn't satisfied with this. "Do you really think you'll be able to help her doctor?" He asked.

Edward reverted to the usual routine for this sort of question. "Of course. Doctor Marwan is very good at his job, and he has a lot of experience. Joan couldn't be in better hands."

Sean gave him a rueful look as they left the room. To Edward, once they had left, this snippet offered an important insight into what Joan had been trying to tell him on Friday. How could he have been so dense? He had been so focused on the voices and this being his special case that he had forgotten all about the music. This was not something he had heard of being reported by any patient with schizophrenia, but he would call in at the library to do some research before going home.

At Joan's bedside Bernadette and Sean were trying to talk to her but knowing what she was going through they didn't try to push her. Joan found it difficult to distinguish between what the demons (for that was how she thought of the voices now) and her parents were saying. Now she had accepted she was possessed, she understood that the demons were external to her, and were not voices whose origin was within her own psyche. That knowledge alone gave her great comfort. But there were at least two conversations going on at the same time. She could distinctly hear one of the demons, the first one, who seemed a lesser power than the others saying *'How does it feel to be alone, Joan? You know you'll never* be allowed to go back to the chapel now, don't you? Never never never . . .' at the same time as her mother was telling her "We spoke to that nice young doctor as we came in tonight, love."

The second one immediately broke in. *'Don't talk to them you silly little bitch. Not if you know what's good for you.'*

Joan wanted to talk to her mum but couldn't. She wasn't sure whether it was the power of the voice or simply exhaustion, but it was all she could do to give her mother an enquiring glance. Bernadette looked at Sean as if to say 'Come on, make an effort, she's your daughter too,' but now the third, the most hateful of the trio, added his poison. *'They only come out of a sense of duty. It's not as though they love you or anything, is it? How could anyone love a piece of shit like you?'*

She ignored it. She heard her dad saying "Yes, that's right. He was asking us how you were before you became ill." She ignored him too. She had to. It was the only way to cling on to her sanity.

Now the first one was back. *'You're on your own now Joan. Completely on your own. Nobody can help you, nobody. Soon you'll be completely powerless.'*

Speaking over the demon Joan heard her mum say "He said that your consultant, doctor Marwan was very good, and that he had a lot of experience. He told us you couldn't be in better hands."

But this prompted the Devil himself to gloat over her impending ruin. *'Couldn't be in better hands? The fools. Not even Jesus will be able to help you now,'* he said. *'You've really blown it, haven't you, you pathetic little slut!*

Suddenly Joan roused herself. She sat up, squeezing her head with her hands as if this might drive them out. "Enough! Stop it. I can't stand it any more!" She shouted.

Bernadette was frightened. Had Joan done the right thing not taking the medication? Should she tell someone? She knew she couldn't. She believed in her daughter and had promised her she would do everything she could to make this exorcism happen. She reached out to stroke her daughter's arm. "Joan, what is it love?"

Joan looked at her mother. Her gaze was vacant. She was all in. "It's the devils. I'm nearly in their power now. They're there all the time, torturing me. It's only a matter of time before they take me over completely."

Sean could not help saying "But the doctor said . . ."

Joan's response was anguished. "What the hell does he know? They say they can help me, but they can't. They can't give me what I need."

Sean didn't know what to say. He had been brought up to think that doctors knew best, but now? "Come on love," he said, almost distraught at his daughter's despair. "They're the professionals. Give them some credit. They might be a little out of their depth, but they're trying their best, I'm sure. We have to trust them to do what they think is best for you."

"Trust them? How can I trust them? They've stopped me from going to the one place where I get any peace. They can't see past their fucking professional egos. The only thing that they can think of is that I've got some sort of mental illness. They've convinced themselves of it, and I'm the one who suffers as a result." Joan seemed to have forgotten about the exorcism. After two days of unremitting cruelty she had again become fixated on the chapel as her hope of respite. She started to sob, terrible wails torn from the very heart of her. "They won't let me go to the chapel any more. Please, I'm begging now, please tell them to let me go to the chapel."

Her father could not bear to see Joan like this. It was worse than learning he had the Parkinson's. He was helpless again. He tried to blink the tears back from his own eyes. "Joan love," he said, his voice cracking with emotion. "We have asked them. They said it wasn't safe unless a member of staff could go with you. You have to be reasonable, there's other people in here as well, you're not the only one who's ill you know love."

She shouted again. A cry of anguish and desperation. "Can't you get it through your head that I'm not fucking ill, I'm possessed!"

Now Bernadette was crying too. "Joan, I know it's not the real you that's talking like this, love, but please, please . . ."

She couldn't finish what she was saying. Joan collapsed onto the bed, clutching her pillow. Then visiting was at an end, and Bernadette and Sean rose, pushing their chairs into a corner, uncertain about leaving, wanting to stay if only they could offer some succour to their daughter. However, they were bundled out of the ward along with all the other visitors. They couldn't see her again until tomorrow. The demons seemed to find it all uproariously funny. The second one was laughing riotously while the first one kept repeating '*Isn't she precious! She's so funny ha ha ha ha . . .*'

*

Joan had been moping around her flat all evening. She couldn't bring herself to phone Ed and he hadn't called her. She glanced at the clock. It was five to eleven. Christ. Where had the evening gone? The phone trilled. She let it ring several times before picking it up.

"Hello."

"Hi Joan, it's me, Ed. Sorry I'm so late calling."

"Oh. Hi, Ed," she said coolly. "What do you want?"

Ed picked up on her subdued tone. "What do you mean 'What do you want'?" He said. "I said I'd call, didn't I?" He waited for her to reply. She didn't. Now he became concerned. "Is everything alright?"

Just knowing that Susan had phoned in a request for Ed had left Joan brooding on it all day. She knew she was probably being ridiculous, but she couldn't help it. She had worked herself up into a state of righteous indignation. "Ed, do you know what time it is? It's nearly eleven o'clock. I've had a fucking bitch of a day and you leave it till now to call me. Do you think everything's alright with that?"

Ed was desolate. "Joan, I'm sorry. I didn't think. But I promised I would call, didn't I? I didn't get off till late myself tonight, but I thought it was important not to let you down."

Now all the tension that had been building within her was released. "So what made you so late Ed? Out at the pub with the nurses were we?"

It sounded like he was being accused of something. "What? No!. As a matter of fact, I stayed behind until visiting to speak to one of my patient's parents, and then I had to go to the library to look something up."

"Not the nurses then?" Still the accusation hung between them.

"No! Why would you think that?"

But she was only working up to what was really troubling her. "Do you know a nurse called Sue?"

"Sue? Yeah, there's a nurse called Sue on Maple ward. What about her?" Ed had a glimmer of what might be coming.

"And I suppose she's young and very attractive?"

Ed's mind was racing. Who could possibly have told Joan that he had been out - which, to everyone in the psychy unit meant *slept* - with Sue? His tone was defensive. "I think she's in her mid 20s, and yes, she's attractive."

"Did you go out with her?"

So someone had told her. He didn't reply immediately. "Yes."

"And did you sleep with her?"

He didn't answer. "Come on, Ed," Joan continued, in for the kill. "There's no point denying it. You did sleep with her, didn't you?"

Edward did not know how this had come about, and he didn't know how he was going to rescue this situation, but he knew that he had to. He spoke very quietly. "I'm not going to deny it. Yes I slept with her. But it was ages ago. Before I even met you. I've never been out with her – or slept with her - since, and I don't want to again."

Although Joan's voice was tinged with a meaningless victory at having been proved right, it was brittle with suppressed emotion. "Well Ed, that's not what she seems to think."

Ed was mystified. "Joan, what's going on? Has she been talking to you or something?"

"Not exactly."

"Well, what then?"

She pulled out a tissue to blow her nose before replying. "Have you ever listened to DJ Mike on the radio and his Sunday morning love song request show?"

"No, never."

Joan sniffed, her voice breaking a little. "Well, Ed, on Sunday, this Sue put in a request for you. Care to know what she requested?" She paused. "When will I see you again."

He didn't know what to say. "Joan, you can't think . . ."

"Right now, Ed, I don't know what I think." Before he could say anything she continued. "Ed, you've got a decision to make. I thought we had something special. Maybe I was wrong."

"No, no! Joan, look . . ." This was a place he had never been in before. He simply didn't know how to respond.

Neither did Joan. She had been in a state of high emotion all weekend, but, for no good reason, this had tipped her the other way Maybe she was just tired and over-reacting, but she couldn't think about it any more tonight. Something restrained her from saying anything that she would never be able to take back. "Ed, I'm tired OK? Call me when you've made your mind up what it is you really do want to do with your life. Only don't leave it too long, okay?" She hung up.

22
Revelation

On Tuesday, Sue was on the early shift. Edward came in at eight – early for him - and waited in the nursing station until she and Viv had finished giving out the medicines. He was clearly annoyed about something, but Sue was not expecting that it could be anything to do with her.

"Sue, can I have a word please?" He said, his voice tight with suppressed anger.

She smiled at him. "Sure. What about?"

"In private?"

He led her to one of the interview rooms and pointedly closed the door behind them. "What did you want to talk to me about Ed?" She asked, all innocence.

He almost shouted at her. "You've got a bloody nerve, you know that?"

Susan was taken aback. "Me? What are you talking about?"

But Ed was in no mood to explain yet. He was still working through his indignation. "Who the hell do you think you are? What gives you the right to interfere in my life?" He was so in her face it was intimidating.

"Ed! Calm down, okay? I've absolutely no idea what you're talking about."

Was she going to deny it? Just let her try. "Really?" She had never seen him like this before. "Yeah, right. So it wasn't you who phoned in to DJ Mike on Sunday and put in a request for doctor Edward Plant at St. Peter's hospital, and asked him to play 'When will I see you again'? I must have got it wrong, mustn't I? It must have been some other Sue in the psychy unit."

Was that all it was? She was almost relieved. She couldn't believe he would get so worked up over something like this. She had always thought his monstrous ego was armour-plated. Could he really be so thin-skinned? "Is that all?" She said, surprise registering in her voice. "Yeah, it was me. What's the problem? Loads of people phone in requests to that show for people they're going out with."

"But we're not going out, are we?"

She was none the wiser. "No, but I wanted to let you know I was still interested, okay, and this seemed, I don't know, a bit more fun than sending you a telegram, alright?"

"Do you know what you've done, you stupid cow?"

Now her temper was starting to rise too. It had only been a bit of fun. She didn't deserve to be treated like this because of it. "Obviously not, Ed. Tell me, what have I done?"

"You've gone and ruined everything, that's what. For the first time in my life I've met someone who really means something to me, only she gets to hear about your so-called harmless little request and now she thinks I'm seeing someone else behind her back. That's what you've done."

It dawned on her then. What had been a bit of a joke now seemed very lame. Why hadn't she listened to Cathy? "Oh." She said. "I'm sorry Ed. I never thought . . . I didn't know . . . That's why you went off early on Friday?"

"That's why I went off early on Friday."

"Shit. I'm really sorry Ed. I didn't mean . . ."

But he was in no mood for an apology. He stalked out slamming the door behind him. In the nursing station Maria raised her eyes at Viv in a silent comment on his behaviour, but Viv ignored her. It made no difference. Maria was compiling her own dossier on the misdemeanours of various members of staff and this one would be filed away under 'intimidation' to be brought out at the opportune time.

Edward paced the ward looking for Joan. He found her in her favoured spot, the quiet corner, sipping a cup of tea. She seemed withdrawn into herself, but there were no longer any signs of sedation. She watched Ed approaching as if she were looking at herself from the outside with the demons giving a running commentary.

'Oh look,' the first one said, 'it's that nice doctor Plant.'

In a sing-song voice the other one added 'She fancies him, she fancies him . . .' again and again.

Then Satan himself. 'She wants to fuck him. That's what she really wants.' The others laughed as if he had made a fine joke.

Then the first one again. 'But she can't get a man of her own, can she?'

'*That's why she wants to fuck her precious Jesus instead.*' Satan replied.

'*Stupid bitch.*' The second one agreed.

Edward's voice was added to theirs. "Joan?"

Slowly she looked up, her eyes coming into focus. "What?"

'*Don't talk to him!*' The first demon shouted at her.

'*He can't help you.*' The second yelled.

Then the awful sneering whipcrack of the Devil. '*And he won't fuck you.*'

Edward heard none of this. "Joan," he said, "I've had a word with doctor Marwan, and he said you can go to the chapel if I go with you. Would you like that?"

All three demons joined together shrieking at her, over and over, telling her no, leaving no room in her mind for anything else.

The tears started by themselves. Joan could no longer hold them at bay. "Oh God, yes please. Thank you."

Edward held out his hand to help her out of the chair. Together they walked off the ward towards the chapel. All the while Joan's face was screwed up as if each step was a new agony. The demons were pitiless.

You don't want to go to the chapel.
Something bad will happen, it always does.
It's a trick to get you in their power.
Don't trust him.
You can't trust him.
He can't help you.
Nobody can help you.
He doesn't even like you.
You like him though, don't you.
How can you be so stupid?
None of them can help you.
There's no point going to the chapel.
Jesus has forgotten all about you.

Viv followed them to the chapel. As they entered Ed witnessed the same change come over Joan that he had seen on their last visit. Now her tears came from relief at this blessed respite Ed told Viv he didn't need her to stay, that he was sure that Joan would be safe with him. Joan spent some minutes on her knees, praying, until Ed joined her.

"Can you tell me about it now?" He said. "The music?"

But now she was here, she felt reluctant to say anything about it. "I don't know whether I'm supposed to. What if I tell you and it breaks the spell?"

The thought occurred to Ed that all she had to do was ask. "Why don't you just ask if it's alright to tell me?"

"Okay." She bowed her head. After a few moments she turned back to him. "It's okay," she said, "I can tell you."

"Tell me exactly what happens when you come in here."

She thought for a second or two. "The voices stop."

"Why do you think that is?"

Her answer was confident. She'd had time to get it all worked out now. "It's because they're pure evil. They're demons. I mean real demons, like in the Bible. This place is suffused with the love and authority of God. They have no power against that."

"Does anything else happen?"

Her face lit up with joy. "Yes."

"What? What else happens?"

She did not reply immediately, but took his face in her hands, examining it intently as if to be sure of his sincerity. Eventually she told him, as if it were a momentous revelation. "I can hear singing. It's Jesus and his angels."

"How do you know it's Jesus and his angels?"

Her reply was simple and sincere. "Because I've seen Him." She took her hands away from his face.

"Can you see Him now?"

She shook her head. "No, not now. I only saw Jesus in the church near where I live, the Sacred Heart."

Edward was curious. "What did he look like?"

"There was a statue. White stone, life-size. It came to life. It was the statue that sang to me."

"And didn't you think this was a bit odd? Didn't you feel even a little bit frightened?"

She looked away from him then. She wondered if he was trying to lead her somewhere she wouldn't want to go. "When you say it like that, it does seem odd, but at the time, I don't know why, it just didn't feel that way. It just felt natural. As for being afraid, it was completely the opposite. I felt utterly safe and secure, held fast in the loving hands of Jesus."

"I see."

She turned back to face him. "Do you?" She took his hands in hers. They were cool and dry. He didn't try to pull them away.

"No, not exactly," he admitted, now feeling self-conscious. "But I've recently learned something about the power of love, so maybe that's a start." They laughed together, nervously.

For a short time they sat together in silence, she absently tracing shapes on his hands with her fingertips. Then he said "This song that Jesus sings, can you sing it to me?"

Her hands grew still. "I'm not sure. I'm not sure I'm supposed to. Anyway, I don't know the words or what they mean. It's some language I've never heard before. What if it stops if I sing it to you?"

"Is that a risk you're prepared to take?"

"I don't know." She looked worried. Briefly, she closed her eyes. When she opened them she said "I think I can try and let you know what the music sounds like, but I can't sing the words."

"That's okay."

She closed her eyes again. Her hands closed on his and she started to hum softly. "Da da da daah da da da da da da da da daah da da . . ."

He recognised it. "I've heard that music before. It's . . ."

But she reached her hand up to his face to touch his lips with her finger. "Sshhh." She continued to hum.

Spellbound, Ed closed his eyes. Joan caressed his cheek with her hand. Neither of them knew where it came from but they were both consumed by a never before experienced ecstasy. Though he wasn't cold he shivered involuntarily. It was like being in a dream. Though the only sound was Joan's humming, the music seemed to grow so that he could hear it in its full majesty with orchestras and massed choirs singing their hymn of praise and power and joy beneath the wondrous radiance of God. It didn't occur to him to question it or to want to end it, he was aware only of the moment, of being, of its divine wonder.

He hadn't noticed that Joan had continued to stroke his face gently with the back of her hand. Now her hand was behind his head, fingers entwined in the curls at the nape of his neck. Very slowly their faces came closer and closer together, faces almost touching. He could feel the softness of her breath on his lips. Then his heart was pounding, his mouth dry, he had only to move forward a fraction . . . He opened his eyes just as their lips were about to touch. At the same instant Joan opened hers. The spell was broken. The music stopped and they jerked apart from each other, each of them horrified at the thought of what they had been about to do.

Joan was the first to speak. "My God! That's how Jesus was betrayed . . ."

"Jesus?"

"With a kiss."

Edward was very embarrassed. This was exactly what Marwan had warned him about. He stood up, breathing hard. "Come on, Joan. We'd better go. We can't stay here all day." His words sounded harsh, clattering after the serene voice of the music.

Joan was unwilling to go back. "Why not?" She replied. "Why can't we stay here, at least for a while longer?"

"I've got work to do. Other patients to look after."

"But I don't want to leave. You know what it means to me to be here now, don't you? And what will happen to me when I do leave. Please? I can't, not yet."

"Can't, or won't?"

Her look was both imploring and defiant. "Both."

"What will happen if I make you leave?"

How could he say that, now that he knew? "You wouldn't do that would you? Not now?"

"You know I can't let you stay here all day."

"You bastard. It was all a put-up job wasn't it? Get me in here, get me to pour my heart out, all for nothing."

He realised he wasn't exactly being fair to her. It was a combination of his sour mood and his embarrassment that was making him act this way. He tried to be more sympathetic. "No, Joan, not for nothing. If we are to help you we need to have as full an understanding as we can get about what's happening to you."

"Help me? What exactly have you done to help me?"

"The main thing is the medication."

"The medication?" Now her exasperation and scorn poured forth. "For God's sake, have you listened to a word I've said? The medication doesn't help. The only thing that helps is coming here."

"The *only* thing? Are you sure?"

"Of course I'm fucking sure!" She paused, shaking her head in disbelief at his obtuseness. "Christ!"

"So as soon as you leave here, the voices will come back, will they?"

"Yes, yes, yes! Only they won't just come back, for hours afterwards they'll punish me for having evaded them by coming here."

"And the medication really doesn't help?"

She looked at him incredulously. "It doesn't do a thing to stop the voices, but it does make me feel a damn sight worse. If you must know, I haven't been taking it for days and not one of you has noticed the slightest difference!"

This revelation sobered Edward. He had invested so much faith in the power of the medication to at least give some relief from the voices. He tried to salvage what he could. "So tell me Joan what's most important to you? Getting rid of the voices or being able to hear Jesus singing?"

This was an impossible question. The fight went out of her. Deflated by defeat she almost seemed to shrink in size. She lowered her head into her hands. "I don't know. It's impossible to know. You can't even begin to imagine what it's like. The voices are Hell. Literally. It's the Devil. I know that now. Somehow he gets into my head and is determined to destroy me. The love that Jesus has for me is all that protects me, but sometimes I doubt even that, it's so awful. But I understand now that it's part of God's purpose for me. He's allowing the devil to torment me as a test of my faithfulness, my willingness to be his servant."

"I think I understand now, too."

Almost shocked by this admission, she turned to look at him. "Do you? You keep telling me you want to help but all that means to you is trying to convince me I'm mentally ill and cram me full of pills. Can you accept that I'm not mentally ill? I think I'm possessed, and the power of this place keeps it at bay. I need a priest and prayers, not a psychiatrist with pills "

She sounded so rational, almost convincing. She had certainly convinced herself. But she had to be wrong. Had to be. "But you have to admit that you've been behaving hysterically at times?" He said.

She laughed bitterly. "How would you behave if the police dragged you out of church? I wasn't hurting anyone, but people just couldn't leave me to find peace with God in my own way."

"Well what about all the trouble you created when you ran away to the chapel here and refused to leave? Is that normal?"

"Is it normal to drag people out of church when they praying?"

He looked at his watch. They had been there for over an hour. He sighed. "Joan, I'm afraid we do have to go, but I promise you, if you come quietly you'll be able to come back tomorrow."

23
For her own good

Edward left Joan in the day room and went in search of Dr. Marwan. He didn't have to look far, he was in his office; Tony was with him. They looked up as Edward entered. "I'm glad you've dropped by, Edward," Marwan said. "We were just discussing Joan Archer. Tony told me you'd gone to the chapel with her."

Edward nodded to Tony, acknowledging his presence. "Yeah. I was just coming to let you know how I'd got on."

Marwan pointed to a chair in front of his desk. "Have a seat. If I can trust my instincts, something tells me this case is about to take an unexpected twist."

"You can say that again," Edward said, pulling the chair up. "So what exactly happened?"

Edward looked from Marwan to Tony. "Well, like we agreed, I stopped the sedation so that when we got to the chapel she wouldn't be so out of it she couldn't think straight."

"And?"

"She became completely lucid again. It's an amazing transformation. It happens instantaneously – as soon as she walks through the chapel door you can see it on her face. If I didn't know better, I'd say I had witnessed a miracle. Just like the biblical stories of Jesus casting out devils."

"Is that what *she* said?" Tony asked.

"Not exactly. But she did say she believed she wasn't mentally ill, that she was possessed by the devil, and that it was happening as a test of her faith."

Marwan steepled his hands on his desk, his forefingers touching his chin. "So far, this fits exactly with our hypothesis about her delusional belief system and how this is driving her illness."

But Edward was no longer quite so sanguine about this. They hadn't seen what a change going to the chapel could bring about in Joan. "Hmm. I must say that you need to see it for yourself to appreciate just how remarkable the transformation is."

Marwan looked at Edward, an expression of curiosity on his face. "It's obviously had a profound effect on you Edward. Did anything else happen?"

Edward hesitated. Could he tell them that he had heard the music too? No. Not when he doubted the evidence of his own senses. He had already rationalised it as the power of autosuggestion or maybe even a hysterical reaction. And he certainly couldn't tell them about the almost kiss. Not if he wanted to be taken seriously. "Well, not exactly," he said. "But she did tell me a lot more about what happens when she visits the chapel."

"What, exactly?"

"She told me that Jesus sings to her . . . personally. He sings and then a choir of angels joins in to sing the harmonies."

Marwan exchanged a glance with Tony. "What does he sing to her? Hymns, sacred music?"

"No. She said she didn't know what music it was. She'd never heard it before, and she didn't understand the language."

Tony tried to make a joke. "So, not country and western then?"

Marwan smiled. For an off-the-cuff remark it was quite good. He tried one of his own. "Or hip-hop?" Not that he knew what hip-hop was.

"Beethoven, actually."

This got their attention. "Beethoven?"

"Yes. I got her to hum the music, and it was unmistakably the *Ode to Joy* from Beethoven's ninth."

Both Marwan and Tony smiled in relief. "Good," Marwan said.

Edward didn't understand. "Good? Why is it good?"

"Don't you see Edward? Although it's not a rational approach to take, this is such a distressing and disturbing case that at the back of one's mind it's impossible to shake off the nagging doubt that this really might be a genuine case of possession. The fact that the music she believes to come from Jesus is something as prosaic as Beethoven strongly suggests that this is all part of a perfectly explicable syndrome. We've been struggling to complete the picture but now we have a large, and possibly conclusive, piece of the jigsaw."

But Edward struggled to see how this could provide that final clue to Joan's case. "So how does the music fit?"

"The music is the alter-ego, as it were, of the voices. It's another manifestation of the auditory hallucinations. Don't you see?

When her environment changes to one that Joan perceives to be 'good', the hallucinations don't vanish as we thought, they metamorphose to suit the environment. It's a unique case, certainly, but utterly consistent with our working diagnosis." He turned to Tony. "Wouldn't you agree, Tony?"

Tony wasn't quite sure, all this theorising was a bit beyond him, but he wasn't about to disagree with such an elegant explanation. "Well, like Salim, I've never seen anything quite like this before, but I'd have to agree with him. It's a complicated case alright, but I've no doubts in my mind that it's schizophrenia. None at all."

Whatever Edward might think, he was in the minority. The truth was he didn't know what to think any more. In the past few days his world had been turned up-side down, and then fired off at a tangent. He was happy for Marwan to take on the mantle of solving this diagnostic conundrum. It was one less complication for him to have to think about. "So, what next?" He asked.

"The most important thing is the medication," Marwan said. "She must continue as planned. This is what will eventually provide the key to her recovery."

"Do you think we should increase the dose?" Tony asked. He was convinced, as were most of the nurses, that the dose had been too low all along.

But Marwan shook his head. "Let's leave it a few more days. When she's been on her present dose for a fortnight, we'll review her progress then."

"She's stopped taking the medication." Edward told them. Surprise registered on both their faces.

"And when were you planning to let us know about this?" Tony's response was to show some irritation at this bombshell.

"I only just found out myself," Ed replied. "She told me while we were in the chapel. Said she hasn't been taking it for days, and that she's been feeling better since she stopped taking it."

"We can't have that." Tony was adamant; patients who didn't take their medicines increased the risk to his staff.

"I agree," Marwan said. "Edward, can you write up her dose to be given as a liquid so she can't spit it out? If she refuses to take it, then we'll have to think again, but let's see what effect this has on her first."

"Sure. I'll do it straight away." That placated Tony. Then Edward added "And what about her visits to the chapel?"

Marwan exchanged a knowing look with Tony. Clearly this was something they had been discussing before Edward's arrival. Edward suspected that Tony had been recommending against Joan being allowed to go. "We were discussing this before you arrived," Marwan told him. "We think that by allowing Joan to visit the chapel, we're just colluding in her delusions. That can lead to the belief on the part of the patient that we think the delusions are real, thus providing external confirmation that serves only to strengthen them. I agree with Tony that there must be no further visits to the chapel. I know it seems cruel, but it's for her own good in the long term."

Though Edward was not convinced, it was clear he would have little say in the matter. It was better to try and ensure it was done with as little upset as possible. "I see. That's going to be very traumatic for her. I think I had better be the one to tell her." He spoke to Tony. "Tony, can you make sure that all the nursing staff are properly briefed on this?"

"No problem." There was nothing more to be decided, and Tony left the room. Edward remained where he was. Marwan could see his trainee was troubled.

"Edward, I sense that you don't entirely agree with this decision? Are you sure you're not identifying too strongly with this patient? Are you sure there isn't something else you want to tell me?"

"No. I . . . It's just that you haven't seen the effect going to the chapel has on Joan. It really is quite profound. I'm just worried how telling her she can't go any more will affect her, that's all."

Marwan sympathised with Edward, but making tough decisions that were in the best interests of patients, though it might not seem so immediately, was something he would have to learn to come to terms with. But not today. It was clear to him that Edward had become over-involved. Once Joan had responded to treatment and been discharged he would take Edward aside for a detailed debriefing of the case. "I'll tell you what, Edward. It's the ward round tomorrow. I'll be the one who tells her, agreed?

*

James O'Hanlon could hardly bring himself to credit the words on the page before him.

> *The existence of demons in the world is a teaching of faith that is acknowledged by all who know and accept Sacred Scripture as a manifestation of the direct inspiration of God.*

He paused in his reading to try and take it in.

> *Diabolic possession is the most serious form of demonic activity for it involves the presence of a demon within a person with the loss of mental, intellectual and emotional freedoms. Exorcism is the rite of driving out the Devil and his demons from a person who has been possessed by them.*

He had always considered himself to be a rational Christian. He had no doubt of the existence of God or indeed the Devil, but was convinced that over the centuries Christians of all denominations had inflicted great evil on many innocent people because of a superstitious attachment to the idea that the Devil could become intimately involved with humans. The time for such superstitions was surely past? He read on.

> *A case of possession is not to be diagnosed lightly. Many of the symptoms of schizophrenia and other mental diseases can be mistaken for signs of possession, especially by those who are gullible or easily led. Priests are cautioned to be as certain as they can be that the person is truly possessed by an evil demon before considering exorcism.*

The next line made his blood run cold.

> *During exorcism, the exorcist confronts the grave risk of becoming possessed by the Devil or demon himself.*

He had kept his promise to Joan. He had spoken to his bishop. The bishop had a duty of scepticism, he told James, to guard against unnecessary or frivolous exorcisms, but James managed to convince him that this was indeed a case that required further investigation by a priest who had been trained as an exorcist. The Vatican took the matter so seriously that it had appointed an Exorcist-in-Chief, an elderly priest who, despite his age, took his duties extremely seriously. Amid widespread concerns among the Christian churches about the growing interest in Satanism and the occult, made all too easy by the rapid expansion of the Internet, it was he who had been the driving force behind the instruction that all dioceses should train a number of priests as exorcists ready to be the Church's vanguard in the fight against such extreme perversions However, Bishop Andrews was one who had been a laggard on this. Like James, he was a rationalist on most matters who thought the time for such superstition was past. But James was an old friend, and he accepted that he would not make such a request without compelling reasons.

"At first I accepted the judgement of the psychiatrists at face value," James said. "They're supposed to be the experts, after all, and they were so confident in their diagnosis. However, there are several very troubling aspects that they don't seem to have an answer for. The first is that according to Joan, their treatment has no effect whatsoever. The second is that whenever Joan is able to enter a consecrated place, like a church or the hospital chapel, the voices are silenced. The third is that Joan herself is absolutely convinced that the voices are diabolical in origin, and she's someone who would not take such a view lightly."

"What do the doctors have to say about that?"

"I've not spoken to them directly yet, I was waiting until you had given permission to proceed, but according to Joan's parents, who are devout parishioners of long standing, the doctors say that Joan is mentally ill and her refusal to accept their diagnosis is a consequence of her illness."

"Very convenient for the doctors," the Bishop observed wryly. The housekeeper brought them tea. They said nothing until he had withdrawn. "The problem is, James," the bishop continued, "that there are no priests in the diocese trained in exorcism."

James poured milk into two cups, then added the tea. "I would have been surprised if there were."

"I'm afraid I'll have to go to Westminster on this one," he said, indicating that he would have to go through the Archbishop of Westminster's office to locate an exorcist. "Funnily enough, the Cardinal agrees with the Holy Father on this, and has ordained a number of exorcists in the past couple of years, so perhaps it won't be as difficult as we fear to find one."

Unfortunately that proved not to be the case. Exorcists were few and far between. After spending a frustrating afternoon on the telephone one eventually was located: a Spanish priest currently in Sunderland, Father Alonso. He could not come. He was very sympathetic, but said he had identified multiple cases of possession in the North-East and dared not leave. He advised James to perform the exorcism himself.

*

That evening, Joan's parents thought she was looking much better. "I do feel a bit better actually," Joan said.

"Are the voices gone then?" Sean asked.

Joan smiled weakly. "No, Dad, but somehow they seem to be less powerful than they were."

"Could the medication finally be working?" Bernadette wondered.

Joan sighed. "The medication hasn't got anything to do with it, Mum. I haven't been taking it, remember. I even told doctor Plant that today. I had a long talk with him in the chapel though, and it helped me to understand what it is I'm going through."

"You mean, this business about having schizophrenia?"

Joan shook her head. "Mum. I haven't got schizophrenia."

"We went to the library and looked it up, you know," Sean said. "It sounded just like what you said was happening to you, hearing horrible voices and what-not."

"Honestly, Dad. I really haven't got schizophrenia."

But Sean had been convinced by the books they had found. Their descriptions of schizophrenia were strikingly similar to what Joan had been going though. "Did the doctor say that?"

Joan scowled. Bernadette intervened. "So how did doctor Plant help you to understand what's happening to you, love?"

"Well he kept trying to tell me I've got schizophrenia, but I just couldn't see how what was happening to me could be caused by some chemicals in my brain. It's too real. Then I realised. This is a test. I'm being possessed by the devil as a test of my faith. Medication isn't going to help with that, only prayer can help me. You wouldn't believe how much stronger I feel after being allowed to spend some time in the chapel today."

"We are praying for you too love, and so is father James. We're all praying for you."

The mention of father James prompted Joan to ask about how her request for an exorcism was getting on. "He told us he was seeing the bishop," Bernadette told her, "but that's the last we heard."

*

Edward and Peter were watching television; not that there was anything worth watching. They had ordered a take-away curry which naturally required a libation of cold beer to accompany it. Edward was expounding on 'his' case. "Actually, I think I'm a fucking genius. Nobody else was able to figure out this case, but I knew we were missing something."

Peter thought Ed was over-compensating for something. He wasn't usually this garrulous. Something about him tonight didn't ring true, but he couldn't put his finger on it.

"Whoop-ee! Since when did you become doctor give-a-shit?" He asked between mouthfuls. "So what happens next?"

Edward drained his can. "Do you want another one?" He asked, heading in the direction of the fridge. As he opened the fridge door he said over his shoulder "She'll be treated with medication, by injection if she refuses. That's what's really needed to take away her delusions and hallucinations."

Peter had often wondered why it was that psychiatrists had achieved such a dominant position in the world of mental illness. Was it because they were so insufferably sure of themselves, like Ed was being now? "But what if she doesn't want the music to go away?" He said. "What if she really is hearing the voice of the Devil and having divine visions? Have you considered that?"

This made Edward think, but not for long. There was no profit and much aggravation in going down that route. No, he had decided to follow the line of least resistance and accept Marwan's reasoning in its entirety. Even so, his response was somewhat defensive. "Divine visions? For Christ's sake, this is the twenty-first fucking century! Anyway, you haven't seen her or you'd understand. We have to do something to help her. The voices are so threatening – she's terrified that what they're telling her about Jesus not loving her might be true – that she'll agree to anything that would get rid of them."

"Only the voices though, not the music?"

"That's a risk we have to take."

"That's big of you," Peter observed, then realised from the expression on Ed's face that he had gone too far. Time to change to a happier subject. "So when are you seeing Joan again?"

Edward seemed not to be particularly interested. "Joan? Oh, Joan. Dunno."

Now Peter knew something was wrong. "Dunno?" He asked pointedly. "I thought this was the real deal, love, commitment and all the trimmings?"

"Me too."

Now Peter understood what had been eating his friend. "So what's up?"

Ed sighed. "I'm not really sure." Peter could sense that this wasn't true. "Oh, fuck it. One of the fucking nurses on the ward went and put in a request for me on the radio. Said she wanted to see me again or something."

"And?"

"Somebody told Joan."

"Oh." That explained a great deal. "So what are you going to do about it?"

But Ed was no longer so sure of himself. "What can I do about it? The ball's in her court."

"And you think you're a genius? You're an arse, that's what you are." Peter picked up his car keys and threw them at Edward. "Look, you moron, you might know the best moves for getting into a girl's knickers, but you know fuck-all about relationships. What you need to do is go round to her flat now, tell her that you love her tell her how sorry you are, and tell her how much you so want this relationship to work."

"Tell her I'm sorry? But I didn't do anything?"

Peter shook his head, his impatience at Ed's idiocy growing. "You think that matters? What matters is she feels hurt for some reason, and you seem to think that you being in the right is more important than the relationship."

Edward stood there, playing with the keys. He had to do something. This being in limbo was awful. "Maybe you're right."

"You know I'm bloody well right."

Ed picked up a jumper and made to leave. "Thanks mate. I really do owe you one this time."

"Forget it." Peter started clearing the dishes. As Ed was leaving he shouted after him "Oh – and buy her some flowers on the way over!"

24
Catatonic

After so many years working in psychiatry, it struck Dr. Marwan as quite odd that this was the first time he had ever had occasion to meet a Catholic priest. "Tea?" He asked as he welcomed his visitor.

James O'Hanlon declined the offer. He felt distinctly uncomfortable. He knew that what he was about to ask would smack of medieval superstition and that to a modern doctor it would be irrational to seek to overturn the discoveries of science with something as insubstantial as faith; he didn't even know whether Joan's consultant believed in God, but he had promised Joan, and that was that. "Thank you for seeing me," he said as he took a seat.

"I don't usually see people who are not relatives unless at a patient's specific request," Marwan explained politely, "but in this case, knowing the depths of Joan's beliefs, I thought it worth having at least an initial conversation. Frankly, at this juncture I am grateful for any help I can get. Hers is a most distressing and perplexing case."

"It's not really a conversation I'm after," James said. "And I don't know if I'll be of much help, at least, not the sort of help you might usually be looking for. I've had a rather unusual request of Joan, one that I think you should be told about, and will need your permission if it is to be granted."

Marwan was intrigued. "What is it?"

"She wants an exorcism."

Marwan thought he had been working in psychiatry for so long that he had lost the capacity to be shocked; now he realised he hadn't. "Out of the question." His reply was purely instinctive. He knew nothing about exorcism, and surprised himself with the vehemence of his reply, but he knew it was the only decision he could make.

The priest nodded. This was only what he had expected. "I thought you might say that," he conceded, "but what makes you so sure?"

Marwan refused to be drawn. "I'm afraid I can't discuss the specific details of Joan's case," he said, pulling off his glasses to polish them, "but you must be aware that for centuries, because of superstitious beliefs about demonic possession it's likely that enormous damage was done to thousands of individuals who were actually mentally ill."

"I accept that," James acknowledged, "but let's be honest. For most of that time, the medical treatments that might have been offered were just as damaging, perhaps even more so. It's only comparatively recently that modern treatments have offered any real hope to people with mental illness, while the experience of possession as a very real phenomenon has existed for thousands of years."

Marwan smiled. "So people like you would have us believe. But we now live in an age of reason. Superstitious beliefs about demons rightly belong in the past. If, as you suggest, possession remains a real phenomenon, why has it never been studied scientifically? Why, in the modern world, has it disappeared apart from a few easily discredited cases?"

"I'm afraid you've been misinformed, doctor Marwan. The problem is that science cannot explain possession, so, very conveniently, it simply states that it does not exist, so that to the world of science at least, it disappears. But it has not disappeared. There are in fact many credible modern cases of possession. And where medicine is impotent, prayer may provide an answer."

"But there you have it, Father." The psychiatrist was confident in his judgement. "In Joan's case, medicine is not impotent."

James found the psychiatrist's condescension irritating. "Joan herself told me that the medication she had been prescribed had had no effect other than to make her feel worse. So much so that she stopped taking it."

"Indeed, but we have taken steps to rectify that. You must understand that in a condition like schizophrenia, a response to treatment can take time. Weeks, usually, but sometimes months. It's still early days yet for Joan."

"So you won't even consider an exorcism?"

"I'm afraid it's not possible. I have a duty to consider her best interests in everything I do. If I agreed to such a thing I would be colluding in her delusions and that could have a serious detrimental effect on her. Medication is what she needs, and time; that, and a calm environment in which to make her recovery."

"Are you so certain of your diagnosis that there's no room for doubt?"

Dr. Marwan shook his head. It had been an interesting conversation, but it could have had only one outcome. He held out his hand. The priest's grip was surprisingly strong.

"Thank you for your time," he said.

*

Marwan got his secretary to see the priest out, then hurried to the group therapy room where the rest of his team were already gathered for the ward round. Joan was now his top priority, and hers was the first case they would consider today. He had only just sat himself down when there was a light knock on the door and Joan entered the room.

Marwan smiled at her. "Good morning, Joan; thank you for coming. Won't you take a seat?" Joan took one of the empty chairs. "Joan," Marwan continued, "doctor Plant told me about the conversation you had yesterday in the chapel." He gave her another smile which he hoped would be reassuring. "I must say your case is full of the most unexpected twists and turns."

This morning the voices had returned with a vengeance. *'Fucking hell.'* The first one said. *'Not again. Dick-head.'*

Then the second one. *'Ignore him Joan, if you know what's good for you, you stupid slag.'*

Joan hadn't heard a word Marwan had said. "What? I'm sorry . . . the voices . . ."

Marwan understood what she was going through. "Don't worry Joan, I understand. It's taken us a while to put all the pieces together, but I think we have a pretty full picture now."

'I told you to ignore him. Why can't you just listen and do as you're told?'

So far the Devil had not made his presence felt today. Now he did. His menacing voice filled her consciousness. *'Don't waste your time on him. How the fuck could he ever understand what's happening to you?'*

Joan tried to focus her attention on Dr. Marwan, but she was finding it almost impossible. "You mean . . ." She began to say.

But she was interrupted by the shrieking of the second demon. '*Shut your fucking mouth you stupid bitch!*'

She shook her head. She knew she wasn't making much sense. "I'm sorry, I'm trying to concentrate, but it's difficult, you know?"

Marwan sympathised. "I take it the voices are very bad just now?"

"Yes."

"What are they saying to you?"

She closed her eyes, frowning with the effort of concentrating. "They're not just talking, they're shouting. They say I'm stupid, you're stupid, you can't possibly understand what I'm going through, and that I mustn't listen to you."

"But when you go to the chapel, the voices disappear?"

"Yes."

"To be replaced by the voice of Jesus?"

"Not exactly."

This was the response Marwan had been seeking. He had planned this interview so that he could direct it precisely to where he wanted to take it. He had a surprise in store for Joan. "But that's what Edward – doctor Plant - told us yesterday. Has he misunderstood?"

Joan shook her head. "No. Jesus doesn't talk to me, he sings to me."

Perfect. This was exactly where he wanted her. Now he would inject a little of what the psychologists called cognitive dissonance, and watch it have its effect. He sprang his trap. "Yes. He sings the Ode to Joy from Beethoven's ninth symphony."

Joan was so shocked that the voices were blocked out. "What? Is that what he told you?" Could he have betrayed her? She glared at him. Out of nowhere, her anger flared. "How could he know that? I've never heard the music before, and the language is strange, like nothing I've ever heard."

Now she noticed the CD player on the floor behind Dr. Marwan's chair. He leaned over and pressed the 'play' button. Music filled the room. Glorious joyful music, with the orchestras and the choirs of heaven singing their exultant hymn of praise. Just like she had heard it in church and in the chapel. Note for perfect note. She was utterly astonished. "But . . . how . . ?"

Now the demons returned. Her head was filled with their harsh gleeful strident laughter.

From the look on her face and her initial response, Dr. Marwan concluded that his little demonstration had had its desired effect. "It's Beethoven, Joan. It's his most famous work, his choral symphony. Sublime, but still Beethoven; oh, and . . . the language is German." He allowed the music to play a little longer then switched it off. "Satisfied?" He asked.

Joan sobbed and lowered her head to her hands. "It's not . . it's not possible." She looked up, as if hoping at least someone would be on her side. "Is it?"

Dr. Marwan was very satisfied. Getting Joan to accept that she really was suffering from a mental illness would be a giant step forward. His demonstration that there was nothing 'divine' about the music, that it was perfectly explicable in human terms had clearly had its desired effect. "Don't look so worried Joan," he said. "Although this might give you pause for thought, it actually helps us It confirms that our suspicions about your condition were accurate. I'm sorry to say that you really are suffering from schizophrenia."

The demons were laughing without pause, their hideous screeching tearing through her mind.

Joan fixed Marwan in her gaze. "No."

Marwan smiled at her. "Yes. And once the medication gets into your system again, we'll start to see a real difference."

But Joan was obdurate. In spite of the shock of discovering that the music had been Beethoven, her conviction returned. If the Bible was the inspired word of God, why couldn't Beethoven's compositions be the inspired music of God? Her voice gained strength as she spoke. "No, doctor Marwan, you're wrong. The medication does *not* help. I felt better yesterday because I was allowed to stay in the chapel. That gave me a lot of strength back. I've slipped back a bit today, but I'll be better again once I've been back to the chapel."

Marwan exchanged a glance with Edward. She noticed it and felt a surge of panic in the pit of her stomach. "I'm afraid that won't be possible, Joan. Not until we see some real evidence of improvement in your condition."

Joan looked at Edward, her gaze beseeching. "You wouldn't? You promised."

Now Marwan spoke very gently. "Joan. It's not doctor Plant's decision – it's mine - do you understand?"

Now her rage erupted. "Understand? Understand? Do you think I'm stupid? Of course I understand. Let me spell it out for you: because of your arrogance, your refusal to accept that you could possibly be wrong, you have decided to send me to Hell! Well fuck you! Fuck the whole fucking lot of you!"

The demons in her head were hysterical.

Edward tried to remonstrate with her. "Joan, please! That's not how it is. It's for your own good. You know that."

'Go on Joan, you tell him. Tell him what a prick he is.'

Joan's fury allowed her to dismiss the voice. "For my own good? How can you say that? You saw me yesterday. You saw how much going to the chapel helps me, what it means to me – and now you're going to take that away from me – on his say-so? He doesn't know me, or anything about me . . .."

But Edward interrupted her. "No Joan. Doctor Marwan is an expert. He's got a lot of experience, and he's recognised a pattern in the way you switch from the evil voices to the voice of Jesus. They're just the extremes of your syndrome and you switch between them depending on where you happen to be. The medication really is the only thing that will help you."

Joan had had enough. She stood, knocking her chair over, glaring at the assembled so-called mental health professionals. "You stupid senseless fools! Who are you to decide what's good for me? I'm going to the chapel now, and none of you is going to stop me."

Maria had been wondering where all this clever-dick stuff Marwan had been so pleased with would lead. As far as she was concerned, he had completely misjudged the situation. Instead of getting the patient to accept she was mentally ill, his tinkering had had the opposite effect, and, more to the point, agitated Joan to the level where it looked as if she might become violent. There was an alarm button set in the wall near where she was sitting. Casually she reached across and pressed it. It would sound in the nursing station and bring people running.

Edward tried again to reason with Joan. "No Joan. Now listen to me for pity's sake. You're not going to the chapel. If you try to go there you'll be forcibly restrained and we'll give you the medication by injection. Now do you understand?"

The door burst open. In walked Tony followed by Cathy and Viv. "Is everything all right, doctor Marwan?" He asked.

Joan collapsed to her knees. She looked from one member of the team to another. Did none of them believe her? They all avoided her glance. She was defeated and she knew it. She was helpless. The demons renewed their onslaught with a viciousness against which she had no defence. She wailed, a cry of fear and desperation in the knowledge that finally she had been abandoned.

Edward picked the chair up for her and helped her to sit again.

Marwan looked grim. Things seemed to have been going the way he wanted, but they had taken an unexpected turn. He was becoming extremely worried about Joan, but tried not to let it show. "Good. I'm glad we cleared that up. Now, is there anything else you would like to ask us?"

The Devil was talking to her, his quiet voice the most chilling thing she had ever heard. *'Before long you'll be completely in my power. Nothing can help you now.'*

She raised her eyes to focus on Marwan. "Please," she pleaded, "come with me to the chapel, and let me talk to you . . . Aaaarrhh!" She broke off, holding her head in her hands, unable to continue. Through gritted teeth she eventually managed to finish what she had started to say: "Let me talk to you without these voices tormenting me."

But his opinion about what needed to be done was fixed. "You know that's not possible Joan."

"Please? It's telling me I'll soon be completely in its power. Please don't abandon me like this."

'What did you expect you stupid bitch?' The second demon sneered.

But Marwan was unswayed. "Joan, I know that this is difficult – if not impossible – for you to understand right now, but the fear you are experiencing is the response of your subconscious to a pattern of delusional beliefs. Taking the medication really is the best thing for you to do right now."

"But it's the voice of the Devil. I know that now. What I need is an exorcism, not medication."

"An exorcism? I know you have strong religious beliefs Joan but I'm afraid an exorcism is completely out of the question."

"I asked my mum and dad to ask Father James . . ."

"That's their parish priest," Ed explained.

Marwan pondered whether to tell Joan that he had already spoken to her Father James. It was essential that she harboured no false hopes about an exorcism. "Yes, I know," he said. "In fact I met him earlier. He told me you had asked for an exorcism, and I told him the same thing I'm telling you, Joan. If he really wants what's best for you, he won't attempt to interfere. And he certainly won't be permitted to conduct an exorcism while you're my patient. Understood?"

"Forget it." Joan said under her breath.

"What?"

"I said fucking forget it, okay?" Her anger was building again.

"Forget what, Joan?"

Her appearance changed subtly. Her eyes narrowed, encompassing all of them in their baleful glare, taking on the ferocity of a predator that was about to strike. They shivered as if a chill had suddenly coursed through them. They felt a premonition of evil, a preternatural sharpening of their senses that told them of a malevolent presence and filled them with inexplicable fear. All except Joan, who simply said "I won't be taking any of your medication." The voice was hers, but its inflexion, its accent, both were alien. They looked at her as if they did not know her.

'*About time.*' The first demon said, feeling the change in her, her spirit diminishing, their power growing.

'*Soon, very soon now.*' The Devil said.

Then the sensation passed. Marwan was the first to recover. "No Joan, that's not an option. If you won't take the medication we'll give it to you by injection. This treatment plan has already been discussed and agreed by the team, and we will not be changing our minds about it. Do you understand?" She made no response. "I said, do you understand?"

Later, Marwan still felt uneasy, they all did. Joan had said nothing more, but withdrew into herself, no longer responding to anything that was said, and needing to be helped from the room, a nurse on each arm to guide her to the day room. They were all shaken by what they had seen. Marwan tried to dismiss it as overwrought imaginations acting under the power of suggestion, but even when rationalised, still he could not easily dismiss the shiver of terror that had him rooted to his chair. He had ended the ward round. It had been too traumatic a session to do justice to any patients following Joan. He asked his secretary to contact Joan's parents to ask them to come in and see him. They were due at any minute.

His secretary ushered them in and returned minutes later with a tray bearing three cups of tea. "Here we are," she said brightly. "Anyone take sugar?"

"Me, thank you," Sean replied. "Just the one, please." He sounded nervous.

Dr. Marwan waited for his secretary to leave. "Mr. and Mrs. Archer, thank for coming in to see me. I'm sure you must be very worried about Joan."

"Very worried, doctor." Bernadette spoke for both of them. "Nobody tells us anything. We're at our wits' end."

"I'm afraid I can't tell you very much myself, but there is something in particular I wanted to talk over with you."

"Yes?"

Marwan started to polish his glasses. "I understand Joan asked if you could arrange for her to have an exorcism?"

The parents exchanged a guilty look. "She did," Bernadette admitted. "We mentioned it to Father James, but he said it was a very unusual request and that he would have to speak to the bishop about it."

Marwan inspected his glasses before putting them back on. "Yes. I think 'unusual' is putting it mildly. What do you think about it?"

"I suppose it seems incredible in this day and age, but Father James said that possession can and does happen, though it's extremely rare. He said an exorcism wasn't completely out of the question."

"I'm afraid it is."

It was the doctor's attitude that annoyed Sean. He was so cocksure of himself. "Out of the question? Why?" He asked.

Marwan had half expected they would be like this. "Possession is a concept that belongs in the medieval mind, not in the modern rational world. It's nothing more than superstitious nonsense. It is a belief founded in ignorance and fear - a way for uneducated folk to explain the inexplicable and, as such, it has no place in modern medicine. Joan is quite simply ill. She finds it difficult to acknowledge the fact, but a fact it remains nonetheless. We owe it to her to be scientific and objective if we are to help her."

Bernadette thought this was nothing but bluster. "Do you believe in God, doctor?"

"As a matter of fact, I do, but that has no bearing on this matter," Marwan insisted.

"But if God can intervene in the world, why can't the Devil?"

Marwan could see where she was trying to take this, but was having none of it. "Despite my belief in the Almighty, I don't believe he intervenes on such a personal level."

Now Sean took up the thread. "Are you saying that there's no such thing as evil in the world, doctor?"

"Not at all. The presence of evil is self-evident. I just don't believe that it manifests itself in the form of possession by the Devil And if I may go further, I must say it's not good for Joan for you to encourage her in such a belief."

"But we didn't encourage her. It was Joan who asked us about the exorcism, we just said we'd talk to Father James about it for her."

"Well I must ask you not to discuss it with her again."

But Bernadette was not so easily put off. "But what if the bishop says it's okay?"

Marwan groaned inwardly. How was Joan going to be convinced she wasn't possessed if he couldn't convince the parents? "It doesn't matter what the bishop says, it won't help Joan, and it will not be allowed to take place here."

"But she could have one after she comes home?"

It had been a difficult day; perhaps the most difficult of his career. He tried not to show how exasperated he was feeling, but some of his frustration came through. "Please, Mrs. Archer; try to understand that by going along with this ridiculous notion you are colluding with Joan in her delusional beliefs. This does nothing but delay the process of recovery. And let me tell you, I suspect that Joan's recovery will be long, protracted, and painful. You really don't want to do anything that could hold her back, do you?"

Bernadette had been put well and truly in her place. "No doctor, of course not."

"Good." So that was settled. Then he remembered his manners. "Thank you. And please, no more talk about possession or exorcism, eh?"

Sean and Bernadette left Marwan's office. He had told them that since they were here anyway, they could look in on Joan. She wasn't in her bed, or in her usual spot in the quiet corner. They found her where the nurses had left her in the day room, just staring into space. They pulled up chairs on either side but she did not acknowledge their presence.

"Hello love," Sean said, "how are you today?"

She did not reply. A single tear trickled down her cheek. She made no effort to wipe it away.

Bernadette tried. "We've just been to see your consultant. He seems very nice, very caring. Seems to know what he's talking about."

Still Joan did not reply or give any sign that she knew they were there. Her parents exchanged worried glances.

"It's a horrible day out," Sean tried again.

Bernadette showed Joan the raindrops on the sleeve of her coat. "Yes, we got wet, look. And that was only walking over from the car park. Good job I had my umbrella, wasn't it?"

Some of the patients were smoking. One of them blew smoke in their direction. Sean coughed. Joan did not seem to notice.

"Are you alright Sean?" Bernadette asked. She said to Joan "It can't be good for you, all this smoke in here." She looked for somewhere to sit away from the smoke. "Shall we go over there, where there's no-one smoking?" Joan said nothing. "Come on love; let's go over there, shall we?"

She took Joan's arm and pulled her up. Joan did not resist and passively allowed her parents to lead her to the other side of the room, shuffling laboriously. "That's better, isn't it?" Still Joan made no response.

Bernadette tried to make light of it. "Tell you who we saw today, love, Maggie Bateson. Didn't you go to school with her daughter? What was her name? Pamela. Yes, that's it, Pamela."

It was like talking to a mute. Sean and his wife exchanged a look of deep concern. "I'm afraid we were told we could only stay for a couple of minutes," Bernadette continued. "Just to say hello, so I think we'd better go now, okay?" When Joan did not reply she got up from her chair. "Well, goodbye love, see you at visiting tonight."

"That's right, love. You take care of yourself, okay?" Sean attempted a feeble joke. "And no running after those doctors, you hear?" As soon as he said it he wished he hadn't.

They each kissed their daughter on the cheek, and left, Bernadette fishing in her handbag for a tissue to dab at the tears that were starting down her face.

As they got into the car for the drive home Bernadette spoke. "Oh, Sean, she looked worse than ever. Are you sure we're doing the right thing?"

"I don't know." He blew his nose. "I'm not sure of anything any more, love."

Bernadette started the engine, gunning the accelerator. "Well, I'm not leaving it here. I'm going to ask Father James what he thinks. Let's go straight round to the church, shall we?"

"Aye, you're probably right, as usual."

"Probably right? I know I'm right. And if she's no better tomorrow, I'm going to demand a second opinion, that's what I'm going to do."

When Sean and Bernadette returned that evening Joan was no different. She was in the same place they had left her, still taking no notice of anything going on around her. They had no greater success in trying to get her to respond than they had had earlier. They remained at her side throughout visiting and left in a state of high anxiety. Only yesterday she had seemed so much better. Was it the refusal to allow an exorcism that had precipitated this change?

Susan had come in on the late shift and noticed the change in Joan. After visiting she went to find her. Joan was still in the same place she had occupied all day, staring into space. Susan shook her arm gently to get her attention.

"Joan? Joan? Come on Joan, it's bed time. Would you like some cocoa?" She asked, gently.

Joan did not respond, but allowed Susan to raise her from the chair and lead her to her bed. Susan drew the curtains. "You get yourself undressed, Joan, and I'll come back in a minute with a nice hot drink, okay?"

When she returned a few minutes later, Joan was still standing exactly where Susan had left her. Susan put the hot drink down on the bedside cabinet and tried to rouse her. "Joan, Joan!" Now she shook her vigorously. "Can you hear me Joan? Please answer me Joan, please?"

But still she was unable to get a response. She wasn't sure what to do. She was the senior nurse on this shift, so there wasn't anyone she could ask. She decided to phone Tony to see if he was at home. He was. "Tony, I'm worried about Joan. Something is very wrong with her." She explained how Joan had been all afternoon.

Tony did not live far away; he said he would come in and have a look. It didn't take him long. When they got to Joan's bed she was still standing exactly where Susan had left her.

"Joan," he said, "Joan? It's me, Tony, the unit manager. Do you recognise me?"

There was no response. Tony lifted her arm so that it was at a right angle to her body. When he let go it stayed where it was.

"Shit."

"What is it?"

Tony stood watching Joan for nearly half a minute to see if her arm would fall. It didn't. Gently he lowered her arm. "I've not seen this for years."

Susan was clueless. "What?"

"This waxy flexibility. Whatever posture we put her in, she'll just stay there, completely passive. I think she's gone catatonic."

"Catatonic? I remember that from my training, but I've never seen it. I thought it was a thing of the past."

Tony led Joan to the bed and got her to sit on it. "So did I. I've only ever seen it once myself, years ago."

"What does it mean?"

"It means trouble. It's like she's gone into a trance. She's cut herself off from us completely. If we're lucky she'll continue to accept fluids, if not . . ."

"Should I tell Ed?"

"Yes, and see if you can track down doctor Marwan. He needs to be told about this as well."

Ed was in a restaurant when his mobile rang. He was with Joan. They had just been to the pictures. Joan was still rather distant and their conversation brittle. Ed was trying to be cheerful. He took the mobile from his pocket, but didn't recognise the number on the screen.

"Hello?"

When he heard the voice on the other end his heart sank. "Ed? Ed, it's Sue."

Why did she have to call him now? He moved the phone away from his ear so that Joan could hear and replied in an exaggerated voice. "Oh hi, Sue. Why on earth would you be calling me? No, I'm afraid we don't have a copy of '*When will I see you again?*' to play tonight." His tone changed, showing he resented this intrusion. "Okay? Sue, I can't believe you'd be calling me when . . ."

Susan cut him off. "Ed! Get a grip will you? This is not about you. Do you honestly think I would have called you if I had any other option?"

This calmed him. "Fine, fine. What is it?"

"It's Joan. Tony says she's gone catatonic, and that you should be told about it PDQ."

"Catatonic? But . . . isn't that . . ."

"Yes, Ed, I know. It's a thing of the past. Only it isn't; it's very much happening here and now."

"Blimey. God, I don't have a clue what to do. Is she alright otherwise?"

"She's still breathing if that's what you mean."

Edward tried to think. "Have you told doctor Marwan?"

"Not yet. Ed, would you mind . . ."

"Yeah, of course. I'll give him a call right now."

"And will you be coming in?"

"Depends what Marwan says. It's not as if I know what to do, or anything, is it? If she arrests or anything, call the crash team. Not anything else we can do as far as I know. I'll call you back when I've spoken to doctor Marwan, okay?"

"Okay. And Ed," she paused, reluctant to remind herself of how angry he had been with her.

"Yes?"

"I really am sorry, you know, about . . ."

"Yeah, okay. 'Bye."

He pressed the disconnect button, and looked for the number for Dr. Marwan.

"What's the problem?" Joan asked him.

He shook his head and pointed to his phone indicating that it was ringing at the other end. But all he got was Marwan's voicemail. He waited for the beep. "Hello, doctor Marwan? It's Edward. Sorry to call so late, but I thought you ought to know that it seems that Joan Archer has gone catatonic. She's physically safe at the moment, but I don't know what I should do about it. I'll wait for you to get back to me before deciding whether I need to go in."

Joan was concerned now. "Your patient has gone catatonic? That sounds serious."

Edward had become quite agitated. "Yeah, it is serious. It's incredibly rare these days. I've only ever read about it, and I've no idea how it should be treated. I'll have to wait until I hear from doctor Marwan."

She reached across and squeezed his hand. It was the first real contact between them. "You okay? You seem a bit worked up over it."

"Yeah. It's just that I feel, you know, responsible. When I told Marwan about Joan's experiences in the chapel he decided she shouldn't be allowed to go any more. Since then she's gone downhill rapidly, and now this."

She pushed her fingers between his. "Ed, you can't go blaming yourself, you know. You do know that, don't you?"

But he seemed reluctant to be convinced. "Yeah. I s'pose so."

"No, I mean it. I warned you about getting too involved. I think you've identified too closely with her, and now you're losing your objectivity. You owe it to your other patients to keep that distance. Without it, you're lost. And you're too good a doctor to let that happen to you, okay?"

He admitted defeat. "Okay."

"Suddenly I'm not hungry. You want to come back to my place?"

25
A reluctant exorcist

Father Alonso had suggested that if Joan's need was so urgent, then James should perform the exorcism himself. Reluctantly, James had accepted that this was the only option open to them. He spoke to the bishop again; he agreed that James should perform the rite but cautioned him to prepare with the utmost care. James had spent all afternoon in the diocesan library reading everything he could on the subject. Much of what was available were *apologia* justifying exorcism and its evolution from early times. There was comparatively little on modern attitudes and the rite itself He paused in his reading to rub the back of his neck. There was a coffee machine in a communal area near the library entrance. Should he have another one? Best not, he told himself. Already he could feel the blood pounding in his temples, probably the result of all the caffeine he had consumed. He resumed his reading.

Exorcism, invoking the power of Christ to deliver demoniacs from the possession of Satan, has been attested since the earliest days of the Church. It is clear from numerous testimonies that Christian exorcism did not involve employing magic or pagan superstitions, but depended on the power of prayer and faith in Christ crucified to give a simple and authoritative adjuration in the name of the risen Jesus to the demon to leave the body that they have possessed and are subjecting to vile torments.

That Christ gave authority to his disciples to cast out demons is attested by all of the synoptic evangelists: 'And he gathered the twelve to him to send them out two by two, giving them the authority to cast out evil spirits . . .' *(Mark 6:7);* 'Jesus called the twelve together and gave to them authority to cast out evil spirits . . .'*(Matt. 10:1); and* 'One day Jesus called together his disciples to invest them with the authority to cast out demons . . .'*(Luke 9:1).*

The efficacy of the exorcism depends greatly on the exorcist. The priest who undertakes the office should be of good physical health and impeccable moral character, courageous, humble, and one who undertakes normal pastoral duties. He must be in a state of Grace, seeking and obtaining absolution before the exorcism, otherwise he invites the Devil to entrap him. The exorcist must never forget that if

the entity is expelled it must return to Hell, an outcome it will do its
utmost to prevent.

The exorcist should not work alone. If possible he should be
assisted by another priest and a doctor. Witnesses, preferably relatives
of the possessed, should also be present.

If on its first utterance the exorcism fails to banish the demon,
the rite should be repeated, as many times as is needful.

He rubbed his eyes, trying to banish his fatigue. That was enough for today. He carried a stack of books to deposit them on the librarian's trolley. Only one would he take away with him: a copy of the *Rite of Exorcism*. He took seriously the advice to obtain absolution before proceeding. He would see Phil Andrews again on his way back to the presbytery. He thought he could kill two birds with one stone. He would ask the bishop to hear his confession, and at the same time ask him to be his assistant in the exorcism.

When he got back to the presbytery there was a note through the door. Bernadette and Sean wanted him to call them urgently. He did so immediately. Things had taken a new and sinister turn. Joan was much worse. Following a confrontation in the ward round in which she had been told she would no longer be permitted to go to the chapel she had withdrawn completely into herself. Now nobody could get her to respond or communicate with her in any way. This seemed to him to have an ominous significance. She had warned that she was almost completely in the power of the demons that had taken possession of her, now it seemed she had lost the ability to resist. Sean and Bernadette would be returning for visiting at seven. They would let him know whether there was any improvement. If not, what could they do? They had thought of asking for a second opinion. He agreed: if Joan had a psychiatrist who was even nominally Christian he might be more sympathetic to the idea of exorcism. If not, even without Dr. Marwan's cooperation, James thought there was at least something that could be done. Visiting was due to finish at nine. He phoned the bishop to warn him he might be needed later that night. Now that it seemed imminent, he expressed his anxiety about taking part. "Don't worry about it Phil," James had said, trying to raise his spirits. "Come over early and I'll hear your confession. We'll be in the only Church in England with two clerics in a state of Grace; we'll be unstoppable."

Since then James had spent his time preparing himself and the church. They would conduct the rite before the statue of the Sacred Heart. This was the aspect of Jesus with which Joan had identified most strongly. He had asked Bernadette to bring a photograph of Joan and some of the pictures of Jesus from Joan's bedroom. They would help to establish a connection with her spiritual presence.

He returned to the book he had borrowed on conducting the rite itself, reading more about the stages an exorcism was likely to involve:

The Presence, where the demon makes itself manifest; The Break Point, often recognisable by the ensuing pandemonium and vitriolic utterances from the mouth of the possessed; The Clash, where exorcist and demon are engaged in a direct contest with the exorcist seeking mastery; and finally, The Expulsion, where the demon is forced to leave in the name of Christ triumphant. All present feel the occultation of the Presence.

He looked at his watch. Eight o'clock. He wouldn't hear from Sean and Bernadette for some time. He had had enough of reading; prayer was what he needed now. He went back to the church and knelt at the altar rail. What should he pray for? Faith? Strength? But this was not about him. In the end it was obvious. He prayed for Joan, that the Saviour would bring comfort and healing to her exhausted spirit.

At eight-thirty the Bishop arrived. James heard his confession and together they went through the rite of exorcism. It was after ten when the presbytery bell rang. Bernadette was clearly upset.

"How's Joan?" James asked.

"Terrible, Father. She just sits there, staring without seeing, incapable of doing anything for herself. She doesn't know me or her dad, and doesn't seem to be aware of anything going on around her. I don't know what it is they've done to her, but it's cruel to see her like that."

That made his mind up for him. If Joan was in such a crisis, something had to be done. He explained what he intended to do.

"Ideally, an exorcism would be performed with the victim present. However, Joan's doctors refuse to countenance an exorcism, so we must do the next best thing. I've been thinking about this for most of today, wondering how to go about it. The Church tells us that God is omnipotent and omnipresent and that if we had the necessary faith we could move mountains. Everything I have read suggests that demons are expelled not because of the physical proximity of the exorcist and victim, but because of the power of prayer and our faith in the Lord. I propose to carry out the rite of exorcism here in our church, seeking the Lord's help not for ourselves, but for Joan. When I command the demon to be gone from Joan's body, it must hear me and, if our faith is sufficient will be compelled to obey. This is not the normal form of the rite of exorcism, but I think it's the best we can do in the circumstances."

"And when do you plan to do it, Father?" Bernadette asked.

"Now."

He led them into the church. Apart from a small red light burning to indicate the presence of the Sacrament, it was in darkness. James switched on the lights above the sanctuary, casting a dim glow through the rest of the church, making it look cold and unwelcoming.

"Before we start the exorcism, Bernadette and Sean must confess their sins and be granted absolution. We must all be in a state of Grace, otherwise we put our own souls in peril," James announced. "Then we'll say mass." Bernadette knelt on one side of the church and made her confession to James; Sean, on the other, confessed to the bishop. Then mass was said, the most solemn and portentous they had ever attended. At stake was the rescue of their daughter. When the mass was ended, Bernadette and Sean took places in the front pew before the statue of Christ; James and the bishop retired to the sacristy. When they emerged James was wearing the white surplice and purple stole prescribed by the rite, the bishop wore a simple alb.

The sanctuary lights were dimmed. Two candles were lit on the side-altar beneath the statue. Six tall floor-standing candles, normally used only on high feast days were brought from the sanctuary to the side chapel and placed to give a semi-circle of light. Bernadette and Sean put a photograph of Joan on the altar and, to either side of it, some of the pictures of Christ that they had taken from her bedroom. All was ready. They were fearfully conscious of the solemnity and power of what they were about to do. It was now very late and the darkened church eerily silent. Unfamiliar shadows cast by the flickering candles played tricks on their heightened senses, and, in the silence, unexpected noises took on a sharpness and clarity that rendered them sinister, no matter how innocent their origin. As he approached the altar, Father James' deliberate steps across the parquet floor echoed sharply. He prostrated himself and said a silent prayer for guidance before getting to his feet and sprinkling each of them with holy water, making the shape of a cross and saying "In the name of the Father, and of the Son, and of the Holy Spirit."

"We'll start with a reading from the Old Testament, from the Book of Job." He opened a small Bible.

> Behold, God will not cast away a faithful man, neither will he help the evil doers.

They listened to the reading in silence, pondering its words that on a new significance in these dreadful circumstances. Then James told them they would read psalm fifty-four together. This would unite them in their purpose. They chanted:

> Save me, O God, by thy name, and judge me by thy strength.
> Hear my prayer, O God; give ear to the words of my mouth.
> For strangers are risen up against me, and oppressors seek after my soul.

This was followed by the bishop reading a short passage from the gospel according to John.

> In the beginning was the Word, and the Word was with God, and the Word was God. . . In him was life; and the life was the light of men. And the Light shineth in darkness; and the darkness comprehended it not.

"From this we invoke the power of the divine Word and the light against the darkness of Hell," he explained. Then he and James positioned themselves before the altar with its photograph of Joan, the bishop holding up the book with the rite of exorcism so that James could read from it. James crossed himself and read in a loud clear voice that echoed around the empty church.

"I exorcise thee, most vile spirit, in the name of the risen Lord. I command thee to get out and flee from this servant of God, Joan, who was claimed for God by his holy Church in the sacrament of baptism, who grew in the knowledge of the Lord in the sacraments of penance and Holy Communion, and who affirmed her faith in the promises of the Resurrection in the sacrament of confirmation." He paused, making the sign of the cross over the photograph. "In the name of the Father, and of the Son, and of the Holy Spirit."

He consulted the text again. "It is the Lord Himself who commands thee, He who ordered thee cast down from the heights of Heaven to the very depths of Hell. He commands thee, who commands the sea, the winds, and the tempests.

"Therefore, thou most evil enemy of the faith, hear the command of the Most High and tremble before it. Satan, harbinger of death, root of evil, kindler of vices, seducer of men, procurer of sorrows, I command thee in the name of Christ to attend and listen. It is fruitless to stand and resist, for thou knowest that Christ the Lord will destroy thy strength. Fear and heed the promise made by He who redeemed Adam's sin, who knows the hearts of men, who was crucified, died, triumphed over the gates of Hell and who lives on in the resurrection."

Taking up the holy water he sprinkled the photograph, saying "Depart I command thee in the name of the Father, and of the Son, and of the Holy Spirit who liveth and reigneth, one God, for ever and ever, world without end."

Before they could reply "Amen," as one the candles were snuffed out, leaving them in total darkness.

Bernadette had been listening awestruck to the power of the words. Exorcism was such a strange intrusion into their modern lives it was almost as if they had been transported back in time. Like many Catholics, she knew that, from time to time, exorcisms were conducted, but never had she witnessed one. She tried to focus on the meaning in the words. Then, without warning, the church was plunged into darkness; a darkness that she knew without any doubt was straight from Hell. She could not stop herself from screaming. It dawned on her that they were alone in this small place, and that Satan was actually there, now, his presence so real it had been able to extinguish the candles. There was a noise like wind soughing through trees and the air felt chill. They were enveloped in utter blackness. Then the noise stopped and all was silent. Slowly she became aware of the presence among them of a brooding malice, a fathomless evil that permeated the very stones surrounding them. It was all around them, and there was nowhere that was beyond its reach. Her skin was crawling, as if from the physical nearness of the evil that had come among them. In the darkness she reached for the assurance of Sean's hand. He must be afraid too, she knew, but he would never show it, not when he knew how frightened she was. He was a true rock, dependable even in the face of this implacable malevolence.

Although he kept it to himself, Sean was terrified. He felt cold sweat trickling down his back. Never had he known such fear. He squeezed Bernadette's hand with an assurance he did not truly feel.

Father James too felt the touch of fear. But he had been expecting something like this to happen. This was surely *the Presence* when the entity made itself known to them. It was trying to frighten them. It meant it was aware of what they were doing. He had placed a torch against the altar rail. He picked it up and switched it on. Its beam revealed anxious faces.

"Do not be afraid," he told them. "This is a sign that we are getting through to it. Just give me a minute and I'll get the candles lit again."

*

In the hospital Joan had been hooked up to a series of monitors that showed her heart-beat, respiration and the amount of oxygen in her blood. A nurse was keeping a solitary vigil at her bedside. All was normal. She glanced at her watch; it was just past midnight. She was glad she had been asked to come in to do a one-to-one, it was easy money. She didn't know the patient, but then she didn't need to; all she had to do was to watch the monitors, and if there seemed any sign of serious deterioration, call the crash team. The patient had been silent and immobile for hours.

The lights were low, too low to be able to read, and the inevitable sleepiness, the curse of night duty, was creeping up on her. Without warning, Joan gave a sharp intake of breath as if feeling sudden pain. She whimpered, and went rigid. The nurse glanced at the monitors. The heart rate was rising, blood pressure increasing, respiration getting shorter and faster. Suddenly the patient's limbs started to convulse in rapid spasmodic seizures. The nurse hit the alarm.

"What is it?" asked the first of the other night staff to arrive. "Is she arresting?"

"No. She's having a fit!"

There was little they could do. The on-call SHO was bleeped in case they needed to administer diazepam, but about thirty seconds later the fit stopped, before she could even arrive, leaving Joan immobile as before, the only clue that anything had happened a sheen of moisture on her upper lip.

*

After relighting the candles, Father James asked Bernadette to lead them in saying a decade of the Rosary. That helped to calm them. "Remember," he told them, "it's the power of prayer and our faith in the Resurrection that are the keys to success. Whatever it is that's tormenting Joan, we've rattled it. We just need to keep at it."

Drawing himself up to his full height he returned to the rite, his voice ringing out in the flickering light, sounding unnaturally loud in the silent church.

"I command thee, thou foul serpent of Hell, in the name of Him who created this world and caused thee to be created, in the name of Him who triumphed over thy power in this world and caused thee to be cast down into everlasting fire: get thee hence from this servant of God, Joan, who desires only to return to the bosom of our holy mother Church. I command thee not in the knowledge and wielding of my own power, but by the virtue of the thrice-blessed Trinity, that thou depart from this servant of God, Joan, whom Almighty God created in his own image."

After relighting the candles, bishop Andrews had resumed his place before the altar, again holding out the book of the Rite for James to see. When the candles had gone out it had taken the greatest self control on his part not to run and hide in a corner, so abject had his terror been. He risked a glance towards Sean and Bernadette. These were good people, ordinary devout Catholics both, blessed with a simple acceptance of the teachings of the Church, praying without rest that their daughter would be delivered from Satan's grasp. He wished he had half the faith they had. He laughed inwardly at the irony of it. Here was he, a bishop of the Church, some people still called him 'Your Grace'. Yet he felt he was far from Grace, so filled was he with doubts. And tonight of all nights he knew he would need a belief in his God so impregnable it would be proof against the Devil himself. Yet he felt so small, so powerless against the terrible might of Hell. What had he been thinking of, agreeing to assist James with this exorcism? He was not made of the right stuff for this. With a jolt he realised his thoughts had been wandering as James moistened a finger to turn the page.

"Therefore thou art commanded to surrender, thou noxious demon of Hell. Surrender: not to me, but to the irresistible power of the risen Christ. He who thou tempted in the desert, He who thou tempted on the mountain, He who thou tempted on the pinnacle of the temple of Jerusalem and who commanded thee to get thee hence to the pit prepared for thee and thine angels.

"Begone, therefore, thou purveyor of depravity, thou seducer of innocence. Surrender thy place to Christ, who hath cast thee and thy demons into utter darkness, there to dwell in thine own filth for eternity.

"Therefore in the name of the Most High I command thee: depart from this woman, never dare again to cross the threshold of this temple of God. Flee and tremble at the invocation of the holy name that causes all Hell to kneel prostrate in fear and submission, to whom cherubim and seraphim with unwearied voices praise, singing, holy, holy, holy, is the Lord God almighty."

He stopped, sweat flowing freely from him. He waited to see if there would be a reaction similar to that which they had witnessed earlier. But there was nothing. According to the manual, they had come to the *Clash*: the voice of the demon should now be silent as it realised it was contending against the servants of the Kingdom of Heaven. Now was the time for the exorcist to gain mastery, but he was exhausted. Was this a sign that the Devil was fighting him? He felt drained, physically and emotionally. He didn't know whether he had the inner strength to continue, but he must see it out to the end. His legs so weak they were shaking, he lowered himself to kneel at the altar rail.

*

In the hospital, after the fit, the nurse watching Joan had redoubled her vigilance. She expected to see her patient sleeping deeply for hours after the convulsion – though how she would tell the difference from before the fit she did not know. There did seem to be signs of dreaming, with Joan writhing on the bed muttering unintelligible phrases, or shouting fragments of words. But apart from that there was nothing. Every hour, heart rate, breathing rate, blood pressure and oxygen saturation were recorded, but, apart from the convulsion earlier, there was nothing of note to report.

*

After a few minutes James felt recovered enough to resume. Now he held a wooden cross before him as a symbol of his authority.

"I call upon thee, most vile spirit, and command thee to listen in fear and awe to this servant of the living Christ who stands before thee at the command and under the protection of the divine Lord. I command thee to depart from this servant of God, Joan, whom thou hast enslaved in thy wickedness; depart ye cursed, into unquenchable fire, which is prepared for thee and thine angels. Depart with all thy deceits and return not, because God has ordained that man be the temple of the Holy Spirit."

He stopped, his throat suddenly completely dry. He could not make the words come. He swayed, clutching the crucifix to his breast.

"What is it?" The bishop hissed. Bernadette and Sean were rooted to the spot, fearful. James waved his hand vaguely, as if to indicate that he would be alright in a minute. He couldn't describe what he felt. His throat had constricted to the point where he could barely breathe. Was this the crisis of the struggle, or was it merely the result of an overworked imagination? He was at the most critical part of the rite – the final command to the demon to leave. He forced himself to continue, his voice rasping with the effort.

"Thou art expelled by the will of Christ's servant, Joan.

"Thou art expelled by the will of Christ's servant James.

"Thou art expelled by the will of Christ's servants Philip, Bernadette, and Sean.

"Thou art expelled by the will of all holy men and women.

"Thou art expelled by the will of the archangel Michael and all the angels and archangels of Heaven.

"Thou art expelled by the Lord God of hosts.

"Thou art expelled by his Son, the Beloved.

"Thou art expelled by the Holy Spirit, the Lord and giver of life.

"Thou are expelled by the Holy Trinity, indivisible, three in one.

"Begone now to the place that has been prepared for thee and all they deceits and do not presume in thy impudence to darken this world again."

*

In the hospital, the alarm on the heart monitor sounded. The nurse ran to the machine. Joan was flatlining. Her heart had all but stopped; blood pressure and oxygen saturation were both falling rapidly. Her breathing ceased. The nurse hit the alarm button and struck Joan hard in the middle of her chest, starting the emergency resus procedure. When help came, she yelled "She's arrested! Call the crash team!"

A nurse arrived with the emergency box and placed an oxygen mask and bag over Joan's face. Together they administered thirty compressions then two breaths. They would repeat this until the crash team arrived. An SHO arrived and made a rapid assessment. She took the adrenaline injection from the emergency box.

*

Utterly spent, James sank to his knees. It was done. But what effect would it have?

26
The inquest

The inquest began at seven the following morning. The night staff had stayed behind, and were waiting in the group therapy room. Tony and Susan were on the early shift anyway, and Edward and Dr. Marwan had both been in since half past six.

Marwan looked grim. He had been called in the night, but had decided that since there was nothing he could do there was no point in coming in. He had asked the ward staff to call Edward to get him to come in early. They had a lot to go through. If necessary, he would review Joan's case from beginning to end.

"First of all," he said, "I want to say thank-you to the night staff, who, I understand, performed heroically. They did all that could have been expected of them, and it's not so much how they responded last night I want to discuss, but what got us there." He looked at Sandra, the senior nurse who had been on duty. "Could you tell us all exactly what happened?"

Sandra looked tired. It had been a long and stressful night. "Well, as arranged, we had extra bank cover from Chris," she pointed to the nurse who was seated next to her, "to provide one-to-one cover for Joan Archer. Chris can tell you better than me what happened."

All eyes were on Chris. She looked like she'd had a night of it too. "For the first few hours, she didn't stir. Pulse, respiration, BP sats, all normal. Then, just after midnight, she fitted."

"Fitted?" Ed wanted to be absolutely sure. "How long did it last?"

"Yes. Full tonic-clonic grand-mal seizure. It didn't last long, no more than a minute I would say. It had stopped before the on-call doctor arrived."

"What did you do?" Marwan asked.

"Just the usual. The convulsion had clearly subsided, so the SHO said there was no point giving diazepam. I administered oxygen, but the sats were okay so there was no point carrying on with that either."

Marwan was taking notes. "What happened next?"

"Nothing much. She seemed a bit restless, tossing and turning and mumbling in her sleep, occasionally calling out, like she was having a bad dream."

"Isn't that rather unusual following a grand-mal?" Ed pointed out.

Chris nodded. "I know, but I didn't know what significance it had. I assumed it was the response of her condition to the fit."

"It's alright," Marwan assured her. "Ed and I have been discussing this. It has us mystified too. Why she should fit when she had no previous history, and why she should show signs of restlessness in her sleep when she had previously been catatonic are conundrums we'll need to think long and hard about." He made another quick note. "What happened next?"

"At about one-fifteen the alarm on the heart monitor went off. Her pulse was virtually at a standstill, she had stopped breathing and her BP and sats were falling rapidly. I started emergency resus and called the crash team. They were there within minutes, and took over from me and Sandra."

"And the rest is history." Marwan concluded for them. He put his pen down. "Thank you Chris, thank you Sandra. Just for the record I think you did a good job. I don't think there was anything more you could have done. Why don't you both go home and try and get some sleep?"

The night staff left. Now Tony found himself the centre of Marwan's attention. "Tony, what exactly happened with Joan earlier yesterday evening?"

Tony frowned. "Well, I wasn't here during visiting, and at hand-over, nobody seemed to have noticed anything wrong. It was only when Susan went to tell Joan it was time to go to bed that she realised something was the matter. She'd been sat in the same chair without moving since visiting. Sue couldn't get any response from her at all. Sue took her to her bed and called me. I noticed the waxy flexibility."

"Are you sure about that?"

"Dead sure."

"Was she taking fluids?"

"Just a little water," Susan added, "but only when she was prompted."

"And how is she now?"

Tony sighed. "She's on the high dependency unit. The crash team were able to resuscitate her on the ward, then ran her over to ICU, but they didn't keep her there for long. From what they tell me she seems to be making a remarkable recovery."

"At least that's something," Ed chimed in. "I called the cardiology reg who saw her. He's completely mystified. Says her heart is completely normal for a woman of her age; no trace of any pathology, and absolutely no reason for her to arrest."

Marwan stood. "Well," he said, "let's go and see this mystery for ourselves, eh?"

On the high dependency unit Joan was propped up in bed with all manner of tubes and wires attached to her. She was staring into space and showed no recognition of Ed or Dr. Marwan. Ed did a quick physical examination, then raised her arm so that it stood out straight in front of her. It stayed where he left it. He waited to see whether normal fatigue would force her to let it drop. When it didn't he gently laid her arm by her side.

"Physically she seems fine. I'll organise a blood and urine screen, U's and E's and thyroid, but I doubt we'll find anything."

"Temperature?" Marwan asked.

Ed consulted her chart. "Spot on. No sign of any infection or injury that could be causing this."

Marwan shook his head, baffled. "Extraordinary. This case. Nothing about it is straightforward, is it?"

"Doctor Marwan, you don't think . . ."

Marwan looked askance at his junior. "You don't think she might really be possessed? Edward. I thought you were an atheist."

"I am. It's just . . ."

"Edward, superstition is the response of the ignorant to the inexplicable. This isn't inexplicable, far from it. It's terribly difficult to find a way to help this poor girl, but we'll do it using medical science, not hocus pocus; agreed?"

"Agreed."

Marwan led Ed from the cubicle. "I'm going to call Professor Morland. He's an old friend, and some years ago he wrote a review of the management of catatonia. Who knows, it's such a rare phenomenon these days he may offer to get directly involved himself. While I'm doing that I want you to arrange for her to be brought back to the ward. And don't worry. People have gone catatonic before, and survived."

By two o'clock, Joan was back on the psychiatric unit, in one of the side rooms, with a drip to prevent her from getting dehydrated. She had been seen by a consultant cardiologist who had pronounced himself mystified, and that Joan was well enough to be transferred back to Maple ward. Marwan was like a mother hen, checking on her every hour or so. "Any results back yet?" He asked Edward.

"U's and E's normal. Nothing else yet."

"What about creatine kinase?"

"I'm afraid I didn't do that. Is it important?"

"The results might be interesting rather than crucial, I would say. Steven Morland mentioned it could be an indication that what we're seeing is linked to neuroleptic malignant syndrome."

"I'll get onto it."

Marwan turned to Cathy. "How are her obs?"

"Nothing abnormal," she replied.

"How often are they being done?"

"Every hour."

"Let's make that every half an hour, just in case."

He turned to go. Edward walked with him. "Did Prof Morland recommend any treatment?"

"He said IM lorasanide might be worth a try. I think we'll leave it a bit longer before trying anything so drastic." He stopped, waiting for Cathy to catch up. "Have her parents been informed?" He asked.

She shook her head. "I don't think so, not yet. We called first thing, but there was no answer. I'll try again in a bit."

"Okay. When they arrive, could you ask them if they would wait to see me before letting them go in to see Joan?"

*

It was mid afternoon when Sean and Bernadette arrived on the ward. They exited Dr. Marwan's office clearly upset but trying to put a brave face on things. At the door, Bernadette paused, turning to ask a last question. "Thank you for keeping us informed doctor. Is it alright if we go and see Joan now?"

Marwan's voice carried from within. "Of course. Just ask one of the nurses to go with you, if you don't mind."

At the nursing station Sean told them what Marwan had said. "No problem," Cathy replied, "I'll come with you. Did he explain her condition to you, that it's very unlikely that you'll get any response from her?"

"Yes."

"She was like that that last night anyhow," Bernadette added

Cathy led them to Joan's room.

The bed was empty. The drip had been pulled out and fluid had leaked all over the floor. The bed clothes were in disarray.

"Where is she?" Sean asked. "I thought you said she couldn't move."

After what had happened last night, Cathy was extremely concerned; it could be heard in her voice. "Can you wait here in case she comes back?" She ran to the nursing station.

She found Maria and Amy. "Maria," Cathy said, trying to catch her breath, "Joan's gone. Call security. I'll organise a search of the ward and then the unit."

"Gone?" Maria didn't seem to understand. "How? When?"

"It doesn't matter how or when, but you know what state she's in. After last night there's no knowing what might happen."

"I'll go and find doctor Marwan," Amy offered.

"And Ed too, if he's about, if you don't mind," Cathy called after her.

Half an hour later, Sean and Bernadette were back in Dr. Marwan's office, waiting to hear whether Joan had been found. Edward stood with his back to them, staring out of the window, fretting. Cathy came in. "She's definitely gone. The whole hospital has been searched. Nothing."

"What about the chapel?" Bernadette asked.

"First place we thought of, but there was no sign of her."

"Well she can't get far, can she?" Edward said, his frustration showing. "She's in a bloody hospital gown, for Christ's sake!"

Marwan was polishing his glasses for the twentieth time. "Have the police have been informed?"

"Yes. But it's hardly a major priority to them is it? All they were interested in was whether she was likely to be a danger to the public."

"Unlikely in my opinion," Marwan thought aloud. "I'm much more concerned about the risk to her own safety. In the state she's in, she's incredibly vulnerable right now."

Edward was upset and angry. Joan was his patient and the case seemed to have lurched from one disaster to another. He was still convinced that had he been allowed to follow his instincts and continue the visits to the chapel, none of this would have happened. His convenient memory forgot about how over-involved he had become. Without thinking, he gave voice to his thoughts. "How the hell did she get out in the first place? I thought nursing staff weren't supposed to go to sleep on duty!"

Marwan spoke sharply; his own nerves were stretched and it came out more abruptly than he intended. "Edward! That's enough of that, thank you. We need to remain calm. Angry recrimination is not going to help Joan. There'll be an incident enquiry afterwards – by people who haven't been involved in Joan's care - but for now all that matters is getting her back safely." He checked his watch. "She's been gone for an hour at the most. Not much we can do but wait." He turned his attention to Bernadette. "Mrs. Archer, are you sure you wouldn't prefer to go home? We can contact you just as easily there, you know."

But Bernadette wanted to stay where she was. If anything happened, she wanted to be among the first to know, not treated as an afterthought as seemed to have happened all too frequently so far. "If it's alright with you doctor, I'd prefer to wait here. This is where they'll bring her when they find her, and I want to be here for her when they do."

"I understand. Can we get you a cup of tea or anything?"

"No thank you, it's . . ." She couldn't hold the tears in any longer. She delved into her handbag for a handkerchief. Dr. Marwan spoke to Sean. "I really do think it would be better if you took Mrs. Archer home. There isn't anything you can do here, and I promise you someone will call as soon as there's any word about Joan."

Sean agreed. He hated being here. Though he had never said so, with its pervading atmosphere of pessimism, he always felt uneasy when visiting the psychiatric unit. Every time he left he hoped he would never have to come back. "The doctor's right love. No sense in just sittin' round waitin' here. Let's go home. I'll give Father James a ring, see if he can come round for a bit, eh?"

"Now what?" Ed asked after they had left.

Marwan was still grim. "We wait."

27
Renewed

Joan was held fast by heavy chains, the weight of the links so great that even if she exerted all her strength she could not move even one of them. She could sense a presence next to her, a dark malevolent will, brooding and calculating. Just the knowledge that it was there and that she was fettered, helpless before it, filled her with a deep nameless terror. She could feel its ice-cold hatred. She knew it was not interested in her physical self; that was the mere window dressing of her temporal life. What it wanted, coveted, desired above all else, was her soul: immortal, unsullied, and, as yet, beyond its reach. The fiend's pangs of yearning were of such an intensity they were like a physical pain, burning, searing; its need so great it consumed all its purpose.

The silence as it pondered how it would obtain what it sought, what it had been seeking for so long, was terrifying. But even worse was Joan's unendurable fear of its touch. It had simply to reach across and she would melt with terror; what resolve she had left would dissipate like mist in a breeze.

She could not move her head, and all she could see was a featureless grey corridor which stretched before her with swing doors at its end. Although the doors had windows, they were opaque, and though she could neither see nor hear anything of the world beyond the doors, she knew it was there, the physical world to which she belonged, where her life was meant to be lived. But she was cut off from it. She could not reach it no matter how she tried. She shouted; a cry for help from deep within her frame, the loudest, most powerful yell of which she was capable. Somebody must hear it. But her voice was denied her. Her cry was silent. She was helpless, captive before this pitiless terror, utterly at its mercy.

Yet something was protecting her, preventing the demon from mounting its final assault on the sacred gates of her being. Try as she might, none of her senses could find this protector, but she knew it was there, it had to be, for she had no defences of her own.

Without warning, pain coursed through her with an agony she had never felt before. Her body convulsed with it, straining against the chains, but she was powerless to do anything other than suffer the excruciating white heat that ran down every nerve fibre.

In her mind she screamed, but still her voice did not obey, and the pain raged and raged and she knew it would never end and hoped she would die so the pain would be gone.

Then, as swiftly as it had come, it was gone. Her body went limp with relief, with no sign that she had suffered other than a sheen of moisture on her upper lip.

The entity that had caused the pain was still there. It knew what great treasure lay within its grasp and desired it like it desired no other thing.

Now it moved. It stood before her, tall and terrible, its hatred for mankind and all its works was visible, seething on its surface in a miasma of filth. But it was no longer paying any attention to her: it was staring intently at the doors. She could feel its rage. Its outcries filled her head, forcing her to mimic them as it mouthed obscenities vile beyond her worst imaginings. Now its skin seemed to be blistering with heat, though she herself could feel only the icy chill of its presence. Its implacable will shouted into her consciousness: "No! She is mine! I will not give her up! I will not!"

Then it was gone. The chains fell away and were gone. How long she lay there afterwards she could not tell. The entity left no trace of its presence and she was at peace, serene. If she chose to, she could walk along the corridor and open the doors, but she was exhausted by her ordeal. Now there was a bright light. It was coming from beyond the doors, which opened, and she floated on air along the corridor and out into the room beyond. There were people there, gathered around a bed, speaking rapidly and loudly. She was looking down on them. There was a woman on the bed, and one of the people was pushing hard on her chest in short rapid bursts. She looked away from the bed seeking the light. It was still there, but receding. And there was the music, the music that her Saviour had sent her, but that was fading too.

Joan didn't know where she was when she woke. She was tired, so very tired. She didn't trouble herself to wonder where she might be, but surrendered to the desire to sleep. She woke again. Although she had no awareness of time there was an insistent thought nagging at her, telling her to get up and out of bed. Now she realised she was in a hospital. There was a needle in her arm held in place by tape, attached to a plastic tube. She pulled it out, and watched in a detached way as fluid spilled from it onto the floor

There was a cupboard on the wall. She opened it and found several pairs of pyjamas, of the old-fashioned kind with jackets and baggy bottoms. She found a pair to fit her and put them on and left the room, walking down the corridor. She made no attempt to conceal her presence, she simply saw no-one. In the nursing station a coat had been slung over the back of a chair, and a pair of sandals left under a desk. She put them on. There were coins in the coat pocket. Nobody paid her any attention as she walked off the ward and out into the world.

She walked as if in a dream. She had no idea where she was going, but knew she would get to where she needed to be. It occurred to her that this was what it was like to have faith, to trust one's being entirely to someone else.

It was a tourist who spotted her, an Episcopalian priest from Connecticut on a tour of English medieval cathedrals. He was panning his video camera up the tower when he saw a figure on the roof. He zoomed in. It was a woman. It looked like she was . . . dancing?

28

Journeys

It was Cathy who brought the news to Dr. Marwan and Edward. "They've found her."

"Where is she?"

"On the roof of the cathedral."

If Marwan was surprised, he did not show it, but simply said "Edward and I will get over there straight away."

Susan called Joan's parents. "Hello? Mr. Archer? It's Susan. One of the nurses on Maple ward? Joan's been found." She paused, waiting for Sean to tell his wife. "No, she's not hurt as far as we know." Another pause. "She's at the cathedral." She could hear Bernadette telling Sean what to ask. "No, I'm afraid she's not in there praying, it appears that she's on the roof. Doctor Marwan is on his way over there now with doctor Plant."

By the time Dr. Marwan and Edward got there, visitors to the cathedral had been ushered out and the surrounding area cordoned off by the police. The two psychiatrists approached an officer standing in front of a hastily-erected plastic barrier bearing the words 'Police. Do not cross.' He radioed to his superior, an inspector who invited them to duck underneath the line of tape.

"I'm Inspector Jepson," he said by way of introduction. "And you gentlemen are from the psychiatric hospital? We've got all the public out of harm's way. It's just knowing what to do about her." He pointed to where Joan was balancing on the parapet above them.

Marwan looked up, squinting in the bright sunlight. "Yes. It's a very complex case. Quite tragic, really."

"Can you give me any details?" The inspector asked. "Could be quite crucial to how we approach her."

Marwan sneezed. Bright light often had that unfortunate effect on him. "I can't tell you much, because I have to protect her right to confidentiality. What I can tell you is that her name is Joan Archer, she's 23 years old, single, lives with her parents, and is a Catholic."

"No boyfriend trouble?"

Marwan shook his head. "No. She's suffering from a severe mental illness, inspector, not going through boyfriend trouble."

"No? What about suicide? Do you think she's likely to . . ."

It was Ed who answered. "We've no way of knowing what's going through her mind right now. She's just been through a very traumatic couple of days. What we really need to do is to get up there and talk to her."

But the inspector disagreed. "I think you'll have to let me be the judge of that if you don't mind sir. I wouldn't want anyone to be put in any unnecessary danger. One of our trained negotiators is on his way from headquarters. They're the experts at talking people down, I think it's best if we wait for them to turn up, don't you?"

On the roof of the cathedral tower, Joan was transformed with joy. She was bathed in the brilliant glow of the late afternoon sunlight and could hear the music of the angels in its full majesty. She had kicked off the borrowed sandals and was dancing to the music, barefoot, arms held high, leaping onto the parapet to perform a pirouette before jumping back down.

Below on the cathedral green a television van and crew arrived. Its camera panned immediately to the roof, and a reporter set herself to find people to interview.

"Oh Christ," the inspector moaned. "That's all we need, I don't think. Excuse me will you, I'd better go and speak to our friends from the media."

This gave Edward the chance to speak to Marwan. "I should be the one who goes up there. She knows me, and I think she could still be persuaded to trust me."

But Marwan would not hear of it. "No Edward. You heard what the inspector said, and I agree with him; I don't want you taking any unnecessary risks."

They watched the inspector remonstrating with the reporter. "No, I'm afraid I can't give you any more information," he was saying. "All I can say is that we have qualified medical staff on hand, and one of our team that specialises in talking people down in these kinds of situations is on their way now. Now, I'm asking politely for your cooperation: please don't do anything to jeopardise that girl's or anyone else's lives for that matter."

A shout came from the tower. Everybody's eyes were drawn to it. "Edward! Edward! I know you're there." Joan was standing on the parapet. There was no rail, nothing to stop her from falling, but she was fearless. "Edward! Edward! I want you to come up here!

There's nothing to be afraid of. Nobody will hurt you – nothing *can* hurt you. Edward! Edward! Come on, answer me!"

The inspector's two-way radio bleeped. He put some distance between himself and the reporter before answering. Then he shouted across to Marwan and Edward. "I don't suppose you know what that's all about, do you?"

Edward waited for the inspector to rejoin them. "It's me she's shouting. She was my patient, and I was developing a good relationship with her before she absconded."

The inspector seemed sceptical. "Good? That's what you call good, is it?"

"Don't be too critical inspector," Marwan said. "It's very difficult to develop relationships in these circumstances. She is a very disturbed young woman. For the record, in my opinion, Edward was doing a good job."

Joan's voice drifted down again. "Edward! What are you waiting for?"

The inspector ignored her. "I'm afraid we have something of a problem."

Marwan raised his eyebrows. "The media?"

"No. They're just an occupational hazard. I'm afraid the problem is the negotiator. He's just been involved in an RTA on his way over. Even though he was driving a blue-lighter, some berk shot a red light and broadsided him."

Edward's response was automatic. "Shit! Is he going to be okay?"

"I think so. Bad case of concussion though, he won't be any help to us today I'm afraid."

Edward didn't hesitate. "I could do it."

"Do what?"

"Talk her down. I could do it. She trusts me, I know she does. That's why she's calling for me."

The inspector was reluctant to put someone else at risk. "I don't know. You've not been trained to handle these situations."

"Maybe. But I am training to be a psychiatrist, and I do know her well. Besides, have you got any better options?"

"Apart from calling out the armed response team? No, not really."

Edward turned to Dr. Marwan. "What do you think?"

Marwan had the same reservations as the inspector. "Edward, I think you're a very promising young psychiatrist, but you're more than a little impulsive. Just remember that if you do go up there, I will share some of the responsibility for letting you go. I agree that you have the best relationship with Joan, and that probably gives you the best chance of bringing her down safely . . . but – for God's sake, Edward, be careful. If you feel in the slightest danger, come down. Nobody will criticise you if you do. Above all, no heroics. I don't want to leave here with two body bags when even one would be a disaster."

Edward grinned. He knew he was the only one who could help Joan now. Only he really understood what she had been going through. "Thanks. I promise I won't let you down." He turned to the policeman: "Inspector?"

Grudgingly, the inspector agreed. "Well, if your boss says you're the best man for the job, who am I to argue? But like he said – be careful, okay?"

Edward handed his jacket to his mentor and walked into the shadow of the cathedral's interior.

29
The transforming power of joy

Inside, Edward followed the signs to the tower steps where he found another sign explaining that the tower was closed for repairs. He ignored it and started to climb. The steep narrow steps of the spiral staircase had him breathless long before he reached the top.

The top of the tower was a square space enclosed by a flat-topped stone parapet about two feet high with thick squared-off posts at each corner. There were holes in the stones where the old safety rails had been removed and new ones were waiting to be mounted.

Joan did not see him when he emerged from the stairwell. She was absorbed in her dance, smiling and laughing with a joyous naïveté.

Slowly she became aware of him. "Oh, Ed. Can't you hear it? Can't you feel it? We're standing in a corner of Heaven come down to earth. It's amazing, wonderful, glorious. I don't know how to express how intense everything is right now at this instant, I just feel so – alive! We're bathing in God's very light. He's with me, holding me safe in the essence of his love and power."

Edward didn't know how to respond. She was lucid, but was she rational? "That's . . . great, Joan," he said, hesitantly. She gave him a chiding look. "No," he insisted. "I really mean it. So you're okay now?"

She was smiling in the fullness of her joy. "Yes Ed. Everything is absolutely okay now, in ways that you would find hard to understand. Even I find it hard to understand." She looked to one side and seemed to be smiling at someone.

"I understand more than you know, Joan. I understand what's wrong with you, and I want to help you."

She turned back to him, still smiling. "How can you possibly understand when you don't believe in God or in me or anything at all apart from your own self? But all that will change – if you'll let it."

They were interrupted by Joan's mother and Father James almost falling from the stairwell onto the roof, both of them out of breath. "Doctor Plant!" Bernadette called.

Edward was not pleased to see them. "Mrs. Archer? Who let you up here? Please – can't you see what a difficult situation this is?"

Bernadette ignored him and spoke directly to her daughter. "Joan, sweetheart. Good news. The exorcism you wanted? The bishop authorised it. Although we couldn't be with you, Father James did it anyway – in the church last night. Both me and your dad took part." She hoped what she said would make sense to her daughter. "Won't you come down now please?"

Joan smiled at her, but said nothing.

Edward was furious. "Oh for crying out loud! Can't you people listen to reason? She didn't need an exorcism, she's mentally ill. She needs proper treatment."

For over two weeks Bernadette had been forced to stand by and watch her daughter go through hell. Now all her pent-up ire and scorn at what she had witnessed poured out. "Proper treatment? Is that what you call it? I saw what you did to her. Your proper treatment was torturing her, not helping her. An exorcism is what Joan needed, and if she has a belief in it, then maybe it will be enough to help her."

"Surely it was worth a try?" Father James said.

Edward knew he had to do something to retrieve the situation. "Look, Father, Mrs. Archer. This isn't helping to get Joan down from here. Why don't you just let me try to get her to calm down and . . ."

A third person came out onto the roof, panting with exertion. It was the inspector. "How did you people get up here? Don't you know that this is a police emergency scene? Only . . ."

Edward broke in. "Inspector – this is Joan's mother and their parish priest. Can't you get them out of here? I did seem to be establishing a rapport with Joan before I was interrupted!"

"Can't you see that this situation is extremely delicate?" The inspector said. He was clearly angry with them. "Your coming up here really isn't helping. We must let the doctor do the job he's been trained to do. I'm afraid I have to insist that you go down. Immediately."

But Bernadette did not want to leave Joan. "No! Please! She's my daughter! I have the right to be here, surely?"

But the inspector was insistent. "Please?" He led the way to the top of the stairs.

In tears, Bernadette was helped from the roof by Father James. All the while, Joan had been standing balanced on the parapet, saying nothing. Only now did she call to her mother, her cheerful voice not in keeping with the high emotions. "Mum! Don't worry! Everything will turn out as God wishes. I love you!"

Edward was becoming exasperated. "Joan, you know you can't stay up here. Sooner or later you're going to have to come down, and the sooner you come down, the sooner we can help you."

She laughed. "Help me? You?"

But he found nothing to be amused at; far from it. "Joan, I know you don't think you're ill, but you have to face facts - you are very ill indeed. I also know that you don't think that what we've done has helped, at least not so far, but you have to give us a chance. Doctor Marwan is a very experienced psychiatrist, and he really is doing his best. He's just asked for help with your case from a very eminent professor. It's just a question of time before we find the treatment that works best for you."

Still laughing, she ran lightly along the length of the parapet. Edward's heart was in his mouth. One missed step and she would be dead. At the end was a thick post, about two feet higher than the parapet. Without hesitating she leaped onto it and came to a perfect standstill. Her balance was astonishing. Only then did she give him an answer.

"Edward. I know you want to help, but you can't. I don't need anyone's help any more – I'm beyond any help that you could possibly give me." Again she glanced to one side as if someone was standing next to her.

But it was Edward's job to convince her to come down. "Joan, can't you stop thinking about yourself for a minute and think of all the pain you're causing to the people who care for you – especially your mum and dad?"

That made her think. Several moments passed before she replied. "I know it's hard for them, but sometimes a sacrifice has to be made. Sometimes it's worth the sacrifice. They'll understand." She turned to her left and spoke. "Won't they?" She seemed to get an answer for she turned back to Edward smiling. "They will," she assured him. "They really will."

"You know the police wanted to come up and drag you off the roof by force."

"You won't let them do that, will you Ed?"

"I said I would try to get you to come down voluntarily, but they won't wait forever."

"They won't have to. It'll be over soon."

This surprised him. "How do you know?"

"I know how it ends now," she said, her eyes shining. "He showed me. Isn't it glorious?"

"He?"

"Jesus."

It seemed to Ed that what Joan was saying suggested she was far from rational. It was fairly obvious that she could still hear at least one voice, which, if Marwan's theory was correct, would have to be congruent with the setting. She was in a sacred place, so it was predictable that she would hear not the voice of the Devil, but the voice of God.

"Is this another voice you're hearing?"

She shook her head in pity for his lack of understanding. "It's not like that any more. They're gone. They'll never have power over me again." She inhaled deeply and turned to look at the panorama that stretched below them. "Behold the wonder of God's creation and be humble." For no other reason than the pleasure it would give her she did a twirl, holding her hands out from her body Edward wanted to rush across and grab her to stop her from falling, but he was rooted to the spot, hypnotised by the joy she had in her very being. When she had had enough she spoke to him again. "Ed, do you remember when I asked you how could you tell what God's purpose was for your life?"

"I remember."

"Well, the music and the voices were sent to me to fulfil that purpose. The music was sent to give me the strength to get through my ordeal. The voices were sent so that I would meet you. It was all ordained. After that it was just a question of understanding and then accepting God's will."

Edward was astonished. In the course of his studies he had read any number of case reports describing in great detail the delusional systems that patients could construct, but never had he come across one that was so complex and coherent in its logic as this. But, he reminded himself, what Joan was telling him was not real, it was a delusion, it had to be.

"Joan," He said. "Frankly I'm amazed that you're so calm. Your case isn't like any that I've ever seen or even heard of, but please trust me when I tell you that you are mentally ill and that you need the kind of specialist help that only we can give you. Please let me help you."

He took a step towards her. She jumped from the post and ran along the uneven surface of the parapet to land on the next one. She showed no sign of fear at what she was doing. How on earth had she become so sure-footed?

"Don't come any closer, Ed," she warned. "I told you that you wouldn't understand, and you won't, not yet. But you will." She paused. "You will."

"And I suppose Jesus told you that as well?"

"You know he did." She looked at him intently making sure she had his full attention. "Ed, there's something else I have to tell you. I know you won't believe me now, but some day you will."

"Go ahead, I'm listening."

"I've been granted the most amazing gift. I've been allowed to experience Heaven while I'm still alive on earth. It's astonishing. I can't begin to tell you about the fullness of peace and joy there is in the presence of Jesus."

Edward could not keep the scepticism out of his voice. "Let me guess, Joan, he's here with you now?"

"Yes. He's right beside me. I'm filled with a love so great it defies description. I know that no harm can ever come to me again. I have his promise."

She cocked her head to one side as if listening, then nodded. When she looked back at Edward he could see her eyes glistening with the tears that were beginning to form.

"Ed, you know what I just said about knowing what God's purpose for my life was? I understand now that what I've been going through was just a preparation for it. I'm not mentally ill; I really have been visited by God. Is that so very hard to believe?"

She did not seem to have noticed that he was edging towards her. He spoke as deliberately and as calmly as he could.

"Joan, I'm sorry, I really am. But you have to face facts, and the facts are that you do have a mental illness, and that you need help. We can help, but you have to trust us – me – to help you."

"Yes," she said. "In the end it's really all about trust, isn't it?"

"Yes, I suppose it is." He moved closer still.

"Ed, do you know what love is?" She paused, but not long enough for him to frame a reply. "God is love. Love is of God, and whoever loves is born of God and knows God. Whoever does not love cannot know God. Do you know who said that? It was St. John the evangelist. Why do you find it so hard to believe, Ed?"

He was now almost within reach of her. "What I find hard to believe in is a god that allows so much suffering and pain to exist in a world he is supposed to have created."

Why could he not understand? "Oh Ed, don't you know that God is the answer to suffering and pain, not the cause of it?"

"God doesn't exist, Joan; I know he doesn't." He held his hand out to her, inviting her to take it. "Joan, you're scaring me. Please take my hand. Please come down."

She smiled at him then. He cared. That meant he did love. Her smile was a lover's knowing smile. She had felt that connection with him, earlier in their sessions in the chapel, and now, she felt complete in him. A mystical union that no-one else would know about, only ever the two of them. But still she had to make him understand and accept what it was that had happened between them

"Ed, I'm in the hands of Jesus now, and everything I do is guided by Him. God's purpose for my life was to save a soul from the dark eternity of despair, and I've very nearly achieved my task."

He edged forward. Her hand was almost in reach. He didn't understand what she was talking about. "Save a soul from despair? Whose?"

She gave him that smile again, of love untainted, unconsummated. She was utterly calm, serene, content. "Yours."

She jumped.

*

She was gone before he could move. Too late, he leaped forward to grab her and almost followed her over the parapet. "No!" He yelled, as if that could stop her.

Helpless, he watched her as she fell, seemingly in slow motion, all the way to the ground so far below. She did not fight her fall, but closed her eyes and clasped her hands as if in prayer.

His shout alerted those below that something untoward had happened. None were able to avert their eyes from her fall. The tower was high and a small eternity passed before she hit the ground.

She fell onto the cobbles at the foot of the tower with a flat sound, like a linen sheet on a clothesline, cracking in the wind. The inspector was the first to get to her, followed by Marwan. The doctor felt for a pulse, but nobody could have survived that fall. He shook his head. Bernadette and Sean were upon them moments later. Bernadette pulled her daughter into her arms, her anguished keening piercing the air.

Then Edward emerged from the cathedral. He was distraught. Marwan wondered if he had made the right decision letting him go up the tower after all.

30

The tricky business of redemption

Some hold that funerals should celebrate the life of the deceased, but this life had ended in tragedy, its youthful promise unfulfilled. Joan's family remembered her as the delightful child with shining eyes whose death left a gaping void that never could be filled. The professionals remembered her as the troubled young woman who, despite their every effort, they hadn't been able to help. They had lessons to learn in the hope that they might prevent a similar outcome in the future.

The funeral was quiet. No flowers. The family had asked instead that donations be made to the priests' training fund. They were grateful for all the support that Father James had given them, and for his fateful intervention, at no little risk to himself. In the church, Joan's coffin was placed before the statue of the Sacred Heart; it was what she would have wished. With Sean on one side of her and Caroline on the other, Bernadette had wept quietly through the entire course of the requiem mass. She still found it difficult to believe what had happened. She had wanted to talk to Dr. Plant, to ask him about those last moments on the cathedral roof, but both of them were still too upset. It would have to wait.

The cortege took them to the cemetery. It was hard enough losing a daughter: Bernadette could not stand the thought of her being burned; she would be interred. Reverently, the undertaker's men lowered the coffin into the earth, before making way for the mourners.

James O'Hanlon, himself greatly affected by what had happened, prayed silently for the strength to see it through to the end. His bishop had advised him to take a leave of absence, but he could not abandon his parishioners in their hour of greatest need. Besides, he needed their solace as much as they needed his. He had tried to prepare some suitable words to say at the graveside, but nothing would come; now he trusted that God would guide his words.

"My dear brothers and sisters," he began. "Some hold that Joan was a disturbed young woman suffering from a severe form of mental illness. All who saw her in the last weeks of her life can attest to the fact that she was indeed suffering greatly. But Joan herself believed she was the victim of a malevolent spirit that had taken possession of her. Either way she was not responsible for her actions, and it is not for us to stand in judgement over her. Rather, we should pray for her soul in the joyful hope of eternal salvation.

"We might see Joan's death as inexplicable: we ask ourselves how could such a lovely young person, with so much to look forward to in her life, and blessed with such a rich faith, die in such tragic circumstances? The medical professionals tell us that she was suffering from a mental illness, but I was witness myself to Joan's claim that she was privileged by the sight of beatific visions. We should comfort ourselves with the knowledge that Joan died utterly convinced that she was placing herself into the hands of God. Hers was a wonderful faith that is denied to so many of us no matter how much we want to believe.

"So now, we commit the body of our beloved daughter to the earth, to the loving bosom of our God, in certain hope of the resurrection.

"Through Christ our Lord."

Each of the mourners took a handful of earth to scatter over the coffin.

There was no gathering afterwards, and the mourners settled into little knots of people, exchanging condolences with the family before going their separate ways.

Three members of staff from the hospital had attended. They had kept out of the way standing together behind the family mourners, conscious of the blame that was being heaped upon them. That was to be expected. The general public did not understand mental illness and were often fearful of it, but that did not stop them wanting to point the finger of blame when something went wrong. After the last words had been said they walked slowly away.

It was a while before one of them broke the silence. "I'm afraid there's going to be a formal inquiry," Dr. Marwan told them. "I was only told about it this morning. Not that there's anything to worry about: I'm convinced we did everything we possibly could."

But Edward bitterly regretted the part he had played. He felt a deep and enduring sense of guilt. "Did we? Did we really do everything we could have done?"

Marwan understood how deeply the experience had hurt his trainee. "We always put her best interests first and acted with the best possible intentions throughout."

But Ed did not want to be convinced. To him, they were guilty of failing Joan. They hadn't listened to her and had rejected her experiences as false. If only they had acted differently. He had played it over and over in his mind, and with each playing, the part he had taken became more and more blameworthy. "We still succeeded in fucking up her life, though, didn't we?" He retorted.

"Ed, you mustn't look at it that way," Tony said.

Edward was angry that he seemed to be the only one with any sense of self-recrimination. Didn't the others feel that they were in any way culpable for what had happened, or were they closing ranks in the face of the inevitable inquiry? He turned on Tony. "What other way is there of looking at it? We were so fucking convinced that we were right that we didn't bother to listen to her. Never once did we give serious consideration to the possibility that she might have been right and we might have been wrong."

Marwan tried to be conciliatory. "I understand that you find this upsetting, Ed. We all do. Suicide is always a bad business, but it's a risk we face all the time when dealing with mental illness."

Whatever the intention, the words had the opposite effect. "*We* face? That's a pretty conceited way of looking at it, isn't it? Some might call it arrogant. I thought it was the victim who faced the risk of suicide, not the spectators."

Edward had been like this since Joan's death. Marwan thought it was now bordering on self-indulgence. "Edward, for your own sake, try to be objective, please. Your own reaction now should show you just how traumatic suicide is for the people left behind. Punishing yourself like this doesn't help anyone. Guilt is a self-indulgent extravagant gesture that you simply can't afford, not if you want to make a career in psychiatry."

But Edward didn't know what he wanted any more. "That's what I keep asking myself. Do I really want a career in psychiatry, after this?"

Marwan hadn't heard him talk like this before. He didn't want to see a promising career thrown away. "Edward, please don't make any rash decisions that you might regret later. What happened is that this was an incredibly complex case and you found yourself being drawn into it more deeply than you should have been. I have to bear some of the responsibility for that myself. I've seen similar close identification with a patient happen before, only most of the time it doesn't have such an unhappy ending. What you have to do is to take it on the chin, learn from it and move on. We can let trauma damage us or use it to make us stronger. The choice is yours."

"Is that what you call it – being drawn in? Joan said that my involvement was pre-ordained. Doesn't that count for anything?"

Marwan had hoped that Edward's viewpoint would have been more constructive, especially with an inquiry to be conducted. "I can understand that you are assailed by doubts right now – that's a normal part of the guilt that we all feel, but please at least try to employ the objectivity that your training should have given you. This was not a pre-ordained cosmic intervention where the forces of good and evil having fought over your patient somehow dragged you into some eternal metaphysical struggle. Joan was mentally ill; there's not a shred of doubt about that in my mind. Suicide, as you well know, is an ever-present risk in many forms of mental illness. In this case, because your patient could no longer resist her delusional beliefs, she took her own life. You have to find a way to deal with that because, if you choose to stay in psychiatry, and I think you should, it's likely to be the first of several such tragedies over the course of an average career."

Edward had no reply to this. Marwan could be right, he conceded grudgingly. The trouble was this experience was making him question everything he had been taught. He didn't know what to believe any more. What had really shaken him was being told that despite their objections, the parish priest had gone ahead and performed an exorcism anyway. He had no way of knowing whether Joan's remarkable transformation was due to the exorcism, but, if it was a coincidence, it was too real to feel comfortable about

They were approaching the road. He said a perfunctory goodbye and went in search of a taxi.

Dr. Marwan and Tony waited for a moment watching Edward as he walked away. "You know, I think he's changed," Tony said.

Marwan agreed. "I think you're right. But I wonder if he realises it himself yet?"

Marwan and Tony had come in separate cars. Marwan reached his first, and bade Tony goodbye. There was a small parcel on the passenger seat. He had forgotten all about it. How ridiculous to forget your own birthday, he chided himself. Though he was in no mood to celebrate, he unwrapped it. It was an i-pod, with a note saying *'With love from Nidhi. Play me.'* A gift from his sister. The gifts she sent were always thoughtful. He put in the earphones and played the first track. After only a few notes he pulled the earphones out, almost panic-struck, his heart beating wildly and his breath coming in short gasps. Be calm, he told himself. It's a coincidence, nothing more. He read the caption on the screen to make sure he was not mistaken. It was The Ode to Joy from Beethoven's 9th Symphony.

Father James was on yet another mission of mercy. Mrs. Aspinall's husband had died three years ago; ever since she had been finding it increasingly difficult to cope, and had recently gone into a rest home. James had been promising to visit for weeks, but somehow never managed to get round to it. He couldn't keep putting it off and decided he would go on his way back from the funeral. It might help to take his mind off things, for a little while, at least. His heart still heavy, he parked his car and walked to the reception area.

He was met by one of the staff. "Hello, I'm Father O'Hanlon. I've come to see Mrs. Aspinall."

"Oh yes. She's been asking for you. I'll take you to her."

James followed her to the lounge. He half expected to find Mrs. Aspinall tranquillised, but there she was, engaged in an animated conversation with several other residents. Her eyes lit up when she saw him. "Oh hello, Father," she said, "you're just the person we need, you can be our chairman with the casting vote." She looked triumphant, as if she expected that her priest would undoubtedly side with her. "We couldn't agree on whether we should play this for the music appreciation group this afternoon. What do you think?" She pressed the 'play' button on a small music centre.

James couldn't believe his ears. Was this God (or Joan) having a joke at his expense? It was Beethoven's ninth. "What do I think?" He pretended it was a difficult decision to make. "I think you should definitely play it."

Of all the mourners, Sean and Bernadette were the first to get home. The house was silent and empty; they felt Joan's absence like a physical thing, like the phantom pain from an amputation. Their mood, naturally, was downcast; Bernadette hung their coats in the hall.

"I think we did the right thing, not having any sort of reception after the funeral," she said, her voice low.

It had taken a great effort for Sean to hold back the tears that had been threatening all morning. It just wasn't the done thing for men to cry in public. "People mean well, but I couldn't have taken much more of it, love."

She pulled him to her and embraced him fiercely. "I know," she said, not wanting to let go, needing the comfort of his arms around her. But they couldn't stand like that for the rest of the day. Slowly she disentangled herself from him. Being active, doing something, anything, any small inconsequential task, was better than just sitting and grieving over what might have been. "You go in the living room and I'll make us a cup of tea."

It was the need for something to occupy his mind that led Sean to put the television on. It was a documentary about pivotal figures in the development of music. They were playing Beethoven's Ode to Joy. He stood transfixed.

Joan's death had shaken Caroline. It had come out of nowhere. And now Joan was gone. Okay, so they hadn't always seen eye to eye, but that was normal, wasn't it? She had nothing to reproach herself for, she told herself. But Joan's death was a powerful reminder of her own mortality, of the slenderness of life's thread. It was the finality of it that was so hard to take. There could never be any going back. There never would be any more good times, only memories. Better not to dwell on this, she told herself, being morbid wouldn't help anyone, and she had to pick the twins up soon. She had to act normal for them; life goes on. She pushed the switch to boil the kettle and spooned instant coffee into a cup. Without thinking she turned on the kitchen radio. It was Classic FM the lunchtime request show. She was shocked to hear 'a request for Caroline from your sister Joan.' It had to be a coincidence, but it was too close, the loss too fresh. She burst into tears. It took her a while to realise what music it was that was being played.

Tony had to go back to work. It was probably the best thing but he was not in the right frame of mind for it. Best to drown himself in paperwork, there was always plenty of that, the only thing the health service wasn't short of. He half smiled at that. Then he remembered what Marwan had said about an enquiry. Things could get quite grim when outsiders came poking their noses around, and strangely, it always seemed to be nursing staff who came in for most criticism. Tony wondered whether he should ask the union for their advice. It would probably be best to get them involved right from the start. He had a contact number somewhere. He looked through the detritus strewn across his desk. Not the tidiest of offices. He imagined what an enquiry might have to say about it: 'It is difficult to see how such an untidy and disorganised office space can be conducive to the efficient operation of the psychiatric unit.'

Susan popped her head in. "Back so soon? How'd it go?"

"About as well as could be expected, I think."

"How'd Ed take it?"

Tony thought for a moment before answering. "Not well. I think the experience has really traumatised him."

Maria was right behind Susan. "'bout time something broke through that thick skin of his."

Tony ignored her, continuing to look through the disarray of papers on his desk. "Sue, have you seen the card with the union rep's details? Marwan told me there's going to be an official inquiry, and I think we should get the union involved sooner rather than later."

Maria was determined to make her presence felt. "An inquiry? Whose idea was that?" Still they took no notice of her.

There was a set of drawers down the side of the desk. Ignoring Tony's efforts, Susan opened the middle one and took out a small plastic box. She extracted a card. "This what you're looking for?"

"How'd you know where to find it?" He asked. She gave him a look that said 'Don't forget we're all in this together.'

"Thanks." He dialled the number.

Getting through to someone with whom he could have a sensible conversation proved difficult. He kept coming back to a message telling him to press '1' for this department, '2' for another, and so on. Eventually he did get through to a person, but they informed him politely but firmly that he had come through to the wrong department. If he would wait, they would try to connect him to the right one. They put him on hold.

His blood went cold. His fingers lost their ability to grip and he dropped the phone. Susan turned at the sound of the phone hitting the desk with a 'clunk'. Tony was as white as a sheet.

"Are you all right Tony?" She asked. "You look like you've seen a ghost." He couldn't reply. She picked the phone up to listen, and dropped it herself as if it were contaminated. "Jesus," she said, as she realised. "It's got to be a coincidence, hasn't it?"

Edward had been given compassionate leave, or, at least that was what they called it. Doubtless it would be extended until after the inquiry announced its findings. Time weighed heavily on him, not having any purpose to his days. He ruminated constantly about how Joan's death might have been prevented. It wasn't healthy, but he couldn't help it. He wondered whether he might be depressed, but couldn't be objective about his own feelings, and anyway, if he was depressed, he probably deserved it. Joan had offered to go with him to the funeral, but he had not wanted her to be there, wanted at least something in his life to be separate from this collision between what he had once believed and what he had found. She had, however, insisted that they meet afterwards. She didn't want him going back to his flat alone, to mope in the solitude of melancholy. She had taken a few days off and booked them into a small country hotel. Although it was only a couple of miles out of town they would be isolated from any reminders of what had happened, and they could be together, go for long walks, and just be: letting whatever healing that could come from their relationship emerge without any outside distractions.

Ed stopped the taxi just outside the hotel entrance. As he was paying the driver, a car pulled out and stopped next to them. Its window was down and the music that was coming from it could be heard clearly. Ed was startled, so much that he dropped the money he was holding and had to scramble around for it on the pavement. He had the frightened look of a rabbit mesmerised by a car's headlights. "Are you alright, mate?" The driver asked him.

Ed tried to gather his thoughts. "Yeah, it's just . . ." He couldn't complete the sentence. The music had taken him by surprise. Although he told himself it was a coincidence, his concentration was gone and he could no longer recognise the denominations of the coins he was trying to give to the driver. In the end the driver had to take his fare from Ed's outstretched hand, like you would with a child. "You take care, now," he said as he drove off.

Ed walked the twenty yards to the hotel reception. Joan had already checked them both in and was waiting for him. He seemed distracted and she looked at him quizzically. "I'm okay," he insisted. "It just wasn't very easy being there, but I felt I owed it to her to say goodbye."

"That's fine," she said, "but it's over now." She kissed him lightly and caressed his face, allowing her fingers to linger on his cheek. She led him to the lift. It was waiting for them, and they stepped in, pushing the button for the second floor. Almost immediately, Ed became very agitated. "What's the matter?" She asked him, taking tight hold of his hand.

"The music!" There was piped music in the lift. It made him feel trapped, claustrophobic. There was no escape. He would be forced to listen to it no matter what distress it caused him. He knew he would never be able to listen to it again without its evoking tragic memories and powerful emotions.

Joan listened. It took a moment to sink in. The door opened It wasn't their floor, but Ed all but fell out, refusing to go back in as if it were inhabited by some baleful influence. "Ed, Ed!" It took a moment to get his attention. "It's a coincidence, nothing more – it has to be – you know that, don't you?"

His breathing was becoming calmer. He nodded, hoping she was right. He didn't mention the car at the hotel gates.

"But what if it wasn't? What if it was real? What if what Joan said to me was true?"

She had no answer to that. They took the stairs to the next floor. She took his hand and led him to their room. As she put the key in the door she turned to face him. "Ed, it *was* a coincidence."

The room was sumptuous, a suite rather than a single room. She threw the key onto a small table and turned to kiss him. Still he seemed absent, distracted, not living in the present. "I know you've been deeply upset by everything that's happened, but now's the time to put it behind you, think about the future, okay?"

He smiled sheepishly. "Okay."

She left him and went into the bedroom, calling back over her shoulder "This place is costing us a fortune. Let's make the most of it. Why don't you see if you can find us a smoochie movie on the telly and we can have a nice romantic afternoon and forget that the rest of the world even exists?"

Ed flopped down on the couch and picked up the TV remote control. Joan came back with a bottle of champagne and two glasses. The TV seemed to be taking ages to warm up. Ed tried pressing various buttons on the remote. Suddenly, the TV lit up and the *Ode to Joy* filled the room, so loudly it was as if the orchestra and choir were in there with them. Edward shrieked and tried frantically to find any button on the remote that would switch the damned thing off, but all of his efforts were ineffective. The music enveloped them in its embrace, a paean of triumph and fulfilment. Now Edward was certain. This was no coincidence. He stopped trying to switch it off and listened, hypnotised, inscribing in his memory its every crescendo, all of its nuances and subtleties. Joan, with more presence of mind, snatched the remote control from him and pressed the *off* button repeatedly, but still to no avail. Only when she pulled the power cable from the wall did it stop.

Anxiously she turned to look at him. She had half expected to find him in a heap of gibbering hysteria, but instead he was calm. He looked amazed, as if he had made a momentous discovery.

"It's true, isn't it?" He said, wonderingly. "God does exist, doesn't he? And what Joan told me, that was true as well."

She went back to the couch, embracing him, tracing the contours of his face as if he were some new creation. "You know what that means?" He said.

She didn't answer. Now was not the time for talking. She put a finger to his lips to silence him, smiling like a mother whose child has just discovered an important truth.

Epilogue

To tell a story is a lonely task. To tell it well, as it happened, without untruths or half truths; to include everything that matters while leaving out unimportant trivia, is not a light burden, or even one that I take on willingly. And if stories must have a beginning and an end, how should the threads of this beginning be unravelled? When will it end? I'm not sure how this story should be told, only that it has taken on a life of its own, possessing me and compelling me to bring it to light. I'm not a writer; I've never written anything like this before, and right now all I have are questions to which I don't have many answers. Did it begin with me? Or with her? The only thing I'm sure of is that it's become a living force inside me, building the pressure until I feel like I'm either going to explode or somehow get the story out. Maybe that's it: just let the story tell itself, absolve myself of any responsibility.

The door opened. Into the room walked a young woman, pretty, with short, dark hair, heavily pregnant and carrying two mugs in her hands. She placed one beside the computer monitor and absent-mindedly pushed the fingers of her free hand into the hair at the nape of the neck of the man who was patiently typing away in his inefficient two-fingered manner. "How's it going?" she asked cheerily, peering at the screen, trying to read through the reflection.

"Not well," he replied grumpily. He sighed and tried to take a sip of coffee, but it was too hot. "I don't think I'm cut out for this; I just don't think I've got, you know: I just don't think I'm any good at it."

She pushed herself between him and the keyboard and sat herself in his lap, cradling her mug in both hands, blowing on the surface of her drink. "Well, at least let me have a look." He put his arms around her waist, nuzzling his face into her back while she read the words on the screen. "It's not bad," she said, "so far." She turned round to face him, gave him a peck on the cheek.

He was not so easily persuaded. "So far?" he retorted, with a pained look on his face. "I've only done one paragraph and it looks like rubbish to me."

"Don't be so hard on yourself," she tried to be encouraging. "What's wrong with it?"

"It's too self-conscious," he sulked, "and it took me all morning just to scrape those few bits together. If it carries on like this, our kids will be pensioners before I'm finished."

She stood up. "Are you sure you should be doing this at all?" She asked. "I remember you telling me that reliving traumatic experiences can be counter-productive, and you *were* traumatised – remember? We're supposed to be making a new start."

"I know. It's just that . . . it's something I've just got to do. If I don't get it out it's likely to kill me anyway. I know that sounds stupid, but it's the way I feel: I can't help it."

She stroked his hair gently. "I know." She straightened up and walked to the door. "I only came to bring you a cup of coffee." She opened the door and paused for a moment. "What do you want for tea?"

He smiled – limply. "Anything. You sure you don't mind?" He indicated the computer screen.

"It's okay, Ed. Really. I understand. I really do. But it's up to you love. You either have to do it or give up. Just make your decision and stick to it, okay?" She closed the door behind her leaving him to his story.

With a heavy sigh he selected the text it had taken so much angst to create, deleted it, and started again.

THE END

Printed in the United Kingdom by
Lightning Source UK Ltd., Milton Keynes
136903UK00002B/64-69/P